ECHOES

of

FORTUNE

The Search *for*
Braddock's Lost Gold

David R Leng

White Publishing, Hanover, MA

Stephen White, Editor

To Winnie.

ACKNOWLEDGMENTS

My wife and children, thank you for putting up with me over the past 14 months of writing this book. Equally important, thank you for indulging me in conversations since I came up with the idea for the book years ago.

To Steve White, my editor, I appreciate your guidance throughout writing my first novel.

To Uhurina Swann, a talented local writer I met through sheer luck. Thank you for allowing me to join your writer's group and for your feedback on the initial rough draft. It was immensely helpful.

A special thanks goes to Steve Stramara for helping me change the final ending. I would also like to thank the numerous beta readers for their feedback, which was critical to refining (and shrinking) this book. The final version of this book is almost half the length of the original draft.

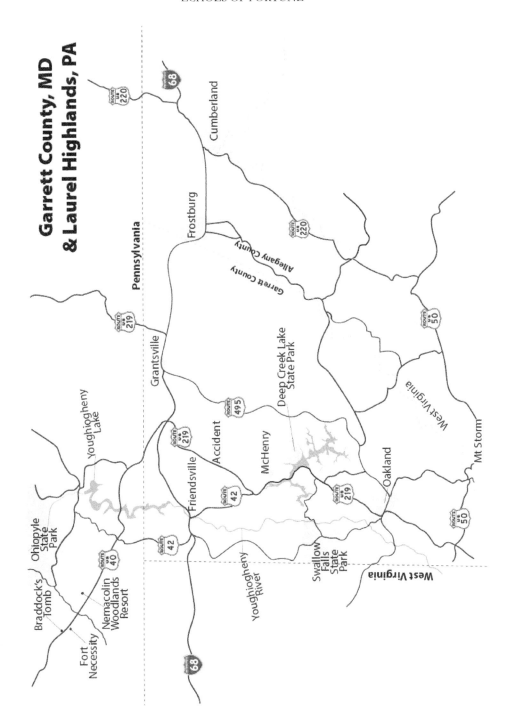

Garrett County, MD & Laurel Highlands, PA

DEEP CREEK LAKE, MARYLAND

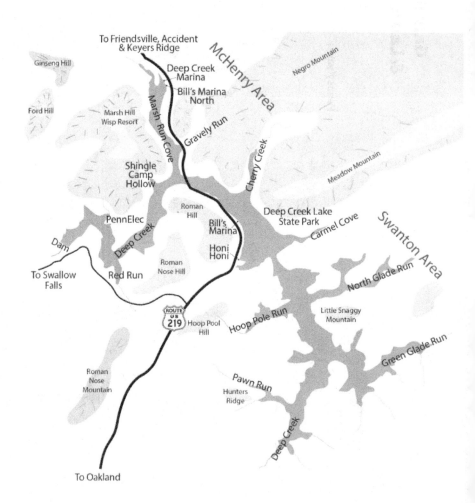

Prologue

Wednesday, July 9th, 1755

Major General Edward Braddock could practically taste the blood of his enemies on his tongue. Victory was at hand. Fort Duquesne would soon be Fort Pitt once more, he thought. *The French will cower before the might of my army.*

The afternoon light flickered through the dense canopy of leaves, casting fractured shadows over Braddock as he spurred his stallion forward. His heart pounded with anticipation: *Only a few more miles and our cannons will be in range.* The General's decorated military uniform hinted at his distinguished career, but his eyes betrayed a weariness earned through countless battles.

"Press on!" His voice, a grizzled bark, sliced through the damp air. "We must catch up with the advance guard!"

Braddock and his Flying Brigade, their redcoats stark against the greenery, surged ahead with muskets and cannons at the ready. The previous day's triumph in repelling the French attack at Camp Monongahela had bolstered Braddock's confidence. *The French and their Native allies would surely think twice before clashing with our might again.*

A thunderous gunshot echoed through the valley, and Braddock's heart jumped. He stood in his saddle, eyes darting around in desperation. Before he could locate the source, a cacophony of gunfire and muffled screams filled the air.

"The advance guard is under attack. Forward, make haste! Crush our enemy!" he roared.

Charging up the path, they encountered Lieutenant Colonel Thomas Gage and his men in full retreat, faces etched with panic. Braddock's force collided with them, uncertainty and confusion sweeping both groups.

"They cut us off! Came at us from all directions!" Gage yelled, his voice strained and breathless.

Shots fired, swords clashed, and men screamed as the unsettling 'whoop' war cries of Native warriors echoed from every direction. Braddock knew the enemy was closing in fast. His voice rose to a desperate scream, pleading for order as madness reigned around them.

"Form lines! Form lines!" he commanded, his face hardening as the distant crackle of musket fire grew closer and more urgent. "Steady!" Braddock roared as unseen assailants unleashed volleys from the forest. Musket balls whizzed through the air, slamming into trees or striking flesh with heavy thuds. "Hold your ground!"

He caught sight of the advancing French soldiers and yelled, "Fire!" Braddock's focus was unwavering. His men flailed as lead bit into his brothers-in-arms, felling them with malicious precision. However, the French line in front of them had not fired a shot yet.

A young soldier's voice, contorted in bewildered terror, reached Braddock's ears. "Where are the shots coming from?"

"Everywhere," Braddock spat, scanning the trees for any sign of the enemy. Phantoms of the forest, hidden foes picking them apart.

"Keep steady! They will cower from our strength and discipline!" Braddock knew the key to survival was maintaining order amidst the chaos. "Reload! Fire!" He continued issuing commands, trying to impose order on the disarray, but every shout, every shot, only seemed to stoke the confusion as the woodland erupted in a storm of gunfire and death.

A thick, pungent fog of gunpowder smoke hung in the air, stinging the eyes and nostrils of the soldiers. The sounds were deafening – shouts and shots rang out, filling the forest with the echo of muskets.

"Form lines! Stand ready!" Braddock's sharp and commanding voice cut through the harshness of battle. His gray hair was plastered to his forehead with sweat as he scanned for the elusive enemy.

"Fire!" A volley thundered in response, the disciplined waves of gunfire pushing back the French soldiers. Another barrage of bullets hailed from the veiled snipers amongst the trees and cut down his men with ruthless precision.

"Steady, lads!" Braddock's command was ironclad despite the mounting horror. The eerie, petrifying cries of the Natives echoed through the woods. Scalps – bloody and grotesque British scalps – nailed to the bark of trees struck a cold terror into their hearts.

"Sir, they…" A junior officer began, but before he could finish, Braddock's horse reared as a bullet found its mark in the steed's flesh. With a violent twist, the General crashed to the ground, dust and leaves clouding his vision.

"Bring up the cannons!" he roared, scrambling upright, his uniform tarnished with dirt and blood. More men surged forward at his call, lining up with unwavering fervor despite the shadow of death looming over them. "Aim into the trees!"

"Prepare to fire!" The cannon crews loaded with intensity; balls and powder were rammed home as the great guns aimed at the concealed enemy. The air vibrated with tension, and acrid gunpowder filled their nostrils.

"Fire!" The command was a thunderclap, and the cannons obeyed, spewing death among the trees with each roar. Braddock's chest heaved as the forest shuddered under the assault. "Reload! Keep firing!" The British lines held, muskets blazing in defiant answer to the ambush. Braddock stood firm, the embodiment of Britannia's might, even as the world descended into anarchy around him.

Cannons belched smoke and fire, the woods alive with the echo of war.

Amidst the chaos, the colonial auxiliaries broke rank, their forms darting between and behind the trees, their muskets answering the shadowy enemy's call.

"Steady, men!" Braddock's voice was commanding and unwavering. "Show them British lead!" The men's volleys sang, but fear crept in, a silent assassin among the ranks. Braddock mounted another horse, his eyes scanning for the French line. They would break, he was sure of it – just a bit more courage and a touch more control.

"Discipline!" he shouted, trying to ignite their resolve. "Fire!" Amidst all the disorder and resounding noise, unheard was the shot that silenced Braddock's orders. It tore into Braddock's chest, flinging him from his mount. The earth met him with unforgiving force. The world spun – a whirl of screams and gunshots. His breath came hard, each gasp a fiery agony.

"General's down!" A cry cut above the rest. His men's faces were a blur of terror as they passed, their bravery crumbling into panic.

"Stand your…" His command died on his lips; he had no strength to yell nor overcome the clamor of retreat, the haunting symphony of the dying who lay scattered like autumn leaves along the road.

"Help… us…" Their pleas reached him even as his own strength waned.

Pain clouded Braddock's vision. The forest whirled, a tapestry of green and red. Through the haze, his eyes found George Washington. The young colonel stood tall amidst the chaos, his voice carrying through the confusion as he barked orders to the remnants of their scattered force.

"Rear guard!" Washington's command was firm, his saddled figure rallying like a beacon. "Form up! Cover the men!"

Braddock's heart hammered in his chest, a combination of pride and desperation. Despite his pallor and evident sickness, Washington was a bastion of resolve. The General's lips parted to shout encouragement, but only a choked gasp escaped.

Then a shot – the sharp blast of a rifle. Washington's horse crumpled, legs buckling as it collapsed. Braddock's gut clenched. *No, not him too.* But Washington was quick, rolling clear even as his steed hit the earth. He

4

sprang to his feet, his red uniform now smeared with earth and leaves, yet his gaze remained locked on Braddock.

"General!" Washington raced forward, his stride determined.

Braddock tried to respond, to rise and meet him, but his body refused. Wounded soldiers fell defending him, their victory turning into their slaughter. And more eerie war cries filled the air – high-pitched, chilling whoops of the Native Americans punctuated each gunshot, each life taken.

The forest reverberated with gunfire; trees splintered from the relentless volleys. Amid the chaos, Braddock refocused upon Washington commandeering a horse hitched to a supply wagon, urging the animal forward with a firm slap on its flank. Washington thundered toward him, his red coat billowing behind him like a cape in the wind. Braddock's breath caught as he watched in horror, fragments of fabric fluttering into the air from Washington's coat, ripped from its very cloth in the wake of enemy bullets.

"George!" Braddock's voice was a hoarse whisper, desperation clawing at his throat.

Pale as death itself, Washington arrived beside him, determination etched deep into his youthful features. With a strength that disguised his illness, Washington heaved Braddock up and crashed onto the wagon bed, groaning under their combined weight.

"I've got you, Sir," Washington's words struggled against the clatter of battle.

"Retreat," Braddock managed to bite out through clenched teeth, his command ragged but explicit. "Order the retreat."

"Yes, Sir. We must first get you to safety."

"George, go to Fort Cumberland..." Braddock's order trailed off as darkness edged his sight, the pain in his chest a constant beacon amidst the dimming world. Lying, staring up, he was unaware if Washington heard him.

The wagon jolted, each rut in the path delivering a hammer blow to Braddock's battered frame. His world shrank to a realm of agony, punctuated by the sharp snap of gunfire. He clung to consciousness through sheer will.

"Retreat!" Even as Washington spurred the horse forward, his voice was crisp with command.

Braddock's vision tunneled, the periphery fading to black, but he couldn't escape the stark terror etched on the faces of his men. The line between order and chaos blurred, mingling with the stench of gunpowder and blood.

"Fall back!" Washington shouted again, his silhouette a blur against the chaos. "Over the river!"

The wagon hit a stone, tossing Braddock into the air and slamming him down, his breath pushed from his lungs. Pain flared white-hot, but seeing his men – his responsibility – scattering like leaves before the wind seared his soul.

"Fire from behind the trees!" Braddock wanted to scream the order, to rally his troops, but the words were but a whisper, lost beneath the clamor of retreat. He realized he had learned a lesson too late for too many of his brave men: *Our tactics are useless against the chaotic and cowardly firing from behind trees.*

Washington's jaw clenched as he navigated the maelstrom. Braddock saw him glance back just once, their eyes meeting in silent understanding – the peril of command, the cost of leadership.

The wagon splashed into the river, cold water dousing Braddock's skin. He gasped, the chill a cruel juxtaposition to the heat of battle they left behind.

"I need cover fire!" Washington demanded, rising to the moment as Braddock knew he would. On the far bank, the young officer directed the remnants of the brigade with grim determination, his own fear buried beneath layers of resolve.

"Men to the trees!" Washington commanded. His figure darted among the men, a beacon amidst despair, orchestrating their desperate defense.

Braddock's gaze lingered on the bedlam, the river's roar serving as a respite from the screams and shouts. They crossed – somehow a miracle and Washington's impromptu plan succeeded, offering a chance for survival.

After what felt like an eternity, the wagon halted with a jolt that sent a fresh stab of agony tearing through Braddock's chest. Through blurred vision, he discerned Washington's towering figure as he rounded the wagon, his face etched with concern and resolution.

"Doctor!" Washington's voice sliced through the din.

James Craik appeared, his medical bag clutched in steady hands. With swift precision, he grabbed a small clear bottle from his bag, doused the wound with alcohol, and examined it, setting Braddock's chest aflame.

"Your lung may be compromised, General. Infection is my greatest fear."

"Can you save him?" Washington's tone was firm, commanding even in the face of uncertainty.

"I'll stitch him up. Keep him comfortable." Craik's hands moved with meticulousness, threading the needles through the skin. "But he needs proper care."

"Understood." Washington nodded and returned his gaze to Braddock, awaiting orders.

"George," Braddock called.

"Yes, General."

"Retreat," he rasped between labored breaths. "Back to Fort Cumberland."

"Understood, Sir. We should continue the withdrawal for your safety." Washington countered. "However, should we send riders to order our remaining troops to join us? They would bolster our ranks for another attack. Our orders were to capture Fort Duquesne and secure the Ohio Valley. It's imperative."

Braddock barked, strained yet forceful, "No, Colonel!"

The words sliced through Washington, causing his head to recoil.

"We must return. Those are your orders now." Braddock's voice, though feeble, carried the unmistakable tone of command. Washington, his silhouette etched against the chaos, stood rigid, awaiting further explanation.

"Retreat?" Washington bellowed the urgency of his words spurred the men into action. "Why, Sir?"

"George, there's more at stake than you realize. It is imperative I make it back to Fort Cumberland. We must go with all speed." The urgency in his own words surprised even himself, but this situation was no place for half-measures or indecision.

Washington's eyes, always a reservoir of calm, flickered with concern. "Understood, General." He turned on his heel and began issuing orders; his voice cut through the lingering gunpowder smoke and the distant cries of the wounded.

Craik finished with the stitches; a makeshift dressing held his torn flesh together. Braddock slumped against the wagon's hard bench. *George's plan may be sound, but we must recover the payroll.*

"Move out!" Washington's order cut through the madness once more. The rhythm of retreating footsteps drummed a somber beat into the earth. And amidst it all, Braddock clung to consciousness, the fate of the mission – and his life – hanging in the balance.

When Braddock peered over the edge of the cart, vast emptiness greeted him where soldiers should have been. Countless injured individuals struggled to keep up with the group. *In less than three hours, I lost over a third of my men...*

His focus shifted, and he closed his eyes, praying their critical new mission would be successful. Every jolt of the wagon sent a fresh lance of pain through his chest, the stitched wound protesting each rut in the path they traveled. His mind raced even as his body begged for respite. *I was right to order the payroll hidden. If it were here today, we might have lost it, and all of this would be for naught; morale would crumble, soldiers would desert, and the crown's efforts in America would suffer or even fail.*

"I must make it," Braddock whispered to himself, gripping the splintered edge of the wagon with what little strength remained. The agonizing throbbing in his chest punctuated the hooves' rhythmic cadence. *The payroll will be lost if I don't make it to the first marker.*

"Keep moving!" Washington's shout echoed from somewhere ahead, his presence both a beacon and a reprimand to any who dared falter.

Where are you, Clarke? Were you successful in hiding it? Where? The wagon lurched on again, and a deeper fog settled into Braddock's eyes.

Chapter 1

Jack Sullivan burst out of the building and raced across the porch like a madman, nearly plowing over an elderly couple on their way in. He sprinted down the sidewalk screaming, "Make way! Make way!" as he started to launch himself over the creek's small bridge. Ignoring the protests of the bewildered tourists, he pushed through and came perilously close to knocking another couple off their feet in his haste.

With lightning reflexes, Jack snatched hold of them to steady the pair before hurtling toward his dark red four-wheel-drive Chevrolet Suburban again. His hand shook as he fumbled with his key fob, only just seizing it prior to it hitting the ground. In one swift motion, he unlocked the SUV and threw himself into the driver's seat. Igniting the engine, he slammed it into gear and floored it. Trying to catch his breath, he wondered in desperation: *Will I make it in time?*

Smashing his foot down harder on the gas pedal, Jack pushed his car to its limits as it roared like a lion. Every nerve in his body screamed at him – this was it. Unable to think straight, urgency compelled him.

Jack raced through the tree and hillside-lined road that snaked through the valley. Periodic glimpses of the river that formed the ravine flashed by in a blur. His focus on his destination caused him to miss the big yellow warning signs to reduce speed and a large black arrow indicating an upcoming sharp bend in the road.

He flew into the turn with too much velocity, losing grip on the tires, and skidded onto the road's shoulder. Instinct took over; he steered into the drift and gunned the engine. The back end slid around with a vicious squeal until all four wheels bit in, propelling him back onto the pavement a heartbeat prior to striking the beginning of the guide rail, which kept vehicles from crashing into the river.

Snapping back to reality, Jack needed to make it to McHenry, Maryland, before he lost his opportunity. However, he had to remain in control – killing himself or totaling his ride weren't options. Taking a deep breath, he slowed down, closer, but still exceeding the speed limit, while replaying the day's events leading to this momentous moment.

* * *

Earlier that day, the mid-morning sun wove through the thick tree canopy, casting Jack in a dance of shadows and light as he made his way up the Youghiogheny Riverbank. The hum of his metal detector punctuated each step, a steady companion on his solitary journey. He stopped, lifting his hat to swipe at the sweat on his forehead, the sunlight accentuating the rugged handsomeness of his features. His dirty-blonde hair was tinged with dampness as piercing blue eyes surveyed the land with an unwavering intensity.

Discarding his coat, he revealed a frame both muscular and adorned in the casual defiance of a Metallica tee and worn jeans. He tied the jacket around his waist, his hands rough from the years of these outdoor adventures.

As the relentless guitar of Pete Townshend of The Who streamed through his earbuds, he pressed on. Despite the shade, sweat trailed down his brow, the riverbank's secrets beckoning him closer.

A beep halted his march, which exposed nothing more than a discarded aluminum pull tab. Immersed in his task and the chords filling his ears, he missed the kayakers floating by as they shouted, "HEY!" or "WOOOHOOOOO!" while waving for his attention.

Jack sighed, shoulders slumping, as he rechecked the spot before continuing up the slope. Disappointment weighed on him as he resumed his climb, the forest's thick embrace challenging his pace. Yet, determination drove him, his gaze catching a glimpse of the red marker stick against a daunting rock wall. He replanted it upriver, signaling another checked area, and ventured further. Despite the day's fruitless search, Jack's resolve hardened; he sought the legend of Braddock's Gold.

Near the river, the drama of rafters rescuing one of their own out of the water caught his eye – a man ejected from the boat, clutching to the rope around their inflatable whitewater raft. A small chuckle escaped him, imagining their potential fate from the chaos of the ferocious rapids ahead compared to the mild ones they just passed through.

Concern now replaced his amusement, and he rushed towards them, offering assistance drowned out by the river's roar. The spectacle ended with the sodden man heaved aboard unceremoniously, working to dislodge the massive wedgie his friends gave as his reward for falling in. Jack's laughter mingled with the din in the air, a momentary reprieve in his quest.

At the water's edge, Jack silenced the buzzing of his phone alarm. Success here today bore the potential of more than the day's earnings; it held the promise of a new future, far removed from the $800 and modest tips of his private tour gig. With a muted press, he postponed the alert, his attention shifting to the task at hand. He adjusted his marker upriver, his first attempt thwarted by stone, the second firm and true. His strides grew brisk as he ascended the slope, driven by the prospect of discovery.

A sharp squeal from his detector cut the air, igniting a surge of adrenaline. Jack crouched, clearing the earth, only to meet disappointment at the surface. Undeterred and guided by the persistent beeps, he unfolded his shovel and delved deeper. Digging in, it reverberated against something solid, sending his pulse racing.

In the dirt, Jack uncovered an artifact of history – an ornate bayonet hilt, its design speaking of the 1700s. Joy and wonder etched across his face as he admired the relic, pondering its origins. *What tale do you hold?*

French or British – what hands wielded you? The absence of its blade only deepened the mystery, hinting at a value far beyond the incomplete find.

After silencing another alarm interruption and scrutinizing his discovery, he placed the hilt in a bag, secured it in his backpack, and scanned the spot again in vain. *Where is the rest of it? Whole, you'd fetch thousands.* Sighing, he set his sights on the looming rock face and closed in upon it.

Repositioning the stick, his irritation with the recurrent notifications was evident in a heavy sigh. The reality of his financial predicament loomed – he had to return to his paid gig or risk the very viability of his pursuits. He disabled the alarm without hesitation and placed a Google Maps pin on his phone. Jack navigated the terrain downriver with less caution, driven by necessity.

Reaching his vehicle, his eyes scanned the area, devoid of people. He changed in stealth and speed into attire befitting his tour guide role – a sharp contrast to his rugged exploration gear. He revealed a physique shaped by sports and adventure, donning black dress jeans, a checkered button-down shirt, and sleek black Nike athletic shoes.

With a final glance in the mirror to tidy up his hair, he embarked on the familiar path to his day job. The discovery of the day lingered in his thoughts, a beacon of hope for a future filled with such endeavors.

Glancing at the clock, Jack groaned; he was running late. *This may cost me.* He accelerated along Sang Run Road, speeding over the bridge across the Youghiogheny River and up the hill towards the Friendsville Road intersection. There, gazing upon The Schoolhouse Earth Store dimmed his spirits. Brimming with assorted trinkets, clothing, and home decor, the store wasn't what disheartened him. It was the memory of Emma, his ex-fiancé and college love, and her delight in shopping here and similar places.

Turning north onto Friendsville Road, Jack's route took him past pastoral scenes and isolated homes. He drove by the scenic Chanteclaire Farm wedding venue, its entrance marked by lush apple and walnut trees. After a few miles, the road descended into the Youghiogheny River Valley towards Friendsville, Maryland.

With no time to spare to stop in town at his apartment to change, Jack was thankful he chose to pack extra clothes. He resumed his journey, exiting the river valley where I-68 intersects with Friendsville Road, heading to Pennsylvania. Twenty minutes later, he entered the quaint community of Markleysburg. As he drove down Main Street with its line of Victorian homes and shops, he reached Route 40, referred to as The National Road or Braddock's Road.

His fingers drummed on the steering wheel in annoyance over the wait for traffic to clear. Stopping long enough, it offered a moment to muse on Route 40's historic alignment over General Braddock's trail from Fort Cumberland to Pittsburgh. Once congestion cleared, he ascended the close to two-mile incline out of the valley. Upon reaching the top, a quick glance at the clock preceded his arrival at Rustic Joe's Coffee House. He parked near the entrance, welcomed by the cool air.

After locking his car, Jack approached the inviting structure, noting the wood and stone façade and heart-shaped holes in the shutters. His sneakers crunched on the gravel as he moved towards the double doors, his reflection meeting him in the glass. Pulling them open, the warmth and the rich aroma of coffee enveloped him. A familiar voice greeted him from behind the counter, the dark-haired girl in an apron, saying, "Hi, Jack."

"Hey, Nancy. How's it going?" he flashed his trademark smile, one that never failed to light up the room.

Nancy's return grin was just as bright. "Doing well. What's the order today?"

"Three coffees," he said, leaning on the counter. "Decaf for me. Got some out-of-towners booked for a six-hour tour, not the usual four. Picking them up from Nemacolin."

"Anything special with the coffee?"

"Keep it simple. Black for me, with packets of cream and sugar to go for the others." He glanced around the café; the rustic charm of barn wood and modern flair of metal accents always brought him a sense of peace. The aroma of fresh coffee blended with the scent of baked goods made his mouth water. "Throw in three muffins and a pair of cookies, too, would you?"

"Coming right up," Nancy said as she moved about the counter. "What are they seeing today?"

Jack collected his order. "Taking them to the usual spots."

He laid a $30 on the counter and grabbed the carrier and bag from her. "Thanks. Your coffee's a big hit with my clients."

Nancy, teasingly close now, quipped, "Is that why I always get a generous tip?"

Jack, preoccupied, missed the playful glint in her gaze. "Yeah, got another tour tomorrow. See you then."

Nancy's eyes followed him to the door, a hopeful note in her voice, "Looking forward to it!"

Jack's journey continued along Route 40, bypassing landmarks like the Mystic Rock Golf Course and the Lady Luck Casino en route to the Nemacolin Woodlands Resort. This destination, a sprawling 2,000-acre oasis nestled in the Laurel Highlands of Farmington, PA, stood unparalleled in beauty.

Jack's SUV glided amidst the resort's serpentine driveway, escorted by an arboreal flourish. His gaze settled on the Nemacolin Resort, its gateway marked by a grand stone gatehouse, intricate carvings, and a wooden roof exuding rustic grandeur. The way unfolded to unveil the Chateau Lafayette, an architectural nod to French elegance, its magnificence reminiscent of European luxury.

Surrounding the Chateau, gardens bloomed in vibrant testament to the resort's meticulous care, a visual feast of flora framing the path to opulence.

At the portico, a valet in navy attire approached. Jack asked, "I'm here for Mr. and Mrs. Werner. Can I park nearby so I can meet them inside?"

"Just ahead, about 50 feet," the valet directed. "Leave the keys in the car in case we need to move it."

Parking as advised, Jack admired the lobby, which exuded luxury with its polished marble floors and a chandelier casting prismatic light. Art and sculptures adorned the space, each piece a narrative of distant realms supported by ornate wood-paneled walls.

The reception desk was abuzz with the soft murmurs of travelers, their faces alight with anticipation. Beyond this nucleus, the area unfolded into a serene lounge, an arrangement of plush seating around a lively fireplace offering a cozy retreat. Here, guests mingled or savored the calm, the fireplace's crackle a subtle invitation to unwind.

As Jack absorbed the elegance, he called out, "Mr. and Mrs. Werner?" His voice carried over the lobby, stirring the quiet near the fireplace, a ripple of expectation through the tranquil air.

A man of distinguished grace and vitality, Mr. Werner stood with an aura of assurance that seemed to defy his years. Even in his mid to late sixties, his tall frame moved with a fluidity born of an active life, his hair a refined peppered dark, signaling a sophisticated edge. With tenderness, he assisted his wife to her feet.

Mrs. Werner greeted her husband's assistance with a smile that radiated kindness and friendliness. Her presence was a blend of classic beauty and the comforting warmth of a nurturing heart, her attire stylish without effort.

Mr. Werner, turning to gather their belongings, picked up two Yeti coffee tumblers and a small paper bag from the table.

Observing in silence, Jack masked his sigh of frustration.

"Mr. and Mrs. Werner, Jack Sullivan. A pleasure." Delivering his apology for the delay without pause and with practiced ease, he cited a traffic mishap on his route. "I trust you haven't been waiting long?"

"Not long at all," Mr. Werner said.

While asked about their preference for the tour's start, Mrs. Werner chose Fallingwater, a decision her husband supported, emphasizing her wishes with affection.

"Fallingwater it is, then." Jack guided them to his vehicle, ensuring both were comfortable prior to joining them. He opened the driver's door as Mr. Werner said, "I told you, Suzie, we didn't need to worry about getting coffee and buying those Yetis. Jack has some coffee for us here."

"Well, better safe than sorry."

Jack replied, "You should at least try it. Rustic Joe's coffee is the best on the mountain. Have you been to the Laurel Highlands before, Mr. and Mrs. Werner?"

"Please, call me Paul. No. We flew in last night from Iowa and rented a car at the Pittsburgh Airport. We're in for a long weekend and haven't seen anything yet. What would you recommend?"

"Well, Paul, there are a lot of things to do at the Nemacolin Resort besides golf and the spa. I suggest doing the Off-Road Jeep Experience if you want some excitement. You get to drive an off-road course in a high-end Jeep. I've heard it's a lot of fun. There is also the Nemacolin Field Club for clay shooting," Jack said.

"If you're keen on exploring beyond the resort," Jack began his rehearsed description, his eyes reflecting the allure of the surroundings, "the area teems with charm. Quaint towns, artisan shops, and abundant parks await. Ohiopyle State Park is a jewel among them, just a short drive away. It sprawls over 20,000 acres, boasting forests, waterfalls, and the vibrant Youghiogheny River. There, adventures range from fishing to whitewater rafting."

Paul leaned in. "Sounds intriguing. What else?"

Jack's smile widened. "Not to miss is Wright's Kentuck Knob, which we'll see after Fallingwater. The Laurel Highlands offer nature's grandeur, nestled within mountains soaring to 3,000 feet, cradling valleys and woodlands rich in green. Spring and summer bring a chorus of wildlife; fall paints the landscape in vivid colors. The Youghiogheny's rapids offer a call to the bold, and Wright's architectural wonders await discovery. It's a sanctuary where nature whispers her secrets."

Suzie's eyes sparkled. "Wow. Where else?"

"Chalk Hill, too, on Route 40," Jack continued, "which boasts eateries, boutiques, a winery, and a festive Christmas store. Oh, and there's the bike trail through Ohiopyle, tracing an old railway all the way from Washington, DC, to Pittsburgh. The Laurel Highlands abounds with experiences."

Suzie nudged Paul. "I told you that you'd like this place, and we should've planned a week here."

Turning to Jack, she said, "A college friend from Uniontown told me about this area."

"That's the ex," Paul said, his smirk playful. "But Suzie, you know I don't like being away from the shop for very long. It's a busy time for orders."

"What do you do, Paul?"

Paul leaned back, a combination of pride and exhaustion in his voice. "I own a machine shop in Cedar Rapids with about 90 employees. It's a constant battle – chasing new clients, sourcing materials, meeting deadlines. And the workforce is another story; people leave without notice, or sometimes they don't show up, forcing me to beg for replacements. It seems like the moment I step away, everything piles up, waiting for my return. Escaping even for a short break is a luxury."

Suzie failed to conceal her irritation in her response, "Let's just enjoy the here and now. The shop can wait until we're back." She paused, her frustration bubbling over. "And can we please not revisit conversations about my ex? It's been over 40 years, Paul."

"Sorry, Suz," Paul murmured.

Seeking a diversion, Suzie pivoted the conversation towards Jack. "Your Trip Advisor profile mentioned you're a Penn State history professor and also in the Navy Reserves. Plus, you're doing tours. What led you down this path?"

Jack said with a modest smile, "In truth, I'm an associate professor and still working on my master's, teaching undergrads in the meantime. And, well, the bills won't pay themselves."

Although piquing Suzie's curiosity, she treaded with care. "Hope you don't mind me saying, but you seem a bit… older for a master's student."

Jack forced a grin and said with resignation and humor, "My mother would agree with you. She's my biggest cheerleader, though, always pushing me to finish."

18

"And how old are you, if it's okay to ask?"

"I turned 31 last month," Jack said.

Suzie nodded, somewhat surprised. "I thought you were perhaps a little older."

"My dad always says it's not the years; it's the miles," Jack laughed, lightening the mood as Paul joined in, chuckling. "After earning my history degree from Penn State during the Great Recession, job opportunities were scarce. I ended up leading tours part-time to make ends meet while pursuing my master's. At the same time, my girlfriend advanced her career in DC and is now the Assistant Director and Curator at the Museum of American History. So, as she's made significant strides, I am still here in the Laurel Highlands."

"It sounds like you are no longer together," Suzie said.

"No, we're not, ma'am. She called off our engagement just over three years ago," Jack said, sorrow in his voice. "Emma was always ambitious, securing her dream job right away. In comparison, I am more relaxed. She found my pace frustrating – I wasn't aggressive enough in pursuing a teaching position, to hasten my master's, or to relocate with her."

He sighed and continued, "The job market was bleak during the recession, leading me to enlist in the Navy to bolster my finances. Plus, the GI Bill helps with tuition. Emma supported me through my naval stint, but our paths diverged a few years later."

"Sorry to hear that," Suzie said with sympathy.

Jack's tone lightened as he shifted the conversation. "On a brighter note, the Navy introduced me to Steve, my best friend. He comes to town often."

"Paul served in the Air Force during Vietnam," Suzie shared.

"I was a mechanic, not on the front lines, but I learned a lot about aircraft parts."

"Did that inspire your move into manufacturing?" Jack asked.

"Somewhat. I enjoyed the work, and my uncle's shop provided a natural step when I returned. I took it over since he had no children."

"That's impressive," Jack said.

"Jack, just so you know, we also struggled when we started out. So don't give up," Suzie redirected. "That's enough about us. Tell me about Steve."

Jack smiled. "Now, Stevie... He's part commando, part engineering genius, with a sense of humor that's just, well, out there. He was my rock in the Navy."

"What made him so crucial to you?" Suzie prodded.

Opening up about his military experiences often proved lucrative for Jack. "I served in the Persian Gulf. There was an unexpected skirmish outside Basrah, and they sent us in to help extract two dozen pinned-down soldiers along the Shatt al-Arab River. We came under heavy fire, and I took a shot that missed my vest and knocked me into the river. I was unconscious. Stevie dove in and pulled me out, revived me, and packed my wound. After my recovery, due to my background in the armed forces, I got lucky and found an instructor job at Penn State's Fayette campus. This allowed me to pursue a master's degree."

Suzie, curious, asked, "But couldn't you have moved to DC with Emma? Pursued your master's there?"

Jack sidestepped, not wanting to explain his hunt for Braddock's gold. "This region has my heart. I'm fascinated by the French and Indian War, exploring the landscape and retracing the steps of those early skirmishes. Emma couldn't grasp my passion for the untamed wilderness here, the history underfoot. That, Suzie, is something the city couldn't offer."

A reflective silence filled the car, and Jack's glance caught Suzie staring at him through the rearview mirror. With a somber tone, "I couldn't leave yet; I wanted to do more here. I tried to make a change with the Navy. You know, a change of scenery sometimes helps you alter your perspective. But as soon as I got out, I desired to come back. She couldn't understand and ended it."

With a muffled sigh, Jack mused: *If only finding Braddock's gold had been more than a dream, things might've been different.*

To ease the heavy air, Jack shifted the conversation. "Did you want to hear something interesting about Route 40 – The National Road we drove on for a bit?"

Curiosity replaced the tension. "Yes," came the reply.

"It started as a Native American trail – Nemacolin's Path. General Edward Braddock expanded it to march his army from Fort Cumberland to what's now Pittsburgh, making it broad enough for the supply wagons and cannons to traverse it. It was also called Braddock's Road afterward."

With enthusiasm, Jack went on to explain why the King sent Braddock to the colonies to expel the French and expand the British territories.

"Braddock was skilled in European battle strategies, yet he underestimated guerrilla warfare tactics used by the French and Native Americans. His reluctance to ally with Native Americans, or perhaps his mistrust, was a significant misstep in the French and Indian War."

Jack's passion for history shone as he spoke, "In comparison, Colonel George Washington, who accompanied Braddock from Fort Cumberland, understood guerrilla tactics better. But it seems Braddock didn't heed his advice. Or, he may have held Washington's earlier entanglement with the French at Jumonville Glen against him. Historians believe that this skirmish started the war with France. Have you heard about that or the battle at Fort Necessity?"

Paul's eyes widened. "No, what happened?"

"The French were fortifying their hold from New France, which is Canada, to Louisiana with forts and trading posts, aiming to monopolize the fur trade. The British colonists, eyeing the same lands for settlement, found themselves at odds with France."

"The British built a Fort Prince George at the fork of the Ohio, Monongahela, and Allegheny Rivers, which is now Pittsburgh. When Washington arrived in 1754, he found the fort taken over by the French, who renamed Fort Duquesne. He asked the French to leave the territory. They, surprise, surprise, refused to depart."

"What did Washington do?" Suzie asked, her curiosity piqued.

"Being a small, outnumbered group, Washington retreated and headed back to Virginia to report. However, along the way back, he confronted a small French group in Jumonville, not far from here. Washington also asked them to leave. A scuffle ensued when French soldiers, led by

Joseph Coulon de Villiers, Sieur de Jumonville, offered a *countering* message to Washington, where they ordered Washington to leave the area instead. This altercation resulted in the deaths of Coulon and nine others. Ultimately, France accused Washington of attacking their small force at Jumonville Glen," Jack explained.

"So, sounds like each side blames the other?" Paul interjected.

"Pretty much. The escalating tensions caused Washington to erect Fort Necessity in June 1754. On July 3rd, a French attack upon the fort marked the onset of the French and Indian War. Many saw Washington's defeat and coerced confession of assassinating Coulon as sparking the war. We could visit these historical sites," Jack said, enthusiasm evident.

"Sounds fascinating," Suzie remarked, intrigued.

"The conflict with the French was far from settled for Washington. He later joined Braddock's to recapture Fort Duquesne. During the march, he suffered from dysentery, forcing him to stay behind. However, despite still being ill, he managed to rejoin the troops just before the disastrous Battle of the Monongahela. Amidst the chaos, Braddock received a mortal wound, and Washington raced in to rescue him. They retreated and were transporting him back to Fort Cumberland when Braddock died on July 13th, on the very road he constructed," Jack narrated.

"That's interesting," Paul said.

"Oh, it gets even better," Jack's voice rose again. "Washington ordered Braddock's burial under the road, marching back and forth until they couldn't distinguish the grave from the road. Not until 1804 did construction workers uncover a body adorned with an officer's uniform buttons, believed to be Braddock. He lies buried between Fort Necessity and Chalk Hill. Shall we visit his grave?"

"Yes, but why bury him like that?" Paul queried.

"To protect his remains from desecration," Jack replied, noting Suzie's discomfort in the mirror. His fingers tapped on the steering wheel while he pondered their next conversation on the scenic drive.

With luck, the scenery changed, "Hey, we're in Ohiopyle, where you want to come for fun." Jack pointed out. "On the left, you've got the visitor center. To the right, White Water Adventurers, and just across the river, Wilderness Voyageurs. They're your go-to's for rafting, kayaking, even bike tours."

"Can we rent stuff there?" Paul asked.

"Indeed," he said. "They've got all you need for a day out. And if you're hungry, Ohiopyle Bakery and Sandwich Shoppe is over there and has homemade baked goods, sandwiches, soups, and salads. Plus, Falls City Restaurant & Pub nearby has a solid selection of craft beers and a great view from their outdoor seating. I like hanging out there on nice days like today."

Nearing Fallingwater, 'Your Song' by Elton John rang from Jack's phone, prompting a moment of distraction as he pressed disconnect. He tilted his head, and a slight furrow appeared: *Why is Emma calling now?*

He continued, "We're almost there. Up ahead is Fallingwater, surrounded by the Bear Run Nature Preserve. Its 5,000 acres of lush wilderness are home to diverse wildlife, including the eastern hellbender, North America's biggest salamander, and even the elusive Allegheny Woodrat."

Pulling into the parking lot, they approached the architectural marvel. "Fallingwater melds with nature like no other," Jack said, admiration clear in his voice. "Its design captures the essence of this place, with windows framing the waterfall views and decks that seem to float above the stream."

They paused on the bridge, taking in the magnificent view of the house and waterfall. Suzie's beaming grin was a display of her excitement. Without hesitation, Jack's hand extended outward before Suzie asked, "Can you please take a picture of us?"

"Of course," Jack smiled, just as his phone rang again to 'Your Song.' With a flicker of concern, he silenced it: *Something's up. However, I don't want to upset my clients.*

"Sorry about that... Ready? Smile..."

Through a modest entryway on the ground level, they stepped onto a terrace framed by stone and wood, leading to the door of Fallingwater.

Inside, the expansive living room greeted the Werners. Its high ceilings and concrete boundaries were magnified by the light streaming through wall-to-wall, floor-to-ceiling windows, unveiling the landscape's grandeur. The room, decorated with elegant and tasteful furnishings, was complemented by a robust wooden table, a commanding stone fireplace, and inviting chairs.

Jack gestured toward the balcony. "The most remarkable aspect here is the balcony and how it's suspended over the waterfall. It's where steel and stone merge, crafting an illusion of floating amidst nature. This place embodies simplicity and elegance, its design marrying the interior with the wilderness beyond."

Suzie's eyes widened in awe, "It's breathtaking."

"Shall we step out to the balcony for the view and a photo? It's a favored spot, aside from the fireplace inside," he proposed.

On the balcony, the Werner's arranged themselves for a picture, the waterfall framing their moment. 'Your Song' interrupted again, but Jack, with a sigh and quick tap, chose to ignore it, focusing instead on capturing their smiles with Suzie's phone.

Returning indoors, he shared the history of Fallingwater, commissioned by the Kaufmann family as a respite from urban life. "In 1934, Edgar Kaufmann Sr., a notable businessman and lover of modern architecture, sought Frank Lloyd Wright's vision for this retreat. In integrating the house with its natural surroundings, Wright's design was both revolutionary and contentious, challenging conventional boundaries between inside and outside."

'Your Song' played once more, and Mr. Werner's patience thinned, his gaze sharpening towards him, who silenced the call.

"Wright envisioned a living space that embraced its setting, blurring the lines with nature," he continued, unaffected.

Approaching the study, they found the room occupied. "Let's pause here; the study's a bit crowded. Would you like to take the photo by the fireplace now?"

Suzie, still captivated by the views, deferred. "Let's wait. I'm not ready to leave these views just yet."

Minutes slipped by, and the people exited the study. The guide greeted him, "Jack, leading *another* expedition through the house, I see?"

"Hey, Karen. Time's tight today; they've got one day to soak it all in. Couldn't linger for your next tour, as much as we'd have liked them to have my favorite guide. Maybe they can join your group after the study?" he asked.

Karen's response came with a light-hearted warning, "Catch up if you can, Jack. You're known for your detours," her smile softening the tease. She turned to the Werners, advising, "Steer him clear of any historical tangents, like the French and Indian War."

Paul smiled, and curiosity piqued; he leaned closer to Jack, murmuring, "History between you two?"

"Yeah… Short and not good. It's a chapter best left unturned. However, she sours over losing tips."

With a wink, "Say no more." Paul gestured for him to continue.

He led the Werners into the study, immersing them in its essence. "This snug study boasts a built-in desk, shelves, and even a window seat – all in Wright's vision for an integrated living space."

They explored for a few minutes before moving on, Jack leading. "Next is the dining room, westward along this corridor. We'll likely rejoin Karen's group there." When they entered the room, he added, "Its windows frame the wilderness with perfection, mirroring the vastness outside."

The dining room revealed itself through its expansive table set and adorned walls, each piece conveying Kaufmanns' desire for harmony with nature.

Jack, ever the guide, seamlessly wove the room's narrative into the fabric of their experience when his phone binged, breaking the moment. A glance disclosed a text, a single word igniting a spark of urgency in his eyes and an opened mouth – "BRADDOCK!"

Paul's gaze bore into him, concern etching his features. "Jack, you alright? Looks like you've seen a ghost."

He stammered, "Not sure, it's just... my ex, Emma. She keeps calling."

Suzie chimed in with firm resolve, "You better call her back. That many calls, it sounds urgent."

Muttering apologies, he excused himself, his call to Emma laced with panic, "Hey, Emma. What's happening? They found what? Where?"

Jack's grip tightened on his phone, his voice infused with sudden haste. "How soon would I have to be there? I understand, but... I'm at Fallingwater, giving an all-day tour. I can't leave my couple stranded... What should I do?"

Observing the unfolding drama, Suzie nudged Paul into action and gestured toward Karen. "Jack, this seems serious. Karen can take over, right? Otherwise, we'll call the resort. Don't fret about us." Paul's question hung in the air as he looked at Karen, who nodded her assent with a smirk.

Jack was still processing but now grasping he had an excuse for ditching the tour. He hesitated before saying, "I'm sorry. But you've already paid... I can return your money."

Paul placed his hand on Jack's shoulder and opened his mouth, but Suzie interrupted. With a preemptive wave, she said, "Don't worry about it, Jack. It's only money."

"You sure?" Jack's voice trembled with gratitude and disbelief.

Paul sighed. "Go, Jack," and he urged with a gentle finality.

"Thank you," Jack whispered.

He returned his attention to his phone. "Emma, I'll be there in less than an hour." With that, he sprinted away, leaving the tour and the house behind.

Chapter 2

While Jack was searching the Youghiogheny Riverbank earlier this morning, contractor Mike Thompson and his crew, Kevin and Shawn, thought they were having a typical day. As usual, they were already behind schedule on their construction project when their day took a sudden turn. The excavator halted with a jolt, striking something unyielding beneath the soil.

"What the hell did I just hit?" Mike bellowed across the site.

Shawn yelled back, "Looks like massive cedar or oak logs, side by side!"

Why on earth are they buried four feet underground? Mike growled in frustration. He attempted to dig around them with the excavator, but something felt off.

He barked at his crew to halt as he jumped from the machine, glancing at his watch with concern. They were immersed in The Lodges of Sunset Village excavation, facing an imposing ten-foot earthen wall. Above them were towering trees on mountainside slopes, its peak a little higher than their position. Behind them was an unobstructed view of Deep Creek Lake glistening hundreds of feet below.

Their dwindling timeline for preparing the site for the next phase of construction drove them to dig in a hurry. They were racing the clock to finish the excavation and the forming and pouring of the concrete footers.

With a sense of haste, they heaved shovels through the dirt, muscles straining and sweat beading, hurrying against a deadline they now needed to unearth the secrets held by the ground. After a few minutes, Mike's face twisted into a grimace as he huffed. "Kevin, get a chain from my truck."

They wrapped the chain several times around the end of one log. Mike attached the other end of it to the backhoe and shouted, "Everyone out! I don't want this breaking and hitting one of you."

Mike climbed into the cab, started it up, and inched the bucket's boom to take up the slack. He then pulled hard, and the excavator's engine roared, but there was no movement. Without warning, the chain snapped. He flinched and shielded his face before it struck the machine's cage with a loud CLANK! *Thank God for the cage.*

Fueled by frustration, Mike's digging grew reckless, the machine's movements a mirror of his agitation. In spite of the effort, the logs remained steadfast but were now bared, presenting a curious barrier to the foundation.

His frantic attempts didn't go unnoticed by his men, perched on the hillside, chuckling at his fervent but pointless efforts. Despite his determination, the stubborn impediment resisted. Climbing out, Mike surveyed the site – five massive logs lay bare, an imposing sight.

"Another chain," Mike ordered, his resolve undimmed. They extracted every log, revealing a baffling twelve-foot-wide gap in the foundation wall.

Puzzled by the discovery, he speculated on the purpose of the buried logs, each a 400 to 500-pound colossal testament to a forgotten endeavor. Shawn's suggestion that something might lie beneath prompted a renewed excavation.

Mike paused, tilting his head as his eyes narrowed. Then his expression softened. "You may be right. Grab the shovels!"

Their shovels soon struck a hard object. Clearing the dirt, they uncovered a wooden barrel, its contents a mystery thudding and clinking within as they rolled it to the basement floor. He instructed Kevin to fetch tools to remove the top hoop ring.

"Let's pop this open," he said, excitement in his voice. The staves creaked as they pulled.

A loud crack from the loosened lid met Mike's triumphant smile. He removed the lid without hesitation, reached inside, and plucked out a deep red coat. "Is this a British Redcoat?" he marveled.

Reaching further, he retrieved a leather-bound book, a protruding paper catching his eye. Unfolding it, Mike saw a hand-drawn map sprawled out before him, detailing familiar landmarks such as Fort Cumberland, the Savage and Youghiogheny Rivers, and a path mirroring Route 40. "We're on one of these trails," he realized, pointing to another line.

After refolding the map into the journal, Mike's eyes landed on the inscription inside the cover, *'Property of Cpt. Lt. Thomas Clarke.'* His fingers traced the words as he absorbed the page's contents.

April 13, 1755

I arrived in Alexandria, Virginia, today from the outskirts of Philadelphia. The town is a bustling port, filled with merchants and traders from all over the colonies. Many have come to join the army.

The mood is tense; we presume we will soon fight against the French and their Indian allies. The Quarter Master was not prepared for us. They found quarters for only some of my men and hope to find some for myself and the others tomorrow.

April 14, 1755

I received quarters in the home of James and Susan Davies. This will suit me till I leave to fight against the French. The father, James, is a fisherman; the mother, Susan, works at the inn as a cook; and their son, John, seems anxious to enlist and go with us to fight the French, but I feel he is too young.

April 15, 1755

General Edward Braddock met with the Colonial Governors today. Following this meeting, Braddock informed us officers that the Governors decided to expel France from the colonies and wilderness territories.

I received orders to gather guns and ammunition and to accompany the General and his army to Fort Cumberland. We expect additional regiments to join us for our campaign to take Fort Duquesne.

Mike looked up, furious. "Dammit, guys! Get me the phone number for the Garrett County Historical Society Museum. We gotta get somebody out here before we finish digging this basement!"

Chapter 3

Sunday, April 13th, 1755

The sun approached the horizon as Lieutenant Thomas Clarke rode with his most trusted men: brothers James and John Miller, George Williams, and Henry Jones. They hoped to reach Alexandria, Virginia, before sunset.

Hoping to arrive in two instead of three days, their push from Philadelphia had been long and arduous, their bodies aching from countless hours on horseback or wagon. Yet, despite their exhaustion, determination to join General Braddock's troops once he arrived, which they anticipated would be any day now, spurred them on.

Clarke was a stocky man with kind, expressive eyes revealing his compassionate nature. His leadership skills were evident in the unwavering trust and loyalty of those who followed him.

George Williams, the wiry scout with a weathered face, rode beside Clarke. George was a resourceful and cunning soldier renowned for his ability to adapt to any situation. Being in the colonies for years, he was familiar with the land and spoke several Native American dialects. "I believe we should hasten, Sir, if we are to arrive by sunset," he said Clarke with a soft rasp.

"Yes, thank you, George. It would be better to rest in a bed tonight."

Clarke's eyes scanned the surroundings and saw nothing unusual. "James, scout ahead," he commanded, his voice hoarse from the journey. "Find the quartermaster. See if he can locate some beds for us."

The Miller brothers looked very similar but were very different. James Miller, the two-year elder, was a fit, handsome man with a square jaw and a mischievous glint in his eyes. Well known for his charm and daring, he was an excellent marksman. On the other hand, his tad taller brother, John, had muscular arms honed from years spent working as a blacksmith before joining the army. He was quiet and introspective but an exceptional fighter. He was distinguishable by his somewhat skewed nose, earned in a past bar fight rescuing James – who, of course, started it.

"Yes, Sir," James replied, urging his horse into a gallop with a nudge of his heels.

Henry Jones, a tall, burly veteran with graying hair, brought up the rear. His dry sense of humor and no-nonsense attitude provided comfort and intimidation to those near him. He was also able to anticipate the enemy's moves with uncanny precision.

Clarke looked around again. "Let's go, men," he said as he prodded his horse to a faster pace.

"Let's hope Braddock's arrival is soon," Jones muttered, more to himself than anyone else. "We've ridden hard for this. I wonder what the Governors will request of the General and us."

"It was a hard ride indeed," Clarke nodded. "I'm not sure what our future path may be." His thoughts drifted to the possibility of war. Serving under General Braddock was an honor, but a responsibility pressed down on his shoulders.

The sun dipped below the horizon, casting an orange glow over the bustling streets of Alexandria as they arrived. They walked through the dim streets, the light of lanterns throwing shadows on the cobblestone beneath them.

In 1755, Alexandria was a busy port town, its narrow streets lined with brick buildings, taverns, and merchant shops. The air was thick with the scent of saltwater, woodsmoke, and the distant promise of adventure.

From down the street, they spotted James as he rode up to them. "Every inn is full, Sir," James said. His lean frame made him appear more like a runner, and his nimble fingers helped him become a skilled marksman.

He continued, "I have not yet found John McLean, the quartermaster. He wasn't at his post, and his staff didn't expect him back till morning. They sent a runner to fetch him and will try to locate something for us. We need both food and sleep, Sir."

"Patience, brother," John said, attempting to calm his sibling. "We'll find something soon."

"James is right. We should dine first," Clarke said, steeling himself against the creeping exhaustion threatening to overwhelm him. "We'll worry about lodging after our bellies are full. With any luck, they'll have some rooms readied for us by then."

"Yes, Sir," George said, steering his horse toward a tavern on the corner. "I've been told that this place serves a hearty stew."

The warm air filled with meat and fresh bread beckoned them inside.

"At last," Henry uttered as he struggled to dismount and then stretched. "Let's hope this meal passes muster."

The men filed into the shadowed establishment, their boots thudding against the wooden floor as they claimed a table near the back.

Their frustration at being unable to secure a bed for the night overshadowed their hunger. Hushed conversations swirled around them, but Clarke focused on the gnawing exhaustion in his bones.

"If we don't have something from the quartermaster soon, perhaps we should inquire with some of the locals," James said through a mouthful of stew.

"There might be someone willing to take us in. Or we could sleep on the wagon," John countered, his voice tinged with resignation.

"No different than last night," James smirked.

Clarke grimaced at the comment and considered options, his mind slowed by fatigue and hunger. "Let's eat first," he said. "Then we'll see what we can do."

Exiting the restaurant, a boy spotted them and approached. He called out, "Lieutenant Clarke, the quartermaster sent a message, Sir."

"What is it, young man?" Clarke asked.

"You must have ridden too fast. McLean wasn't expecting you 'til tomorrow and can only provide lodging for two."

"Thank you, son. I'm afraid we'll be in the wagon again. I cannot sleep in a bed when my men have none."

John looked at James and turned to Clarke, "George and Henry can take the beds, Sir. We'll stay with you."

"You heard the brothers; go with the runner. We'll meet you at the town hall in the morning."

"Thank you, Sir," George and Henry both replied as they followed the runner.

With aching limbs, Clarke and the brothers resigned themselves to a restless night huddled together in their cramped wagon, the cold night air biting at them through their blankets.

"Tomorrow will be better, men," Clarke said, his breath forming a frosty cloud as he stared up at the starry sky. He pulled out his journal and scribbled down an entry detailing their journey, late dinner, and current predicament.

Monday, April 14th, 1755

Dawn was crisp and clear, and despite their discomfort, Lieutenant Clarke rose early, rubbing stiffness out of his joints before he and the brothers set off to meet the rest of his troop. The blankets helped with warmth but not comfort.

Arriving at the town hall, George and Henry were waiting for them, looking well-rested.

"Morning, Sir," George called out.

"Morning," Clarke said. "George and I are going to scour the town. We should obtain more provisions. Henry, you and the brothers should wait here for the quartermaster. We don't want to go through another cold, restless night."

"Yes, Sir," Henry said.

"What are you thinking for, Sir?" George asked.

"We will need some additional food, powder, and shot. Henry, find out what the Supply Officer has. George and I'll get some food to supplement our rations for the march."

Clarke's resourcefulness and keen eye for detail served him well as he navigated the crowded streets, procuring provisions for his men with an efficiency born from years of experience. Turning to George after he haggled with a vendor, he said, "We won't go hungry today if our host is short, and we'll have reserves."

Satisfied with the purchases of fresh bread, salted meat, apples, and nuts, they returned to the rest of the group.

It was late afternoon when they arrived back at town hall. "Did the quartermaster find proper lodgings?" Clarke asked.

"Yes, Sir," John replied. "George and Henry will remain where they are, and we are to stay at the home of the Davies – James, Susan, and their son, John."

Clarke chuckled, "As if one James and John wasn't enough, we'll have two."

"Sir, to avoid confusion, I suggest you call me JT and John, JD, when with the family. Those are our initials."

"Excellent idea. Any orders for us?"

"Yes, Sir. We're to be here tomorrow for the Governors meeting. We are on guard at the rear of the building."

"Find any powder and shot?

"The stores are thin, Sir," Henry said. "They informed me that we would learn more about it then."

"Very well. I say we head off for the day and take advantage of being able to bathe and rest so we are fresh in the morning. We should be back here at sunrise, men."

By the time they reached the home of the Davies, the sun had almost set on the modest, two-story house. A warm glow emanated from its windows, beckoning them closer. An engraved wooden sign hung above the door, reading, "Davies Residence."

"Appears promising," John said.

"No matter the quality, we are their guests. We need to be courteous and well-mannered. Understood?" Clarke asked as he lifted the brass knocker and rapped on the door.

The door swung open to reveal James Davies, a stout man with kind eyes and a welcoming smile. Beside him stood his wife Susan, her dark hair pulled back into a neat bun, her hands folded in front of her gracefully.

"Good evening, gentlemen," James said, his voice warm and inviting. "Are you the officer and his men we are to house?"

"Indeed, we are," Clarke replied, nodding in respect. "I'm Lieutenant Thomas Clarke, and two of my men: James, who we call JT, and his brother, John, or JD. We're here to serve General Braddock, and I am proud to do so again. We appreciate your hospitality."

"Ah, yes, we've learned of your long ride," Susan said, her eyes scanning the weary faces before her. "You must be exhausted. Please, come inside. We've plenty of room for you."

"Your kindness is most appreciated, ma'am," Clarke said as he stepped over the threshold, his men following close behind.

"Dad," a young voice said from the corner of the room. A rather tall, young teenage boy appeared in the doorway, wide-eyed with excitement. "Are these the soldiers? Can I join them?"

"John, hush," Susan chided. "You're thirteen, far too young to be thinking about signing up for the army."

"But, Mother, I'm almost as big as some men already," he protested, puffing out his chest.

"Easy now, young man," Clarke said, placing a hand on John's shoulder. "Your mother is right. You may be large enough, but thirteen is still too young for a soldier. Give it a few more years; perhaps you'll be ready."

"Besides, we need you here," James added, ruffling his son's hair. "The family business won't run itself."

"Okay, Dad," John sighed, his face falling with disappointment. A determined gleam told Clarke this wouldn't be the last they'd hear of his ambitions.

The men settled into their temporary lodgings and shared stories and laughter with James Davies and his son; Clarke felt grateful for this unexpected respite. The warmth of the hearth and the kindness of their hosts offered a brief reprieve from the uncertainty ahead. For tonight, they would rest with ease.

Susan called everyone to dinner. The flickering candlelight cast a warm radiance over the room as Clarke, the Miller brothers, and the family sat around the worn wooden table. The aroma of Susan's cooking, an irresistible mix of roast pork and fresh bread, was in the air. The exhausted yet eager men delved into their meal, their spirits lifted by the company of their gracious hosts.

"Tell me, Lieutenant," James Davies said, wiping his mouth with a cloth napkin, "there are rumors we are going to war with the French. Is this what brings you and your men to Alexandria?"

"Not sure," Clarke replied between bites. "The Generals are to meet with the Governors tomorrow. But, we intend to follow Braddock if the decision is to take action against the French."

"Ah, yes, it is what I feared." James Davies nodded. "I imagine it will be a long, bloody fight if they do."

"Indeed," Clarke said. "We'll do whatever it takes to ensure the safety and prosperity of our colonies."

"Your men have quite the camaraderie, Lieutenant," Susan said, smiling at the lively scene before her.

"Yes, Mrs. Davies. They're like family to me – we've been through so much together."

In a quiet moment, James Davies pulled Clarke aside. "Lieutenant, I understand that some of your other men have found quarters elsewhere in town."

"That's correct," Clarke said. "We didn't want to impose on your generosity. Rest assured, they've located suitable lodgings."

"Good," James nodded. "Please let them know they're welcome to join us for meals. We're happy to help in any way we can."

"Thank you, Mr. Davies. Your hospitality is indeed appreciated."

Later that night, Clarke sat at a small desk near the window, the moonlight streaming in as he penned a journal entry detailing the day's events. The soft sounds of his men's steady breathing filled the room, mingling with the rhythmic scratching of his quill on paper.

Chapter 4

Jack's mind, although clouded by the adrenaline of a moment, snapped back with a fervor. He couldn't believe someone found artifacts linked to General Braddock deep within Garrett County. *How did Braddock's troops venture so far off course to the south near Deep Creek Lake? What does it mean? Could this have something to do with the treasure?* Jack retraced his route, driving back toward Friendsville and onto the lake and the town of McHenry.

In a bid for more information, he reached for his phone.

"Hey Siri, call Emma Wilson." The call went directly to voicemail.

Again, he tried. Again, voicemail. Undeterred, he left a message urging her to share any additional details she might have.

He decided to try his best friend. "Hey Siri, call Steve Johnson."

Steve's voice crackled through after a few rings. "Dude! Whazzup?"

Jack's enthusiasm bubbled over. "Stevie, you won't believe what…"

But Steve cut him off. "I already know, man. Emma called me. So, keep it together. Don't let the treasure fever make you sloppy, even more so around the locals. Remember, you suck at poker. You can't bluff worth a damn."

Steve's words were a bucket of cold water, but he realized Steve was correct—the thrill of the chase needed to be tempered with caution. "You're right. And way to squash my excitement. WHOA!" he screamed as he swerved to miss a pickup.

"You okay, Jack?"

"Yeah, just some idiot wasn't looking and started pulling out in front of me."

"Hey, drive safe for a change." Steve shared more details, "Emma found out a contractor uncovered a barrel, with an officer's journal among the finds, all buried deep under logs. At least the contractor was smart enough to call the local museum. Hurry, we both know how these things can go missing."

Jack's worry mirrored Steve's. "That's troubling."

"Emma's worried you'll obsess over this so much so that I'm on my way to keep an eye on you. I'll be there in less than four hours. Oh, if the commander calls to check on you, you may not want to answer the phone or say you're recovering from your emergency appendicitis surgery. My last day consulting for his project at the yard was tomorrow, anyway. We were almost wrapped up, so no one cared."

"Okay, wait... four hours. I thought you were arriving early next week. When'd you leave?"

"Over an hour ago. Emma called after the second time she tried to call you. So, I hope you got a better couch for that shit hole you call an apartment."

"I've got an option for you if that doesn't cut it for you – a bathtub doubling as a makeshift waterbed," he chuckled. "Nah, I went all out on a top-tier air mattress for you. Thanks for coming. It'll be great to catch up."

"Jack..."

"Yeah?"

"The discovery of this barrel confirmed your theory. I can't believe you were right!"

"Of course, I'm right," Jack's laughter filled the air. "But what am I right about?"

"Considering McHenry's location, well over ten miles *south* of Braddock's supposed path... It confirmed your theory that Braddock buried the treasure on the way to Pittsburgh, not while retreating, and

40

did it after Washington fell ill. They would've veered south, evading French territories. Yet, the distance – they might've lost their way after burying it or ended up captured. It's still possible it was already discovered by others over time."

"You might be onto something. However, the barrel's burial suggests they weren't under immediate threat. The real test will be inspecting the site. I'm betting on finding clues within the barrel or journal."

"Let's hope," came the hopeful reply. "Oh, and Jack?"

"What now?"

"At the site, introduce yourself as Emma Wilson's recommendation from the Smithsonian. She's positioned you as a seasoned local archaeologist. This should give you an edge over any competition. Be diplomatic and assure them that the Smithsonian will return the findings. Your Penn State credentials will also bolster your standing."

"Since when did you become so strategic?"

"It's Emma's playbook, not mine," he admitted with a lightness. "Emma's knack for diplomacy."

"True enough," Jack agreed.

"Call me when you get close. I'll update you on my whereabouts."

"Will do. See you soon."

As he neared the lake, the countryside unfurled, with the last farms fading behind and the Klotz Corn Shack marking the journey's rural charm. Navigating a final turn around a prominent hill, Deep Creek Lake's expanse came into view, with Marsh Hill standing sentinel. Unlike any other in Maryland, its prominence was undeniable, hosting the Wisp Resort. It towered almost 700 feet above the water but still allowed the ski slopes and golf courses to butt up against the waters, much like the ski resort at Lake Tahoe.

Passing Fun Unlimited on Friendsville Road, Jack merged onto Garrett Highway, a scenic route into McHenry. The Mountain Coaster at Wisp, emerging from the woodland to weave down the long slope, caught his eye. With the windows down, the distant sounds of joy from the coaster's riders echoed in the valley, a prelude to the adventures awaiting him.

Nestled within the foliage-covered expanse of Garrett County, the area was a haven for outdoor enthusiasts beckoned with its myriad activities – from hiking, biking, boating, and fishing to world-class whitewater rafting. Yet, Jack's attention was elsewhere, fixated on a mission that led him along Route 219. His gaze lingered on the pristine waters of Deep Creek Lake, a jewel under the expansive sky, alive with boats and laughter.

Before long, the County Fairgrounds appeared, bustling with the energy of a barrel racing event. Passing it, Jack veered onto Cabin Lodge Road towards his destination at the Lodges at Sunset Village. He parked, closing his eyes for a moment of calm as 'Your Song' rang out from his phone.

"Hey, Em, I just arrived," he said.

"Jack, I tried to call you as soon as Bill O'Connell from the Garrett County Museum called me. Given your expertise in history, particularly with Braddock and the French and Indian War, and your proximity to the lake, I called you. But this is not your treasure hunt. The discovery at the site demands a professional archaeological approach. Document everything in detail, as if it's a formal dig. I know you lack a full team's resources, but do your best to photo and protect what you can."

He masked his annoyance with a terse, "I will, Em."

Emma pressed on, "I've since arranged with the museum director for you to gather the items to bring to the Smithsonian. We'll authenticate, preserve, photograph, and catalog every item. After that, the museum will receive the artifacts back."

"Understood."

"And Jack…"

"Yeah, Em."

"The contractor. He's behind schedule and wants to finish the basement and foundation, so please be quick about it. If you delay him too much, he may just start digging, and we could lose artifacts."

"Got it."

"The site's historical significance is paramount. I've got you a week to

42

review it all to determine if there is something that can help you with your treasure hunt. Please bring all the items to me by next Friday, or I'll be in the hot seat here. In essence, I got you a brief head start on any leads the barrel might hold."

Jack absorbed the complexity of his task, understanding the delicate balance of preserving history and racing against time. "Understood. I'll make sure we don't lose anything to haste."

"Thank you."

"And, Emma."

"Yeah, Jack."

"Thank you. It means a lot that you're helping me like this," Jack's voice appreciative, his thoughts on their shared past.

Emma's warm and genuine tone responded, "Of course. I hope this brings an end to your Braddock mystery. Closure or treasure, it's time you found one." However, her voice cracked near the end as if she was becoming emotional.

Thanks to Emma, his years-long hunt for the treasure appeared to be on the verge of a breakthrough. Her involvement stirred up a sea of memories, highlighting the distances now between them.

Jack collected his thoughts, steeling himself for the day's unexpected journey. Reaching for the door handle, ready to step into the sunlight, his gaze caught on an unforeseen distraction – a rather striking woman standing by his car, her eyes fixed on him.

Chapter 5

Exiting his Suburban, Jack took a deep breath to steady his excitement.

"Are you Jack Sullivan from the Smithsonian?" the woman asked. "I'm Sally Adkins, Garrett County Historical Society Museum's Director."

Composing himself to hide his confusion as Sally was not his anticipated, Bill O'Connell. Sally, mirroring his age, bore an effortless elegance, her light mocha skin and dark hair framing her slender features. Yet, Jack's resolve didn't falter; he adopted his professional demeanor, stepping forward with a confidence that demanded attention. Hand extended, he said, "Pleasure to meet you, Miss Adkins. I'm Jack. Here's my card. Wasn't aware you'd be here to welcome me."

"Call me Sally. Hope I didn't startle you. I was about to walk over to the site and saw you sitting in your Suburban. Thought I would introduce myself. I figured I'd wait to determine if you were the person they sent. And," she paused, "I'm concerned about our artifacts leaving Garrett County."

He met her worry with a steady yet firm tone. "I understand your concern, Sally. However, the Smithsonian aims to preserve these items before returning them to you. They're in good hands."

"Hoping things remain that way and the artifacts do come back."

"Would you like to join me at the site?"

"I would, but I'm not dressed for digging. Can I stay and observe?"

He nodded, strode to his vehicle's rear, and rushed to swap his shoes for his trusty, mud-speckled brown boots. With a practiced hand, he retrieved his treasure-hunting kit: a backpack, metal detector, knife, shovel, and cloth bags. Inhaling, he sought to quell his rising anticipation. Today, he might edge closer to the legend of Braddock's lost gold, a quest leading him to scour the region. The hatch closed with a definitive thud, echoing off the distant mountains.

Jack's gaze swept over the landscape as he approached the dig site. Beyond the excavation, the forested slopes stretched upward, cradling the mountain's peak. His eyes traced westward, across the Garrett Highway, to where the lake's Marsh Run Cove lay nestled, a vista of tranquility beneath them. Opposite, the Wisp's ski slopes take full advantage of the elevation change. The sun was low enough to cast shadows. The breathtaking scene reminded Jack why he loved the Deep Creek area.

Nearing the excavation, Sally misstepped and started to tumble, but Jack's quick reflexes steadied her.

"Are those your only shoes?" he asked, eyeing her impractical heels.

"Yes. I didn't plan for fieldwork today," Sally said.

He nodded. "I always keep boots in my Suburban for days like this."

They found the contractors clustered around the unearthed wooden barrel at the pit's brink. Their hands were busy with something he couldn't lay his eyes on.

"Will you men stop playing with the red coat!" Sally's voice cut through the air.

The workers paused. One lowered the British uniform he'd been handling and did not return her glare.

"Guys, I'd listen to her," Jack boomed. The sudden attention startled Mike, the foreman.

"Who the hell are you?" Mike snapped, then softened, "Sorry, the delay's got us tense. You're the Smithsonian guy, right?" He turned and told his team, "Put it down."

Facing Jack, "We've uncovered some items from one of General

Braddock's men that might interest you."

Descending into the excavation, he extended a hand to Mike. "Jack Sullivan," he introduced himself, offering a business card, and gestured towards Sally. "And this is Sally Adkins from the Garrett County Museum."

Mike embodied the contractor archetype – tall and solid, with the requisite steel-toed boots, reflective vest, hard hat, and eye and ear protection hanging around his neck. He offered a gloveless handshake to Jack, introducing himself with a nod toward Sally in the distance. "Mike Thompson. I know Sally," he said before gesturing to his crew, Kevin and Shawn. "I hope you can make quick heads or tails of this. I have to finish the basement so we can pour the foundation and get back on schedule."

"Thank you for reaching out to the museum. Did you take some pictures of how you found the items?"

"No, we did not."

Kevin interjected, "But I wished I had some video. It was something." He started to laugh.

Turning back to Mike, Jack asked, "Would you and your men be able to help me with the process?"

"Sure, I still have to pay the guys for about another hour and a half before their workday ends. So, I would like to try to get some work out of them for once," Mike replied, laughing as he bent and picked up a shovel.

Gathering around the unearthed barrel, Mike extracted a leather-bound journal with care, its age evident in its appearance. With shaky hands, Jack captured the moment with his phone, remarking on the journal's condition.

After placing the journal in a clean cloth bag, Jack requested Mike to display a found red coat for a photo. The crew's mocking expressions while they looked at Mike did not go unnoticed by Jack. He said, "Why don't the three of you stand together and hold the jacket for the picture? That way, we can document who found it."

"Thank you," Kevin scoffed, dripping with sarcasm, joining Mike and Shawn with their prize held between them like fishing contest winners displaying their impressive catch.

Jack's attention shifted to the barrel's astonishing condition after centuries underground, marveling at its preservation before refocusing on the group for the photo. Curious about the barrel's contents, he learned of additional finds – buttons, coins, and lead ammunition. He documented these with care, each item a whisper from the past.

At last, Jack sought to examine the discovery site firsthand. "Would you show me where you unearthed the barrel?"

Mike strode across the basement, his finger directing attention to a distinct depression in the earth. "Right there, you can see the hole the barrel sat in."

Jack documented the scene with his camera before turning. "Found anything else?"

"Nothing."

Beside him, Kevin shifted and avoided eye contact again while Shawn threw him a wary glance.

He eyed Kevin with suspicion. "Nothing?" His tone was sharp.

Kevin's confession spilled out. "I'm sorry! I just took one coin, thinking it wouldn't hurt. There were several, after all." He produced a blue-green, oxidized copper coin from his pocket.

Jack inspected the coin, revealing King George II on the front of the half penny and Minerva with her owl on the reverse. "We should return this to Sally and the museum; maybe they can do something else for you," he said.

"That's possible," Sally added.

After photographing the coin, he set it into a bag and inverted the barrel lid to serve as a clean surface for the artifacts. He swept the metal detector over the area surrounding the hole and got a prompt, loud beep. Digging with his knife, he found a rusty sliver of metal, an old bayonet blade, but no hilt. He documented this find as well.

Jack placed the blade beside the coin bag, took more photos, and resumed his search with the detector. Despite scanning the vicinity and the walls, silence ensued. The tension of expectation gnawed at him. Nothing turned up in the piles of dirt or the expansive hole.

He turned to Mike and asked, "Would you and your men gingerly scrape away soil to discover if we can find anything else?"

"Can do."

The three men went to work, scraping scoop after scoop of dirt. Jack continued checking the basement floor and walls, but his detector made no sound. His stomach churned with anticipation and dread. He checked new mounds and the giant hole, but nothing.

Growing impatient with the slow pace of hand digging, Jack said, "Mike, could your backhoe broaden the search area with tiny scrapes of dirt? My detector can pick up small items even six feet underground. There might be more here. Just take care with the excavation."

"Sure thing," Mike agreed.

While relocating the barrel, a figure in jeans and a gray hoodie observing from the edge of the pit entered the corner of Jack's eye. Mike shaved into the basement wall, but Jack couldn't shake off his unease about the stranger who moved for a better view up the hillside. He secured the journal, coat, and coins in his backpack and threw them on his back.

Mike expanded the hole with precision, doubling its size in thirty minutes. The soil amassed beside them as Jack swept the area with his metal detector, its silence a heavy verdict. Knowing the day's dwindling work hours, he asked, "Should we continue?"

Jack, caught in a moment of indecision, weighed the slim chances against the concern Mike would charge him for their time. "Maybe a bit more," he suggested, hinting at a deeper search below the already unearthed layers, driven by the tale of the buried logs and the potential treasure beneath.

Mike's machinery roared back to life, delving deeper at Jack's behest; however, they uncovered nothing but earth. Fifteen minutes later, the operation halted, leaving them staring into the deepened void.

"I think we're done. Sally, what do you think?"

"In all likelihood, you're right, Jack. If we haven't found anything in the gaping hole, there's nothing else here."

"Sally, Mike has my phone number in case he comes across something in the next day or two while finishing the basement. Mike, I'm sure I can say this on behalf of Sally as well; we appreciate you and your guys doing this for the museums."

"Yes, we do, Mike," Sally said. "When we get the artifacts back, we'll have a new exhibit opening party that you and your men can attend as our honored guests."

"You're welcome. That sounds great," Mike said with a broad smile, but his attention pivoted to making money as he looked at Jack. "I'm assuming I can go back to digging?"

"I don't see why not," replied Jack, "as you shut down for the day, I'm going to scan the around the hillside for anything else. Would your men be willing to carry the barrel up to my SUV on their way out?"

"Without a doubt. I'm going to move the piles out of the basement for a little bit while you search. If I do some prep now, I can start forming footers tomorrow first thing."

Sally's departure, with a promise of communication from Jack, marked the end of their collective hope. The day's search, ambitious in intent, concluded. Although disappointed that he did not find anything else, Jack's expectation of reviewing the journal further for clues about Braddock's treasure made the day's efforts worthwhile.

He slotted his earbuds in, his attention returning to the expanse surrounding the excavated basement. Not long after, Ozzy Ozbourne's 'Crazy Train' blared from his phone. "Where you at, Stevie?"

"Closing in, about an hour away. Where to?"

"My place. Pizza tonight?"

"Sure thing."

"Deep Creek or Mountain State?"

"I like Deep Creek Pizza better."

"Same here. I'll keep scanning and grab the pizza on my way back."

"See you soon," Steve signed off.

Pizza ordered; Jack's gaze lifted from his phone to a retreating figure in a hoodie. He wove through the site with his detector, pausing only to acknowledge Mike's departure.

Severed and solitary above the excavation, a colossal tree on its side caught his eye. Despite the presence of several other felled trees, a massive six-foot thick trunk stood out. A pang of sorrow struck when he gazed upon the sacrificed giant white oak until he encircled it and spotted the significant rot. He estimated the number of rings and the tree's age to be about 400 years old.

Another twenty minutes yielded little but nails next to the adjacent cabin. Jack packed his gear and the barrel into his SUV and drove down the Garret Highway, a very short distance north to Deep Creek Pizza. The aroma of just baked pizza greeted him even before he stepped inside, promising a well-earned meal.

Dinner was now secured, and he navigated the scenic Garrett Highway, diverting down Friendsville Road and relishing its curves for the fourth time today. Descending the steep hill, he veered right prior to the bridge over the Youghiogheny River. Soon, Friendsville unfolded in front of him – a tapestry of Victorian homes and historic buildings against the verdant backdrop of the river valley.

The town's charm, its restored Victorian elegance and stonework, always made him grin. He peered at the river and the families smiling and enjoying the swimming, fishing, kayaking, and the serenity and beauty of the water. In contrast, others strolled or hiked along the river trail, a picturesque ending to Jack's day.

Swinging onto Maple Street, the quiet, small-town appeal greeted Jack: a few shops and businesses nestled within. A convenience store, hardware outlet, post office, restaurants, and cafes made up the serene streetscape. Then he glanced at Precision Rafting Expeditions and All Earth Eco Tours. He mused how the tranquil area transformed into a lively bustle on Saturdays when Deep Creek Lake released water, attracting crowds seeking whitewater excitement on the river.

The eateries, brimming with guests from nearby lodgings, contrasted with today's calm. Moments later, he parked beside a brick edifice that housed the Appalachian Valley Natural Products store beneath several apartments, including his own. Retrieving his backpack and a pizza from the car, he secured the door behind him and approached the building's end to enter.

Ascending the stairs to his apartment, a familiar musk welcomed him. The dated decor reflected comfort and nostalgia, with 70s-90s style furniture and timeworn appliances. He heated the oven for the pizza and tossed it in. On the way to the porch, he admired the framed memories: Steve and him on a boat in Iraq, a family photo of his mom, dad, little sister, and himself in front of Cinderella's castle at Disney World, and together with Emma on Mount Washington overlooking Pittsburgh when he proposed.

He opened the porch's glass door, the overlook offering a view of Main Street's stillness, save for a couple heading towards the Friendsville Public House. The spot, renowned for its craft beers and hearty meals, distracted him for a moment from the serenity of his perch.

As he settled, the fresh air eased the day's weight off his shoulders. Anticipating Steve's imminent arrival, he savored a minute of peace, a silent homage to the simple joys of his home and this community.

A familiar voice shattered this tranquility. "The pizza better be hot; I'm starving."

Chapter 6

Tuesday, April 15th, 1755

Clarke woke before sunrise with his thoughts focused on the much-anticipated meeting of Colonial Governors. He and the Millers dressed, ate with the Davies, and headed to the town hall. Upon arrival, the sun's glow peeked out over the horizon, casting a golden light on the mist-covered streets. George and Henry joined them, and they took their posts.

The council started early, and word spread that the General would address his officers following its conclusion. The sun reached its zenith when a hush fell over the crowd, and all eyes turned to the makeshift stage erected at the center of the town square.

Major General Braddock stood tall and imposing, his graying hair and piercing eyes commanding the attention of all present. He cleared his throat and began to speak, his voice booming throughout the square. "Gentlemen, the time for us to act is now. The French have encroached upon our territory and are trying to claim it as their own. We must be swift and decisive to repel this threat and secure our lands."

A murmur of agreement rippled through the crowd as the General continued, outlining the urgency of their mission. "We are ordered to expel France from our territories. My men are to proceed against Fort

Duquesne and reclaim it in the name of our king. I expect nothing less than your complete dedication and unwavering loyalty in achieving this objective. We have much to prepare so we can go on to victory. We are now going to hand out orders."

General Braddock paused, scanning the assembly before locking eyes on Clarke. "Lieutenant Clarke!"

"Sir," Clarke saluted. "My men and I stand ready to serve. What are your orders?"

"We require additional arms and munitions. You and your men are to travel, gather weapons, powder, and shot for our troops, and mobilize for the march to Fort Cumberland."

"Yes, Sir."

"Colonel Washington, have Lieutenant Robert Davis and his men report to Clarke and assign enough personnel to carry out their vital task. Time is of the essence. Washington, give Clarke his list and treasury."

"Yes, Sir."

Braddock continued addressing the crowd, handing out orders to officers. "Men, we cannot afford any delays."

Clarke understood the importance of their objective and the need for swift action. When he turned to his trusted companions, the same resolve reflected in their eyes.

He was about to issue orders when he heard, "Lieutenant Robert Davis reporting."

"Glad you could join us, Robert. Who's with you?"

"I present William Thomas, Edward Smith, and the twins, Thomas and Samuel Rogers."

"Nice to meet you. We are awaiting our list and funds."

Washington arrived, presented Clarke with a small chest and papers, and said, "Here is your list of supplies and the necessary money to acquire them. You must leave at once and return as soon as possible, Lieutenant. What we received from England was insufficient to arm all the local militia marching with us, and what we need is not in Alexandria. You will ride to the neighboring towns to gather more, so we divided the task. I ordered Lieutenant Williams and his four men to head to the west. Therefore, Clarke, I'm ordering you to send half your men to Baltimore and the other to the south. Be back no later than three days."

"Understood, Sir," Clarke replied, taking the chest and papers from Washington.

Clarke turned to his group. "Alright, we have an assignment to complete. George, how long should it take to Baltimore?"

"Six to seven hours, Sir. That's at a decent pace."

"We have a long road ahead of us, and our success hinges on speed. This is the 14th. I say we head out now and reconvene by the evening of the 16th. We'll still have time to head out again if we need more supplies. James and John take two of Robert's guys and secure provisions for our journey. The rest of us will prepare the horses and wagons. Meet us at the stables." The men nodded, understanding the gravity of their orders, and set out to fulfill their assigned duties.

Clarke's troops dispersed into the crowds of people. He moved through the bustling town, his mind reviewing the supplies they needed to obtain – rifles, ammunition, and gunpowder.

Approaching the stables on the outskirts of Alexandria, Clarke understood reinforcements were coming to join General Braddock's campaign to take Fort Duquesne. The mere thought of these additional regiments bolstered his confidence.

"More men, more firepower," he muttered beneath his breath, a determined glint in his eyes. "We'll show the French what we're made of."

Before long, the horses and wagons were ready, and the men returned with supplies and provisions. Clarke and his men rode north to Baltimore and Davis to the south.

They arrived in Baltimore after sunset and found stables and an inn. Once fed, Clarke retreated to his room, read the latest letters from his wife and sister again, and still contemplated what to say in reply. He recorded his journal entry and called it a night.

Wednesday, April 16th, 1755

Clarke and his men prepared to search for arms while the dim sun rose behind a bank of clouds. They walked towards the city's edge. The streets were quiet except for the occasional rooster crowing or a dog barking.

Hoping to find the necessary tools and weapons, Clarke led his group to a large forge on its outskirts. Stepping into the darkened building, the sharp scent of burning coal mingled with the metallic tang of molten metal assaulted their nostrils, and the clanging of hammers against anvils filled their ears. A weathered man emerged from the shadows, his face already coated in layers of soot and glistening with sweat.

"What can I do for you, gentlemen?" he asked, eyeing them with concern.

"We need rifles, ammunition, and gunpowder," Clarke replied, his tone firm and business-like.

The old man stroked his beard, "I might be able to help you out, but it won't be cheap."

"We won't pay a king's ransom for the king's orders. However, we can offer you fair compensation."

"Very well, let me see what I have." The blacksmith disappeared into the back of the forge, returning a few minutes later with a cart stacked with weapons and several ammunition crates. "This is all I have."

Clarke inspected the weapons and ammunition, nodding his approval. "Excellent. We'll take the lot."

The smith named his price, and Clarke countered. After they agreed, Clarke handed over funds from the chest. "Much obliged," the blacksmith said, counting the coins before stashing them in a wooden box. "You fellas, stay safe out there. You can get powder down the street."

After a few more stops for rifles and gunpowder, they exceeded their goal. Clarke turned to his men and said, "I suggest we ride now and into the night lest we risk being robbed."

Henry replied, "I agree, Sir. We have too much to store somewhere safe."

Clarke and his men set off towards Alexandria.

Thursday, April 17th, 1755

Clarke and his men arrived after sunrise. They were offloading the last powder keg as Robert and his troop appeared.

"Robert, you look like you're ready to collapse."

"Lieutenant, we obtained most of our list before we were out of funds. We rode in haste, fearing the theft of our supplies if we stayed another night."

"We did the same. We only arrived an hour ago."

"We visited the towns of Dumfries, New Marlboro, Falmouth, Matomkin, Stratford, and Leeds. That is where our money ran out. Leeds has more arms should we need it."

"Let's see what you got," Clarke said as he took the register from Robert. The two tallied up their combined purchases. "It appears we have exceeded our orders, well-done men. I say we all turn in and meet for dinner tonight at the inn."

While dusk settled, Clarke, Davis, and their men gathered for a meal, their laughter and conversations filling the air. Several figures of authority approached — their presence commanding silence.

Sir John St. Clair, flanked by Colonel Thomas Dunbar and Captain Horatio Gates, stood before them. Clarke rose, and his salute was mirrored by his men.

"Lieutenant Clarke," St. Clair said, tinged with genuine respect. "Your reputation precedes you. The efficiency and dedication of you and your men are commendable in exceeding orders. It's an honor to align our efforts with such capable soldiers."

Clarke felt a surge of pride. "Thank you, Sir. We're eager to do our part in this campaign."

"Coordination will be key in this endeavor, and we must ensure our efforts are well-integrated," Dunbar said, offering his hand, which Clarke accepted.

"Indeed, Colonel. My men and I stand ready to assist in any way we can," Clarke affirmed.

Gates, nodding in approval, said, "Your expertise in logistics will be invaluable, Lieutenant. Together, we shall overcome the French and reclaim our fort."

"Thank you, Sirs. It may interest you to know," Clarke said, seizing the opportunity to demonstrate his unit's diligence further, "Lieutenant Davis reported there are additional munitions in Leeds available, should our operations require it."

Dunbar's response was a thoughtful nod acknowledging the strategic advantage. "That is indeed welcome news. I will discuss this with Washington. Lieutenant, be ready to lead a retrieval at dawn. For now, enjoy your evening."

"Yes, Sir," Clarke said, resuming his seat as the officers departed.

Friday, April 18th, 1755

In the morning, Washington ordered Clarke and George to report to the officers' meeting, with George available as a translator for their Native American allies. The colonel also resupplied them with gold so that Robert's group, along with the Miller brothers, could obtain additional supplies.

Over the next two days, Clarke immersed himself in the strategy session. They poured over maps and discussed supply lines, unit coordination, and contingency plans. A prominent Native American warrior and leader briefed them on the movements of the French soldiers and their usual patrol routes. Despite the enormity of their task, Clarke's confidence grew as he witnessed these commanders' collective experience and skill.

Saturday, April 19th, 1755

Washington walked up to Clarke amidst the second day's stir. "Lieutenant, your efforts have not gone unnoticed. You've lived up to your reputation. Join me for dinner tonight," Washington proposed with a nod of respect.

"Yes, Sir. It would be my honor," he said, a sense of pride swelling within him.

Clarke learned that day that England rallied an immense army of almost 2,400 men. He was to set out with Braddock and Washington to Fort Cumberland in the morning. Some troops already departed; the rest were to follow in the next few days.

That evening, entering the low-lit dining room, the savory aroma of roasted meat filled his nostrils. The flickering candlelight cast shadows on the walls, creating an atmosphere of anticipation.

"Lieutenant Clarke," Washington gestured to the chair in front of Clarke as he walked around to the other side of the table, placing his back against the wall. When Clarke took his seat, he felt a sense of awe at being in the presence of this ambitious young officer.

"I trust you've completed your preparations for tomorrow."

"Indeed, I have, Sir," Clarke replied. "It has been remarkable how fast soldiers filled Alexandria. Our forces grew stronger by the day."

"Yes, it is impressive," Washington said, taking a sip of wine.

While the meal continued, Washington recounted the harrowing tale of his long journey to Fort Pitt, where he discovered the French had taken the fort, and the skirmish at Jumonville on his return, where he had narrowly escaped death. Clarke hung on to every word, aware of the historical significance of their current objective.

"Though we were victorious that day, it was only the beginning of a much larger struggle," Washington said. "Now, we must take the fight to the enemy and expel them from our lands."

The two officers shared stories late into the night, and Clarke's determination and purpose seemed renewed. This war wasn't about land or political power but about England and its people's futures.

Sunday, April 20th, 1755

Clarke's voice pierced the crisp morning air, rallying his troops as they prepared to depart. "This fight is for us, for those who will follow. We march not just for victory but for a future worthy of our king and country."

With resolve in their eyes and dedication in their ranks, Clarke and his troop, side by side with Lieutenant Davis and his contingent, commenced their campaign. United in purpose, they rode out to confront the French, their spirits steadfast, their aim clear – to claim their territory and shape the course of history.

Chapter 7

When Jack opened the door to his apartment, his best friend, Steve Johnson, embraced him. Although Steve was slightly taller than average, he was endowed with a large muscular frame with chiseled features and an ebony complexion, giving him an air of mystery. His eyes flashed with infectious energy, and a large, easy smile lit up his face. His dockers and tight-fitted polo shirt accentuated his physique.

Relieved, Jack welcomed him, "It's great to see you, Stevie. I hope you didn't waste a trip and this journal holds something. The site didn't offer much."

Steve brushed off the concern, "I had time off, and I was already coming to see you."

"Yeah, but next weekend."

"Any extra day with a friend is a bonus. Let's dive into that journal while we eat."

"*After!* Don't want Emma yelling for ruining things with sauce stains."

Steve replied, "Yell at you? I saved you from the river in Iraq, but I couldn't save you from Emma if you did that. She would kill you." They both laughed.

Pulling the pizza out of the oven, Jack's curiosity about Steve's recent activities surfaced. Steve, now collaborating with their former commander, who was now a Rear Admiral, explained his work in enhancing naval training and designing advanced patrol boats. Their shared combat experiences inspired this project, aiming to create vessels equipped to counter modern threats through increased agility, armor, and technological sophistication.

"So maybe next time, I won't have to drag your ass out of the water," Steve said while laughing.

"Okay, okay, how many times will you hang this over my head? That's twice already."

"Well, I guess I'll have to stop… someday, but I can't right now; it's too much damn fun busting your chops!" After Steve stopped chuckling, he said, "We hope with more tech, we can identify and fight or defend against threats quicker."

"Sounds like you have your work cut out for you," Jack replied as he grabbed the near-empty box and placed it on the counter. He washed and dried his hands before sitting at the table to open the cloth bag. With anticipation high, he sat down to explore the artifacts, hopeful for discoveries yet unveiled.

Jack started to set the items out, the bayonet catching Steve's immediate attention. He seized it, taken aback by its tarnished state – what was once a gleaming weapon now lay dulled by corrosion, its edges blunted and pitted with rust. Beneath the decay, its historical significance was undeniable.

"This is incredible. I can wash the dirt off and oil it for protection. I could help preserve it that way."

"Not right now," Jack said. "We'll pick up some oil tomorrow. Also, please make sure your hands are clean before you handle the journal. And wipe the pizza sauce off that blade, will you?"

Jack unveiled more from his backpack, including a red coat that was in good condition despite its centuries under the earth. The jacket bore the now faded scarlet of 18th-century British officers, its wool thick yet remarkably intact.

The coat's grandeur was apparent in its double-breasted front, adorned with gold buttons, though some were missing, presumed lost over time, or were in the barrel. Its high collar promised warmth and protection, while gold braided cuffs added a touch of prestige. The tailored coat snugged the wearer's body, with a slim waist and flared skirts that would've reached down to the knees.

Jack and Steve admired the craftsmanship, the embroidery, and the ornate details. "Looks like a lieutenant's coat," Jack surmised. Although tempted to try it on, he realized it would not fit him.

Steve was distracted by the coins on the table. "How much do you think these are worth?"

"Between seven to ten thousand for the coins alone. That's why the entire treasure's value could be millions."

"Then let's not dally! Open the journal!" urged Steve.

Jack set aside the jacket with care and picked up the journal. A large, folded piece of paper sticking out from it captured his attention. Unfolding General Braddock's mapped route to Fort Duquesne, he found it laden with sketches and a dashed line marking their path.

"See this, the markings are the trail they took. It starts at Savage River, winds by Little Meadows, and follows the mountain's bends through Garrett County to the barrel."

"Where's it go then?"

"One heads south and west... I'm guessing it crosses the southern part of the lake. The other goes northwest and north. Likely following today's Route 42 to Sang Run, aiming for the Youghiogheny. They could have planned on following that trail so they could catch up with the troops at the Great Crossing or on the way to Pittsburgh."

Steve leaned in, excitement bright in his eyes, "And the treasure? Where's it marked?"

Jack scrutinized the map a few moments before sighing, "No 'X' marks any spot here, I'm afraid. Our best bet lies within this journal for further clues."

With a gleam of mischief, Steve declared in a mock-pirate tone, "Aye, those be cunning pirates burying their loot. Let's not dally, mate," he said, followed by a hearty chuckle.

Jack played along, "Aye, they were crafty."

Laughter faded, and Steve's curiosity resurfaced, "Why did you say they *planned* on heading north?"

"I'm guessing they never made it back. Clarke's choice to hide his coat and journal hints they feared French and Native American pursuit. By hiding his officer's insignia and possessions, he'd reduce the potential of being tortured if captured. If they buried the treasure, it would appear as a patrol, not on a secretive quest."

"Understandable. So, where's the gold most likely location?"

"It's somewhere nearby, I'd wager. Otherwise, they'd have headed north much sooner. They most likely followed the Native American trails as it would have been quicker and easier for them. Once they successfully buried the treasure, you would think they would turn northward and rejoin the army. Yet, without full knowledge of these paths, it's hard to say. But, this map hints at possibilities, though."

Jack spread the journal's remaining contents on the table. "There's… Four letters," he said as he unfolded each. "Two from Clarke's wife, Elizabeth; one from his sister, Sarah, calling him Brother Thomas; and one Clarke wrote to Elizabeth, but he never sent it."

Jack read the first letter. *"To my love, Thomas, I hope this letter finds you well. I miss you more than words can say, and I worry about you every day while you're away. The children are always asking for you, little Celia, the most. She is growing up so fast. Junior has started school and is doing well. Robert continues to be mischievous, and Catherine never leaves his side. As for Celia, she had a cough for a few days, but she is fine now.*

"It is hard to manage everything alone while you're away, but I am trying my best. Your mother and brother William have come to help with the children and the farm. They have been a great help to me, and I don't know what I would do without them.

"Please take care of yourself, my love. I know you're strong and brave, but you are in my thoughts daily. Remember how much we all love you and how much we need you to come back home to us. Yours always, Elizabeth.

After folding the letter, he picks up the second letter and starts, *"My Dearest Thomas, I hope you are well in health and spirit, even though I know you must be struggling with the hardships of war. I write with a heavy heart to tell you Little C has become very ill. The fever has taken hold of her, and she cannot keep anything down but sips of water. I fear for her life and pray for her recovery every night.*

"The children miss you, and I am doing my best to care for them in your absence. Your mother and brother William have been a great help, tending to the farm and looking after the children. But the heavy rains this year have made it harder to plant crops, and we may not have a bountiful harvest. I am concerned about our future, but I know we'll persevere with the Lord's grace.

"My love for you grows stronger every day, and I long for the day when you return home safe to us. Take care of yourself, my love, and know we all love and miss you. Yours always, Elizabeth."

"Well, I hope Little C, whether it's Celia or Catherine, recovered," Steve said with some sadness.

Jack scanned the letter and said, "The one from the sister is rather dark."

"Dear Brother Thomas, I hope this letter finds you well. I am writing to express my concern. Fears of a coming war and your safety weigh heavy on my mind. I pray every day for your safe return home.

"I must inform you I noticed something that troubles me greatly. Our brother William has been showing a great fondness for your lovely wife, Elizabeth. I have been keeping a close eye on them, and while nothing has happened yet, I fear his admiration for her may lead to trouble.

"Please do not take this as an insult to your wife's character, for I know her to be a faithful and virtuous woman. I believe it is my duty as your sister to bring this matter to your attention. I'll intervene if necessary.

"I pray you can return home soon and set things right. Until then, know you're in my thoughts and prayers. Your loving sister, Sarah Thomas."

"No bad news on Little C there, but something is up with his brother," Jack said.

"You said there's a fourth letter?" asked Steve.

"Yes, here it is. It is to Clarke's wife."

"*June 23rd, 1755. Dear Elizabeth, My precious, if you're reading this, I'll not be returning home to you and our children. I hope my fellow soldiers find this concealed letter and it makes its way to you one day. I pray you and our children will have a long, joyous, loving life. I'll miss you all more than words can express.*

"*Please care for the children, and I hope they will not give you too much trouble. I'll only be able to look down upon their smiling faces from heaven.*

"*I am doing well, but I must admit, I am tired of being at war already. Although we have faced no battles with the French, we have had some skirmishes with small forces we come across from time to time. I dream of the day when all men can live in peace.*

"*I must express my concerns about my brother William. Though he is helping with the farm, I fear he may become too attached to you, and his motives may not be correct. Please be cautious around him, my love. I trust you, but I worry the loss of his wife, Mary, from consumption may have left a massive cavity in his life and heart he might try to fill with your affections.*

"*Give my love to our children and my regards to others. My tears are pooling on the ground as I ponder I may be leaving you and the children behind. I cannot stop the tears from cascading down my face. I love you, always, Thomas.*"

Steve's voice broke the silence, "It's unsettling. He prepared for the worst, leaving a note for his wife for the General to send. Yet, he didn't share his endeavors here in McHenry with her. We should dig deeper into the journal."

Jack nodded. "He was bracing for the end. Had he returned, the letter would've been unnecessary. Fears of French or Native American assaults must have loomed large. Hiding it in a barrel was his assurance it would find her hands. I couldn't imagine writing something like that."

"I can't believe the strength it would take," Steve murmured. "So the journal should hold the key to any buried secrets."

Jack opened the journal, the past unfolding. "Odd, but clear, Captain Clarke, started the journal lieutenant but lacked a captain's attire. His entries begin in Alexandria, Virginia, at a pivotal moment before the governors' decisive action against France. His entries are succinct, detailing the mobilization of troops and resources, the General's directives for armament, and the necessity of sufficient wagons and horses for their supplies. He recounts interactions with notable figures – Sir John St. Clair, Col. Thomas Dunbar, Capt. Horatio Gates, and even dining with Col. George Washington on April 19th, 1755, that's the eve of their departure to Fort Cumberland."

"There's fewer notes after they crossed the Potomac River and arrived at the fort on Saturday, May 10th. Here's an interesting one. May 11th, he notes, *Braddock made several significant decisions. He decided to leave behind some of his artillery and supplies to lighten the load for his troops and order important repairs to the fort's infrastructure.*"

"I'm beginning to understand why Braddock chose Clarke to take some men and follow the trail to where they buried the barrel," Steve said. "It appears he had the trust of General; he's always near him and informed on what's going on."

Jack continued to flip through the pages, stopping to read:

"*Thursday, May 29th, 1755, with General Braddock leading the army, we left Fort Cumberland with a force of almost 2,400 British regulars and local militia.*"

"Here is another interesting one. *Thursday, June 19th, 1755. We're leaving Little Meadows and crossing Little Youghiogheny River.*' Today, we call it the Casselman's River in Grantsville. *'Colonel Washington is suffering from flux'*... that's dysentery. *'It is severe, and he can't continue. General Braddock decided to leave the Colonel behind with a large regiment of almost 300 men. They're to rejoin us when Washington recovers.*"

"Oh my God, I was right. Here it is. *'The General called me to the edge of the camp and handed me one of Colonel Washington's personal maps. He promoted me to captain and asked me to organize a small unit for a mission, and Lieutenant Davis and his men would be under me again. We're to follow one of the trails to the southwest, find a secure place to protect a cache, and return to join the army in time for its march upon Fort Duquesne. Only I am to convey its final position to the General.*"

"I knew you were right," Steve exclaimed. "After Washington's illness left him out of the picture, Braddock must have hidden the gold."

"Seems so," Jack said, his eyes alight with the thrill of confirmation yet shadowed by the unsolved puzzle. "Still, knowing this brings us no closer to the treasure itself, but it does shed light on the map's origins. Perhaps Washington, familiar with these lands or informed by fur traders, enriched his map with routes known only to the Native Americans. Let's see what more this journal reveals."

Diving back into the worn pages, Jack's voice turned somber, "*'Saturday, June 21st, 1755 – A decision I made today cost Samuel Rogers his life. I often ponder if patience at Little Youghiogheny might have spared us, yet the urgency of our mission drove us to gamble. His death is my burden to bear.'* Quite foreboding, isn't it?"

"It was," Steve said, his mind pondering the possibilities. "How did Samuel meet his end, I wonder?"

"Perhaps an ambush at the river crossing?" Steve speculated. "What's next in the journal?"

Jack turned the page. "*'Sunday, June 22nd, 1755 – By evening, we discovered a strategic, elevated spot near a marsh, securing our encampment for the coming nights.'* This must be the barrel's resting place."

"*'Monday, June 23rd, 1755 – Today, we found the ideal hiding spot for the treasure. I shall brief the General.'* Yet, no clues to its exact location," Jack sighed.

"Was hoping for more," Steve said.

"Only one more entry remains," Jack said, flipping ahead only to find the subsequent pages barren. "It's from Tuesday, June 24th, the day following his last letter. It reads, *'A morning marked by chaos and tragedy preceded the fulfillment of our task. I dispatched Lieutenant Davis to set the first marker. I await his successful return.'* It appears this was his final word."

"Anything else there, Jack?" Steve asked, his eyes wide.

Jack's fingers paused his scan of the journal, and he said. "There are pages missing. Some torn from the end of his entries, and others are missing from the back. Hold on! There's cryptic writing on a page near the back, covered in letters!"

He read '*NILHR ALEWT BTHVE SLOAR EAHUY OIEXB SFIGS TERMW ORTUI ILETT RNAAG MRDNB SOHES RRHAI EDETA ETNSD ERESI LKBRO HYNKD OAOTT EARAO YEHUN WARNI TNURR ITTLL EDLHD GI.'* "The first letter, N, is much larger than the rest. This has to be a code."

"Hold up. I'm curious about two things: What kind of code? And you mentioned a *first* marker?" Steve raised an eyebrow, "How many markers are there?"

Jack chuckled, "You cannot count, Mr. Three Questions. Regardless, I'm hoping it's not 'The Great Cipher' – a nightmare of one used by the French and British. It's a beast with hundreds of symbols replacing words. Without the codebook, it's a dead end. This doesn't fit that mold; we're looking at plain letters here."

"So, what's the verdict?"

"We might be dealing with a Vigenère Cipher," Jack theorized.

"That means?"

"It's all about the keyword," Jack said. "Imagine encoding the word 'Code' using 'Word' as our key. You match letters to numerical values. You shift them by adding those numbers together, and – voila – an encrypted message. In that example, 'C' plus 'W' is... 'X' as 'A' equals zero. Deciphering is just the math in reverse. The trick's finding *the* key."

"How do we crack it?"

"Might be in a personal letter or something only Braddock knew. His wife's name, perhaps, or a secret between Braddock and Clarke," Jack pondered.

"Could a computer sort it out or break it?" Steve asked.

"Excellent idea! Check the app store," he agreed.

Steve grabbed his phone.

"Could it be Playfair Cipher..." Jack asked, then shook his head, "No, it's too early for that, and again, we'd need a key."

A brief silence fell before he dismissed another possibility, "It's not a

Cardan Grille cipher either. No perforated card to slide over text and reveal hidden messages."

Now scribbling notes, Steve asked, "How do you spell that first cipher?"

"V-i-g-e-n-e-r-e."

"Found an app. $2.99. Downloading now."

"Wait!" Jack's sudden interjection halted Steve. After a thoughtful pause, he speculated, "Spelling it out sparked an idea – what about a Scytale Cipher?"

"What's that?"

"Imagine coiling a long strip of paper around a round object, like a spring. You write a few words of your message across that spring, placing one letter in a separate segment of the strip. You rotate it, write more, and repeat until you complete writing out your message. When you finish, you unroll the strip, and the letters are all out of order. You write the now-coded vertical letters across a sheet of paper, and it looks like gibberish until you reverse the process to decode it. It's an effective code since the length and number of words written on each horizontal line on the coil vary. You cannot assume that every so many letters is the next letter in the sequence."

"Got it!"

"Let's try writing the code vertically and use a rolled sheet of paper to simulate a similar-sized rod to align the words. It's simpler, and it might be our key," Jack proposed, eyes gleaming.

Steve replied, quick and eager, "Let's give it a go!"

"Fetch the tablet and pen from the counter, will you? I've got an idea. And while I'm jotting it down, please find my scissors," Jack called out.

Jack scribbled onto the paper, his focus unbroken until Steve, reading his needs, offered the scissors. Without a word, Jack sliced the paper into three precise vertical strips.

Pondering aloud, Jack asked, "The diameter for wrapping this... Could it have been a wagon wheel spoke, perhaps?"

Steve said, offering a spark of ingenuity, "Looking for something cylindrical? Why not a rifle barrel? They're standard in circumference, aren't they? You're lucky. I thought to bring the tape."

"That's likely. It would be the easiest option for Clarke," Jack replied, his attention fixed on securing the strips with tape. He rolled another sheet of paper lengthwise into a makeshift tube to mimic a barrel's circumference.

"Grip this tube at both ends. We need to simulate a rifle's circumference to coil the code around. We can fine-tune the tube's size to decode the message," Jack instructed, his mind centered on the cipher.

Wrapping the strip around, it was clear the alignment was off. "Let's widen it a bit..." However, that appeared not to work. "No, shrink it a tad," he said, seeking the perfect fit.

Steve adjusted the tube's size moment by moment, a silent dance of trial and error between them. Tightening then loosening, they searched for the correct orientation.

With one final adjustment, the letters aligned, and the first word emerged. "Next!" Jack shouted, the cipher unraveling before them. He transcribed the sequence of letters, each rotation revealing another piece of the puzzle. "n e x t m a r k e r b u r i e d h i l l s i d e s o u t h of i n d i a n t r a i l b e l o w l a r g e s t t a l l e s t o a k t r e e a t t h e b e n d w h e r e t r a i l t u r n s n o r t h b y m a r s h a n d t o w a r d y o u g h i o g h e n y r i v e r."

Jack gazed at it and read it aloud, "Next marker buried hillside south of Indian trail below largest tallest oak tree at the bend where trail turns north by marsh and toward Youghiogheny River."

With despair in his voice and without lifting his gaze to meet Steve's, he muttered, "This must've been the clue placed at the first indicator to lead us here, to this barrel. It means this barrel has to be the second marker."

Frustration creased his brow as he rifled through the journal's pages in a fury, searching for a semblance of another code. Jack's voice rose in anger and defeat, "There's nothing left! No other code! The journal ends here! We're back to where we fucking started! We've got nothing!"

Steve took up the journal, his eyes skimming through it for something, anything, Jack might have missed. A knock at the door shattered the silence stretching between them.

Jack's sigh carried his frustration. "Perfect, Mrs. Walker's going to complain again," he grumbled, standing to answer the door. With a tone of preemptive apology, he opened the door, "Sorry about screaming, Mrs. Walker."

The expected reprimand never came. "Although I heard you scream, Jack, I'm not here to complain about noise," she replied.

His reaction was immediate, mouth falling open and eyes widening as he looked upon the woman in his doorway, disbelief washing over his features.

Chapter 8

Minutes earlier, Emma Wilson arrived at Jack's apartment, her gaze drifting from the windshield to her own hands clasped atop the steering wheel and narrowed to the bare finger that once promised forever. Closing her eyes and with a few deep breaths, she braced herself to encounter Jack for the first time since their engagement dissolved.

She reflected on how Jack had stumbled upon an article after graduation and how it ignited the initial pursuit of General Braddock's gold. It started as an adventure together. The lush trails and the murmuring wind seemed plucked from a tale of old. Yet, what began as a shared quest morphed over time into Jack's solitary obsession. His fervor for the hunt deepened with every map, historical document, or idea. The greater time they spent apart – her in DC, him in the mountains – the deeper his fixation became.

The quest consumed the space between them and relegated their once-shared dreams and dialogues to the background. Emma had tried to be supportive, but Jack's increasing and relentless pursuit left her feeling sidelined. His neglect of familial obligations, save for compulsory holiday appearances, and his irritation at their visitations underscored the toll his obsession took. Their relationship seemed to dwindle to a mere casualty in his search for the gold.

Their final argument had ended with Jack storming off with gear in tow, making clear his priorities. Emma's desire for their first simple day on the lake that late summer sunny day had been overshadowed by a clue he deemed critical. His determined departure left no room for her, only the hunt.

I hope I can help bring closure to his addiction; one way or another, Emma stepped out of her car.

Dressed in form-fitting black jeans and a soft yellow blouse that accentuated her slim yet curvaceous figure, Emma's presence was undeniable. Her dark hair cascaded in waves, framing a face marked by striking features and expressive blue eyes. She radiated a confidence that was as compelling as elegant. In other words, it would be almost impossible for anyone not to notice Emma Wilson.

Gathering her bag, she ascended the stairs to Jack's apartment, catching snippets of conversation between Jack and Steve. A sudden outburst from Jack paused her hand mid-knock, her heart a tumult of anticipation and trepidation. The moment stretched, the door swung open, revealing Jack, his dropped jaw in utter astonishment.

"Although I heard you scream, Jack, I'm not here to complain about noise," she said to break the ice.

He stared at Emma in uneasy silence for what felt like minutes before she stepped inside and set her bag near the door. Steve, engrossed in a journal and letters at the table, looked up with a puzzled expression while Jack's intense gaze fixed on her without faltering.

After a few anxious seconds, Jack broke the uncomfortable hush, tense yet curious. "Emma?"

"Jack," she answered, her voice quivering.

Steve chimed in with a touch of sarcasm. "So the two of you know each other?" His chuckle filled the room.

After another moment, Steve raised an eyebrow. "Thank you for asking about me. But, this is awkward."

She felt a flush creep up her neck. "Yes, I suppose it is."

The tension hung heavy until Steve, with his typical humor, attempted to lighten the mood. "How was your drive, Emma? Before this gets weirder, should I go out on the porch to let the monkeys fly out of my butt?" referencing a comedic line from *Wayne's World* to ease the reunion's discomfort.

The joke drew smiles from Jack and Emma, breaking the ice.

She turned the topic to their discovery. "Sorry for dropping in unannounced. I was concerned about the artifacts and their effect on *you*, Jack. Knowing your focus on finding the treasure made me think I should be here to… look out for you. Besides, it saves you a trip to DC. So… what have you found?"

Jack looked at her, recognizing that familiar determination and altruism he still missed. "We found a barrel and a broken bayonet blade, but it's a dead end. The journal confirms the treasure but offers no further clues."

"How about I take a look?" she asked and took a seat at the table. While Emma poured over the journal, her stomach protested, heard by all, leading her to ask, "Do you have anything to eat? I ran home after work, packed for a week, and drove straight here. I've been running on Diet Coke and peanut butter crackers since breakfast."

"A week?" Jack echoed, surprised and somewhat daunted at the thought of her extended stay.

"Yeah, I've not visited for some time, and I missed the lake and… the two of you since… well," Emma said.

"He knows," Steve's sarcasm sliced through again, but Jack offered what little food he had, apologizing for the sparse bachelor fare. "We could go over to the Public House if you want to get something to eat and drink. We can hit a grocery store tomorrow."

Standing, she grabbed the pizza box, unveiling its last fermenting slice that had been sitting for hours. "Given your drinking habits, I am not going to a pub tonight. I refuse to play babysitter to drunks. I'll make a turkey sandwich instead," she said as she rifled through the fridge.

"Seems she's got us pegged, Jack," Steve said, his grin broad and mischievous.

Emma assembled her sandwich, her curiosity piqued. "Jack, why the outcry of disappointment when I arrived?"

"We reached the journal's end and found some entries about their local activities but no specifics. There was a code we hoped would reveal the treasure's location. We cracked it, only to learn the 'next marker' lies south of the trail, where it turns north, on a hillside below the largest, tallest tree," Jack recounted, frustration veiled as he gestured to the map.

He said, skepticism lacing his tone, "They hid the barrel on a hillside by the path indicated here. White oaks can endure centuries, yet over 250 years have passed. That once dominant oak may now be indistinguishable or gone; the other trees would've grown up around it. However, there was a six-foot wide oak at the Lodges, a few feet bigger than the rest, which signifies that was *the* location. With the area's transformation by lake and farm developments, our search now feels impossible if we have to find another tree that fits all of those clues."

Steve interjected, "The barrel's burial – several feet below, under hefty logs – suggests an intention to obscure and protect. According to the journal's final entry," he took the journal and flipped the pages, "*We completed our task. I had Lieutenant Davis place the first marker.*' The buried journal implies it wasn't the initial marker. Hence, our quest is now for a another clue – or the treasure itself."

Peering over Steve's shoulder at the note, Emma said, "It's clear that they made their efforts here a secret by encrypting their clues. Since they hid the journal, they must have completed their goal. At that time, they knew the treasure's location. So its existence isn't in question, just its whereabouts."

"Correct," Jack said, "but the real mystery is whether it remains undiscovered. Did Clarke reclaim it and not need to recover his journal? Or does something in this barrel lead us to another marker or the gold itself?"

"Nevertheless... is it still there?" still Emma muttered.

Jack's theory hinted at a larger narrative. "Braddock's hasty retreat, death before reaching the first clue, and soldiers' looking in the area after the war are proof the treasure's still here. Had it been found, the rumors and searching would've ceased."

The comments spurred some deep, silent contemplation.

Finishing her meal, Emma took command. "I thought about it. We have to find that treasure, or the thought of it will haunt us forever. I side with Steve; this barrel hints at something we've overlooked." Resolute, she proposed they revisit the journal for missed clues, excusing herself to refresh and slip into pajamas.

* * *

Steve squinted at Jack, a smirk playing at the corner of his mouth. "So, did I lose the sofa, or did you lose your bed? She won't be checking into any hotels, that's for sure."

Jack pressed his lips together, eyes flitting between Steve and the couch, "Let's wait and see."

With some resignation in his tone, Steve sighed and said, "Alright, which do you want? The letters and map, or the journal?"

"Give me the letters," Jack said, his voice steady.

In silence, they delved into the artifacts, scouring for overlooked clues.

Emma emerged from the bathroom, clad in athletic shorts and a loose tank top, causing Steve to catch a glimpse of her figure. At the same time, Jack was engrossed in his journal until he came across something at the back and exclaimed, "Incredible!"

Steve, misinterpreting the exclamation, chided him, aiming to ease an imagined tension. "Easy, Jack. You're making Emma uncomfortable."

Jack glanced up, his eyes dancing with amusement. "No. Not what you think, Steve. Look here," he gestured towards the journal's back, where residual impressions of letters were next to the missing pages. "Grab a pencil and the tracing paper in the drawer by the fridge."

Steve moved to fetch the supplies, his curiosity piqued. "What's the plan?"

Jack explained the process of creating a rubbing to reveal the hidden letters, his tone blending excitement with concentration. While they worked, letters emerged on the paper, forming a sequence that seemed familiar yet disjointed.

Frustration knitted Jack's brow, recognizing the pattern of 'a l l e s t o a k t r e e' down the edge. "It's the same message we decoded before,"

76

he concluded, disappointment tingeing his voice, confirming Emma's earlier suspicion.

Emma leaned closer, her interest piqued as she examined the journal. "There might be more here," she said, pointing to faint markings on another page.

Jack took another peek, and his excitement renewed. "You could be right, but it's hard to tell. Grab another sheet of tracing paper, Steve."

"Just call me Mr. Watson, why don't you, Sherlock?"

"Sorry, Steve, you're more than an assistant. Please grab it," he said, smiling.

With a light hand, Jack applied the side of the pencil lead to the tracing paper once more, revealing what were not lines but slashes through the text. "Seven of them," Steve said, both men pondering the new clue's significance.

"Yes, seven," Jack said, laced with frustration. "However, it's the letters we need to decipher. Beyond a scattering of Os, Ts, and something that could be Cs or Ss, the patterns offer no hints. Some slashes stretch wider, suggesting varied word lengths."

Emma reached out, her voice hopeful. "Let me try, Jack." She moved under the kitchen's brightest light, scrutinizing the journal, only to return, her optimism dimmed. "I can't see anything else," she said.

Settling onto the sofa with the map and letters, Emma's posture – a bundle of concentration with the journal propped against her knees. "Guys, there's something about the barrel we missed. Did you leave something in it?"

Jack's curiosity piqued. "Nothing. Why the interest in the barrel?"

Emma pieced it together aloud. "Clarke tore out a page with the code, likely sending it with the men who hid it at the first clue. So, what do we know? We could not find another cipher like the one they used for the 'First Marker.' Clarke made an effort to bury this journal and his jacket, which hid everything that the French could have used to determine more about their mission and where they buried the treasure. All of this together means the final clue to finding the treasure must have been in the barrel and, therefore, must be in these documents."

Jack said, "Yes, but what is the clue is the problem."

"It's late," Emma said, her voice tired yet determined. "Decide on sleeping arrangements, Steve. I'm claiming the couch tonight. A break might refresh us, bring new perspectives."

Unaware of the implications, Jack offered, "You can take my bed, Em. Unless you prefer to sleep with Steve."

Steve's grin was swift, but Emma quashed the joke with a laugh. "I don't think so, Stevie. Jack, I only need a blanket and a pillow. And Steve's too much of a gentleman to try anything."

"Damn the morals my parents repeatedly beat into me," Steve chuckled.

"Let's set up the air mattress for you, Steve," Jack said, moving to retrieve the necessities.

While Steve handled the pump, Jack searched for entertainment. "No Pirates game tonight. We've got a replay of the Penguins clinching their... ahem... fifth cup against Nashville."

"Pure luck," Steve countered, the proud rivalry in his tone. "Pittsburgh just edged out my Capitals in seven games."

Jack's retort was swift, playful. "Well, maybe 2018 will be your year... to lose to us for a third year in a row!"

Emma's voice cut through their banter, her focus unwavering. "Enough, boys. I need quiet to think."

Jack flipped through the channels, landing on a familiar sight. "Stevie, *Jurassic Park's* on HBO. Up for it?"

"Sure," he replied.

"Not bad timing," Jack said. "Looks like we're 15 minutes in. Emma, volume okay?"

Emma, absorbed in her journal, didn't look up.

A half-hour later, when Dr. Grant, Dr. Sattler, and Dr. Malcolm were having lunch in Jurassic Park's visitor center, and Hammond, the owner of the park, joined them to discuss cloning science, Emma bolted upright on the couch with one of the letters in her hand.

"Jack, this letter from Thomas – see anything strange about it? Given seven slashes means seven keywords, right?"

Jack scooted closer, the letter now commanding his full attention. Emma's finger hovered over certain words, prompting Jack's realization. "How did we miss this?"

"What's up?" Steve asked, his curiosity piqued.

Emma nudged Jack. "Tell him."

Jack traced the peculiar words. "Take a look at this. Some letters that start a word are bigger than the rest, like P in *precious* here and *concealed* there. It's subtle."

Steve frowned. "Meaning?"

"It's a code. *'Precious'* hints at something valuable, *'concealed'* or hidden. We're talking hidden treasure," Jack explained.

Emma pointed again. "*'look down upon'* – *'down'* must be a clue."

"Down... Down... Wait, on a map, down is south."

"So we have to go south of the barrel."

"Yes. And I can see *'As I leave you behind,'* *'behind,'* and *'tears cascade,'* *'cascade,'*" Jack said.

"That's five," Steve counted. "Hidden Treasure, Behind, Cascade, South."

Emma pondered. "What does 'Cascade' mean? And the others?"

"Cascade is something falling," Steve said.

Jack mused. "Cascade... *'tears cascade'* sounds like a waterfall. The treasure's behind a waterfall."

"Sounds right," Steve said. "But we're missing words."

Jack revisited the letter. "*'may have left a cavity in his life.'* The 'C' in *'cavity'* – is it larger?"

Emma leaned in. "It seems so. What could that mean?"

Jack spoke more to himself than anyone, his voice low, "Cavity... hole. South, behind a waterfall, in a... Not a hole, no. The word starts with 'cav,' which hints at a cave, perhaps."

"That's it, a cave," he reasoned aloud. "There are two main theories about the treasure's hiding spot. One myth has it buried beneath a massive oak that blazes gold every autumn. That one matches the barrel under the largest oak. That huge, six-foot-wide tree I saw on its side at the scene had to be the legendary tree."

"Jack, that does fit," Steve said.

"The other theory suggests a cave burial near water, along a river or creek. There've been some people who went missing and were later found dead in caves in the region. Police presumed they were spelunkers, people who like to climb in caves, but some believed they were looking for the treasure. This clue – a cave concealed by a waterfall – aligns with that."

Jack raised his head, "Being hidden by falls might explain why it's still lost. People have searched the area around the National Road from Grantsville to Pittsburgh. My recent focus, the Youghiogheny, didn't reveal the treasure yet because I've never looked behind any waterfalls."

"Where to first?" Steve asked.

"Garrett County is known for its waterfalls. Muddy Creek Falls in Swallow Falls State Park, the tallest in Maryland at 50 feet, hides a rocky recess behind boulders, almost a cave."

"There are the falls along the Youghiogheny, including Upper and Lower Swallow Falls and Tolliver Falls," Jack detailed.

"How about Gap Falls?" Emma said, "You took me there once."

"You have a good memory, Em, but Gap Falls lies northwest. We should start there and search the Yough for other falls," Jack said.

"Jack, you've cracked it!" Emma beamed, embracing him in triumph.

Yet, Steve's words cut through, "Hold on, we're missing a word. The letter had seven slashes."

The realization dimmed Jack's excitement, "Right again." They revisited the letter, and after a moment, Jack muttered a curse.

"What's wrong?" both Emma and Steve asked.

"Here, *Please be cautious.*' The 'C' stands out."

Worry shadowed Jack's expression as he exchanged looks with his friends. "Cautious... It implies danger awaits, maybe traps or natural hazards in the cave. We must comb through everything for hints on what dangers lie ahead."

"You're onto something," Emma conceded, her voice heavy with fatigue. "It's very late, and I'm exhausted. Tomorrow's another day – early breakfast and off to chase waterfalls and hidden caves. I'll dig deeper into the letters and journal on the way."

Her eyes held Jack in a poignant pause, and her face softened in regret, "The treasure's out there, Jack. I'm sorry I pushed you to cut back on your search."

Jack rose, a soft resolve in his posture. "It's alright, Em. Back then, we didn't know it was real. Come morning, we'll look together." He paused at the bedroom door, casting a final, understanding gaze at Emma before disappearing inside.

Emma's eyes, brimming with unshed tears, reflected her turmoil – the pain of their estrangement.

Steve reached out and squeezed Emma's shoulder, and his breath caught in his throat as he struggled to find the right words. "I know how much your breakup affected both of you," he said, his voice cracking with emotion. "The one thing I learned in life is it's never too late to do something." He walked over and turned off the lights, leaving her to her thoughts.

Chapter 9

Restlessness plagued Jack's night, his thoughts ensnared by hidden treasures and burgeoning feelings for Emma. The abrupt ring of his phone shattered the silence of dawn, pulling him from the clutches of sleep. Through bleary eyes, he noted the faint hint of light seeping around the blind, a stark reminder of the early hour. Someone used the hack by calling twice to bypass his phone's silent mode – signaling urgency.

Groggily, Jack answered, not recognizing the caller ID. "This is Jack. What's up?"

A voice erupted in anger, "What the hell did you do to my site?"

Confused, Jack asked, "Who's this?"

"It's Mike Thompson. I've arrived to find my excavations in shambles, walls and floor excavated, and the excavator's engine is still warm. What were you up to?"

"I'm clueless about this. I left 20 minutes after you. My night was pizza and TV with friends in Friendsville, nothing more."

"We have a problem. Get here, now."

"I need time – to wake everyone and drive over."

"Make it as fast as you can," Mike pressed, "I've got a day's work destroyed."

When the call ended, the full severity hadn't dawned on Jack.

Springing into action, Jack rallied Emma and Steve in the living room, urgency in every word. "We have to move – trouble at the site."

Emma and Steve snapped to attention, and their sleepiness dispelled by concern. "What happened?" Emma asked, gathering her things as Steve fumbled out of bed.

"I'll tell you on the way," Jack instructed, grabbing swim attire in a frenzy, "Pack swimsuits and towels. We're getting wet at the falls."

"Are you kidding me? I haven't even eaten yet," Steve protested.

Jack's insistent, "Sorry, no time!" He grabbed a mesh bag with snorkel gear from his closet.

"Okay, okay," Steve replied.

"Come on!" he urged as he headed out the door.

"Who did it, and what were they doing?" Steve asked, while they stomped down the steps like a herd of elephants.

"I'm stumped," he said. "My gut tells me it was the hooded guy who seemed very curious about the dig and barrel. Or perhaps another treasure hunter heard about General Braddock's artifacts and hoped we missed something."

They jumped into Jack's Suburban, and he ignited the engine and pressed the accelerator.

"Remember the two tales about the treasure's hiding place: a massive tree or a cave? We now know both were true," Jack asked. "Secrecy was a tall order with an army as vast as Braddock's. Soldiers probably heard rumors and might have sought the gold after that or the Revolutionary War when it was more peaceful."

Emma nodded in agreement.

Jack pressed on. "Heck, back in the Civil War in the spring of 1863 – Confederate forces disrupted the B&O Railroad and stormed Fort Alice. Some people speculated they were also after the gold to fund their efforts."

"That's a piece of history I missed," Steve quipped, half-joking.

"Who can say what the contractor and his employees disclosed about the findings? Word spreads like wildfire here. I'll suggest to Mike that rumors of the barrel's discovery might have lured treasure hunters aiming for black market profits."

"That could work," Emma contemplated, reaching for the journal.

The radio played a poignant song. *"...people can be so cold? They'll hurt you and desert you, yet steal your soul if permitted. Oh, but don't allow it..."*

"Spot on. Name that tune, Jack," remarked Steve.

Jack joined in, his voice cracking, *"Just call, and I'll show up, yes, I will. You've got a friend."* Their rendition of James Taylor's song filled the car until they reached the Lodges.

Once parked, Jack proposed, "I'll approach first, given Mike already met me. I hope the way I introduce you might convince him of our innocence."

"We'll follow your lead," Steve said.

Emma concurred.

Descending to the basement, the scale of the additional excavation astounded Jack. The hole in the wall was more than double in size, and the floor in front of the hole was now six feet deep. However, the person who did this was not reckless; their efforts were precise.

Approaching Mike, Jack extended a hand, "Morning, Mike. Any idea who did this?"

Mike's hand stayed by his side, "My money's on you. You were the last one here, scouring the ground for more artifacts."

"In our earlier call, I mentioned I was there for a bit before grabbing pizza and meeting Steve at my place. Here's the receipt as proof. I would like to introduce you to Navy Lieutenant Commander Steven Johnson. And this is Emma Wilson, the Smithsonian Museum of American History Assistant Director and Curator, whom I think you spoke with over the phone. Emma joined us late evening to examine your discoveries."

Mike's eyes widened in surprise and then narrowed, a crease forming between his brows, "Apologies, it's just... losing all of yesterday hit hard. I arrived early to make up time, and now today's wasted on repairs. I had to cancel the cement delivery, incurring extra costs and delaying us till next Wednesday. I must rely on my crew to manage without me while I'm away with my family."

His sigh cut through the silence, mirroring Jack's own discontent.

Jack's hand found Mike's shoulder, offering a steady reassurance. "It's unfortunate. Had the perpetrator been less cautious, the damage might have been irreparable. It's also possible teens took your dozer for a joyride."

"Whoever it was, they knew how to handle an excavator," Mike speculated.

Steve, bewildered, asked, "But for what purpose?"

Emma expressed her sympathy, "It's troubling, Mike. News of your find might have attracted opportunists hoping for black market treasures."

"You might be right," Mike conceded. "Take a look around; perhaps something will catch your eye. In the meantime, I'll refill the holes. Keep an eye out for something of interest."

Agreeing, Jack proposed a plan. "I'll watch from the left; Steve, Emma, take the other side. With us spread out, we might spot something."

Mike paused after moving the piles of soil to the top of the excavation. "Notice anything?"

Both Steve and Jack confirmed, "No, nothing."

Mike suggested they head out and said, "I'll reach out if something comes up."

Their departure was fraught and filled with concern, "Sorry this happened, Mike. Take care."

On the way to his vehicle, Jack rattled off the breakfast options, "Perkins, Coffee Traders, Canoe On the Run, The Casselman Bakery, or into Oakland for 3rd Street Diner, Denny's, or do we kill a morning at Englanders, Emma's favorite."

Without hesitation, Emma opted, "Englanders! My treat!"

"My vote goes with the person paying," Steve laughed. "We can always search tomorrow, Jack."

Leaving The Lodges, Jack steered south onto Route 219, and Emma's eyes lit up while gazing at the lake. "Look, there's the Wisp! I've missed skiing there."

Jack smiled, reminiscing. "We had a great winter. I hit the slopes several evenings and weekends when I could. Steve even braved joining me a few times."

"True, but I switched to snowboarding this year – less painful falls," Steve said, voice full of pride.

Emma beamed. "I've got to join you guys next time."

Through the rearview mirror, Jack caught Steve's vast grin.

Crossing the bridge over Deep Creek Lake, Emma was giddy as a schoolgirl, "We should get out on the water. Think we can rent a boat tomorrow?"

"We'll see what we can do," Jack tempered her expectations, suspecting this hunt could last for days or weeks.

Emma's nostalgia filled the car. "Things have not changed here, have they?"

"Everything moves slower here. It's the tranquility that keeps me here," Jack said.

"It's perfect," Emma said.

Passing familiar landmarks, Emma recounted memories of Traders Landing, High Mountain Sports, and more, her enthusiasm peaking upon seeing the Honi Honi bar. Spotting the day's lineup, she couldn't contain herself. "No way! Queen City Funk & Soul this afternoon, and The Stickers tonight! We have to go; we can't search in the dark!"

"Okay, okay. We'll go," Jack laughed, entertained by her zest.

Without warning, Jack's expression darkened. "Oh, no!"

"What's wrong?" Emma's mood shifted to concern.

"I'm supposed to lead a tour later."

"Can't you cancel it?"

Jack was reluctant and conceded, "Yes, but it'll hit my Trip Advisor ratings. I better do it now, though." Handing his phone to Emma, he instructed her to navigate the cancelation process.

"Your passcode?" she asked.

"Hold out my phone, Em," and Jack opened it using his thumbprint.

Once in the app, she hesitated. "What's the excuse?"

86

Steve said, "I told our Commander that Jack had an emergency appendicitis surgery."

"Works for me," Jack said, his voice a blend of relief and a subtle hint of guilt.

Emma voiced her concerns, skepticism lacing her words. "I worry that they might ask for evidence. Why not say, 'Sorry, not feeling well, with stomach aches and chills?' They'd likely assume it's a bug, and the customer would want to avoid any chance of catching it."

"That makes more sense," was the agreement.

Nearing Oakland, the heart of the county, the town unfolded in its historic splendor. The streets were a canvas of the past, with grand homes echoing the late 19th and early 20th centuries and small businesses offering a glimpse into the town's vibrant community life.

Gliding through Oakland, Jack's car turned on Center Street, where charming shops basked in the morning sunlight. Another turn to Second led them to look at the train station, a structure steeped in history. Animated with enthusiasm, Jack shared, "That marvel is the B&O Railroad Station and Museum. Its benefactor, John Garrett, the namesake of this county and a friend of Lincoln and a railroad magnate, built it. He and his railroad contributed much to the Union's victory."

The station, with its majestic red-brick façade and white accents, each element narrated the tales of a bygone era.

At the traffic signal, the distant whistles and chugging of trains from yesteryears echoed in his ears. He looked up at the two-story building; large arched windows graced its structure, casting playful shadows that revealed glimpses of an interior bathed in natural light.

Continuing their journey, they passed the Garrett County Historical Society Museum and a series of stores until they reached Englanders. The diner, a favorite among locals, welcomed them with its nostalgic aura.

Inside, a vast collection of antiques greeted them. Emma paused, enchanted by an ancient porcelain tea set, its beauty undeniable.

Before touching it, Steve intervened, his hunger overriding his patience. "Let's eat first, Emma," he urged, grabbing her arm.

She protested, her fascination with the set undimmed. "But Steve, look at it. It's not any tea set; its design shows its regal past, perhaps European royalty. Imagine the tales it could tell." Her eyes sparkled with the romance of history encapsulated in delicate china.

Steve's gentle tug elicited a laugh from her, who raised her hands in a playful gesture of defeat. "Alright, alright. I've learned my lesson about coming between you and your insatiable hunger. Please try to keep your breakfast bill under twenty dollars."

"Yes, ma'am!" Steve replied with mock solemnity, looping an arm around Emma's shoulders as they navigated through the aisles of oddities and memorabilia toward the diner section.

The diner, nestled at the store's rear, welcomed them with its cozy embrace, its booths upholstered in vinyl, and the walls adorned with vintage décor, invoked a charming retro ambiance. The air was rich with the aromas of sizzling bacon, fresh eggs, and brewing coffee, while a menu boasted an array of staples – burgers, fries, milkshakes – alongside more novel offerings like lobster mac and cheese, all available throughout the day.

Finding the place quiet after the morning rush, they claimed a secluded booth. Unnoticed by Emma, Steve's smile was a silent herald of his matchmaking schemes as he strategically sat in the middle and left no room beside him.

"Is it too early for a milkshake?" Steve asked, unable to conceal a smirk with his menu.

A warm blush spread across Emma's cheeks when she realized the ploy after she slid into the opposite side.

At that moment, Jack's attention shifted, catching sight of the hooded figure making their way toward their booth behind Steve.

Chapter 10

Thursday, May 29th, 1755

D awn promised clear skies and a gentle breeze, perfect conditions for embarking on their crucial military campaign. The first light cast a golden glow upon the walls of Fort Cumberland as General Braddock and his army began to awaken. The air was thick with anticipation as the soldiers prepared for their expedition to Fort Duquesne. Washington paced at the General's tent, his face flushed.

"Colonel Washington," Braddock called out, firm yet tinged with concern. "You must conserve your strength for the campaign."

"I'll be fine, Sir," Washington replied, his voice weak but determined. "I won't allow this illness to hinder our progress."

The sun rose higher, casting its warm rays upon the bustling fort while General Braddock led his 600 men out of Fort Cumberland. At the head of the procession, Braddock's stern expression and commanding presence captured the attention of every soldier. He rode atop his steed, back straight, and eyes fixed on the path ahead. His graying hair caught the sunlight, highlighting the lines etched into his face by years of war and responsibility. There was no mistaking the relevance of their task and the expectation each man would play his part to ensure its success.

"Men," Braddock bellowed. "Today, we embark on a journey which will test your resolve and courage. However, I have faith in your abilities, and together, we'll retake Fort Pitt and expel France from our lands! We fight for King and country!"

"Sir, we won't let you down," Washington said, his eyes burning with conviction despite the sweat beading on his brow.

As the men cheered and prepared to set off, the young Colonel felt a sense of pride in their shared purpose, even as his illness threatened to undermine his contribution.

With a nod from Braddock, the vast column of soldiers began its steady advance, a sea of red and white uniforms stretching beyond their line of sight as the rhythmic pounding of boots against the earth resonated through the air.

The army marched onward, and Colonel George Washington rode alongside Braddock, his gaze fixed on the horizon. Within the ranks were future American Revolutionary War Generals Thomas Gage, Charles Lee, and Horatio Gates, with Daniel Morgan and Daniel Boone serving as teamsters.

The young Washington's blue eyes shined with unbridled ambition. He sat tall and proud on his horse, his confident stride a stark contrast to the fatigue etched on the faces of the men around him.

"Quite an impressive sight, isn't it," Washington said, casting a sidelong glance at Braddock.

"Indeed," Braddock replied. "Just wait till you experience the full army complement at Little Meadows."

Lieutenant Clarke rode behind the General, his eyes darting between the two officers and the treacherous terrain ahead. The journey from Fort Cumberland would be arduous as the soldiers battled against the rugged landscape and exhaustion. The dense forest threatened to swallow them whole, while perilous cliffs and steep inclines tested the limits of their endurance.

The soldiers' boots sank into the soft ground, their uniforms covered in dirt and sweat. Their breaths became ragged and labored, and each step forward displayed their unwavering determination. Despite their fatigue, a fire in their eyes – a shared sense of purpose bound them together in their struggle.

After six days of marching, the column arrived at Laurel Hill Creek and caught up with another brigade. They didn't make camp but pressed on the following day to Little Meadows as the General was anxious to meet up with the rest of his forces.

Because the army had to widen the path to aid its advance and accommodate the passage of the wagons and cannons, this slowed progress and used up a lot of resources. Braddock ordered the empty wagons to return to Fort Cumberland, where they could load up with more supplies.

Marching onward, Clarke admired the tenacity of the men, yet he realized Washington wasn't quite himself. With his flushed face, a fever burned within him. It appeared Washington refused to succumb to his weakness, unwilling to let anything stand in the way of his duty.

"General," Washington said, his voice a hair above a whisper. "I know I haven't been at my best these past few days, but I assure you, I will see this through to the end."

Braddock regarded him for a moment, his steely gaze giving away nothing. "I have no doubt, Colonel," he said, firm yet reassuring. "Remember, we're all in this together. You don't have to shoulder the burden alone."

"Thank you, Sir," Washington replied, the words heavy with gratitude.

Following two days at Little Meadows, the entire army assembled. The officers met and made plans.

Wednesday, June 18th, 1755

The soldiers pressed on as they continued their progress through the unforgiving wilderness, their hearts pounding in unison with each stride.

The sun hung low in the sky, casting long shadows across the rough terrain as the soldiers trudged onward. Sweat dripped from their brows, their faces streaked with dirt and determination. While they marched, the men exchanged weary smiles, offering words of encouragement to one another.

"Keep going, lads!" shouted Sergeant Thompson, his voice hoarse from the exertion. "We'll make camp soon enough, and you can rest those tired bones."

"Thank God," muttered Private Malley, wiping the perspiration from his brow with a grimy sleeve. "I don't know how much further I could go."

"Ah, but this is nothing compared to what awaits us at Fort Duquesne," said Corporal Jameson, grinning despite the weariness etched upon his face. "It's there we'll earn our stripes, boys! We'll be heroes when we're done!"

"Heroes indeed," came a voice from behind the group, and they turned as Colonel George Washington rode up alongside them, his horse's hooves kicking up dust as it moved. In spite of his pale complexion and apparent illness, Washington's eyes shone with determination.

"Carry on, men," Washington replied, nodding in approval. "Your fortitude is an inspiration to us all."

He urged his horse forward, falling into step beside General Braddock. The General glanced over at Washington, noting the younger man's fever-bright eyes and the tremor coursing through his body.

"Colonel, your dedication to our cause does not go unnoticed," Braddock said, gravelly but sincere. "You must remember to care for yourself as well. A commander is only as strong as his weakest soldier and in your current state…"

Washington's jaw tightened; Braddock's words wounded his pride. He understood the General was right – he needed to ensure his own health to be an effective leader.

"Thank you, General," Washington replied and paused to steady himself. "I'll heed your advice."

"Good. Our goal is of the utmost importance. I need every man at his best," Braddock said. "We shall not falter."

Washington nodded.

The sun dipped to the horizon; the weary soldiers began setting up camp for the night at Shade Run. They erected tents with practiced efficiency while others gathered firewood and prepared a simple meal to nourish their exhausted bodies.

"Pass me a peg, will you, Lieutenant?" James Miller called out to Lieutenant Robert Davis as he secured the corners of their shared tent. The young officer tossed him the wooden stake, his smile never leaving his face despite the exhaustion felt by all.

"Here you go! Another day closer to our objective, right?" Davis said, wiping the sweat from his brow.

"Indeed, Lieutenant," James replied, raising his hammer above his head and driving it downwards with determination. The sound of metal striking wood echoed through the camp as James drove the peg into the ground with firm strokes. Each hit was loud and clear, matching his resolve and confidence. "We'll see this through, no matter what it takes."

Seated near the crackling fire, Colonel Washington ladled a steaming portion of stew into his bowl, the savory aroma mingling with the scent of wood smoke. Beside him, General Braddock, lost in thought, stirred his meal.

"General," Washington ventured, breaking the silence between them, "what are your thoughts on tomorrow's march?"

"We must press on, Colonel. The terrain may be unforgiving, but we must push on with speed. Still, the men need rest. We'll break camp after another full day of rest."

"Very good, Sir," Washington replied. "Our mission's success hinges on our ability to adapt and overcome."

"Indeed," Braddock said. "Now get some sleep, Colonel. We'll need your strength tomorrow."

Thursday, June 19th, 1755

Dawn broke over the eastern mountains, and the camp came alive with the sound of soldiers preparing for the next day's trek. Amidst the bustling activity, the sharp scent of gunpowder and polished metal emanated throughout camp as each soldier tended to their weapon with care. Their deft hands moved over muskets and bayonets, ensuring they were in prime condition for whatever challenges lay ahead.

Colonel Washington sensed the heavy burden of responsibility upon him, strengthening his determination to complete the mission. "Keep up attention to detail, men," he called out, stern but encouraging. "The success of our campaign lies in your hands."

"Colonel," General Braddock said, approaching Washington, "it's time to address the troops."

Braddock stepped forward, his boots crunching on the forest floor. The camp fell silent; every soldier turned their focus toward the imposing figure before them.

"Men," Braddock's powerful voice boomed throughout the camp, demanding their full attention. "Today marks yet another crucial step in our journey to Fort Duquesne. We face an enemy unlike any you have encountered in the past – the unforgiving wilderness itself, greater than we have seen thus far."

He paused, allowing his words to sink in. "I have faith in each and every one of you. Your dedication to this mission, your unwavering commitment to our cause… these qualities will lead us through to victory."

The soldiers listened, their eyes fixed on Braddock as his speech stirred their hearts. They felt a renewed sense of purpose; a fire ignited within them. "We can all see that building a road for cannons and wagons is slow. I'll be splitting our army and creating a flying brigade of 1,300 men to move ahead and clear our path quicker so the rest of the men and supplies can catch up. This will lead us to a faster victory! We set off at first light."

A chorus of cheers erupted, their spirits lifted by Braddock's rousing speech. They resumed their preparations with a renewed sense of urgency, and their movements became swift and purposeful.

Colonel Washington witnessed Braddock's words galvanizing the men, his heart swelling with pride.

The day continued with oppressive heat, the thick air heavy with humidity. The sun's rays were unrelenting; sweat dripped from every inch of the soldiers' bodies.

Although the sun setting brought relief to the men, concern arose in the morning as Braddock needed to address his troops again.

"Attention!" Braddock barked. The men snapped to attention, their expressions a mixture of anticipation and dread for the challenges ahead.

"Men," Braddock said, his eyes scanning the ranks. "I have grave news. Our esteemed Colonel Washington is ill with a severe case of flux. He won't be able to continue with us at this time."

A murmur rippled through the troops at the mention of Washington's illness, and concern etched onto the faces of many.

Inspiring them with his youthful energy and unwavering determination, the troops viewed the young Colonel as a beacon of hope.

"However," Braddock said, raising his hand to quell the murmurs, "we cannot allow this setback to deter us from our mission. We must press on and trust Colonel Washington will recover and rejoin us in due course."

Braddock paused, allowing his words to sink in before issuing his orders. "I am leaving a regiment of 300 men behind with Colonel Washington. They'll remain with him until he recovers and join us as soon as possible."

"Sir, yes, Sir," came the resolute chorus from the soldiers.

"Good," Braddock nodded with an expression of concern. With Washington unable to continue, the success of their objective rested even more on his shoulders. He could not – would not – let his men down.

"Let's move out!" Braddock ordered, spurring his horse into motion. The troops followed suit, their unified footsteps resounding through the wilderness during their march, the absence of Washington's presence like a gaping wound refusing to heal.

Braddock worried for the young Colonel as they pressed onward, his thoughts drifting to Washington's flushed and feverish face. He had conveyed his orders, and now all he hoped was that fate would be kind to them all.

Another scorching day met Braddock and his forces amid their westward advance. Clarke wondered what was on the General's mind as he was quiet much of the day.

The sun dipped below the horizon, casting the encampment in a warm, golden glow. Braddock stood at the edge of the camp, his arms behind himself, holding a roll of parchment. His face betrayed his inner thoughts, showing his heavy concern as he stared into the vast wilderness stretching before them.

"Clarke!" Braddock called out, his voice loud and urgent.

He strode up to the General, and Braddock said, "I have a secret task for you, one of utmost importance. Walk with me."

"I trust you above many others as you have served with me for years and have never questioned my orders nor failed me. What I ask of you may sound peculiar, but it is the only resolution I can think of for something that troubled me for weeks."

"Anything, Sir," Clarke said.

"I want you to take and hide the army's payroll and gifts somewhere safe," Braddock whispered. "It must be done in secrecy, and only you and I shall know of its location. I had a copy of Washington's map made. Take it!"

Holding up his hand to stop any questions, he unrolled and pointed at the map. "You will see the trail back near Little Meadows; it goes southwest, west, and then turns north to meet us on our route. It takes you away from the French-controlled territories."

"I see it, Sir."

"We cannot afford to have the payroll and valuable trinkets in the wrong hands, which could be used against the crown. I want you to find a secure place to hide the bulk of the payroll and all the bribes. A place that can be described easily in code, such as a cave or under a large tree. If you don't pass something suitable along the way before the trail bends north, hide it near the turn so we know the general area."

"Sir, I don't understand," Clarke said, raising an eyebrow.

"It's simple," Braddock said. "You will bury the chests and set markers on your path to the final spot with coded clues so we can retrieve the cache should you not rejoin us. Hide the first marker at the start of the trail. You will spot the massive oak tree at its turn. Conceal a code under a marked rock as to the whereabouts of the next marker we need to find. Markers must be difficult to discover by accident. Take only a few trusted men with you – men who can keep their mouths shut. Understood?"

"Yes, Sir," Clarke said with concern. "Won't the troops become upset when they hear they will not be paid until after the campaign?"

"I've considered this. That is why I'll keep a small chest, a very manageable and less risky amount. With the separation of the troops to form the Flying Brigade, we do not need all the payroll with us now. We should have enough to get us to Fort Duquesne, and after our victory, I can have you safely retrieve the chests. And since the path you'll follow is behind us, I'll inform the men you are returning the rest to Fort Cumberland for its safety since we left a sufficient number of men behind to protect it. This way, the chests will cease slowing us down, and I will ensure that the enemies of the King cannot get their hands on it."

"Excellent, Sir."

"Don't worry. I expect you to meet me on the battlefield again, Captain Clarke."

"Understood, Sir. Wait, Sir, did you call me Captain?" Clarke asked.

"Consider it a field promotion. Here's a letter. I put in for your promotion, but it will take a while for your official papers to arrive from England. Sorry, I don't have another coat to offer you, but I've let the other officers know."

"Thank you, Sir. We'll leave at first light."

"No, leave before, fewer eyes," Braddock said, a flicker of relief crossing his stern features. "Make sure to use care when you choose your men. Your mission's success – and your men's safety – depends on it."

"Lieutenant Robert Davis and his men performed well for me on our last task to obtain munitions. I'll request him again, Sir."

"I don't know his men, but Davis has a good reputation."

"I'll take him, Sir. I request he and his guys be outfitted like mine and mounted for speed. We still have our narrow wagon, which should serve well to carry the… cache."

"Yes, make it so. And make sure the men under your care have tight lips. Goodnight, Clarke."

"Sir," Clarke saluted, turned, and left to inform his men.

"Godspeed, Captain," Braddock whispered into the night, hoping fate would smile upon them as they marched toward the uncertain future. While night fell, Braddock returned to camp, convinced entrusting this task to Clarke was the best course of action.

Friday, June 20th, 1755

In the darkness before dawn, Clarke realized he had not slept well as he woke frequently to ponder his assignment. His group set off east in stealth to find the trail's beginning. Glancing back at the camp, his fellow soldiers were still fast asleep and unaware. The strong bond among them was evident and gave him an enduring sense of camaraderie.

"Good luck, men," Clarke whispered under his breath as he turned back to look at his journey ahead. His steely resolve carried him forward.

They rode in silence for a half-hour when the sun began to greet them. Clarke said, "With the light of a day, I believe we can now risk some conversation. I wanted to let you know you were hand-picked for this sensitive task. We are expected to complete this quickly and join our brothers in taking Fort Duquesne."

"Captain," Davis said with a firm nod, his eyes shining with steadfastness. "I am honored to be chosen for this task. You can count on me and my men to see it through."

"Very well," Clarke said, relief in his voice. "Teamwork will determine the success or failure of this undertaking and could mean the difference between life and death for us."

"Understood, Sir."

"George explored much of this region before. He'll take point."

"Will do, Sir," George replied. "Suggest we make haste while we can. Once on the trail, we may move slower and must be quieter."

"Excellent point. You heard our guide. Let's go," Clarke ordered as he spurred his horse on.

The cool evening air rolled in as Clarke and his men trekked deeper into the forest, the tall trees forming a protective canopy above them. The dappled sunlight filtered through the leaves as Clarke's keen eyes surveyed the terrain, searching for the path leading them south and away from the army's main body.

"Sir, it starts here," George called out. He pointed at a slight perceptible indentation in the earth – a subtle sign they were on the right path.

"Good work," Clarke praised.

"But first…," Clarke scanned the area, spotting the massive tree a few dozen yards from the turn. He grabbed a hatchet from his pack and walked toward the oak, passing a large rock. Stopping, Clarke tilted it with two hands and set it back down. He turned to the tree and used his hatchet to break off a small portion of bark facing the stone. He rolled it over and struck the rock with the hammer side, leaving a noticeable chip taken out of it.

"Men," he said as he walked back to the group. "Once we place the next marker, I'll send a few of you here to place a note under the rock for the General. Please remember where this is and cover your tracks to and from the trail when you leave."

Using his hands to push leaves and underbrush around, Clarke covered his footprints.

George rode ahead.

"Men," Clarke said, "we follow this trail. Stay sharp and keep your eyes peeled. We're venturing into remote territory with no possibility of rescue, so any mistakes made will be magnified. Let's move out."

As if an ominous sign, the winds picked up as they progressed along the trail, and dark clouds rolled into the area.

James Miller, their best marksman with an uncanny ability to blend into his surroundings, dismounted, moved forward and to the north, and moved from tree to tree, ensuring no one followed them. His brother, John, kept a watchful eye on their provisions and equipment.

"Sir," George rode back to meet them and called out. "I see lightning ahead. Further, we'll come upon a large field."

"Yes, it would be good to be out of the woods with a storm coming,. and we don't want the horses to bolt. I agree. Make camp as soon as we are clear of the trees and tie up the steeds."

"Yes, Sir."

The wind howled through the forest as a shower began. The rain continued to increase as they reached the broad opening before them.

"Hurry, men, let's set up," Clarke ordered. They set up their tents and secured their horses.

"Sir," Davis said, entering the tent. "If you don't mind me asking, how did you come to earn General Braddock's trust?

Clarke hesitated for a moment. "It's not something I often speak of, but a few years ago, when he was a lieutenant colonel and I was a private, he decided to join us, his scouts, on an operation during the Siege of Bergen op Zoom. We found ourselves trapped, separated from our troops with only a handful of men. With no other option, we fought side by side to survive, and only the two of us did. I warned him against joining the undertaking, so it appears he trusts my judgment and knows I would die for him."

Davis nodded. "Quite a story, Sir. I hope one day I can earn your trust as well."

"Keep up the good work, Davis, and you will," Clarke replied, clapping him on the shoulder.

Clarke regaled stories of his previous campaigns, entertaining his men as the storm outside intensified. During the conclusion, the skies cleared. They stepped out of their tents, and the sun began to dip below the horizon, painting the sky with a fiery palette of reds and oranges. Unfortunately, this peaceful moment would be all too brief, as far in the distance, he gazed upon the gathering of additional dark clouds.

Turning to the journey ahead, the trail across the field led them to a valley and into the mountainous wilderness. In the post-storm silence, the roar of a rushing river in the distance troubled him. Pulling out the map from his breast pocket, he realized they soon had to cross the rain-engorged Little Youghiogheny River.

"Rest up, men. We have a major barrier to pass in the morning."

Chapter 11

Jack's adrenaline surged as the hoodie-wearing man approached Steve from behind. With a rapid glance to the side and upward head movement, Steve nodded, indicating they were on the same page. Without raising suspicion, Steve slid his hand across the table, palming a knife, and concealed it under his napkin. Simultaneously, Jack pressed his hand against Emma's thigh under the table before reaching for his own knife in his pocket. They were ready for whatever might come.

The figure neared and lowered the hood, revealing not a threat but a tall, sturdy young man with a warm gaze and a tentative smile. Jack's heart calmed, the anticipated danger melting into confusion and then relief.

The man looked more like a farmer than a foe, with his light brown hair cascading in waves over his forehead. His blue eyes sparkled with intelligence and energy, a stark contrast to the hostility Jack expected.

"Are you Jack Sullivan?" he asked.

"That's me," Jack replied, guarded. "And you are?"

"I'm Ben Baton. Sally Adkins from the museum said I might find you at The Lodges. The contractor called her this morning after misplacing your number. She thought there might be a connection between Braddock's treasure and the journal and feared that someone might, well, not be nice about it based on the previous night's events. I tried to meet you there, but you had already left. Sorry for following you."

"You couldn't call because?"

"I think I wrote your number down wrong," Ben said, presenting a slip of paper.

"Yeah, you flipped two numbers. She called you… because?"

"Well, that's a bit of the story. My last name, Baton, would be pronounced Batun in French. My grandfather's grandfather's grandfather, Jean Baton, was Le Commandant, or Commander, of a squadron. Working with several Native Americans, he captured a small group of British soldiers led by Lieutenant Robert Davis, which included George Williams, Thomas Rogers, Joseph Moore, Thomas Clarke, and Henry Jones. May I sit down?"

The waitress approached, and Emma seized the moment to order, her hunger speaking volumes. Jack gestured for Ben to take a seat and ordered the same hearty breakfast as Emma.

Steve slid over, grabbed the menu again, and scanned it. "I don't know why I even looked at it; I'll have your delicious chocolate…"

Emma interrupted and completed his order, laughing, "Chocolate chip pancakes, sausage, and orange juice in addition to coffee. You're as bad as me with favorites."

"You know me too well," Steve chuckled.

Ben settled with a coffee.

Once the waitress departed, Jack looked at Ben and said, "These are my friends, Steve Johnson and Emma Wilson. You may or may not know, but Emma works with the Smithsonian, and she sent me here after they found the barrel."

After a brief exchange of handshakes, Jack pressed on, "There has to be more as to why Sally thought we should meet. What are you holding back?"

"You're right to be doubtful," Ben conceded. "I know Sally from our local school. She's aware my family has been searching for Braddock's treasure since the Revolutionary War because my grandfather used to frequent the museum looking for new clues. I sometimes joined him. After the Revolution, Jean Baton, an ally of the Americans, settled near Sang Run. You should also know several other veterans from the squad that captured those soldiers settled in Northern Garrett."

"We suspected that. Any idea how many?" asked Steve.

"I don't know. The treasure's not a secret. It's believed the stretch from Fort Cumberland to Braddock, Pennsylvania has been searched or developed along Braddock's Road."

"That's why I focused my search off the beaten path," Jack said.

"Likewise. Heck, even the British found out about it back in 1954 when a British archivist was cataloging documents. A group of men showed up and searched for Braddock's gold, and after two years, they returned home empty-handed."

"That's news to me," Jack said.

"Those men canvassed from Little Meadows to the west, employing my grandfather who moved north of the Route 219 and 40 intersection, oblivious to the one truth he safeguarded."

"And that is?" Steve asked.

While the waitress delivered their drinks, Jack paused the conversation with a gesture, resuming it as she departed.

"Jean's unit caught Davis and his men near Friendsville. Native guides determined they came north along the Yough. That's why we searched the area along the Yough. After decades of looking, my father, Michel Baton, grew skeptical of the treasure's existence."

Emma sympathized, glancing at Jack, "That's understandable."

"Before he died, my grandfather shared everything he knew. After high school, I settled by Fork Run, dedicating more time to the search."

"That's driven you further south?" Jack asked.

"Yes. Jean was eavesdropping on the British soldiers when one cautioned, 'No matter what happens, don't reveal our purpose here.' Another retorted, 'Doesn't matter. They'll never get in, even if they find the cave,' and a fellow captive silenced him with a kick. Their whispers and them not divulging purpose what drove these suspicious soldiers so far south of Braddock's Road – it all connects."

"What became of those prisoners?" Emma asked.

"My family passed down that they went to Fort Duquesne, and there was a prisoner exchange later on," Ben said.

In a hushed tone, Jack leaned closer, "Sally was right to bring us together. Your story aligns with what we discovered in Davis's barrel. The treasure lies hidden in a cave west of the barrel, or marker as they called it. It's a critical piece of the puzzle for us."

Ben sighed. "Useful, though I hoped for more."

Jack continued, "Let's put together what we now know. We know from the journal that Davis hid a coded clue for Braddock to find upon his return to Little Meadows. The British archivist must have discovered something relating to Little Meadows, which explains why the British treasure hunters believed Braddock's men buried the treasure between Little Meadows and the spot where Braddock died. However, they believed Davis buried the gold near Little Meadows or along the road. We now know that Davis hid a coded clue along the road near Little Meadows that marked their departure point. This now explains why no one has found the treasure – everyone's been looking in the wrong direction as Davis's path to hide it was toward Garrett County."

Ben nodded.

"Diving deeper," Jack whispered, "we believe they backtracked to leave codes at each indicator pointing their way to the final burial spot. We deciphered the final one last night to reveal the final clue."

"What code, what clue?" Ben leaned in.

"It was a Scytale Cipher," Jack said, realizing Ben might not know the term, and explained the coiled encryption method.

"We found the message 'Payroll buried inside a cave west of the marker.' After we left the site this morning, we headed to Oakland to see if we could find a map to help identify caves in the area to search. We figured we'd check county records and the museum. We came to Englanders as it's Emma's favorite breakfast spot in town."

Ben's expression fell, and he shook his head. "Well, this sucks. I already knew you were searching the area before you saw me at the excavation site. I mentioned others are looking for it, too, and it's easy to spot them. Last weekend, I saw you using your detector along the Yough while I was exploring on the other shore. You were in the zone with your earbuds."

Emma lightened the mood. "He's got your number, Jack."

"The music keeps me focused and connected to my phone, so I won't miss my alarm when I need to leave to give tours or head to Penn State."

Bensaid, "Sally thinks I can aid your search. Despite exhaustive searches by my family and others, no caves have yielded the treasure."

Jack's optimism waned, "We might be at an impasse, or worse, beaten to the find. Did your efforts include digging and detectors?"

"Both," Ben said, "My grandfather, like his ancestors, explored them all. Yet, a concealed or undiscovered cave remains our last hope."

Jack nodded, his expression earnest. "Let's dig up any maps we've overlooked. Surveyors might have charted the land, but they weren't scouring with metal detectors or spelunking in search of secrets. There might be a map we missed, or we'll have to double back to those caves west of McHenry."

Breakfast arrived, and their focus on the quest lifted. However, Ben's drooping posture and the distant gaze as he stared into his coffee betrayed his sense of a dead end. Years of tracing his ancestors' journey, combing through every inch of the land they once roamed, seemed to weigh on him.

Ben took a slow, deliberate sip, the silence hanging heavy between them. His head tilted, and he said, "Hey, there might be another angle to explore."

Curiosity sparked in the group's eyes.

"You recall how I told you the Native Americans aided my ancestor in capturing Davis?"

Nods all around encouraged him to continue.

"What if we sought insights from the descendants of those tribes? They might hold clues or ancestral records."

Jack considered the suggestion but said, "The Iroquois and Seneca once thrived here, but displacement scattered them. Finding their ancestors in this area might be challenging, and they would have to know the story."

Yet, inspiration struck Jack. "But, if we retraced the Native trails Davis's men used, it could lead us to the cave. They'd stick close to avoid losing their way. Discovering those trails could be the key."

Emma leaned forward, eager. "A map of those paths could be the key. It's our most promising option."

Steve said, "If we can't find a map, revisiting the caves Ben searched before is still a fallback. We might uncover something overlooked."

Ben chimed in, "Count me in. I'm familiar with the terrain."

Jack's smile was genuine. "Yes, your local knowledge will be invaluable."

Mulling over their situation, a sliver of doubt lingered with Jack. Despite needing Ben for his intimate knowledge of the area, Jack couldn't shake off a niggling distrust. Could Ben's information be a double-edged sword? The idea of a detailed map, revealing caves and perhaps waterfalls too, began to take root in his thoughts.

Brightening at the prospect, Jack proposed, "Steve, accompany Ben to the museum. If Sally's there, maybe she can help unearth a map of Native trails. Emma and I will scour the county archives."

"So that's the plan. What do you think, Dirk?" Steve asked.

He replied, "Uh... I think we need to pull a Panama!"

"A Panama?" Ben asked, prompting Jack and Steve to laugh.

"A Panama? No! No Panama!" Jack and Steve said together, laughing harder.

Emma and Ben looked at them with puzzled and amused expressions as if they were trying to understand a foreign language. Steve gave them a questioning and sarcastic look, his eyebrows raised, and his mouth twisted in a smirk. He spread his hands out and palms up, head shaking as if to say, 'What's wrong with you?' before being forced to clarify, "Alright, alright, alright. Are you not a Matthew McConaughey fan? In his movie *Sahara*, he was Dirk Pitt. It was a hysterical scene with Dirk and his friend Al Giordino before they blew up their boss's speedboat."

Emma laughed, "Leave it to them to quote a film about an obsessed treasure hunter."

"Yeah, but didn't they the Confederate Gold Coins in the end?" Jack said, laughing as well.

"The two of you watch way too many movies," Emma shook her head, smiling.

The sun climbed towards its zenith as Jack and Emma parted ways with their companions, an uneasy suspicion about Ben gnawing at Jack's mind. He couldn't shake the thought that Ben might have hidden agendas, maybe coveting the gold for himself.

On Route 219, away from Ben's hearing, Emma stopped Jack, her grip firm on his hand. "Why pair Steve with Ben? Why head to the county building when we suspect the treasure lies south, by a waterfall? Aren't you afraid he might hurt Steve? We should be heading towards Swallow Falls!"

"I had two reasons," Jack said. "First, I don't fully trust Ben. He seemed to be warming up at breakfast, but I couldn't be sure. He's likely to lower his guard around Steve more than he ever would with me."

Jack paused and chose his next words with care, "Then there's Sally. If she's working with Ben, she'll recognize him and maybe even assist when they get there. It's also possible she's not in league with him. She might know the correct owner of the journal, either from conversations with you or Bill, and she was there when the contractor called the museum about it."

Jack's eyes narrowed as he considered the web of possibilities. "Ben didn't know Clarke was the ranking officer. Steve might unravel that at the museum, even more so if Sally's there."

"You're not worried about Steve? If Ben tries anything..."

A slight smile tugged at Jack's lips. "Steve would relish the chance. If Ben made a move, Steve would handle him without breaking a sweat." His expression sobered. "Yet, the real play here is about time. This delay lets us track down an old map we need, one that pinpoints falls and caves. The risk is that Ben will learn what Steve uncovers at the museum. It's a gamble, but one we need to take."

Crossing Route 219, Jack took Emma's hand, a gesture not broken until they neared the county building. Diving into the archive, their search was fruitless till Emma stumbled upon two intriguing maps. One was a 1789 map showing two caves; the other from 1925 only showed one.

Emma said, "However, I don't see creeks or waterfalls. What if Clarke had their directions wrong? I'll take a picture, so we could also use it as a decoy with Ben."

"Great idea, Em. We may need that. John and Gabriel Friend, father and son, fought in the Revolutionary War and settled at 'Friend's Fortune,' now called Friendsville. John discovered the cave named after him. I'm curious. What happened to the second cave? Could Friend have been looking for it as well?"

"Hey, this map is from 1798. See the Native American trail where we found the barrel? It goes northwest for a bit, then turns north to meet the Youghiogheny River at Friendsville, like the one in the barrel."

"Check this out," she motioned to the map's lower edge. "It references *Portions of this map were copied from a map drawn by George Washington before the Seven Years' War.'* The barrel's map had two paths: west to northwest, then north, and another south to southwest. This trail is the Seneca Trail. Yet, this one reveals an additional one veering off the southern one near McHenry, winding west before heading north. Deep Creek Lake's northern valley appears to overlay a junction of trails, with ones along both sides of Marsh Hill Creek."

"You're spot on. Snap some shots of it and send them to me."

Jack and Emma's phones buzzed. Jack's expression fell as he read the text from Steve with a map of Garrett County. It mirrored their Native American trails but included Interstate 68, Highway 219, and Deep Creek Lake.

Emma voiced their shared suspicion, "Someone layered the modern landmarks over this map."

"I think you're right. Let's keep this between us until we're with Steve. It might hold clues we need, and it's best if Ben stays in the dark."

"Do the paths go near Swallow Falls?"

Leaning together to view the document, Emma's head pressed against

Jack's shoulder with her arm around him as they scrutinized the map. Moments later, they identified trails weaving along the Yough River, Muddy, and Swallow Falls. Emma couldn't hide her excitement, which was evident in her tight embrace. "We've found something!" she exclaimed, while Jack reciprocated with a reserved hug. His thoughts were now divided between their breakthrough and a possible rekindling of their romance.

"We could head back and throw Ben off the scent," Jack proposed, drafting a message to Steve about their promising but still incomplete search. Steve responded he needed a half-hour more.

Turning to Emma, "Should we continue here, or do you fancy a quick detour to Englanders?"

Her eyes danced with thought before landing on Jack. "Let's look a bit more, then swing by Englanders for 10 minutes."

Jack's chuckle betrayed his doubt. "Like you can only spend 10 minutes there. But let's keep looking."

They parted ways among the aisles, Jack's eyes tracing each title in detail. A brief search later, he stopped, drawn to a particular volume. With a triumphant tug, he beckoned, "Emma!"

"What is it, Jack?"

Jack unveiled a book titled *The Caves of Maryland* by William E. Davies, filled with an exhaustive catalog of underground wonders. "Here," he said, turning to the table of contents, "Davies categorizes the caves by county. For Garrett, we have Crabtree, John Friends, Muddy Creek Falls Shelters, Sand Cave, and Woods Place."

He leafed through the book, capturing photos of the pages. "Crabtree's massive, situated on Backbone Mountain's north, miles from the Youghiogheny's source. A stream winds through it, but the entrance isn't near the falls. It's a long shot, given the distance south and the terrain. We'll reconsider if needed."

"Sounds good."

"John Friends Cave is closer, by Sang Run along the river. Its walls bear names from the 1750s, and it shows signs of prior searches. Worth noting, but likely picked over."

Emma, drawing close, rested her head on Jack's shoulder. "We might revisit if we're short on leads."

"Perhaps. The Muddy Creek Falls Shelters are intriguing – two sandstone caves near Swallow Falls State Park. I only knew of one. One's twenty-five feet deep; its neighbor was a little smaller. Both merit a look."

"Sand Cave, near Backbone again, hints at Native American activity through digs. However, like Crabtree, it's too distant, their communities having faded by the late 1700s."

A potential lead caught his eye. "Hey, Woods Place Cave. It's reportedly four miles north of Oakland and east of Swallow Falls road, with terraced steps descending 50 feet to a veiled passage. Despite Davies's efforts, he couldn't find the cave. That's our target."

Locking eyes with Emma, Jack's smile conveyed unspoken promises. "Our search today was fruitful, wasn't it?"

Her gaze meeting his, she mirrored his grin. "It was."

In the pause that followed, Jack, breaking the quiet, ventured, "How about we celebrate with a trip to Englanders?"

Emma embraced Jack. "Thank you!"

Chapter 12

Leaving Jack and Emma behind, Steve and Ben turned to walk down 2nd Street, taking in the vibrant Art déco storefronts. Their journey led them to the Garrett National Bank, an ornate limestone building from the 1880s that now houses the County Historical Society Museum. With its maroon awnings beckoning, they paid for admission and stepped inside, surrounded by historical artifacts and tales of the local area.

"Let's look around; maybe we'll uncover something interesting," Steve said, his tone masking a thread of unease over Ben's presence.

In the Log Cabin Room, they began shadowing a tour led by a man Steve believed to be in his late eighties who navigated the space with an unexpected spryness. The room was a portal to pioneer life, adorned with log walls, a stone fireplace, and the dim light of oil lamps illuminating the relics of bygone days. Despite the authenticity, no maps or detailed documents were in sight.

They followed the group through each roomed exhibit – the B&O Railroad and John Garrett, The Historical Hotels, Schools, Arts and Recreation, Industrial, and Victorian times – but found nothing that aligned with their search, rooted in the wrong time periods.

Upon entering the Military Room, Steve's eyes lit up like a child in a candy store – the walls, adorned with medals, weaponry, and historical photographs, narrated stories of bravery. Mannequins, dressed in uniforms, stood as silent guardians of the past. Steve, moved by the legacy of service, reflected on his own familial ties to the military.

"You a military buff?" Ben asked.

"Yes, I am." Realizing Jack didn't give his background to Ben. "My dad and granddad were in the Navy. My grandfather fought in World War II. I find military history fascinating because of the family connection."

Ben suggested a detour to the gift shop and its neighboring display room. That room doubled as an archive and displayed exhibits that changed over time or with the seasons. He hoped that nestled among the curiosities might lay the clue they sought.

The gift shop, full of local lore, captured Steve's attention. He went straight to the racks of books. Titles like *I Love Deep Creek Lake!* and *Garrett County History* promised insights yet left trails and caves uncharted. *Travel Through Garrett County's Past* was full of pictures but skimped on anything about the 1750s.

Amidst the history, *Garrett County Graves Volume 1* stood out – a peculiar find that drew a chuckle from Steve, even more so when he spotted its sequel, *Volume 2*.

A hand on his shoulder interrupted his exploration. Sally Adkins introduced herself as the museum director. Steve looked around, but Ben was absent. She asked, "Is there something you're looking for or I can help you with?"

"I'm a bit of a history buff and like to hike," Steve explained, "I wonder about any resources on local trails, perhaps those tracing back to Native American routes?"

Sally smiled and said, "Books, no. But a map… yes. It isn't what you might consider a true hiking map, but it shows Native American Trails and some landmarks, such as main roads and Deep Creek Lake."

"May I see it?"

"Yes. Plus, it's only $10 if you'd like to purchase a copy." Sally unfurled a map on the counter, showing a weave of paths that captivated him.

"I'll take it! Can I first grab a photo of it and send it to my buddy?" He took a quick picture and texted it to Jack while Sally rolled it back up.

Steve pulled out his wallet, handed her $20, and said, "Keep the rest as a donation. I enjoyed your museum."

His phone buzzed with a message from Jack about a promising lead, hinting at uncharted caves. Flashing what he hoped was a charming smile, he noted Sally's unadorned hand. Steve pondered his next move and messaged Jack to prolong his stay. "Any recommendations on what else to see here?"

"Perhaps I can show you in The Military Room? Some artifacts are not labeled or fully described," Sally said, her smile inviting.

They moved towards the exhibit, and Ben's absence lingered in Steve's mind. However, the opportunity to learn more about Sally and the museum she helmed intrigued him. "So, how did you come to run the museum?" Steve ventured, curiosity piqued.

"Well, teaching history at high school doesn't cover the bills, and helping with my mom's medical expenses makes it harder. My business minor came in handy, though, and landed me a job here for extra income. When the director stepped down, somehow, I got bumped up. Not that there was a line for the position," Sally laughed. "It's a small team here, lots of volunteers passionate about giving tours. It's not a gold mine, but it helps me get by, and I enjoy it."

They walked through the Military Room, and Sally shared stories about the exhibits. Steve hung on her every word, but his curiosity peaked when they approached the Custer and Crook display. "Considering what Custer and Crook did, displacing the Native Americans west, why display artifacts of theirs?"

Sally paused, weighing her words. "It's complicated. General George Crook was temporarily buried in Garrett County. He served under President Ulysses S. Grant. Despite never speaking up during his military career, he spent his last years advocating against the mistreatment of Native Americans. Then there's Custer..." She gestured towards a case with their artifacts, trying to bridge the historical narrative.

"Yeah, but showcasing them? Isn't that controversial?"

"That's the complicated part. It shows that sometimes people are forced to do things they don't want to do, and later do their best to make up for it when they can."

"So, he learned from his mistakes and made an atonement."

"Exactly."

"Hmm."

An employee approached Sally with an issue, cutting the tour short. She apologized to Steve and began to leave.

"No worries, I've learned a lot. Thanks, Sally." After a slight pause, he added, "You into country music?"

Her eyebrow rose. "Yes. Why?"

"Friends and I are hitting Honi Honi to listen to The Stickers tonight. Want to join us? I think we'd have fun, and you would save me from being the third wheel."

She smiled, "I know the band. Sure, sounds like a plan. See you at 8:30."

Left alone, he examined the Gatling Gun until Ben found him. "There you are. Anything from Jack and Emma?"

Checking his phone, he handed it over. "Look at this. They discovered something. We have a bit before meeting at Jack's truck."

Ben scanned the text. "A cave? That's new. Let's grab them and check them out."

"We spent almost three hours here, and it's pushing two. We'll see what Jack and Emma want to do next."

Exiting the museum, Steve surveyed the bustling street to see if there were any signs of Jack and Emma. While they walked, he turned to Ben, his curiosity peaking. "I lost you back at the museum. Where'd you vanish to?"

"I buried myself in the display room and archives behind the gift shop," Ben said. "Came up empty, though. You?"

A sparkle lit up Steve's eyes as he unfurled the acquired map. "I hit the jackpot! Surprised you missed it, given your roots here."

Ben paused, a flicker of discomfort passing over his face. "Well, museums... they're not my scene. Kind of eerie to me."

Steve, puzzled, pressed on. "You? Avoiding history and artifacts? Thought that'd be right up your alley."

Ben shrugged, his voice laced with an elusive undercurrent. "History's fascinating, sure. I'm more for living it than studying it. Besides, treasure hunting's more my style. Wouldn't think to look for clues in some paper rolled up for sale."

Steve detected Ben's avoidance. Switching gears, he said, "Sally showed it to me."

A brief, guarded expression crossed Ben's features. "I must have missed her. Would've been nice to thank her for the intro to you, Jack and Emma."

Sensing he was hitting a dead end, Steve proposed they catch up with Jack and Emma.

Reaching Jack's Suburban and finding it deserted, Steve let out a light chuckle. "Should've guessed."

"Guessed what?" Ben asked, trailing behind.

Rounding a corner, they spotted Jack, a bundle of nerves, outside Englanders. Steve noted the bouncing of Jack's leg – a sign of his impatience.

"I should've figured Emma would be shopping," Steve said, earning a perplexed glance from Ben.

Approaching Jack, Steve perceived a change in his friend's usual urgency. Jack normally would have pushed Emma out of the store and onto the next search destination. He now appeared to be indulging her interests like Englanders and the Honi. It dawned on Steve that Jack was attempting to balance his quest with Emma's happiness, perhaps to secure her cooperation or rekindle something deeper. A wistful thought crossed his mind: *If I could only find my Emma.*

Jack, lost in thought, looked up. "Sorry, while we waited for you, Emma insisted on a 'quick' browse. I suggest we make plans for dinner."

Their shared laughter left Ben perplexed. Steve, seizing the moment, spread out the map. "Given we have time to kill, we should take a look at this. If my hunch is right, the cave you sent a photo of is nearby, just off the trail leading from Buffalo Marsh to Friendsville, close to Ginseng and Sang Runs.

Ben's impatience surfaced as he interrupted their banter. His suggestion of retrieving Emma and venturing towards the cave hung in the air.

Jack flashed wide eyes at Steve and said, "Emma's looking at the antiques. By the time we're ready to head out and then get there, it will be after five o'clock, and we'll only have a limited window before dusk. I suggest starting at 9 AM tomorrow," he proposed, seeking Steve's concurrence.

Knowing Jack was starting to brush off Ben, Steve, not wanting to make it appear as if they were brushing him off, said, "I'm with Ben. That's two or more hours, which could yield the cave. It may be best if you took charge, if you know what I mean."

"Let me go in and ask her."

Jack's return from the store brought Emma's verdict – a morning start was best. "Ben, give me your mobile number, and I'll text you the photo of the map we found. As you live near Sang Run, you'd know better than we do where we should meet in the morning. What do you think?"

Ben's reluctance was evident. "To come this far and wait?"

Jack leaned in, confiding, "Emma's… well... Let's say it's best not to ruffle her feathers."

Steve interjected, smoothing over the tension, "We're keeping her on our side. We don't want her inviting an army of Smithsonian archeologists to search. So we have to trade carefully."

Ben agreed but was reluctant, so they exchanged contact information. Jack sent him the map.

Restless, Ben commented about setting off alone.

"It's your call, Ben. We're here for a while, and dinner plans with Emma could extend our stay. We'll be at the Honi tonight if you're looking to regroup," Jack said, laying out the evening's potential unfolding.

"Who's playing?"

"The Stickers."

"What kind of music?"

"Country."

"Wish it were rock, but country's alright. I might catch up later," Ben said, moving toward his pickup parked outside the diner. The lifted, bright red Dodge Ram passed them and disappeared down the road, vanishing within moments.

Steve glanced at Jack, his voice laced with mock concern, "You're not going to let Emma know I sort of sided with you on her... 'personality'?" He air-quoted the last word, his smirk evident.

"That'd be a surefire way to get us both killed."

They hadn't settled long when Emma emerged from Englanders. "Did you know they ship stuff now?" she marveled.

"Is there anything left for them to sell?" Jack said, and he and Steve smiled, shaking their heads in amusement.

"So, what'd I miss?" she prodded.

"Well, after checking in with you, we told Ben you'd rather start fresh tomorrow. We kinda made it seem..."

Steve jumped in, smoothing over Jack's attempt, "We commented that crossing you wasn't wise – said you could bring your own team of archeologists."

Emma's laughter filled the air. "Good save, Stevie. Makes sense to use me as the deterrent. Keeps Ben at arm's length but within sight."

"Precisely," Jack concurred.

Steve hinted, "There's more. I've got a date tonight at the Honi."

At this, Emma and Jack shared a look of piqued interest, silent questions hanging between them.

Linking arms with both men, Emma steered them towards Jack's car, curiosity burning bright. "You're spilling the details, Stevie," she insisted. "We're off to Swallow Falls, right?"

"Yes, Ma'am," they echoed in unison.

Chapter 13

Jack, Emma, and Steve veered off 2nd Street, their eyes catching the historical allure of the B&O Railroad Station. The terminal boasted an imposing steam engine, with a black and silver body shimmering under the sun's embrace, and a red caboose, with its quaint, round windows beckoning visitors with its charm.

Their journey continued along Herrington Manor Road, the landscape unfolding into a picturesque blend of the Oakland Golf Course and dense forests. They exchanged tales of their archival finds with Steve, most animated about a caves book and a map detailing ancient trails.

Shifting gears, Emma quizzed him about his evening plans. "So, Steve, who's the mystery date tonight?"

His response was cryptic, "You both know her, but only Jack met her."

"Hold on... Sally Adkins?" Jack asked.

"Spot on," he said.

Emma's curiosity was piqued, and she asked, "Why her? Did Ben set you two up?"

"Nope. She found me at the gift shop. Surprised you didn't mention how attractive she is."

"Yeah, Jack. Why didn't you tell us about her?" Emma said with a smile.

Jack squirmed, trying to determine if she was being sarcastic or jealous, so not knowing which, he replied, "Focused on the barrel's contents, I guess. Plus, I didn't think she held a candle to you."

"Treasure, understandable, and a compliment. Nice save," she laughed as she touched her hand to Jack's shoulder.

Steve recounted Sally's odd timing, never appearing with Ben. "She was beginning to walk away when I invited her to join us at the Honi tonight, hoping to learn more."

"I'm sure that's what you were thinking, Stevie," Emma said, dripping with sarcasm before laughing.

They drove over the Swallow Falls State Park Bridge with the windows down; the thundering rush of river over rocks below accompanied the distinct sound of wheels on the metal grate surface. They caught brief glimpses of families frolicking in the water and scrambling up the cascade.

Turning into the park, the towering oaks, pines, and hemlocks surrounded them. They paid their dues at the gate and found their way to the parking lot.

Jack suggested a change into swimsuits. On their walk, he voiced concerns about Sally and Ben's mysterious connection and the caution they needed. "Given Sally's role and her odd link to Ben, we should be careful. Agreed?"

Both replied, "Yes."

Emma, practical as always, chimed in, "It's a small museum. It's possible they're dedicated to guest experiences. Tonight, if she shows, we'll dig deeper."

With a shared nod, Jack and Steve parted ways with her, heading to the restrooms.

In the privacy of the restroom, he probed, "Did Sally catch your eye that much?"

"She did. Either you buried your head in treasure maps too long, or maybe Emma's set the bar high for you."

Jack thought about the possibility but redirected, "We still need to figure out her link to Ben."

"Perhaps. But maybe I can charm it out of her and also get lucky tonight."

"As usual, you'll try to be the ladies' man and… crash and burn," he laughed.

Emerging, they stashed their clothes in the Suburban. Jack armed himself with the tools of their treasure hunt – a metal detector, shovel, and snorkeling gear.

"Do you think we'll be too conspicuous?" Emma asked.

Jack surveyed the dwindling parking lot. "Let's say we're looking for a lost bracelet from a day at the falls. Simple."

They ventured under the Swallow Falls Canyon Trail sign, the gravel-covered footpath ushering them into the embrace of nature. The whisper of leaves and the murmur of the river were their companions.

Emma breathed in the forest's essence, a shared memory with Jack. "I always loved this place. The fresh scent of the trees, the sounds of the cascading water. Very few places like this exist to explore, swim, and hike."

Jack agreed. "I cherish these moments, Em."

They headed down the path cut through the thick forest. Yet, glimpses of the Youghiogheny River below teased them as they approached, its waters dancing over rocks and logs. The echo of the rushing current grew more intense until they reached the impressive sight of Muddy Creek Falls' fifty-foot plunge.

Descending the man-made steps to the base of the falls, they stood awestruck, the mist kissing their faces, the roar enveloping them.

"Wow," Emma whispered as she leaned into Jack, "Too bad we're not here to enjoy it."

"Next time," he promised with a smile, envisioning a day free of pursuits.

They advanced cautiously, supporting each other against the slick rocks, the ambiance turning cooler as they navigated through shadowed areas. Climbing a rise, they approached a fissure guarded by boulders.

Steve pointed. "This is the place."

Narrowing through the passage, they found themselves in a veiled alcove of the cave, its formation from the creek's persistent erosion.

The waterfall's murmur welcomed them, a constant echo within the damp, algae-adorned walls. The moist earth mingled with the stone was heavy and pervasive.

Sunlight snuck in through a crevice above, illuminating the cave's modest interior, marked by an arched ceiling and rugged walls. They moved with deliberate steps, eyes combing every potential nook for hidden treasures amidst the debris scattered by the fall's might. The roar of water drowned out any chance of easy conversation.

Their search commenced in mutual silence. Jack with his metal detector, Steve tapping the walls, and Emma inspecting under the rocks, all to no avail.

Breaking the quiet, Steve announced his frustration with the barren floor. Jack joined them, his expression mirroring their disappointment. "Emma and I have been here before, not looking for treasure, though," he shared, a tinge of regret in his voice. "We're only finding rocks today."

Emma said, a playful warning to Steve's wide grin, "Don't let your thoughts wander too far."

"Should we go on the other side of the boulders and scan underneath Muddy Creek Fall's face?" asked Steve.

"Yes. Niagara Falls erodes three feet a year but faces more water at continuous, faster speeds. I would think over 250 years that Muddy Creek may have only eroded backward five or ten at best."

Outside, Jack led the way, his determination undimmed. He ventured into the pool beneath the falls, a beep from his detector promising. Slipping on his dive mask, he plunged into the chilly depths. Below, sifting through the gravel with his hand, his efforts yielded nothing. Scanning, the device beeped again.

"Shovel, please."

"Tell me where," Steve obliged, scooping up sediment to examine on a nearby rock.

Observing a couple intrigued by their activity, Emma explained they were searching for her lost bracelet, a keepsake from her mother. They wished them luck and departed after capturing a moment with the falls.

Another beep led to another scoop by Steve, but Jack's subsequent scan fell silent. He approached the pile on the stone slab, the detector's alert guiding him to uncover a coin amidst the gravel.

"Look what I found, a Buffalo!" Jack smiled as he held the nickel up to look at it.

"Jack's buying dinner!" Steve exclaimed.

"Why not! This 1937 D Buffalo, very good shape, might be several hundred bucks."

"No shit?" Emma asked.

With a large smile, "Yep. So, no matter what, we made some money today!"

Jack surveyed the surroundings once more, finding only silence and stillness.

"This is as sensitive as it gets. It can find something through six feet of rock," Jack said while stepping out of the water, his expression clouded with disappointment. "With the rocky terrain, even if we hit on something, digging it out would be a nightmare without heavy equipment. That's inviting trouble and maybe the authorities. Let's head down to the smaller cave by the creek."

They moved to the next location, a sheltered cavern down the stream. Despite a thorough search, the cave's solid base and walls offered nothing of interest.

Switching off his detector, Jack concluded, "It's unlikely anything was here. The solid rock and inconsistent water flow would've made concealment difficult, not to mention thousands visit here a year."

"So, where to?" Steve asked.

"Let's follow Muddy Creek towards the Yough, looking for either waterfalls with potential hiding spots behind them or deep pools to conceal a cave."

The journey was challenging, with steep slopes and the need for careful footing on rocks and roots. Reaching a point where Muddy Creek met the Youghiogheny River in a thunderous roar, they climbed a large boulder. The spectacular clash of rivers, where the spray sometimes leaped feet into the air. Despite the dramatic scenery, no hidden waterfalls were in sight downstream.

They continued upriver, aiming for a spot Captain Clarke might have chosen. Nothing matched their requirements until they arrived at Lower Swallow Falls. The falls spanned the river with a 10-foot drop with a massive flow on the far side, a quieter center, and natural steps on the right with a fraction of water spilling down them, stirring their excitement.

Steve gazed in awe and said, "This place never ceases to amaze me."

Jack reminisced, "This whole area is underwater in spring or after heavy rains. There's not much flow today. Remember when we crossed the river at the top and leaped from the outcropping into the 20-foot-deep pool below?" He pointed towards a cliff by the waterfall, emphasizing the pool's depth and the overhang.

Nodding, Steve recalled the adventure as Jack prepared the detector again.

"Time to dive in," Jack said, securing his snorkel. He passed Emma a pair of goggles, who laughed, deflecting them toward Steve. "Navy guys are built for this."

Jack and Steve stepped into the water, adjusting their fins with a focus sharpened by the challenge ahead. They battled the river's current, each stroke full of determination, holding their equipment tight. They found solace at the center waterfall's base, taking refuge on an underwater ledge.

Catching their breath, he handed the detector to Steve, clearing his mask and preparing for the dive. Steve eyed him with both anticipation and concern.

"Be careful," he cautioned.

Jack nodded, his resolve clear. "Will do." With a final deep inhale, he disappeared beneath the water's surface.

* * *

Steve's eyes followed Jack's progress under the waterfall, the roaring cascade almost drowning out his unease. He tracked the submerged silhouette sliding along the wall, diving deeper.

Please don't do something stupid, Jack.

* * *

Cold and dim, the underwater world challenged Jack as he approached the bottom. Leveling out, he moved across the bottom until a shadowy cavern emerged. His heart pounded. Inside, darkness swallowed the limits of sight. His lungs were now burning, and he surfaced and gasped for air, a sharp contrast to the calm he'd left below.

"You were under for close to three minutes. Anything?" Steve's voice reached him across the river.

"Yes!" Jack replied, excitement lacing his breath. "I found a recess, a tiny version of the one at Muddy Creek Falls. I need a second look."

"Why are your eyes shut?" Steve asked.

"Adjusting them to the darkness for when I dive down again."

The creases in Steve's forehead from his worry appeared as he asked, "Are you sure?"

"Yep! I know where to go now. It's deep, but I'll be quick."

Steve hesitated but relented. "Just... be careful."

Jack's breathing calmed, and he took the detector in his hand. He navigated by touch into the waterfall's roar. Diving again, he entered the cavern's embrace, its darkness more foreboding than before. He moved deeper, and the strong current forced him in. Dread filled Jack as he went further into the recess, but the desire for treasure trumped his notion to turn back.

* * *

Steve glanced at his watch as Jack dove and vanished into the cave, the water's cascade echoing in his ears. Impatience edged into Steve's vigil; each second ticked slower than the last. Battling the force against him, he held firm, but after three minutes, unease spiraled into fear.

At the fourth minute, Emma's distant shout, "Go get him!" jolted Steve. With a deep breath, he plunged into the depths below.

* * *

Submerged in silence save for the muffled roar of water, Jack groped his way through the darkening recess. The hunt for the elusive treasure propelled him forward, though visibility waned. Jack's body shuddered, and pain seared as his head collided with a rock above him. He recoiled, dropping the detector. Muffling a cry, he realized expelling air would be his end. Eyes coming to focus, he discovered the water's current forced him into a tight cavity with no room to twist around, his breath depleting.

Forced to crawl backward in retreat, Jack turned and retrieved his detector. The dim light revealed only a barren void – no chest, no treasure – only the stark realization of the cave's emptiness. Panic clutched him, the dire need for air eclipsing all else. Desperate, his feet slammed against the wall like an Olympic swimmer making the last turn of a gold medal race, propelling him toward the exit. His world dimmed as Steve appeared.

* * *

With no sign of Jack, Steve's worry mounted as he approached the entrance. Without warning, Jack darted past him and raced for the surface. The brief relief transformed into horror as Jack's body went limp, the metal detector fluttering to the bottom. Steve lunged forward, fear coursing through his veins with every stroke. He enveloped Jack, battling the current that sought to claim them, forcing them out of the depths and into the sun.

Emerging, Steve's grip around Jack was vice-like, his free hand slapping Jack's face, begging for consciousness. "Jack. Stay with me!" his voice was raw as he hauled them toward the shore. Time ceased moving until Jack's sudden gasp shattered the spell, almost causing him to release his grasp. "Jack... Jack...," his tone was thick with urgency, relief flooding him as Jack showed signs of life, redirecting to a nearby ledge for safety.

Jack's ragged voice asked, "What happened?"

"At least you didn't need mouth-to-mouth this time. You scared me, Dude. You were underwater for an eternity. I dove in after seeing you shoot out of the cave, and then... nothing," Steve recounted, the panic still evident.

Catching his breath, Jack pieced it together. "Hit my head... got stuck," he paused, "too far back."

126

"You're okay now. Find anything?" Steve's concern shifted to curiosity.

"Nothing. Rocks and silence," he sighed. "And Dude?"

"Yeah, Jack?"

"Remind me, when I go diving for nothing, I should bring dive gear and an air tank."

Steve chuckled and nodded in understanding. "Well, when you're ready, we can head back to land to rest more. Oh, and Jack?"

"Yeah?"

"You're making a bad habit of having me haul your ugly ass out of a river."

"I'm glad you're here, my friend."

Steve concurred, and they hurried to Emma. She rushed to Jack, embracing him like a mother reunited with her long-lost child. Tears streamed down her face as she scolded him, "What were you thinking? I couldn't bear to lose you."

"I'm here, thanks to Stevie," he reassured, trying to lighten the moment.

Emma's broad eyes conveyed her concern. "You had us terrified. Promise me, no more." She pulled away from him, and when her hand brushed the back of his head, it came away smeared with blood. "You're bleeding! Let me look."

Emma directed him to sit on the ground. Brushing her fingers through his hair, she found a small, puncture-like cut with a large knot forming on his head. "Let's sit a little while and make sure you don't have a concussion."

"Yes, ma'am," was all he said.

They all gazed at the moving water, and Emma said, "So, what'd you learn in the cave?"

"I'm an idiot?"

"Yes, we already knew that. But what's in it?"

"Nothing. Even if Clarke could have seen the cave, there's no way a chest or barrel survived the current, not over centuries," he mused aloud, skepticism painting his voice as he considered the logistics of hiding treasure behind the waterfall. "If it was shallow when they arrived, maybe, but still…"

Steve raised an eyebrow. "So, a waterfall stash is out?"

Jack wasn't so quick to dismiss. "Here, yes. Something has to be in the letter to his wife, more than those few words. 'Cascade' and 'tears pooling' – they hint at a hidden entrance in a pool behind the falls. It's the perfect concealment."

Emma interjected, her curiosity piqued. "You thought the treasure was here because…?"

"Because it's invisible to the naked eye. Above-ground caves? They would have been picked clean by now. However, a submerged cave," he gestured towards the water, "that's where the secret lies. I think we were going in the right direction with this cave here. That's why I pushed too far here. I think the cave we're searching for with Ben tomorrow and the one from the book has some possibility, but a waterfall is the marker."

Steve joked, "An invisible cave, huh? What's next, Big Foot as the guardian?" His laughter echoed, a playful roar bouncing off the valley walls.

Emma laughed despite herself. "So, we're banking on a hidden cave. Behind a waterfall or sunk deep in a pool?"

"Yep," Jack confirmed, his tone more serious. "The treasures remained undiscovered because the cave is hidden. We haven't come across the right one yet. We keep moving."

Their spirits lifted by Jack's determination, the trio considered their next steps. "We're burning daylight," Emma pointed out, a practical note in her voice. "Let's not waste any more time."

Agreed, they were about to set off when Steve halted. "Wait, Jack's metal detector. Who's diving for it?"

"Not Jack," Emma said, her head jerking to eye Steve, who begrudgingly accepted the challenge. Moments later, he resurfaced with it, triumphant. "See, quick in and out. That's how you do it, Jack."

They strolled down the path, enveloped by the symphony of rustling leaves. Approaching Upper Swallow Falls, the distant laughter of children mingled with the cadence. They paused to admire Balanced

Rock, a 20-foot-tall and 25 to 30-foot-wide geological wonder. Like a floating formation out of the movie *Avatar*, it defied gravity, balancing on its minuscule base, a tiny fraction of its size. Families lined up and snapped pictures with it in the background.

The waterfall commanded attention, its cascade splitting the river's breadth, tumbling into a chasm veiled by a misty spray. On its far flank, a display of joy unfolded as families embraced the thrill of a natural water slide. Amidst the grandeur, time stood still, their senses absorbed by the spectacle.

They studied the cascade in the middle, finding an area beyond it. However, upon closer inspection, they realized it might be too shallow to hide any treasure. Steve smiled and snatched the goggles, declaring, "It's my turn for adventure."

Squeezing past the waterfall's barrier, he navigated the slippery shelf. His laughter broke the air as he exited, saying, "Felt like I was power washed! Nothing behind it – nothing."

"Let's head upriver," Jack proposed.

The trek to Tolliver Run tested their resolve. They eschewed trails for the river's wild embrace. The crystal clear water unveiled the riverbed's secrets as they journeyed.

Reaching Tolliver Falls, where the creek kissed the river, they found the cascade plunging into tranquility – a stark contrast to their quest's fervor.

Their focus narrowed to the mission, and they probed the depths of the falls. Jack snatched the goggles and detector. Reaching through the rush of water, air from a recessed area was behind it. "I'm going in," and disappeared into its might. After a few suspenseful moments, Emma turned to Steve and asked, "Should we follow him?"

"We should."

Emma was reaching into the water herself when Jack emerged, striking her arm. Jack's eyes were wide open, his mouth ajar, and he appeared in shock.

"Did you find it?" Emma's voice held a blend of hope and skepticism.

Jack's grin dissolved the tension, "No, I was joking. I'm glad to be alive."

Emma's retort was swift, filled with annoyance and relief, "Stick to treasure hunting, Jack. Leave the comedy to Steve."

"Okay. It was large enough to hide it but would be too exposed. Someone would spot the treasure in a dry spell with little or no water falling to mask it. No luck with the detector, either. I'm still betting on it hidden in a deep pool behind a waterfall. This one was too shallow."

"Yeah, sorry, but I have some good news," Jack added.

"What?" they asked together.

"We can cross Swallow Falls State Park off the list. We made some money, and it's time to clean up to grab dinner and see The Stickers!"

"Well, I'm happy now," Emma replied.

Steve lingered at the edge of the falls, his gaze fixed on the cascading water before turning, a touch of frustration in his voice. "Not the news we hoped for. I'm all for a meal, but Swallow Falls turned up empty. What's our next move?"

In the ensuing silence, Jack, with a spark of resolve, broke through. "Another waterfall, we need to find one. Gap Falls and National Falls Rapids are to the north," he mused, tracing invisible lines in the air as if mapping their journey. "I mentioned them because there are more along the Youghiogheny and its tributaries. We'll dive into the maps tonight, chart our course."

"Alright, but let's head out. I'm hungry," Emma said, hand to her stomach.

In unison, they responded, "Yes, ma'am," their voices carrying respect and anticipation, oblivious to the twists the night might unfurl.

Chapter 14

The sun dipped lower, bathing the valley in a golden hue. A heavy silence accompanied their return to the Suburban. The day's quest ended in disappointment, yet Emma sought to lighten the mood. "They say the journey matters as much as the destination. At least we've narrowed down where the treasure isn't."

Jack agreed. "Edison once said, 'I didn't fail. I found 2,000 ways not to make a lightbulb. I only needed to discover the one way to make it work.' We need to find that one cave."

Steve, ever the jester, said, "And hey, we didn't lose Jack. Plus, I've got fresh material for ribbing him about his latest rescue."

Jack the SUV as Steve searched for a baseball game on the radio – Pirates leading the Brewers, much to their surprise.

On the way back to his apartment, Jack noticed that his two friends were soon fast asleep. Emma, first to shake off the weariness, ran up the steps and headed for a shower, seeking solace in its warmth. Exiting, draped in a towel, she called out, "Next!" before disappearing into his room.

Steve, seizing the opportunity with Jack still sleeping, freshened up. By the time Emma reappeared, dressed to kill in a black dress and heels, he couldn't hide his admiration.

"Wow, Em, stunning!" he praised.

"You look like you're ready to make an impression with Sally, putting your guns on display with your tight shirt and shorts."

With a big smile, he said, "You better believe it," he flexed his arm while running his hand over the side of his head like he was smoothing his hair.

Jack, roused by their banter, showered and dressed with determination. Uncertain, Jack stepped into the bedroom doorway bare-chested, water dripping down his chest, holding a Hawaiian and a polo. "Which one, Em?"

"I don't think so, Magnum," she chuckled. "You look better in the polo."

Steve's bright smile appeared, and he whispered after Jack entered his room, "Who's kidding who? You want to see his guns."

Emma blushed and said with a grin, "Shhh. Stop it," as she waved her hand downward as they headed out the door.

After parking, they made their way between Uno's and the Honi Honi, descending onto a deck by Deep Creek Lake, where a sensory panorama awaited. The moonlit waters reflected, and gentle waves cradled the docked boats. Laughter mingled with the soft clinks of cold drinks while the air carried a blend of grilled delicacies and the fresh scent of the lake, whetting appetites. Emma, giggling, directed their attention to the outdoor bar's decor – a gorilla and an alligator adorned the rooftops, watching over the patrons scattered across the lawn. Here, amidst the fiberglass giant elephant and whale and a wooden pirate ship, families and children played.

Jack navigated the crowd for beers as Emma and Steve claimed a table to the side of the stage, vacated just in time for The Stickers' performance. The crowd's energy surged as the band opened with 'Countrified,' their country rock melody, which even captured Steve, who found himself swaying and singing for the first time.

With drinks and menus distributed upon his return, Emma initiated a toast, "To today's adventure and the treasures we're yet to find."

Their clinks sealed the sentiment.

Orders placed, they waded into memories of past exploits, the night's ambiance – soft lights and distant conversations – crafting a perfect backdrop. Jack, catching Emma's laughter and the sparkle in her gaze, sighed and felt a pang of nostalgia for their shared history.

His phone's vibration pulled him back; a message from Ben indicated he had no success that evening searching. "Guys, Ben wants to meet at 9. He thinks the cave is near Steep Run Creek. It's west and a little south of where the marker was. Let's go, only in case that's it. Plus, it keeps him close. What do you think?"

Emma scrutinized the map, breaking the silence. "It somewhat aligns with the legend, tracing the Native American trail by the river. It's worth checking, and he might offer more clues."

"We'll aim for 9:30," Jack decided, confirming the time via text. Ben's brief "K" sealed their plan.

"Steve, your thoughts?" Emma prodded, noticing his distraction as he scanned the premises.

Roused by Emma's touch, Steve apologized, his attention elsewhere, hopeful for Sally's arrival.

Emma offered reassurance, "She might still show."

Their meals arrived, diverting attention to the vibrant Honi Honi ambiance, their movements syncing with the background music. After eating, Steve's gaze caught Sally navigating through the dancers. Her presence, accentuated by her attire, drew him towards her, and he escorted her to the table.

"I see you made it, Sally," Jack broke the ice. Sally's eyes opened, and her head shifted back, appearing shocked.

Taking their seats, Steve said, "Sally, these are my friends. You met Jack, and I believe you also spoke to Emma Wilson over the phone. I came into town to visit Jack for vacation, and with what was discovered yesterday, Emma drove up last night to take the items to the Smithsonian. Jack and Emma went to college together, so she called him to go to the site."

"Oh, makes sense," Sally said.

"We've eaten. You want something?" Steve asked.

"I ate already, but from the looks of it, I need to catch up on the drinks."

"What'd you want? It's quicker for service at the bar than wait for a server."

"I'll take a strong vodka and watermelon punch, please."

"More beers, Steve," Emma asked, raising her bottle.

"Emma, I'm so glad Bill put us in touch after he called you," Sally said. "When he informed me the Smithsonian was sending someone, I worried we'd lose a prized historical display. Thank you for taking on the task of preserving the items for us. We could do it, but our small museum doesn't have a lot of time and resources."

"You're most welcome. We are not looking to 'grab' artifacts bound for a museum for everyone to enjoy. We don't like pieces going to collectors."

"I agree," Sally said.

"By the way, who's Bill?" Jack asked.

"Bill's behind the Smithsonian call," Emma shared intrigue in her voice. "My understanding is he's a 94-year-old volunteer with a lifetime rooted in the county."

"He's a relic himself and knows the area better than anyone," Sally said, steering the conversation. Changing the subject, she added, "So, the two of you met in college?"

"Yeah, we're both history majors, so we had a lot of classes together. After graduating, I got a job teaching near DC, and Jack was a substitute teacher at Uniontown High School before getting his position at Penn State. We stayed in touch."

"Steve?"

"He's my friend," Jack replied. "He's also from Uniontown and became friends with Emma when he visited me at college."

Sally probed deeper. "That's nice. So how'd you keep in contact over the years?"

Emma squirmed when she said, "It's... a bit complicated."

"Oh, I take it that you dated?"

"Yes, we broke up a few years after college as the distance was too great, and we remained good friends after."

Sally's eyes widened as she nodded, starting to understand the relationship. "So, Jack's not really here as a museum employee but a trusted friend who knows history, or is he an archeologist?"

"Well... Sort of both. Jack has an uncanny knack for absorbing details about history, which his classmates, like me, found rather annoying." A smirk crossed her face as she shook her head, "He knows more about history than anyone else I know. He's recently been researching the French and Indian War and has spent a lot of time searching this area for... artifacts. And..."

Jack interrupted, "Hey, last summer, I found a canteen and an axe from that war along Braddock's march near Bear Camp. So, you can count on me for any historical intrigue." Jack started to stand, "Excuse me, I need to make a pit stop."

Seeking Steve, Jack relayed their conversation to him, omitting their naval history. "What if Sally inquires about your profession?"

"Say I'm a mechanical and electrical engineering consultant for the government. It covers our Navy connections if it comes up."

"Works for me."

* * *

Steve slid back into his seat; he procured vodka for Sally and beers for them in tow. "So what did I miss?" he asked, his gaze flitting between the faces at the table.

"They filled me in on how everyone met. Pretty amazing those two stayed friends," Sally remarked, turning towards Steve with curiosity sparking in her eyes. "I've caught up on their stories; what about you? What's your line of work?"

"I'm a consultant, a mechanical and electrical engineer for government projects, including the Department of Defense," he explained.

Sally leaned in, intrigued, and asked, "And what does it involve?"

"I'm involved in designing or tweaking military gear, though I'm limited in what I can divulge," he replied, noticing Sally's drink was almost empty, her attention more on the alcohol than the conversation.

Checking his phone, he offered, "Let me see if Jack can grab another drink for you."

"Thanks. How about a dance in the meantime?" she asked as her drink was now empty.

"Sure, I'll give it a shot," he said, setting his beer aside to join her on the floor.

* * *

The music washed over Emma as she watched Steve and Sally dance. Their laughter and seamless moves spoke of a growing closeness, stirring both envy and yearning. She envied their carefree joy and longed for the thrill of new love and the depth of a committed relationship. Her career was fulfilling, yet her personal life was empty.

Jack's return, drinks in hand but concern etching his features, snapped her from thought. "Everything alright?" he asked with gentle inquisition.

"It's nothing," she said, forcing a grin as she glanced back at the dance floor. "Look at Steve. I'm glad Sally made it."

Jack, still concerned but nodding, set down the bottles as the two returned, laughing and sweating with their labored breathing.

Sally took another large, animated swallow of her vivid cocktail.

Steve, in contrast, savored his beer more contemplatively. "I'm happy you're having a good time," he said with a measured smile.

Without hesitation, an energized Sally seized Steve's hand, urging him to join the lively crowd. Emma looked on at their departure to the floor with a bit of longing.

Jack's presence became tangible as his hand touched hers, bringing a warmth both comforting and intrusive. "You look like something is bothering you, Em."

"I'm fine," she replied, realizing Jack had seen through her facade.

"I know you better than that. How 'bout we dance?" he proposed, his voice a blend of softness and persuasion she found irresistibly inviting.

"Okay," smiling. She paused before taking Jack's hand. Once on the deck, he spun her around. Although she believed they were friends now, some uncertainty was in her mind. They moved to the beat of the music, and she lost herself in the moment.

He whispered, "You're still the best dance partner I've had," bringing a flush of warmth to her cheeks, to which she replied, skittish, "You're still quite the dancer yourself."

The evening unfolded with an intensity of revelry. Sally and Steve appeared to draw closer with every tune, while Emma and Jack discovered themselves almost in competition with their friends.

The pumped-up crowd cheered as 'Girl in a Pickup Truck' ended, and the lead singer announced the next song would be their last. He asked if they should make their way back to the table. Sally and Steve were still dancing, lost in their own little world.

"Let's stay," she said, her smile reflecting her renewed spirit.

The band's shift to playing 'Slow Dance' prompted him to ask, "You still want to dance?"

Emma looked at him, smiled, and replied, "Yes."

Their bodies pressed together, and Emma's heart raced as Jack enveloped her in a familiar comfort. She rested her head on his chest, embracing the music and the moment, and perceived glimpses of a past love in his gaze. The room's vibrancy encased them, the dance floor their world within a world illuminated by the soft, colorful lights above.

Amid the evening's relaxed cadence, Jack's attention darted to a stranger seated at the far edge of their table, who stood and turned away. Concerned, he checked Emma for her purse, finding it slung over her shoulder. A wave of relief passed through him as he redirected his focus on her, enveloped by the music's tender grip.

The Stickers played their final note, and the Honi Honi bar began to empty. "Why don't we finish our drinks before we head out," he said.

"Sounds good."

They returned to their spot, soon joined by Steve and Sally, draining the last glasses together.

Sally's words slurred with warmth, "I had a grea' ime, guysh... Losh of fun."

Steve smirked when he glanced between Jack and Sally when he agreed, "Indeed."

Sally, her voice drowsy, asked, "Wherrr ya livin'?"

"Friendsville," he replied.

She pondered, her speech muddled, "Migh' be too mush for me t'drive to Accident tonight. Can ya drop me off, Emmma?"

"How about I drive you? That way, you won't have to fetch your car tomorrow. Jack can follow and take me to his place afterward," Steve proposed.

Gratitude flashed in her eyes. "Thang you'v," she stammered.

They exited the bar, and the foursome paired off. Steve and Sally were arm in arm with hushed laughter while Jack and Emma shared a silent moment. Reaching Sally's car, she whispered a secret to Emma in a hug.

Curiosity aroused, he asked as they distanced themselves, "What did she tell you?"

Emma's grin was infectious, "She said we shouldn't follow them. She'll drop him off in the morning."

The new couple departed, and he turned to her and asked, "Steve's in for a night, isn't he?"

She chuckled, "Looks so. Was he okay to drive? You switched to soda, and I'm far from sober."

"He's fine. He milked his beer for the last hour."

With a gentle smile, Jack changed the conversation, "More important, did you enjoy tonight?"

"I did. Thank you."

"Let's make this a habit."

A shared grin sealed the promise as they drove back to Friendsville.

During the ride, she said, "I managed to ask Sally about Ben while you were not there."

Curious, he asked, "How did you bring it up?"

"She inquired about everyone, so I reciprocated. She was a new teacher when Ben was navigating his high school years, and she described him as a good kid from a struggling family. She mentioned their fascination

138

with Braddock's gold, chuckling over the 'eccentric' grandfather's museum visits and his playful offers of reward for any treasure-hunting tips. Sally didn't give the impression she took their possible success as very realistic. My chance to delve deeper ended when Steve reappeared, whisking her off for a dance."

"So, she's aware of the search, but whether she reached out to Ben remains unclear."

"Yep. She referred to him as a 'nice kid' suggests nothing beyond casual acquaintance."

"So, we're left questioning Sally's motives for contacting him."

"It might be irrelevant. If she did reach out, she intended to connect Ben to you."

"Likely so. Still, we must be careful around her. It will be harder if Steve continues the relationship with her."

"I would hope so, considering Steve's overnight *plans* at her place."

"Life's unpredictable..."

When they arrived at Jack's apartment, he led Emma inside, and they sat on the couch and talked and laughed, reminiscing about old times and catching up on each other's lives.

When the clock struck midnight, he said, "We should turn in, Em."

"I guess so."

Leaning in, his embrace was warm, and his voice carried a note of genuine joy, "Having you here means a lot. I've missed this. But we have a full day's search tomorrow, and it would be best if we rested. So, goodnight, Em. Do you want the bed?"

"No, I'm good. Goodnight, Jack."

His parting glance lingered, filled with unspoken words, met by Emma's knowing smile.

Silence settled as Jack retreated. Emma paused in contemplation. She stood to prepare for the night and slipped on a nightshirt. Her scowl focused on the couch, and with a resolved sigh, she approached Jack's door, opening it to the possibilities of the night.

Chapter 15

Captain Thomas Clarke stretched, staring at the golden hue bathing the field before him that morning. The group stirred from their restless slumber, rubbing their eyes and stretching their limbs. Breaking camp, they intended to make up for the time they lost during the storm that consumed the late afternoon and evening of the day before.

They pushed their horses as they rode down into the valley. Although the rain abated overnight, it left them to deal with its torrential aftermath – the swollen, raging waters of the Little Youghiogheny River. They had to cross the one-hundred-foot-wide, engorged waterway.

It wasn't the distance concerning Clarke as he approached the bulging banks; it was the intense roar of the water. He surveyed the churning rapids with a furrowed brow, his fingers tapping against his thigh.

"Damn this infernal rain," he muttered under his breath.

"Captain!" George asked, "May I look at the map?"

He squinted at the chart and studied it with utmost scrutiny. After a few minutes, he said, "Sir, if we head further south, we might find a shallower crossing. However, we'll lose considerable time, which we don't have."

"Agreed," Clarke replied, his piercing eyes never leaving the torrent.

"We must attempt to cross here. The Natives picked this spot for a reason. It has to be the easiest place."

The rest of the team exchanged cautious looks, their thoughts consumed with worry for their cargo and their own well-being. They were aware navigating a rushing river was perilous, but they also understood the urgency of their mission.

After a moment of contemplation, Clarke straightened and spoke to the men, "We have no other option. We are pressed for time and should try here."

George stepped forward. "Sir, I'll volunteer to take a rope across and tie it to a tree. It'll provide a safety line for someone to grab should they fall in."

"Thank you. Your courage is commendable."

The group prepared to face the dangerous crossing, and Clarke saw the piercing stares or concerned faces of his troop displaying a growing sense of trepidation. The river's relentless current roared like an untamed beast, daring them to challenge its fury. Yet despite their fear, they steeled themselves for the task ahead, their determination unwavering.

With the rope end snug in his grip, George rode into the churning waters of the Little Youghiogheny River. The horse's body tensed as the cold water rose, but he coaxed it on.

George turned the horse to face the onslaught of the current. In the middle, the depth caused the steed's belly and George's boots to become drenched in its chilling embrace. The eyes of his worried comrades bore into his back, their trust in him fueling his determination.

Once pushing up the bank, he tied the rope to a tree and moved to the water's edge. "Hang onto it," George shouted over the river's roar, his voice filled with authority and concern. "Whatever you do, don't let go."

Clarke turned his attention to the wagon; he realized the water would rush over the bed, risking the precious cargo and provisions. "We must lighten the wagon and use our horses to carry everything over."

They divided up the items and secured the two payroll chests to the sides of Clarke's large steed.

Clarke was next, and he walked his overloaded horse with firm grips on the stirrup and safety rope. One by one, each man began to follow George's lead, gripping the reins as they waded into the treacherous currents. Their faces were taut with concentration, and each man was well aware that a single misstep spelled disaster.

William was the last to cross, pulling the wagon into the water. The torrent jerked and turned the cart around, dragging the beast and rider downstream toward ferocious rapids. He gritted his teeth and dug his heels into the horse's flanks, urging it to press against the flow. Despite his efforts, the poor creature was no match for the river's power with such a force bearing down on it. "Cut the harness," Clarke screamed, "Save the horse!"

He realized his mistake: *I should have tied two horses to it.*

William hesitated for an instant, torn between his knowledge the cart made it easier for them to travel and his love for his stallion. The fear in the animal's neigh drove him to action. He drew his knife and jumped into the raging waters. Hanging from the stirrup, he sliced one strap before swinging himself underwater and under the hitch. He surfaced and freed it from the wagon's weight with a single, swift motion.

As the water swept the cart away, it snagged the safety rope, breaking it. Clarke's heart raced as he gazed in horror; the carriage, robbed of its constraints, entered the rapids. He cringed as it went over a drop, lost forever.

Clarke looked back as William attempted to stand; his tall, lean frame appeared almost fragile as the raging waters threatened to overwhelm him. He fought against the relentless current and tried to reach the reigns of the horse when an unexpected surge of water forced his ride backward and sent him tumbling into the churning torrent.

"William!" Clarke cried out, his eyes expanded with fear for the fate of his comrade.

Without hesitation, Samuel Rogers, the quiet and unassuming giant, leaped into the roaring river after him. The quiet giant's muscles rippled beneath the surface as he battled the furious flow. Every fiber in his body focused on reaching the struggling marksman.

"Samuel!" his twin brother, Thomas, called out, anxiety etched on his face as his sibling risked his life for another. As he drew closer, the danger of their situation became all too clear. The relentless currents threatened to drag both men under, and their desperate struggle to stay afloat sent waves of panic through those ashore.

"Grab hold of me!" Samuel yelled, his deep voice faint over the thunderous crashing of the river. William, his face contorted with effort and fighting to keep his head above water, reached out a trembling hand toward his would-be savior. Their fingers brushed against each other, the sensation like an electric jolt coursing through their exhausted bodies.

The men on the riverbank held their breath as they witnessed the intense battle for survival. Clarke's face turned pale, and he let go of his horse's reins, rushing down the shore to assist in the rescue. His heart beat faster in his chest with one of his comrades in grave danger.

"Come on, Samuel!" Thomas muttered, his eyes flicking between the raging torrent and his twin brother. He clenched his fists, willing strength into his sibling as if by sheer force of will.

"Almost there," Clarke murmured, choked with emotion until Samuel reached William. His deep concern for both of his men was evident in every line on his face.

Samuel yelled, 'Grab hold of me!' His boomed over the thunderous roar of the river. William fought to keep his head above water, his face contorted with effort. He extended a trembling hand toward his would-be savior.

Finally able to grab hold of him, Samuel helped William to get his legs upright under himself. They tried to propel themselves towards land. The onlookers, paralyzed by fear, urged their comrades on in the treacherous waters.

The captain screamed, "Hold on! We're coming!"

Samuel and William continued their desperate struggle for safety. The others searched for any means to assist them.

George scoured the bank for a sturdy branch or something to aid their friends. He spotted the shortened, broken rope still secured to the tree. He grabbed it, tied it to his waist, and forced his way into the river.

"Keep going!" Clarke yelled, voice cracking. "You're not far from George."

They fought against the river's relentless pull. Their muscles strained, and gasping for breath. They inched closer to safety. The group moved to the edge of the river with fearful anticipation.

"Almost…there…," Samuel panted, eyes locked on the shoreline. They pushed through the current with everything they had.

"Samuel! Look out!" Clarke shouted, his eyes widening in horror. He spotted a large log hurtling toward them on the surface. The warning came too late. The branch slammed into Samuel's leg, and he roared from the jolt of pain surging through him. He gritted his teeth, knowing it broke his leg. He fought the anguish to maintain his grip on William. *Letting go means certain death for both of us.*

Clarke grabbed and mounted a horse.

"Keep pushing, Samuel!" William urged, his voice strained from exhaustion and fear. "We can make it!"

Glancing down, Samuel's heart raced in his chest upon seeing his thigh bone protruding from his pants. A sudden realization struck him: his time was running out. The agony grew along with the river's fury, escalating with every passing second; the relentless force gnawed at their survival: *Time is running out.*

One leg broken and the other wedged against a large rock – grasping he wouldn't make it, given his injuries – he had to try to save William. His breaths became ragged and desperate, each an unwanted reminder of the dwindling window separating life from death. He spotted George, the taunt rope keeping him a few feet out of reach.

Samuel gasped, "You must swim towards George. I am going to push you."

"What about you?" William shot back; his eyes filled with concern as his body trembled with exertion.

"Never mind me," his tone was urgent and laced with authority. "My leg's broken, and I'm bleeding out. You have to get to safety."

"I won't leave you here!" he protested. His grip slipped under the immense pressure of the current and cut short his words.

"Trust me," Samuel implored, his eyes locked onto those of his comrade. "You don't have a choice."

The river surge grew around as if to punctuate his point and threatened to swallow them whole. Clarke sprinted to George's horse. But in a heartbeat, Samuel made a decision defining the essence of his character – a decision born of selflessness and an unwavering commitment to others.

"Listen to me!" he cried out, summoning every remaining ounce of his strength. "You're going to make it out of this alive – I promise!"

Grabbing William's waist with both hands, with his last ounce of strength, he launched William upwards, almost free of the river, and into the arms of George, sacrificing any chance at survival for the sake of his comrade.

The moment Clarke rode into the torrent, the current take took Samuel in its cruel embrace. What appeared like a strange sense of peace washed over Samuel – a calm acceptance of the fate now awaited him.

"No!" he screamed, reaching out in vain as the river's grip snatched his friend away.

Horror set in as the raging water swept Samuel deeper, his body battered by the ruthless rapids. His head smashed against a large boulder; the collision snapped his neck to the side. Clarke hung his head in sorrow once the lifeless corpse began floating face down.

They would honor Samuel's final wish, no matter what it took. With this thought burning like a beacon in his mind, he fought his way to the shoreline, determined to finish their mission.

"Brother!" Thomas cried out, his voice choked with anguish, racing forward as if to enter the river himself. George grabbed his arm, halting him in his tracks.

"No," George said with resolve, his eyes glistening with unshed tears as he embraced William. "We can't help him now. We need to focus on what's ahead."

Clarke and the others started to pull them to shore.

"Damn it all," William cursed, his fists clenched as he fought back the rising tide of emotion threatening to overwhelm him. "His leg broken. He knew he wouldn't make it; he was bleeding out. Yet he still did everything to save me!" The waterlogged fabric of his clothes clung to his shivering frame, serving as a reminder of the sacrifice made by his friend. He looked up at the sky, which appeared to mirror his turmoil, the dark clouds churning overhead.

"My brother wouldn't want us to give up," Thomas asserted, his gaze lingering where his brother vanished. He inhaled, steeling himself for what lay ahead. "He died so we could continue our mission. We can't let his actions be in vain. We need to carry on for him."

"Ok, let's press on," Clarke declared, his jaw set with determination as he tried to shove aside the pain in his chest. "We'll finish this, not only for ourselves but for Samuel, too."

The muddied shore of the Little Youghiogheny River bore witness to the sad group as they began to reorganize their belongings. The waters were now a living nightmare, its currents tainted by the loss of their friend. Together, they steeled themselves for the challenges remaining ahead, sorrow weighing on their shoulders yet tempered by a renewed sense of purpose.

Clarke knelt by the river's edge, watching the distorted reflection of his face ripple across the surface, a ghostly reminder of losing a man. He bowed his head and said a prayer.

"Here's your pack, William. You may also want to change." George said, handing it over while casting a wary glance at the torrent. He shivered, the cold air cutting through his damp clothes, but the chill in his bones ran deeper than any earthly frost reached.

"Thanks," He replied, yelling to be heard over the river's roar. Staring down it for a moment, it seemed heavier than before, and he started to dress.

"Thomas, did you find your brother's belongings?" Clarke asked, his gaze shifting to the quiet soldier searching the area.

"Y-yes, Sir," He stammered as tears flowed down his cheeks as he bent to retrieve it. He clutched his twin's bag to his chest. "He left them on the shore. I have them right here."

"Let's take it with us so you can return them to his family. When we have a chance, I want to write a letter to his wife," Clarke said. He looked around at his men and recognized they had to keep moving forward. With a slow, measured breath, he resolved to press on. "Alright, let's move out."

He thought: *Samuel didn't hesitate to put his life on the line. I can't let it be for nothing.*

"William," He muttered, noticing his friend's clenched fists. "We're all upset, too. You don't have to shoulder this burden alone."

"Losing him was my fault," William replied, his voice strained. "He jumped in to save me."

"He made his own choice," Thomas interjected, his eyes filled with understanding. "You had the most difficult crossing with the wagon. He knew what he was doing and would have done the same for any of us."

They looked at Thomas; his eyes moved to his brother's pack as he said, "We need to keep going."

"Let's do it together," Clarke declared.

Emboldened by their shared resolve, the group pressed forward through the damp undergrowth.

The dense forest on the other side of the river swallowed every sound, including the wind on the leaves above. The atmosphere was heavy with sorrow, and each man's breath created a swirling mist, hanging in the air before vanishing into the dampness. Their horses' hooves squelched through the mud along their relentless ride, the path before them shrouded in shadows.

"Keep up the pace, lads," he called out, subdued yet firm. He glanced back at the group, noting the grim expressions etched onto their weary faces. William's eyes were distant, staring farther as if something invisible was beyond the trees.

James lost his usual mischievous glint while his brother, John, rode in silence, his introspective gaze cast downward.

"Captain," Davis muttered but determined. "The men are exhausted from the river. We need to find a place to rest."

He looked at the lieutenant, his piercing eyes searching the younger man's face before nodding and said, "Very well, but only for an hour."

"George," Williams called out, snapping the scout from his thoughts. "I think this is a decent spot. It's not much, but it should do."

He walked over and looked around. The elevated, open patch of ground was dryer than the path they were on. "Perfect," he said as he patted William on the back and tied his horse to a tree.

William stared into the distance, reigns in hand, next to a tree. Henry walked up and offered, "Here, let me help you. Get some rest."

"Thanks," William muttered, his voice hollow.

Clarke found a place to sit and pulled out his journal. The realization of Samuel's death tightened his chest. *He saved William, but at what cost? A man lost his life because of my decision.*

He penned a letter to Samuel's wife, Margaret, to express how her husband, her love, made the ultimate sacrifice by saving another man.

After he finished writing, he looked at each man; the softened faces and frowns of his men spoke to Clarke of their mourning, but the guilt preyed on his mind. However, they were brooding more than resting. He sighed: *We must keep moving!*

He walked over to Thomas, "Please put this with your brother's things."

"Yes, Sir."

"Men, let's move on," he commanded.

After they were on the march, Clarke said, "Thomas, I'd like to learn more about your brother. Would you care to share a story with us?"

Thomas looked up, and his face changed from sadness to a smile. He said, "Well, back when Samuel was courting his wife, Margaret, one day her dad found them in his hayloft. The farmer chased him for almost a mile with a pitchfork in hand... and my brother only had enough time

148

to put his breeches on," he laughed. "So, there he was, running down the center of town, bare-chested and barefooted. When the farmer caught up to him, he said Samuel had to marry his daughter, or he would challenge him to a duel..."

Chapter 16

Jack teetered on the edge of sleep as the muted creak of the door drew him awake. Emma stood framed in the doorway. Her long, thin nightshirt failed to conceal her figure silhouetted by the soft yellow hue of the kitchen light behind her.

"Something wrong, Em?"

"No... scoot over. Your couch wrecked my back last night, and your bed's big enough for two. I'm too beat to mess with the air mattress."

A flicker of confusion crossed Jack's features, his mind racing. Was she hinting at a reconciliation, or was this comfort and convenience? While she settled beside him, Jack made to vacate the bed, murmuring, "I can take the living room."

"Stay," she said, her voice hesitating. "Being here, with you... It's stirred up by how much I've missed us. Life in DC's been lonely. I don't know what this means for us, but staying with you feels... safe. For now, let's be friends. It's a matter of comfort. That's all this is. I hope you understand."

His expression softened, though a trace of bewilderment lingered. Holding back, he decided to let her lead. "I do. I've had a hole in my life since you."

She moved over, putting her hand on his chest; he wondered: *Is she doing this?*

She placed a kiss on his cheek, murmuring, "Goodnight," before turning away and curling into the blankets.

"Night, Em."

Jack stared into the darkness, the possibility of reigniting old passions wrestling with the reality of Emma's words. He resolved to tread carefully, the night's revelations ushering him into a restless sleep.

* * *

Dawn filtered through the blinds, bathing the bedroom in gentle warmth. Emma awoke entangled with Jack in an unintentional embrace, her head resting upon his chest and her leg draped across his. A momentary smile flickered across her lips from the contentment and familiarity of lying next to Jack. That was until the previous night's foggy memories surged back, her feeling of inappropriateness overcoming her comfort and turning into regret.

Fearing awakening Jack, she was held captive by the rhythm of his calm breathing and the occasional soft snore; she hesitated, caught between the desire to stay and the need to escape this delicate moment. Emma's eyes widened again, catching herself looking from his handsome face down his chest toward her leg draped over him and paused at his boxers. Now afraid of another uncomfortable situation that was evident, with painstaking care, she disentangled herself and retreated to the sanctuary of the bathroom.

Staring at her mirrored reflection, she dwelled upon the possible implications of her actions and was on the brink of tears. Yet, Jack's integrity in not taking advantage of her drunken vulnerability sparked a fleeting smile as she reminisced over the joy she experienced from her relationship with Jack before it unraveled.

She stretched, and her resolve wavered. *Can we only be friends? Or is this more?* The questions hung heavy in the air, unanswered.

With a deep breath, she returned to the bedroom, finding Jack still deep in slumber. Deciding to start the day at least by making breakfast for them, she ventured to the kitchen, only to find milk and Life cereal. *We did not stop for groceries.*

Perched on the sofa and staring out the window, Emma became

absorbed in thought; her mind wandered through their collective history – the good and the bad. His obsessions had once pushed her to the background, a situation she wasn't eager to revisit. However, she wondered: *Am I falling for him again?*

The rustling of Jack's stirring broke her thoughts, and she approached his door. "Good morning."

"Mornin'," he replied, walking to the couch. "What are you doing?"

"I went to make us breakfast," she said, gesturing to the kitchen, "but we have nothing."

"Sorry, we forgot to stop." Climbing out of bed, he walked over and gave her a quick hug. "You want to go to The Rolling Pin Bakery in Accident, or I can run down the street for eggs."

"Let's go with eggs and whatever else you can find. That way, we're here when Steve gets back."

Jack turned and headed to the bedroom. She admired the view of his broad back and muscular legs. A warmth came over her as she realized she still desired him, but she wanted to remain cautious.

Upon his return, she rejected his offer to cook with a chuckle, "I prefer my eggs not to be crispy and my bacon runny, Jack. But why don't you help me?" Together, they discovered a rhythm in the kitchen, a dance of companionship hinting at a deeper connection still simmering beneath the surface.

They made breakfast, and laughter and shared tales filled the room. Caught in Jack's easy company, Emma pondered the possibility of rekindling what once was. Their banter between bites turned to the day's plans – looking for a cave with Ben and other sites should time allow.

"With all of us searching, if we spread out but keep in sight or within earshot of each other, we should complete the entire area by noon," Jack said.

She nodded. "That makes sense. However, Steve's being late worries me."

"I'm not sure. Why don't you relax outside and keep an eye out for them while I tackle the dishes?"

Taking a seat on the porch, the crisp morning air and the chirps of birds accompanied her concern for the overdue Steve.

* * *

Steve woke with a pounding headache, and his world was a blur. Seeking an answer as to how he was naked under a sheet did not overshadow his gaze upon Sally, also bare, her dark hair cascading down her shoulders. Her slender form and smooth skin were captivating and arousing. His fragmented recollections of the night left him confused about the night's conclusion.

Sally stirred, turned, looked at him, and said, "Thanks for last night. You were, well… amazing." She pressed her lips to his. Parched, yet they melted into his with the faint trace of vodka mingled with the salt of their sweat. He felt the gentle caress of her breasts against his chest.

"It was… unforgettable," Steve managed, his mind a whirlwind of absent memories.

"What time is it?" he asked, trying to anchor himself to the present.

"Thinking of leaving so soon? Come on. We had a lot of fun last night. Don't you want to have some more?" Sally purred, running her hand down Steve's chest.

He hesitated, but he couldn't deny his attraction toward her. He had always been weak regarding women, and she was the most beautiful woman he had ever been with… or may have been with.

"I wanted to tell Jack so we're not rushed," he said, playing with her hair.

He mentioned possible breakfast, and the day's plans of a hike or boating appeared to interest Sally, but her obligations called her away. "I can't. I have to be at the museum soon," she said, regret tinting her voice. Glancing at the clock, she added, "It's past 8:30. I need to go, and as much as I'd love to… continue, we don't have time without making me late, even though I'd enjoy it."

She sat up, "But I'll call you after work to find out where you are at."

"I'd like it if you would come."

"If that's the case, promise me you'll make it happen again tonight. And

153

yes, I would like to see you again later today." She stood, wrapping a blanket around herself. "Sorry, we have to get dressed and go," she turned and opened a dresser drawer to pull out some clothes and left the room.

Not quite understanding what was going on, he got dressed.

* * *

Jack joined Emma in enjoying the morning air on the porch, anticipating Steve. With a grateful peck on Emma's cheek and another "thank you" for breakfast, he inquired about Steve's whereabouts.

Checking the time, she jested about Steve's fate – dead or delighted, likely the latter, attributing his absence to Sally's charm from the previous night.

Their concern lingered with their impending 9:30 rendezvous with Ben when a car halted at their curb. Steve and Sally shared a prolonged farewell kiss. Jack whispered to Emma, "I'll take that as a sign of an enjoyable night for them both."

"Stop it," she muttered back.

Steve's gaze met theirs – their pierced stare of worry and haste – as he stepped inside.

Emma's piercing glare confronted him, and she questioned him about his night's adventure.

He admitted to being swept up in the morning's moments with Sally and his feelings of guilt for his tardiness.

"What's for breakfast?" he asked, only to learn he'd missed out on eggs and bacon. They urged him to opt for cereal instead.

As Steve shoveled spoonfuls into his mouth, he tried to fill the void of his missing memories from the previous night. His hands shook as he recounted the events to Emma and Jack, explaining how they arrived at her apartment and began indulging in bourbon with her while engaging in flirtatious conversation. They played a two-person drinking game of 'Flip, Sip, or Strip,' but everything went dark, a blackout that left him naked in her bed this morning with no recollection of the final events.

"I can only recall bits and pieces – maybe half an hour to an hour. My head was pounding so hard when I woke up. It's the worst hangover I've ever had," he said with a grimace.

She let out a sarcastic chuckle. "What did you drink?"

"Just bourbon. Yet I've never felt this awful afterward," Steve replied, unable to face her.

"Beer before liquor, never sicker," she said dryly.

"No doubt."

"What did you guys talk about?" Jack asked.

Steve's voice faltered, the mystery of the night haunting his every word. "After talking about the museum, all I recall is her deflecting to the game; afterward, it was a blur. I have no clue how I ended up in her bedroom or anything that followed." He massaged his temples, a gesture of utter bafflement. "I found ourselves naked. We scrambled to put our clothes on and leave. I'm at a loss – I don't remember if we even had sex."

In disbelief, Emma's eyes widened. "You're telling me you have no memory of being intimate despite the circumstances?"

"Unfortunately," Steve said with a deep sigh.

Her disappointment was a sharp, "Stevie, this isn't like you."

"I know. Believe me, the last thing I wanted was to forget a night like that," he countered, the frustration evident in his voice.

Jack, eager to steer the conversation, dove in. "Did she question you for information about our discovery? The journal or our findings?"

Steve shook his head. "Nothing comes to mind."

"Any mention of our plans for the day? What we uncovered?"

"Nothing."

"The drinks? Who handled them?"

"I did. Opened a new bottle and served us both. She treated them like shots and asked me to pour her another each time she drained it."

"The glasses?"

"Regular clear ones."

"Why this interrogation, Jack?" Emma asked, a frown knitting her brows.

"Jack's trying to piece together if she was fishing for information," he said, attempting to lighten the mood with a chuckle. "For the record, she didn't pump me for details this morning, if you catch my drift."

"Steve!" she reacted, her hand meeting his shoulder in a playful slap.

"If it's what you're thinking, I doubt she drugged me. She downed one of my drinks during the game as hers was empty, and I topped them both off again."

"Were you exhausted? Yesterday was taxing," Jack posited.

"Not early on, but at one moment, I felt tired well after we sat down. Yet, falling asleep doesn't make sense; I'm too heavy for her to move me if I was unconscious," he reasoned.

"Nothing else she inquired about?"

"No, but she did express interest in joining our plans for the day when I mentioned texting you guys for breakfast and hiking or boating. Didn't press further, though. She was interested in going out on the lake after her work."

"Sorry, I was trying to jog your memory with these questions," Jack said, his gaze now looking downward in thought.

"Like I said, we're good. I think Sally's nice, but she's an aggressive girl, if you know what I mean," he said with a broad smile.

"Steve!" They both exclaimed, and Emma slapped him on the shoulder again, but it was not playful this time.

"In any case, Ben and Sally don't sound entangled," she said. "She calls him a 'nice kid.' Still, she might be leaking him information."

"Nice kid, huh? So, *no* competition for Sally's affection there," Steve quipped, eliciting a chuckle.

"You need to freshen up before we leave?" he asked, shaking his head.

"Yeah, I need a shower."

"Make it quick," she demanded, but chuckled as she said, "And maybe wash your mouth out with soap, too."

"Steve, lock up behind you?" he asked. "Emma and I will start the car and meet you at the curb. We're already going to be late."

Chapter 17

Steve bounded into the Suburban, his smile infectious. "Let's roll," he chimed, catching Jack and Emma exchanging looks hinting at a rekindled flame.

Jack steered onto Friendsville Road, the vehicle climbing from the valley towards Deep Creek, only to veer west on Bishoff Rd, much to Steve's confusion. "Thought we were heading closer to the lake?"

"It's quicker this way. It's near the Upper Yough River Boat Put-In, where we last hit the rapids," Jack said.

Understanding dawned on Steve as they traversed the scenic bluff, his thoughts drifting to Sally amidst the changing landscape.

Jack said, "To the north, we're passing Gap Hill on the right, which is where the John Friend Cave is. On the left is Ginseng Hill, and from the map we found, we will be searching somewhere on the slope from here to the next peak to the south, Upper Ford Hill."

Without much of a pause, Jack added, "Hey, that reminds me of a fun fact."

"Yes, Sheldon," Steve quipped, their collective chuckle at the *Big Bang Theory* sitcom reference. Emma just sighed.

Jack started, "A group of famous industrialists called The Vagabonds camped near here. You familiar with them, Steve?"

"No."

Emma just grimaced and shook her head.

"Well, the Vagabonds camped together every summer for several years. The naturalist John Burroughs passed away a few months prior, so they had a new member join them. The story goes that just after sunset, Henry Ford was the last one to arrive at the camp near here in 1921 in his brand new, shiny Model-T. Before he could even shut off the engine, two men came running over to the car, beaming as they looked upon it with great admiration. The first man quickly stooped over, ran his hands over a tire, and said, 'It looks like you couldn't have made it here without my tires, Henry.' The other man studied the headlights, turning and gazing around to see how well they lit up the area in the dark, and said, 'I think my headlight may have been more important than your tires. And they appeared to have done the job for you.' Ford got out of his car, looked upon, and shook the hands of his two friends, Thomas Edison and Harvey Firestone. He grinned and replied, 'Well, I guess you two are fishing for a thank you for your part in helping me build my cars.'

"They were laughing when Ford looked past the two men, and his eyes fell upon a shadowed figure sitting fireside," Jack continued, "when Ford asked, 'Who's the new guy?' Edison glanced backward and replied with a wave of his hand, 'Oh, he's no one important. He's just *the* President, Warren G. Harding.' They continued to laugh until Harding stood, illuminated by the headlights, and straightened his coat before retorting, 'Well, I figured I was invited here to interview you three *chumps* to select one the most deserving for the position of First Bum. And it will be a difficult choice from what I can see.'"

Steve and Jack laughed, and Emma smiled, saying, "Really, Jack? I've only heard that something like a hundred times."

Grinning from ear to ear, Steve stared at Emma and said, "What do you mean? That's a new one for me. But that was a joke, Jack. What's the Fun Fact?"

Emma laughed, saying, "Oh, you two are killing me. Stevie, do you have to goad him on like that?"

"Absolutely!"

Jack didn't pause, "The fun fact was that it was Firestone and Edison who noticed the powerful rivers and creeks in the county. Some believe they sparked the idea to build hydroelectric dams and create Deep Creek and Youghiogheny lakes."

Steve's response, lighthearted but mocking, "Thanks, Sheldon," came as he beamed and nodded his head in amusement. Emma just smirked and shook her head in defeat.

They arrived almost 15 minutes late. Ben greeted them with a stern expression on his face. "Glad you decided to join me," he said. "We've got a lot of ground to search today. I'll take us up the hill where we can start."

They jumped into Ben's crew cab truck and drove toward the location marked on the map. While walking, Ben explained what they would be undertaking. "The cave lies between two creeks, separated by a mile, with us over half a mile uphill from the river to the peak. It'll be a long search back down."

Jack proposed the efficiency of fanning out within sight of each other to cover the area faster, a suggestion Ben accepted. Spread across a vast swath of land, they navigated the uneven terrain, the scant vegetation aiding their exploration.

Moving through the trees was not tricky despite the landscape and no trails to follow. Their eyes had very little problems scanning the area, and it didn't take long.

Ninety minutes later, Steve's voice cut through the silence, "We're close to the hill's base. I caught a glimpse of the road. We're almost a quarter mile or so away and have yet to uncover anything."

Emma echoed the sentiment, "Same here."

Jack, ever the strategist, proposed a shift in tactics. "I think it's time to rethink this. Let's look at the maps."

Huddled around Steve's chart and Jack's phone, Ben, Steve, and Jack scrutinized it while Emma surveyed their surroundings. A sudden insight from her redirected their focus. "Guys! Down there," she gestured, "There's a large break in the trees, a spot where the light is shining through."

Their eyes followed her indication. Ben was the first to find optimism. "That has to be it. Let's check it out."

They descended toward the brightness, the sun their beacon, until they struck a dense wall of greenery. Struggling through thick underbrush, they stood at a ledge, a clearing unfolding fifteen feet beneath them. They pressed onto a slope strewn with boulders as far as a singular, monolithic stone slab barred their way, an anomaly in the landscape.

"This is it!" Ben exclaimed. "The entrance must have caved in."

The discovery left Jack pondering. The river's roar below and proximity to the Native American Trail on their map were compelling, yet the expected waterfall or stream was absent. The possibility of the landscape's evolution over the past 250 years puzzled him.

"How do we get in?" he asked

Steve answered, "I have an idea. Ben, you have a winch or rope?"

"I think so, in my truck."

"Who wants to go fetch the stuff?"

"I will," Ben said. "No one else touches my truck. I'll also grab some tools we might need." He turned and raced off to his truck.

The three friends debated their next steps. Re-examining Steve's map, Jack theorized, "We might be southwest of the intended marker, and we're close to a trail. But it's the lack of a waterfall that puzzles me. The letter references a waterfall as a landmark... perhaps there is one in the river below, and they viewed this as behind it? Yet, I think we kayaked this stretch, so I do not recall any large drop-off. Maybe the treasure is buried here? Might they have collapsed the entrance to hide it? It's in a bowl-like depression, so it's possible there was once a waterfall back when they were here. Maybe there were heavy rains or melting snow that made one. I don't know, but my gut says this cave's not it."

"The waterfall's missing, sure," Steve pondered, "but imagine if a cave lies here. Although it was on that one map, it's possible no one's searched this before."

Emma chimed in. "I think we should still look inside it."

"Let's split up," Jack said. "Someone should assist Ben with the gear;

the rest of us start removing rocks."

Emma volunteered to help Ben while Steve and Jack strategized on liberating the massive center stone as they cleared many rocks. About 20 minutes later, Steve proposed, "The slab might tip forward with proper leverage at the back. He mentioned having tools; I'm hoping for a come-along winch?"

"That would indeed be ideal," he agreed, eyeing a sturdy tree for anchor.

Clearing debris from the collapsed area, they prepared for Ben and Emma, who arrived with ropes, digging bars, and a large hydraulic truck jack but no winch.

Steve grabbed the jack and said, "Great idea! We'll use it to tilt the slab enough to reveal what's behind it."

They placed the jack between the vertical rock and the face of the drop-off. Pumping the handle, it strained to budge the stone, but the moment they were about to give up, the slab started to nudge, inching the slab with each push of the jack's crank. Steve wedged smaller stones to maintain the gap as he repositioned the jack. After repeating several times, the rock appeared as if it was about to fall. Ben secured ropes around it, taking hold of it with Emma, while Jack and Steve's muscles rippled, applying force to the digging bars.

The monolith quivered, stopped, and surrendered with a thunderous rumble, smashing the surface to unveil a hidden opening, leaving Ben and Emma with their mouths open.

* * *

Jack led the way to the entrance, signaling the others. Ben, ready with flashlights, handed one to him and prepared to delve into history.

Before entering, Steve cautioned, "Let's ensure no other stones are at risk of collapsing."

"Good point, Stevie."

All remained firm after testing. Ben darted through the opening with the eagerness of a seasoned explorer.

"Grab the detector," he reminded Steve.

He turned to Emma, who was staring into the void, her head and shoulders rocking back and forth. This movement was Emma's tell: *She's scared.* Approaching, he enveloped her in a reassuring embrace. "Em, you okay to do this?" he asked, recognizing her fear.

"I don't know," her head moved to look at the ground.

"Since you are somewhat claustrophobic. Would you feel better if you waited outside?"

"I don't know," she said, looking up at him.

"I think you should stay here."

"Why?"

"This collapsed before. If something happens and we need help, you'll have to show rescuers where to find us. Plus, you're safe here."

Jack's soft kiss landed on her forehead, her eyes brimming with emotion. "You're right, but you better come back."

Armed with a flashlight and a digging bar, he ventured into the cave's narrow mouth. The beam of his light revealed the rugged, untouched walls, and the floor bore the smoothness of water's long-ago passage. Using the bar for support, he prodded the ground, listening for the telltale echo of hollow spaces beneath.

The tunnel led them over 100 feet into the heart of the cave, opening into a vast chamber where the darkness swallowed the ceiling. The cool, musty air carried the sound of water dripping, echoing as it journeyed to the cave's depths.

Their eyes scanned the cavern for any hint of treasure. Deeper within, Jack's light caught on some markings – the unmistakable sign of past human presence. A name etched into the stone brought laughter from him.

Ben and Steve approached, and Jack pointed – *Henri Baton, 1803*. Ben, moved by the connection to his ancestor, captured the moment with his phone.

"Well, with my ancestors searching this cave before, I'm betting we will not find anything," he conceded, though the discovery itself brightened his spirits. "I think Henri was likely Jean's grandson, maybe great-grandson. Remember, Jean caught the British soldiers. I need to check with my dad for his exact place in our family tree," he said, staring at the inscription.

"Alright, Ben," Jack replied. He then turned toward the opening and yelled to assure Emma of their safety. The group's exploration became more intense, tapping, examining, and scanning the cave's walls and recesses for over an hour without success.

Emerging into daylight, they found Emma absorbed in playing a game on her phone. "Nothing, Em," Jack said.

"Not quite," Ben corrected, sharing the discovery of his ancestor's name. The excitement of the find, however, did little to convince them of any hidden treasure being within.

"I'm hungry, and it's past lunch," she declared, breaking into their reflections.

"Ben, can you drive us to my SUV?"

"Yes, but what's next?"

"Eating, then planning. If not here, are there any other caves?" Jack speculated.

Ben shook his head. "No, none that match the clues, south of Friendsville or west of the barrel."

"Let's eat and think it over," she suggested.

Turning toward Ben's truck, a faded red pickup raced away, tires screeching.

"Who was that?" Jack asked, curiosity piqued by the sudden departure.

"Not... sure," Ben said with his head tilted and eyes narrowed.

Steve pondered aloud, "Maybe they were after something valuable in your truck."

He dismissed it and said, "No, everything of value is safe, locked in the back."

Jack felt some concern. "Whoever they were, it's still concerning," he mused, the notion of unseen eyes watching them unsettling. "We're off to grab some food. Join us?"

"I'm going to... visit my dad; he'll be excited to hear about the inscription. I'll catch up with you later. We can figure out where we look afterward."

They arrived at Ben's truck, followed by a short ride and a brief exchange. Ben was off, leaving them at Jack's Suburban, pondering their next move.

With the pickup disappearing into the distance, Jack turned to the others. "Lunch? Afterward, we head south. The book hinted at a cave in the area; it might be our best shot now."

Steve's enthusiasm was immediate. "I'm in! Hungry as always!"

Emma's disappointment was quick. "I was hoping for some boating this afternoon. You're right, and it's best without worrying about Ben."

He assured her, "We'll find time to boat, Em. I promise."

Steve, ever curious, sought direction. "So, where to, guys?"

Jack's brows furrowed as he thought: *Did we miss something in the cave? And who's pickup was it?*

Chapter 18

Exiting the lush valley, the trio's spirits, dampened by an unsuccessful treasure hunt, shifted to unease when greeted by storm clouds gathering over the open farmland. Jack's remark about their fortunate timing to avoid boating was a small consolation.

The drive to Garrett Highway was a quiet race against the looming darkness promising rain. The distant flicker of a Burger King sign caught their eyes, a beacon for their growing hunger.

"Let's make it quick," Jack said, guiding the truck into the lot.

"About time, I'm famished," Steve chimed in, his hand on his stomach.

Inside, the aroma of burgers and fries filled the air. They lined up, decisions made in the silence of anticipation.

Emma opted for a Spicy Crispy Chicken Sandwich and a Diet Coke, Steve for a Double Whopper without tomatoes and a chocolate shake, and he also ordered a Double Whopper but with a Coke. "Lunch is on me," he announced, paying with a handful of crumpled bills.

They exited the restaurant to find the sidewalk drenched and heavy raindrops pounding on the roofs of the parked cars. Rivulets of water streamed across the parking lot, gathering in deep puddles and overflowing the drains.

"I think we better eat in," she said.

"I think we run for the SUV. It's right here," Jack replied.

"Why?" she asked.

"After eating, we can look at the maps to finalize where to head next. I don't want people overhearing us."

"Okay," Steve said, sounding disappointed.

The three walked the covered sidewalk to the Suburban, hugging the building to avoid the rain. After unlocking his vehicle, they made a mad dash to enter it.

"Jack, I already had a shower this morning," Steve laughed. "Don't worry, I should be dry by tomorrow."

They took large mouthfuls for a few minutes until Emma broke the silence, "Stevie, you said you're seeing Sally again?"

"She said she'd call after work to figure out where to meet us or what we'd do tonight. So I hope she calls."

"You like her?"

"I guess. I wish I remembered more about last night. I would like to know her better. Is that what you mean?"

"Yes. I'm glad to hear it," Emma said, turning to Jack. "So, where's the cave?"

He unrolled the map and traced the trails with his finger, "You can follow the main Seneca Trail here. It runs from the southern point of the county along the Youghiogheny River, turns east, and crosses where the lake is now before heading north and intersecting with the Cumberland Trail. After the marker, it heads to meet Nemacolin's Path, the Braddock Road."

"The Cumberland trail appears to be what Clarke and his men followed from the Little Meadows Camp. And they buried the barrel near the intersection with Seneca."

Jack scrutinized the map further.

"Cross-referencing the book's description with the local creeks and the clues, only two spots match. Deep Creek, behind the dam, lies north of Oakland and is northeast of Swallow Falls Road. All streams feeding the lake converge here, hiding a waterfall back then. If Clarke ventured south along the trail and veered west and north on this trail, he would have rejoined the army following the trail next to the Yough to Friendsville, where the French captured him. They might've believed themselves south of the marker.

"The second location follows the main Seneca trail, is more likely. It skirts the lake and crosses near Hoop Pole Run and Pawn Run; the latter is a significant stream basin south of the barrel and east of Swallow Falls Road.

"Yet, I propose we start with Deep Creek. It's closer and spans only about a mile. We can search its vicinity for any waterfall within an hour."

Steve was eager. "Let's go. The rain's easing up. We can eat on the way."

They set off, the lake now deserted after the storm. The journey transformed as they left Garrett Highway for Lake Shore Drive, the road meandering through woods alongside the shoreline. For almost a century, the lake's banks witnessed the rise of both modest cabins and sprawling estates. Soon, they veered onto Mayhew Inn Road, stopping at a gravel patch around two miles later.

"People fishing use this parking spot, so we won't draw any attention," Jack said, noting the rain diminished to a drizzle. "Ready?"

"I am," Steve replied.

"Suppose I have no choice," Emma half-joked.

They trekked to a fenced area near the dam. "We'll follow the fence to the creek," Jack said.

Arriving at the stream, she asked, "Why is there no water flowing?"

He explained, "The original massive Deep Creek is now behind the dam and used for emergency overflows or controlled releases. We're searching for what once was an active waterfall, so we are looking for a drop-off that would have been a waterfall into a pool of water. The original areas with pools of water will still exist; there's just no flow of water to see a waterfall today."

Trudging next to the creek, they soon encountered a stretch of shallow, pooled clear water, its bottom in view. A quarter-mile later, the pool ended at a cliff, its depths obscured.

"This looks promising," he said. Descending through the trees, they confronted the eroded face of the falls.

"It was a waterfall," Jack concluded. "No cave in sight, but the depth of water at the bottom of the falls might have a place to hide it. Let's search the banks before considering a swim." Their efforts proved fruitless.

"I guess I'm due for a dip," Jack quipped, regretting the absence of his swimsuit.

Stripping to his tighty-whities, he bared his chiseled physique and waded into the creek, detector in hand.

"I like the view, Jack," she joked at his expense as she bit her smiling lip and didn't blink.

Navigating the slippery stream bed, he approached the waterfall's base, the chest-deep, chilly water enveloping him. Below the waterline, he spotted a large rock against the cliff. *Are you hiding something?*

He dislodged the stone, revealing a small opening. Diving, he probed the cavity, finding nothing but its sides. Surfacing with a smile, he relayed his findings to Steve and Emma.

"A cave, perhaps?" Steve suggested.

"I'll check its depth," Jack said, urged by Emma's cautious plea.

He squeezed through the entrance, and the cold current flowing across his bare skin hinted at a lengthy passage. Yet, he reached the back wall as soon as he started. Despite his efforts with the detector among the cracks and stones, the cave revealed no secrets.

"It's a dead end, only five feet deep," he yelled, disappointed. "Nothing here."

"No worries," she consoled. "Let's look what's further down the creek."

Jack shivered, and Emma used her Jacket to wipe excess water off him as he redressed. Setting off again as the light rain ceased, the sunlight began to slice through the clouds. The stream narrowed, the surrounding trees and rocks drawing closer. Their silent march led them to the Youghiogheny River in the distance, signaling the next chapter of their quest.

With no additional drop-offs on the creek, they decided to return.

Turning toward their SUV, the ominous rustling from the bushes behind them sent shivers up their spine.

"Shh! Listen," Steve murmured.

The rustling intensified, morphing into something of imminent concern. A large black bear tore through the brush and halted a mere hundred feet away.

They froze, their gazes locked on the bear, which appeared uncertain. It sniffed, the glare of its turning head settled on them. As if in slow motion, Jack edged to the front of the group, his arms creeping to grasp his backpack. Pulling it around and rotating it, his eyes widened when he found his bear spray can was no longer clipped to the bag.

With a roar, the bear charged. Jack threw his hand to his pack, grabbing and extending the collapsible shovel.

"RUN!" Emma's voice pierced the tense air.

"NO!" he yelled before muttering, "Make yourselves larger, and don't move." Swaying his pack and shovel and saying, almost in song, "Hey bear… we're moving back."

Steve crept in front of Emma, elevating the metal detector.

The bear ceased and stood, eyeing and sniffing to determine the danger they posed but also showing its size as a clear threat. Amid the heart-pounding standoff, Jack maintained his calm, continuing to appear enlarged.

He continued their snail-paced retreat, his voice steady, "Hey bear; hey bear. We're backing up," his backpack still in one hand and shovel in the other. The bear's demeanor shifted, returning its four paws to earth with a splash but maintaining focus on them.

Much to his surprise, the bear appeared to respond to Jack's tone, tilting its head and sniffing the air. Encouraged, he took another slow, small step back, and the bear didn't react. Steve joined him, never taking his eyes off the large animal. After a few tense moments, the bear turned and walked away towards the bushes, vanishing into the foliage. The group let out a sigh of relief, and Emma collapsed onto the ground, her body trembling with adrenaline.

"Are you alright, Em?" Jack comforted her with a hug.

"Yes, just shaken," she replied, her breath evening out. "That was something."

"Let's head back to the SUV," Steve suggested, squinting as he scanned their surroundings. "No telling if there's more around."

During the trek back to his Suburban, the encounter caused Jack's mind to race.

"So, I take it you've faced bears before?" Steve asked, breaking the silence.

"I have. When we return home, please remind me to clip another bear spray onto my backpack again. I think mine got knocked off in the cave today."

"Ready for the next site?" he asked, eyeing Emma for her accord.

A nod came as her response, tinged with humor. "With two sailors for protection, what's to fear?"

They piled into the car, the day's dance with the bear still tingling in their veins. However, as they drove further, he gripped the wheel tighter, and his thoughts shifted to the mysterious pickup truck by Ben's. *Is someone watching us?* He craned his neck, staring at the rear-view mirror, seeing a blue Subaru and an old, faded red or burgundy truck. He couldn't determine and pondered: *Is it the same one from the cave?*

Jack pushed the accelerator hard.

"Jack, why the rush?" Emma's voice broke through, tinged with worry.

Chapter 19

Emma's piercing glare lingered on Jack, an unspoken question in her eyes.

Sensing her scrutiny but not understanding why, Jack tapped the map cradled in his lap in reassurance. "I'm making sure no one is following us. And trust me, Em, I've done my homework," he said, his finger tapping the chart.

Steve couldn't resist a jab, flicking a fry at him. "Our fearless leader leaves nothing to chance," he said, the sarcasm thick in his voice.

Jack's response was both annoyed and amused. "Hilarious, Steve," he said, the corners of his mouth betraying a reluctant smile.

Their journey took a swift turn as they veered onto Garrett Highway, and he pressed the accelerator hard, sending everyone lurching back in their seats. The SUV turned again, this time on Sand Flat Road before anyone questioned the sudden increase in speed.

"We'll shake off any tail."

Emma's rebuke was quick, "Please don't crash, Jack. Who do you think is following us?"

"I thought I saw the pickup that was next to Ben's truck behind us. It looked to be the same color, but why risk it?"

Steve's wide eyes and pouted lips sent a clear message – he worried that Jack was overthinking it.

They sped across the open farmland, turning on Boy Scout Road. After a short distance, Jack eased the SUV into the Pawn Run Bar + Kitchen's lot.

Checking the road they drove in on, Jack seemed satisfied. "No one's on our tail."

"That's a relief," said Steve, tension easing from his voice.

Jack outlined their next steps as they gathered outside the vehicle. "The stream heads east towards the lake," but instead pointed at a dense cluster of trees westward amid a large field. "I think that's a decent place to start before we search the creek toward the lake. If that patch was level, the farmer would have also cleared that area. So, there might be something there. "

With a plan in action, he grabbed his gear, passing the metal detector to Steve. Emma looked on with a bittersweet ache in her heart. Her love for him battled with her frustration over his addiction to treasure hunting, which often left her an afterthought. Still, she managed to smile, taking her flashlight.

"Ready to go?" Jack's voice pulled her from her thoughts.

Steve slapped Jack's back, "Absolutely."

"Alright, let's go," she pushed through her feelings, determined.

They didn't need long to reach the trees, fanning out as they entered. Jack led, eyes keen for any hint of the cave, while Emma and Steve trailed, scanning the grove and creek. The search was thorough but quick, the land revealing little more than dips and humps in the terrain. Disappointment hung in the air; their exploration yielded nothing.

They pressed eastward, crossing the road and leaving the bar behind for the forest's embrace alongside the stream. The wilderness challenged them with its dense foliage, steep climbs, and uneven ground, yet he guided them with a steadfast resolve.

Wading through the undergrowth, they sought any hint of the cave, their path mirrored by the creek, swollen from recent rains but devoid of any waterfall.

"Nothing," Jack's voice betrayed his growing impatience.

"Should we call it quits for today?" Emma ventured, shaking her head in concern

"Are you kidding? We're on the brink!" his gaze didn't waiver from the distance.

"Ease up, Emma," Steve intervened, his wide grin an attempt to relieve the tension. "We might be on the right track!"

With a sigh, she relented.

They pushed forward, fueled by the prospect of discovery.

While they traversed, Steve whispered to her, "Still no waterfall in sight."

"He's ignoring the obvious," she murmured in response.

"We'll call it a day when we reach the lake," he proposed.

"Agreed."

The terrain demanded their full attention, with Jack leading and the others trailing, each absorbed in thought.

The sun dipped, casting elongated shadows across their path as Steve halted, his focus drawn to a peculiar formation on a distant slope.

"Jack, wait," Steve's shout was soft through the wind's melody. He pointed towards it. "Looks like a recess in the hill behind those boulders. Is that it?"

Spurred by possibility, Jack surged ahead to approach it, leaving his friends to try to keep up. Concealed by the rocks, a deep depression into the hillside hid a moss-veiled entrance, a silent invitation to the earth's secrets below.

"We've found it!" he exclaimed, revealing a hidden archway through the greenery.

Emma eyed the narrow passage with a piercing stare, a foreboding aura emanating from its depths. "Where's the waterfall?" she asked with hesitation.

"This has to be Woods Place Cave," he countered, undeterred by the discrepancy. "The lake's nearby, and the cover has several drop-offs. I'm guessing a waterfall exists downstream where we haven't reached yet."

Steve's shrugged glance towards her spoke volumes.

"Are you sure about this?" Emma's doubt was evident, her gaze alternating between the unassuming entrance and her companions. The cave's opening was devoid of grandeur or easy access, concealed by nature itself, but the absence of the falls deepened the mystery.

"Yes," Jack affirmed, his tone laced with conviction. "This must be the place, right off the Seneca Trail. We're east of Swallow Falls and four to five miles north of Oakland."

Steve, catching the certainty in his voice, conceded, "He might be onto something, Emma. We should check it out. Do you want to stay behind?"

She hesitated at the cave's mouth, head ebbing. "No." With a reluctant glance at him, she said, "I'd rather stick with you. My terror of bears trumps my fear of enclosed, dark, creepy places. Let's do this."

The trio approached the cave, flashlights ready, excited, and concerned. Emma found herself questioning her readiness to face the cavern's secrets, yet she stepped forward, motivated more by solidarity with Jack than the lure of discovery. The entrance enveloped her.

Inside, the chill and damp air surrounded them, and the persistent drip of water played a haunting melody. They marveled at the natural beauty, a corridor carved over millennia adorned with stalactites and stalagmites that captured the flashlight's glow. The cave demanded their attention, forcing them to navigate its narrow passages with care.

"This is incredible," Emma whispered, awestruck by the subterranean marvel. "To think this was under us all along. I wonder how the author missed this?"

"It's a mystery," Jack said, his concentration unwavering as he searched for signs of the treasure. "Though, we need to keep moving. The gold won't find itself."

Steve nodded, his attention split between the metal detector and the path ahead. "Let's not slow down."

Noticing Emma falter, Jack offered a reassuring touch. "Are you alright? We can head back if you're not up for this."

Her eyes met his, a silent strength in her gaze. "I'm okay."

He said with a serious tone, "Just promise me one thing."

"What's that?"

"That you'll continue this with me to the end. You're not only my partner in this; you're my anchor. I need you with me."

She paused as she considered his words, and her response came firm and resolute. "I promise." At that moment, she believed she wasn't playing second fiddle anymore.

"Great," he said, a new determination in his voice. "Let's find that gold."

The search persisted, yet the detector remained silent, a foreboding quiet that deepened as they ventured further into the cave's narrow embrace. Something ethereal urged them forward, a call too insistent to ignore.

The passage constricted, and Jack, leaning into the diminutive gap, assessed their next move.

"This might be it," he deliberated aloud, eyeing the narrow path. "It looks too snug for Steve or me. Emma, you're the only one who might fit. Can you do it?"

Emma's gaze fixed on the daunting crevice, her head ebbing again.

"Of course," she said, albeit with a tremble betraying her fear. "Give me a moment."

Her resolve solidified under Jack's watchful eye, the impending challenge morphing into courage. She had to face her fears, not over the cave's shadowy depths, but her own hesitations. This was her time to shine, fueled by the belief that his faith in her was not misplaced. *Jack must believe I could do this, or he wouldn't have asked.*

"That's my girl," his encouragement came like a light in the dark. She did not realize Jack spotted the shift in her demeanor; her anxiety appeared washed away.

"Alright," she affirmed, her voice now a beacon of determination. "I'm ready."

"Be careful," his tone carried a touch of concern. "Remember, we're right here."

"Thanks," she managed a brave smile, her gratitude whispered into the dark. "I won't let you down."

Emma navigated the passage with a dancer's grace, twisting and contorting through the tight space. Each movement away from Jack and Steve was a step into solitude, yet her resolve never wavered.

For Jack. For me. For us, she repeated like a mantra.

Emerging into a vast cavern, she admired its sublime grandeur. "Wow," she whispered, the sight stopping her in her tracks. The enormous and cathedral-like cave filled her with awe: the walls, a kaleidoscope of earthy tones lit by her flashlight, holding centuries of secrets. Cool and musty air was a reminder of the cave's ancient presence.

Regaining focus, she checked the detector: *Let's do this*. She started her meticulous search, the device sweeping over the ground with hopeful anticipation.

"Come on," she muttered, her determination unyielding as she combed through the area. Her steps, each measured and purposeful, were unwavering. Her concentration was on uncovering what might lay hidden in the embrace of the timeless walls.

Her flashlight cut through the darkness, revealing a terrain of jagged rocks and boulders appearing as if placed they were by careful thought. Emma moved cautiously, avoiding the sharp edges and leaping over crevices that threatened to engulf her.

"Jack, can you hear me?" Her voice echoed, and she hoped her friends would respond.

"We're here," Jack replied, "You, okay?"

"Yeah. This place is huge," she replied, her words tinged with frustration. "I'm still looking."

She pressed deeper into the cave, facing a new challenge as the ground started to slope downwards. Attempting to hang on to the damp walls, Emma's chest pounded, and her mind intent on avoiding a dangerous fall.

One step at a time, she coached herself, her breathing labored in the heavy silence.

Determination fueled her, pushing back the creeping fear and doubt with each careful advance.

"Come on, give me something," she murmured to her metal detector, sweeping it over the uneven surface.

A sharp beep shattered the stillness, sending her mind racing.

"Jack! Steve!" she called out, alive with excitement. "I've found something!"

"What is it?" Jack's voice carried his urgency. "Need us?"

"No," she replied, wondering about the logistics of their passage.

Hoping against hope, she wished this discovery would be their breakthrough – not for wealth, but for the potential life together.

"Focus," she whispered before slipping and crashing to the floor.

Undeterred, Emma got up, dusted off, and homed in on the signal. She uncovered an object within the rocks, her hands trembling as she cleared the debris. Her fingers met the cold touch of metal. She yearned for treasure but endured the disappointment of discovering a small shovel head.

"Damn," she cursed, her frustration surging. Following that, a thought struck her. *A shovel here? Someone must have tried to bury something here!*

She smiled as another beep emanated from the metal detector. Kneeling, she placed her flashlight to spotlight the area, whispering encouragement to herself. Her fingers found a metallic shard, another piece of the shovel, under the light's glare.

Despite her hopes, no more beeps in the vicinity. *Where could they have hidden it?*

Turning, her flashlight's beam scanned the walls and caught something in a recess of the far side – a small wooden box. Her heart skipped with excitement. With cautious haste, she approached and knelt beside it; her wide eyes of excitement were clear.

"Jack! I found a box!" she shouted. Without thought, she pulled out her phone and snapped a photo.

"What's inside?" Jack's voice echoed with curiosity and anticipation.

Adrenaline surged through Emma, her hands trembling as she pried open the crate. A jolt of shock replaced the enthusiasm.

A handgun stared back at her.

This was far from her hopes. Not hesitating, she closed the lid, and her thoughts swirled with confusion and dread. *A gun? Here? Why?*

"Jack! Steve!" she yelled, and it echoed off the cavern walls. "Something's here, but... you need to see it."

"What?"

"A gun," she managed, her tone quivering.

His response was immediate, stern. "Don't touch it. Use something else to grab it."

"Got it, I have a bag. I'll finish up and head out."

Shaken, Emma took another photo and completed her scan, finding nothing more.

Navigating back, Jack's hands stretched out to guide her out of the passage.

She handed over the bagged gun, but his embrace was both comforting and apologetic. "You were brave. It must've been terrifying, doing that alone."

"You rock, Emma," Steve said, offering a reassuring shake of her shoulder. "You okay?"

"I'm a bit rattled. Why would someone hide it here?"

"I'm not sure," Jack murmured.

After opening the bag, his tone shifted to grave, "This isn't any handgun. It's a Colt Anaconda from the 90s or early 2000s." He examined it using a rag from his backpack, noting, "It's loaded. Wait, no, two chambers empty."

The possible implications of the discovery settled on Emma. *A loaded gun, concealed here, but why?*

Steve broke the silence. "We should leave before whoever's gun this is, happens to return for it."

"No, I need to check if Emma missed something," Jack insisted, eyeing the passage.

Emma's glare was sharp. "I didn't miss anything as I checked everywhere."

"I can find something," he persisted, moving towards the corridor.

Steve grabbed Jack's arm and was harsh in his intervention, "Jack, it's not there. We have to figure out what to do with the weapon."

Jack conceded with a heavy stare. "Emma, you ready to go?"

"Yes. More than ever."

They hastened their exit from the cave, although Emma could not stop her mind from racing the entire way: *Who hid the gun? Why?*

Descending to the creek, they followed it to the lake and discovered nothing more.

Steve's reality check was sobering. "No waterfall, Jack. If this were Clarke's cave, someone would have found the treasure. Face it, people were in it already. What now?"

Jack sighed, his optimism waning. "I'm out of clues and ideas, so I'm not sure what our next steps are."

In silence, they returned up the hill, the day's outcome evident in their demeanor. However, amidst the disappointment and concern over the gun, Emma hid her surge of pride in facing her challenges head-on.

The day's last light faded when they arrived at the bar's thinned parking lot. Jack stopped, his head snapping back as soon as they were within sight of his Suburban. His voice cut through the twilight, "What the hell?"

Chapter 20

Captain Thomas Clarke's boots sank into the damp earth while the sun crept over the horizon, casting shadows stretching like dark fingers across the forest floor. A mist from the night's rain hung in the air as he led his men along the narrow trail, their footsteps muffled but still echoing through the dense foliage. The atmosphere was thick with the scent of wet leaves and soil, mixing with the faint tang of sweat from the weary soldiers.

"Keep up the pace," Clarke called over his shoulder, his voice firm yet encouraging. Exhaustion built on their faces, but they needed to press forward. They had a mission to complete, and the responsibility and concern wore heavy on Clarke's shoulders.

Edward Smith wiped the moisture from his brow and replied with a weak smile. "Aye, Sir. We'll follow you anywhere."

Clarke's lips curved into a grateful grin at the remark.

The day wore on, and the landscape shifted. The trees thinned out, giving way to a more open plain extending before them, while to the north, fields of tall grass waved in the gentle breeze. This enabled them to remount their horses. The trail turned westward, and the terrain became less rugged, signaling they were on a plateau.

"Look, Captain," Thomas Rogers said, pointing towards the distance where higher peaks loomed, their curved, tree-lined edges cutting into the sky. "We've come quite a ways, haven't we?"

Following Johnson's gaze, Clarke took in the far-off mountains. "Indeed, we have. Yet, we still have a long road ahead."

After riding a few more hours, he called out, "Let's take a quick break here to catch our breath and regroup."

His men threw themselves onto the soft grass, their weariness evident. Clarke walked a short distance away, his eyes scanning the landscape as he considered their next move. He understood pushing forward was crucial, but he also didn't want to risk the well-being of his troops by driving them too hard.

George approached and whispered, "Captain, a word?"

"Of course."

"I'm sorry to ask this, Sir, but are you sure Braddock wanted us to follow this trail so far south? We don't want to end up lost. We are further south than I have traveled before."

"That, too, crossed my mind," Clarke said as he pulled out the map. "It appears we are on the correct path. I don't see any other way starting near Little Meadows, which goes southwest off the road to Fort Duquesne and turns north. There's one near Bear Camp and another at Great Meadows, but both were closer toward Fort Duquesne."

George took the chart. "I see the other trails. In looking at this spacing, I think we may have come further south than the map indicates. However, this course crosses the Little Youghiogheny, which we did. I don't believe we missed any paths turning north."

"I wondered if the General wanted us to take one of the others. Did he give us the wrong starting point? I also think it's possible someone copied it from a fur trader versus a drawing from a survey, or they were in a rush."

"True, Sir. That would explain it, but we're more removed from French-controlled areas." George looked up and around, pointed, and said, "Off into the distance, there's a gap in the mountains to the northwest; the path may head that direction."

"I see the opening as well," Clarke replied as he looked toward it, "We have two choices: go back or forward? My gut tells me to proceed. The sun continues setting in front of us, so we're heading west, not south. I estimate we have walked 10 miles. We haven't found the Youghiogheny River yet. If we do before turning north, it would mean we are on the wrong trail. However, finding the river would give us a clear path to rejoining Braddock."

"Agreed, Sir."

"Thank you, George," Clarke said, clapping George on the shoulder before returning to address the rest of his troops. "Alright. Let's move."

Clarke led his men across the plateau when an unexpected figure emerged from the tree-lined hill to the south. A Native man, adorned in traditional clothing, strode without hesitation toward them, his eyes meeting theirs with warm curiosity. He gazed on as the man approached, noting the ease and grace of his movements as though he were one with the landscape itself.

Clarke's eyes scanned the treed area beyond the Native but failed to spot anyone else. Turning to George, he said, "I think we should assume others are in the forest with him, and they cannot learn of our true mission."

George nodded, "I agree, Sir." He dismounted and turned to greet the man.

"Niyáwë skënö (Hello)," the man called out, his voice rich and warm yet tinged with caution. George stepped forward, his knowledge of Native dialects making him the ideal interpreter.

"Niyáwë skënö," George dismounted and greeted the man in the Seneca language, offering a slight bow of respect. "Ho'ken kari'sere. Ka'yahs ken ken ti? (We are here in peace. What is your name?)."

Clarke dismounted and stood next to George.

The man smiled and replied in English, "Thank you for showing the courtesy of speaking my language. I am called White Hawk of the Seneca Tribe. What brings you to our lands?"

"This is Captain Clarke," George explained, nodding toward Clarke, who stood tall and proud beside him. "We are on patrol to ensure no French are in the area causing problems."

"Hmm, most kind of you," White Hawk nodded. "You are on a trail my people have used for generations. It can be dangerous if you don't know the way. May I offer you some guidance?"

"Your help would be much appreciated," Clarke said, grateful.

"First," the Native said, gesturing toward a nearby creek, "many waters are tame, but with a little rain, they can sweep a man away."

Clarke cringed at that comment.

He described Buffalo Marsh, warning them of its deceptive allure. "It looks solid, but getting stuck in the mud is easy. Do not cross it."

"Thank you," Clarke said, noting the dangers. "Any other areas we should avoid?"

"Indeed," White Hawk said, pointing westward. "Ahead, you will find deep water; it can be dangerous. Crossing it tests the bravest man." He paused and said, "Several trails take you to the mighty Youghiogheny. Do not attempt to float down the river; man cannot go many places. It is both friend and enemy. Once you reach the river, turn north. The area past it is not friend to the white man."

"Your guidance has been valuable, White Hawk," Clarke said, extending his hand in gratitude. "We'll take your advice to heart. Thank you."

"May the Great Spirit guide you on your journey," he replied, clasping Clarke's arm before stepping back, his dark eyes shimmering with wisdom. "May you find what you seek."

White Hawk retreated into the forest from whence he came, and a sense of awe at the shared connection struck Clarke, however brief. He now understood the challenges ahead were far more significant.

Clarke turned to his men, "Let's press on," as he mounted his horse. May you find what you seek. Did he hope we would run into the French, or did he suspect us of doing something else? We need to find a place to hide the payroll without delay.

The once distant high peak grew more prominent when they reached where White Hawk indicated the trail branched off into two distinct paths: one to the south and one to the northwest. Before them, at the base of the mountain, lay a long creek with deep pools. Nearby was some marsh-like terrain seeming ready to swallow anything or anyone foolish enough to venture too close.

"Which way, Captain?" George asked.

Clarke took a moment to consider their options, his thoughts consumed by the Native's advice and parting comment. He recalled the warnings of treacherous creeks, impassable rivers, and the dangers lurking within the swamp.

Scanning the area, he assessed their situation. The sun dipped lower in the sky, and the western mountain cast shadows across the creek. He looked to the northwest and gazed upon a gap where the trail may bear them north. While turning south, the mountains blocked much of the view a mile or so away.

He continued to rotate, and an enormous white oak tree drew his eyes toward it. Perched near the top of the high hill, a few hundred feet above them, it towered fifty or more feet higher than the surrounding trees like a sentinel, its branches outstretched as if offering protection. Clarke remembered General Braddock's order to find a place close to the bend when the trail turns north.

"Men," he called out, his voice carrying with authority, "this is it. The perfect spot for our second marker." He pointed towards the regal oak, his determination echoing in his words. "This tree will serve as our watchtower. From there, we can view the surroundings and defend ourselves from the high ground."

"Sir," Davis said, his tone tinged with admiration, "An excellent choice. From an elevation, we'll have a clear advantage."

"Indeed." He nodded. Realizing a strong position may make all the difference in their survival and success. "Let's go to work."

Climbing to the base of the colossal oak, Clarke marveled at its grandeur and gnarled bark. Almost four feet in diameter, he wondered how many storms this mighty tree withstood. No other one was over two feet.

"Captain," George said. "How do you want us to set up the defenses?"

"Take down lower branches from the trees or gather them from the ground to build a perimeter wall," he said, his mind already racing with plans for fortification. "Keep watch for any signs of danger. If anything approaches, sound the alarm."

"Understood, Sir," George replied.

The soldiers scurried into action, allowing Clarke a moment of quiet contemplation. They were far from home, guided by a mission that appeared almost impossible to achieve. However, they stood beneath a tree resembling a beacon of hope.

"Are you alright, Sir?" Davis asked, his brown eyes filled with concern.

"Never better," he said. "We've secured our camp to work from. Now, we must find the best place to hide the payroll."

"Sir, I think we should let the fire burn out now, before sunset," George said.

"Agreed."

The sun approached the horizon, and Clarke's men settled into their temporary home. The night sky was a vast expanse of darkness, with the bright pinpricks of stars serving as a celestial backdrop save the bright, near-full moon that rose in the opposite direction. A dimming but warm glow emanated from the campfire embers at the heart of their camp. The residual scent of burned wood mingled with the earthy aroma of the forest surrounding them.

"Settle down, lads," Clarke called out, gesturing for them to gather around the fire. "We've earned ourselves a bit of respite after today's hard work. Who's got a tale to share? Something to lift our spirits as we stare into the face of uncertainty."

"Aye, I've got one," Henry Jones said with a wry smile as he stroked his graying beard. "It's a story of bravery and wit from my younger days when I served under old Captain Ironfoot himself."

"Did you make up that name, Henry?" Robert Davis teased, his infectious snicker spread through the others.

"Quiet now, let the man... tell his tale," Clarke said, a grin tugging at his mouth's corners.

He regaled them with his account, and the laughter continued as the men enjoyed his story of how a small group of soldiers drove a superior troop of French out of a captured town and how the local maidens showed how 'very' appreciative they were of being liberated.

Clarke's attention turned away as soon as Henry spun his tale, and he glanced at the massive white oak tree looming above their camp. He pulled out his journal, opened it to the back, and started to pen an encoded message to describe the location as clearly as possible.

After he crafted the note, he ripped pieces of paper into stripes and wrapped them around the hilt of his bayonet. Clarke wrote the clues on the strips and unwrapped them. He transferred the now jumbled letters onto a page in the back before closing it. He looked up, realizing each man contributed their own tales of triumph and failure, providing some reprieve from the stressful mission, and the men seemed to be looking at him.

"Captain," George called out. "Why don't you share a tale with us? Something from your past we might not know."

"Very well," Clarke said, taking a deep breath as memories surfaced. He walked over to the glowing embers and ignited the strips. He stomped out the remaining cinders. "I'll tell you about the time I narrowly escaped a band of French soldiers in the dead of night, with nothing but my wits and a bit of luck to guide me."

Recounting his harrowing experience, he was grateful for the men who sat before him – those who chose to follow him into danger, trusting in his leadership and ability to bring them all home.

"Here's to our journey and each other," he said at the end of his story, raising a makeshift cup in a toast. "May we face whatever lies ahead with courage and determination, knowing we stand united in purpose and spirit."

"Cheers," the troop chorused, echoing his sentiment as they raised their cups together.

The air was a symphony of nocturnal sounds as Clarke lay on his improvised bed, the earth beneath him providing an unforgiving mattress. The odor of burnt ash mingled with the dampness of the soil, creating a heady aroma filling his nostrils. The moon's glow cast shadows upon the faces of his resting men.

"Sir, where do you think we should hide the payroll?" asked Edward Smith, breaking the silence. He had been quiet throughout the journey, but recognized the keen intelligence behind his thoughtful eyes.

"An excellent question, Edward," he replied, propping himself up on one elbow as he considered their options. "We need a secret and secure spot, somewhere our enemies would never think to find it."

"Perhaps we could bury it by this massive tree," Robert Davis said. "You said it would serve as our marker, and I can't imagine anyone would suspect such a conspicuous landmark."

He weighed the idea in his mind.

"That's worth considering. I think this will be where we place our second marker," Clarke replied, his gaze drifting upward to the sprawling branches of the white oak. "This tree is obvious from the trail below, and it's where it turns north. I have written the code to direct Braddock to this spot. Soon, I'll order two riders to place the coded message under the rock we marked."

"Very good, Sir," Robert said. "Where shall we hide it?"

"I'm not sure yet." *Whatever we decide, we must be quick*, he thought. *Time isn't a luxury.*

"Sir, I think I have an idea," George said, his voice steady and confident. "Why don't we divide up and search?"

Clarke considered the suggestion, impressed by George's resourcefulness. "It's a promising option and will speed things up. We'll separate at first light. Robert, you and your troop go north. My men will take the trail to the south. Explore till mid-afternoon and return here before sunset. If we find no other place, we may need to bury the payroll here."

"Excellent, Sir," George replied, settling back to rest.

"James, can you take the first watch? Thomas, William, and John will follow," Clarke said. With their course of action tentative, he allowed himself to relax, his body lying on the firm ground beneath him.

Darkness enveloped the camp, and anticipation lingered in the air like the scent of the dying fire. He closed his eyes, his thoughts drifting to the task awaiting them at dawn — the crucial decision would determine the success or failure of their mission.

Chapter 21

Emma, puzzled, followed his gaze to the Suburban. "What's wrong?" Absorbed in the situation, Jack ignored her question and dialed 911.

His voice, steady but edged with urgency, filled the dim light of the Pawn Run Bar's parking lot. "We've just come back from the lake. Someone slashed my tires. We found a cave – with a handgun inside, missing two rounds. We need police assistance and a tow truck."

While they waited for the cops, Emma was distraught, chewing on the ends of her fingers. Jack prepared for their arrival by gathering their equipment and stashing it with the metal detector beneath the SUV's hidden cargo door.

Head ebbing, Emma's voice trembled with concern. "Jack, who would do this? Does it tie back to the gun? Could Ben be behind this, angry about us searching without him?"

"I can't piece it together, Em," he said, his mind a whirlwind of possibilities. "But I don't think they're connected."

The distant wail of a siren cut their speculation short, heralding the police's arrival. Emma's tension eased, hope for answers dawning.

Lieutenant Carl Allen, tall and authoritative, stepped out with Officer Mike Barnes, his presence commanding yet reassuring.

"Mr. Sullivan, we're here about your report of a slashed tire, and a found handgun?"

"Call me Jack. Yes, it's all four tires," he said, gesturing toward his vehicle.

As they explained, the officers zeroed in on Jack and Emma, but they omitted commenting on their treasure hunt.

While Allen jotted down their details and backgrounds, his expression shifted upon learning of their naval duty.

"You're not our usual type of call we receive about at a bar," he said. "Thank you both for your service."

Jack ran his hand through his hair and said, "Thank you. We appreciate what you do as well."

Allen's gaze lingered on Jack. "I've heard your name earlier. Your historical find... It's caught people's interest, and so has the trouble at the excavation site."

Jack changed position, unease growing. "Appears so."

The Lieutenant leaned in, serious. "The artifacts you uncovered caused some buzz. Some people are not happy with the Smithsonian's involvement."

Emma opened her mouth, and Allen signaled for silence before she said anything. "Your activities might be attracting unwanted attention. Many in the area heard the legend of the treasure. While your searches aren't illegal, be careful."

"Thanks for the advice," Emma's voice quivered, her eyes mirroring her concern.

"Anytime," Allen said, extending his card. "Should you need it, don't hesitate to reach out. Given the details of your situation, I don't believe we have any more questions. However, someone might be trying to send you a message. Rest assured, we're on it." He closed his notebook and continued, "For our next steps, we have to inspect where you found the gun. We've also arranged for a tow. Could one of you stay behind with Officer Barnes?"

Steve stepped up and accepted Jack's keys.

"Mike, would you mind checking the bar for any surveillance footage?" Allen asked, preparing to accompany Jack and Emma.

Emma tensed as they approached the cave, her worry for Jack compounded by the potential dangers looming larger. Jack's demeanor struck her – his jaw set, brows knitted, eyes determined. *Does he understand the peril we're now facing?*

Upon reaching the cavern, Emma and Allen navigated the narrow passage to the far cavern, leaving Jack behind.

"This is quite the adventure, Miss Wilson," he said, navigating the tight space.

"Likewise, Officer Allen," she said.

"Call me Carl."

"Emma."

As she approached the crate, her heart sank; it lay in ruin, its contents and surrounding stones scattered. "Looks like someone was here," she pointed, her voice laced with worry.

"Indeed. This wasn't your doing?"

"I can show you the photos of what I found."

"Later. So somebody else is familiar with this place," he deduced, scrutinizing the scene.

After documenting the area and collecting evidence, they rejoined Jack; Allen summarized, "Looks like they smashed the crate when they saw the gun was missing and probably didn't want anyone to find anything else."

"Or they covered their tracks," Jack asserted, his fists balled in resolve.

While Emma observed the men, apprehension surged over her. *Although this treasure hunt is exciting, what are we risking? How much danger lies ahead?*

Jack's voice, firm with conviction, cut through her thoughts, "We won't let them stop us."

Allen nodded, impressed. "You should still stay vigilant and please notify me immediately of anything that comes up."

"We will," Jack said as they departed the cave, leaving its ominous shadows behind.

Emma's intuition told herself: *We have more at stake than gold.*

* * *

While Emma and Jack were off with the Lieutenant, Steve stared at Barnes on the deck, his arms crossed, an uneasy sensation gnawing at him. Barnes, seated opposite, poured through the bar's surveillance footage on a tablet.

"This your first time dealing with found firearms and vandalism?" Steve's attempted humor, his laughter forced.

"I'd love to say it is," Barnes replied, his eyes never leaving the screen, a playful grin on his face. "Truth is, it's a first. I may be wrong, but it seems someone's got it in for you."

Steve mulled over the thought that perhaps they wanted the treasure for themselves, considering Jack's intense preoccupation with it. The idea of buried riches had a potent allure that might push individuals to their limits.

"Be cautious," Barnes cautioned. "I'm afraid that the closer you get, the higher the risk."

Steve mulled the comment over: *He may be right.*

A tow truck rumbled up. An immense, flannel-wearing, grease-marked man stepped out of the truck and greeted them with a nod. "Need a hand?"

"Yes," Barnes replied. "Could you rush new tires for their vehicle? They're stuck otherwise."

"Of course," the driver said, inspecting the tires. "I work as a mechanic, too. We've got your size in stock. Give us an hour to replace them." He handed Steve a card and a receipt.

"Appreciate it," Steve said, slipping it into his pocket. "Mind giving me a call when you arrive? I'll cover the cost."

"Sure thing."

With the driver loading the Suburban onto the flatbed, Barnes returned to the surveillance footage.

"Look at this," he pointed out, showing a pickup on the screen.

"That's the same truck we saw near the cave we found with Ben Baton's earlier this morning," Steve said.

Barnes's pen moved, jotting something down about Ben.

On the tablet, they witnessed a hooded figure exit the vehicle, eyeing them from a bar's deck. After the three friends crossed the road and headed down the trail toward the lake, they approached Jack's truck. They brandished a knife, their gloved hands noticeable.

"Is that Ben?" Steve said the first thing that came to mind.

They watched as the person struggled, trying to stab a tire several times before flattening the first. They damaged the rest and disappeared from the screen when they followed the three toward a cave.

"Go back to when they started to cut the tire," he asked.

Barnes asked, "Is that Ben Baton?"

"No…," Steve glared at the video, noting the figure's slighter build and different movements. "That's not Ben. Ben's strong; he wouldn't have had an issue slicing the tires."

"You sure it's not Ben Baton?"

"Positive."

The video never revealed the assailant's face.

"Once again, are you sure it's not Ben Baton?"

"Yes. That person is smaller," Steve said, with anger, "They are tracking us, and I think they're attempting to make us suspect Ben by wearing the same hoodie he does. We need to uncover their identity."

"Right," Barnes said. "Keep in touch and let us know if anything happens."

He nodded, his understanding of their predicament sinking in. They were on the brink of a significant discovery, yet the increasing dangers shadowed his excitement for their safety.

* * *

Twilight embraced the sky, and its ominous final glow settled over the group huddled around the table. Lieutenant Carl Allen, alongside Officer Mike Barnes, faced the three friends with a somber air, and the absence of Suburban was a silent testament to the lurking threat.

The Lieutenant spoke next, his tone a mixture of authority and concern. "We've gone through your statements and the video. It appears someone's working against you."

Jack's hands tightened into fists and repeated gruff sighs; his frustration was evident. He agonized between his unwavering quest for the treasure and the guilt of involving Emma and Steve.

A glance at Emma revealed her worry, deepening the lines of her face.

"Be careful," Barnes cautioned. "My concern is that this may not be a game to your adversary."

"Perhaps we should pause our search," Steve leaned over and whispered to Jack, his hand massaging his neck, hinting at his stress.

Before Jack countered, Steve's phone disrupted the moment. "Hey, Babe," he answered, attempting to keep the mood light.

"Work was a marathon. I need a drink. Are you at Honi Honi?" Sally said.

Steve navigated the conversation towards their immediate situation. "No. We ran into some car trouble. Could you pick us up at Pawn Run Bar and drop us at Glotfelty Tire? I'll explain later."

"Of course. I'll meet you shortly," she said.

Steve relayed Sally's imminent arrival. Jack's mind, however, was a tempest of doubt and anger, shifting on his feet. Emma's reassuring touch calmed his storm within, although her furrowed brows and head movement spoke otherwise.

Allen broke their thoughts, saying, "As you have a ride, we will head out. We'll contact you if there are any developments or if we need anything else from you."

The trio paced or stared at each other as they waited for Sally, their concern over the events evident.

Sally pulled up, and the window slid down, "So, do I have to play catch up again?"

Steve laughed as he got in her vehicle, "Unfortunately, no. Jack's tire indicator went on after turning off 219. We were heading here, as it was closer for you to meet us for dinner. One tire was almost flat, and the others were losing air."

"We were behind a scrap truck on the highway. I think something fell off," Jack said.

"Unreal! Sorry to hear about it," Sally said, her head tilting. "So, I take it you had an eventful day?"

Jack seized the chance to gauge her insight. "Are you referring to our morning's search with Ben?"

Intrigued, she leaned in. "So, you're helping Ben?"

"It's more like we struck out with him today. We went through the artifacts with him, and based on the journal, he figured the treasure had to be in a cave along the river by a Native American trail near Gap Run."

"We searched and found a collapsed cave entrance and opened it. Unfortunately, there was nothing inside other than we found Ben's ancestor's name carved on the wall in 1803. He said he was going to let you know."

"I didn't hear from Ben today, but it sounds like quite the morning adventure and something special for him, I'd reckon."

Jack wondered: *Was Sally's response hinting at a shared excitement for Ben's experience?* He seized the moment to probe into Sally and Ben's relationship, "I was pretty impressed he figured that out from the artifacts," Jack said. "We didn't find anything looking like clues. What did you think about the journal?"

Confusion furrowed her brow. "What do you mean?"

He elaborated, "Yesterday, when Mike was trying to figure out who dug up his site, I suggested he check with his guys about who they told about the discovery. They said they only spoke to their wives. However, Kevin also suggested I ask the 'museum lady.' He said you looked through all the stuff. That's why I asked for your thoughts."

Her puzzlement deepened. "I didn't see them up close, Remember? Kept my distance. I was not dressed right for the excavation site. Is this an accusation?"

Realization dawned on Steve, and he took action to correct Jack's misstep: "No, no, it's a misunderstanding. We thought the guy was deflecting. If you recall, Jack said he tried to take a coin."

"Sorry, my bad. Today's whirlwind had me forgetting you arrived after me," Jack conceded.

"It's alright; today has been troubling for you," Sally dismissed the tension with a wave of her hand.

A brief silence fell before she quipped, "So, no treasure means you're not picking up the check tonight?"

They laughed.

Emma sought to avoid the day's disappointments, "Time to move on. Let's focus on the evening instead."

When arriving at the repair shop, Sally's departure came with a promise of meeting later, leaving Jack, Emma, and Steve in the semi-darkness outside the lit garage.

"Let's head in," Steve motioned towards the glow where Jack's vehicle awaited.

Inside, a brief update from the mechanic hinted at a short wait. "Your SUV will be ready in a few minutes," he said.

"Thanks," he replied and unloaded his stress with a stretch.

She spotted his distress, pulling him aside for a private word. "Jack, it's tough, I know. Please don't let today consume you. We're narrowing down the possible places, at least."

His frustration was in his voice when he confessed, "It's hard not to feel so close yet so far. Now, I'm worried about the risks I've put both of you in. It's just the thought of someone beating us to it..."

"Jack, look at me," she whispered, lifting his chin to align their gazes. "We need you with us, here... now. My fear is you're losing sight of what's important, caught up in this hunt."

"She's got a point," Steve said, having overheard as he drew near. "We're concerned. You should consider stepping back and taking a breather. Don't worry about us; we can handle ourselves."

Jack exhaled, the truth of their words settling in. He nodded with gratitude in his eyes. "I appreciate you both. I'd be lost without you two."

"Then it's settled," Emma smiled. "Tomorrow, we switch gears. Something light, something to ease our minds."

"That's the spirit!" Steve's enthusiasm was infectious. "How about a day on the lake? Us, the boat, the sun, and the sky. No hunts, no pressure. Sound good?"

Jack's forced smile widened, a spark of reluctant acceptance. "Okay."

The mechanic, rag in hand and streaked with grease, approached them. "SUV's ready," he said, tossing the keys to Jack.

"Thanks. What do I owe you for the tires?" Jack asked.

"Already taken care of – your guardian angel covered it," the mechanic gestured towards Steve.

"I owe you one again, Stevie," he said, his grin tinged with irony.

"Forget it. We'll square up when we strike gold," Steve whispered, slinging an arm around Jack's shoulder as they left the garage.

Climbing into their refreshed ride, Jack caught the lake's serene glimmer in the distance through the moonlight. Emma and Steve's advice resonated with him; a break from their quest was necessary. Yet, as night enveloped them, a sense of unease gnawed at him.

"Tomorrow's a new day," Jack said, the road stretching before them. The Honi Honi Bar awaited, promising a night to unwind and reset. *Will this delay allow our competition to get ahead of us?*

Chapter 22

The bar's inviting glow pulled them inside, where laughter, music, and the aromas of cooking burgers and beer spills mingled. The day's frustrations started to vanish as Jack, Steve, and Emma stepped into the bustling atmosphere.

"Steve!" Sally called, waving from a table near the stage.

Steve beamed, "Hey, Sweetie," sliding in beside her, their closeness undeniable. "Appreciate the beers," he nodded towards the drinks awaiting them.

Eyeing the trio's drained expressions, "Rough day?"

Emma managed a smile. "Yeah, a bit. Time to unwind now."

"To a fun night," Steve raised his bottle, prompting a round of toasts and sips, the evening's relaxation beginning to take hold.

Turning to Sally, Steve asked, "We're going boating tomorrow. Care to join us?"

"Yes, thank you. I'd love to!" She kissed him on the cheek.

Jack put his already empty bottle down, enjoying the night's embrace, and waved for more drinks. Emma's concern surfaced, "Could you slow up, Jack?"

"I'm just trying to relax, Em," he snapped. "It's our night off, and so is tomorrow."

Steve tried to lighten the moment, whispering to Emma, "Guess we're driving tonight."

She whispered back, "Appears so."

* * *

While the night deepened, Jack's unspoken discontent stewed, and he retreated into drink after drink, seeking forgetfulness. Emma and Steve exchanged concerned looks, their conversation deliberate in avoiding the topic of their quest.

Emma looked at Sally, realizing she appeared more at ease, and her drinking was moderate. *Maybe she was nervous about meeting the three of us yesterday.*

Turning, she looked upon Jack and his struggle to stay coherent, and she decided that was enough. "Jack, let's go home."

"Ahh-weady?" he slurred, swaying a tad in his seat.

"Let's go, buddy," Steve urged, steadying him with a firm hand.

"Fiiine," he conceded, leaning on Steve for support.

"Steve, take care of him, please," Sally whispered, kissing him goodbye. "I need you well rested, ready to apply my suntan lotion."

He grinned, "Yes, ma'am. We'll pick you up in the morning."

"Goodnight, Sally. Sorry for the chaos," Emma said, offering a parting smile before trailing Steve and Jack out.

She replied, humor in her voice, "No problem, Emma. And Steve, I'm counting on you to make it up to me tomorrow, repeatedly."

Emma smiled, masking her shock at Sally's innuendo.

The moon bathed Jack's apartment in a spectral light as Emma and Steve, supporting a staggering Jack between them, navigating the steps to his door. Inside, they eased him onto his bed, where he collapsed into the pillows with a subdued moan, the day's exertions catching up.

"Thanks for your help," She murmured, gratitude lacing her tone as she gazed at Jack's prone figure. "I'd be at a loss without you."

"It's nothing. That's what friends are for, right?" he replied, a genuine smile reaching his eyes.

Emma paused, her concern evident. "I'm worried. He's becoming too fixated on this treasure. Even though we found that cave in the book, he missed clear signs like the lack of a waterfall. He's been slowly getting

199

more obsessed with the treasure, and today, he was something else. He's almost like he was years ago."

Steve's agreement came with a concerned glance. "I've noticed it as well. However, abandoning him isn't an option. I think he's over his head and doesn't comprehend it."

"How do we help someone when they're sinking and don't realize it?" Her voice broke, blinking back the tears.

"Tomorrow, we'll take a boat out and show him life beyond treasure hunting," he proposed, his tone both soft and resolved. "If that doesn't work, we'll keep trying until it does."

"Okay, but I don't believe I can face this again," she said, nodding despite the concern in her chest. "Some fresh air and relaxation might clear his head."

"Let's hope," he said, rubbing the back of his neck. "We should call it a night."

"Yeah, thanks again," Emma said, giving him a quick embrace. "Goodnight, Steve."

"Night, Emma."

* * *

The door ajar, Steve lingered in the subdued glow of the living room, the distant sounds of Jack's soothing breaths reaching him as she settled in. The path they treaded was fraught with peril, yet abandoning Jack was unthinkable after what they had been through together.

"Come on, Jack," he whispered, pleading for his friend, his brother in all but blood, to rally back to them. "You're stronger than this."

Sighing, he closed the door without a sound, severing the connection to their collective strife, and submerged the room into darkness with a flick of the switch. The night lay before him, its shadows veiling the road ahead. Still, amidst this uncertainty, one truth stood resolute: their bond, forged in love and loyalty, would carry them through.

Perhaps this would be enough.

Chapter 23

The morning light tried to pour through the curtains when Emma found herself in the doorway of Jack's room. She observed him as he lay, the remnants of last night's excesses evident in his disheveled state. The memory of the previous evening's debacle troubled her, a stark reminder of the deep-seated issues of why she called off their wedding. Despite it all, she wasn't ready to give up on him.

"It's time, Jack!" she exclaimed.

Jack groaned into consciousness, squinting and cursing as Emma threw the blinds open. The harsh sunlight pierced straight through to his hangover, eliciting a pained shriek from him. She smirked at his discomfort, though her amusement over payback for the night before faded as she witnessed his struggle to sit up, a pang of sadness replacing it.

Steve's voice sliced through the morning, laced with sarcasm. "Enjoying the sun?" His tone sharpened. "Hope you feel as bad as you made last night for us."

"I'm up, but I feel worse than when you rescued me from the river," Jack confessed, rubbing his temples.

"Really? Which one? And that bad?" Steve raised an eyebrow.

"Iraq. And, yes."

"Doesn't matter!" Emma said, pushing a coffee into Jack's hands. "Because we're not missing a day on the lake. You promised."

He shrugged, his voice flat, "Fine, fine. I need the day to recover from this, anyway." His soured disposition was evident in his slumped shoulders and his distant eyes.

Shifting gears to more pressing matters, Steve hinted at the peril of their quest, "We now know others are looking for the treasure, so the journal is not safe here. We should either hide it or keep it on us."

"Agreed," he said, now more alert. He led them to the corner of the room. "See anything?"

"No," Steve replied.

He revealed a hidden compartment in the floor below, pulled back the carpet, and lifted a board to reveal a small fire safe. "Does this work?"

"Perfect," Emma affirmed.

The conversation shifted to Sally's role in their plans. Jack hesitated, his gaze flickering toward Stevie. "I understand, Stevie," he said, voice low and measured, "but she's too close to Ben. She might slip."

"Jack's right," Emma agreed.

"Okay," Steve conceded, disappointment clear. "She's still coming today, and she knows we are looking. I guess we'll need to be careful around her."

"Agreed. Let's make the most of our lake day," Emma said, a soft smile breaking through. "Jack can figure out a new path for us to follow tomorrow."

Jack's eyes widened as his stare locked onto her, lips pressing into a thin line. She recognized his expression and intense concentration: *Jack just thought of something important.*

"Right," he sighed. "When do we leave? I need to… dress and gather some things."

"Sally's expecting us in an hour," Steve replied, setting the day's plans into motion.

Emma's eyes followed Jack, his attention anchored to something other than the day on the lake. He gathered pieces linked to their quest, scattering them on the table amidst household items repurposed as makeshift weights for the sprawling museum map. His fingers skated over the map's contours, then flitted across his phone's screen, a ballet of thought and deduction.

"What's got you?" Emma asked, her voice a blend of curiosity and mild irritation, observing his determined hunch. "Thought we shelved the treasure hunt for today."

"Something you mentioned reminded me of what you said back at the county archive. It sparked an idea. I'm piecing it together... *for tomorrow*," Jack said, glancing toward her before his gaze returned, intense and engrossed, to the scattered papers of his investigation.

"Okay, but just for a moment. Anything promising?" she leaned closer, trying to catch a glimpse of his discovery.

"Maybe," Jack replied, his mind already racing ahead. "Need a bit more time on this."

"We're short on time, Jack. Sally will be waiting."

"Five minutes?"

"Fine."

He dove back into his comparison, his scrutiny now split between the map and a letter to Clarke's wife.

"Find it?"

"I think so." Satisfaction tinged his voice as he secured the artifacts into a hidden niche beneath the floor.

Shifting gears, Jack moved to his closet, beginning to pack with purpose. Towels, floats, and snorkeling gear landed on his bed. "Anyone up for tubing today?"

"Yes," Emma and Steve's enthusiasm matched.

After pulling out a hefty towable tube, he darted around to gather and don his swim attire. "Steve, can you grab the cooler?"

"On it."

"Let's roll," he said, leading the way out.

She caught the distant gaze in Jack's eyes as they walked to the car. "Penny, for your thoughts?" she nudged him, curious.

"Ah, pondering what we might've missed," Jack said, his smile not quite reaching his eyes.

"Let's leave it for another day. Today, we unwind," she pressed, hoping to steer his mind towards their leisure day.

Jack's agreement came, but Emma realized the treasure's lure was strong. His pursuit wouldn't pause until he explored every avenue. They drove to fetch Sally, and she leaned into the day's promise, wishing for his clouded thoughts to clear.

They arrived to find Sally ready, dressed in shorts and a tank top, her long black hair pulled back in a ponytail. She smiled as she climbed into the back of the truck and kissed Steve, her eyes bright with anticipation.

"Hey, guys," she chimed in, shaking Emma's shoulder. "Thanks for the invite."

"Anytime," Steve replied, wrapping Sally in a casual embrace. "Happy you're here."

Emma stared at them, a knot of jealousy tightening. Perhaps she should bridge the gap with Jack, considering she was the one who called off the engagement. He could be hesitant for the same reason.

Shrugging off her doubts, she turned to him. "Don't forget to stop by Shop N' Save. We need snacks and drinks for the boat."

"Got it. Ooh, and ice for the cooler," Jack said, as if on cue.

They hustled through the aisles at the store, loading supplies into their cart. After a brief trip to the liquor store for extra beverages, they packed up and headed to Bill's Marina. Tucked in the lake's heart, the marina awaited, where they would pick up their pontoon for the day's adventure.

Jack handed their reservation to the clerk, who glanced up and said, "Boater's license?"

After a search through his wallet, he presented his license. The clerk nodded and gestured for them to follow, leading them straight to their pontoon.

"Wow, this one's impressive," Emma said as they boarded the boat, complete with a roof deck and water slide. "Never seen one quite like this. Can't wait to hit the water."

"Only the best for our ladies!" Steve boasted.

"Let's go," Jack said, a smile playing on his lips as he ignited the engine.

The boat purred to life, and they drifted from the dock, leaving the mundane behind for the promise of fun and relaxation.

Above them, the sun cast the lake into a radiant sheen, framed by the soft sway of verdant trees. The day was tailor-made for friends to revel in. Jack steered towards Deep Creek State Park, and Emma settled back, letting the sun kiss her skin, her hair dancing in the breeze.

Sally twirled her sunscreen overhead, graceful and deliberate, like a Jedi with a lightsaber. "Heeyyy, Stevieee!" she called, her voice lilting through the air. In a split second, Steve appeared by her side, catching Emma by surprise. Sally peeled off her clothes with a teasing flourish, unveiling a tiny bikini clinging to her stunning figure, even drawing an admiring glance from Emma. Steve's fingers danced across Sally, tracing the contours with lotion while laughter bubbled among them, echoing their shared joy.

Emma considered joining the theatrics but chose instead to relax, content in their happiness on the water. While nearing the park, Jack's attention shifted, circling the boat with his eyes flicking between the helm and the water to his side.

"What's up, Jack?" Steve leaned out, scanning the lake. "Looking for something?"

"I... thought I saw a big turtle," he said, distraction in his voice.

"Wow!" Emma's tone filled with excitement. "That'd be amazing to see."

"I adore turtles," Sally said.

"Keep an eye out for it," he said.

However, as the turtle remained elusive, Emma spotted that Jack's focus was on the gauges, not the surroundings. Approaching him, she wrapped her arms around his chest. "Everything all right?"

"Yeah," he said.

"I need you to be with us, here, now," she whispered, eyes pleading for his presence.

"Okay, Em," he said, redirecting the boat towards the park's Carmel Cove with renewed purpose.

Releasing Jack, she called out, "Hey, who wants to give the tube a spin?" She pointed at the inflatable raft tucked away at the boat's stern.

"Excellent idea," Steve chimed in with excitement. Together with Emma, they started inflating the tube. Their shared laughter dispelled Jack's earlier gloom.

"It's set!" Emma said, fastening it to the tow rope. "Who's up first?"

"I am," Steve replied, stepping forward. His chiseled physique became evident as he slipped into the life jacket. Jack secured the rope to the back of the boat and tossed the tube into the lake. Steve scampered aboard, his movements eager and unrestrained, reminiscent of a child's delight. Grasping the handles, he leaned back as they gained speed, laughter and shouts escaping him while the tube danced across the cresting waves.

"Check this out!" he yelled, trying a bold move of flipping over, which sent him crashing into the water with a spectacular splash.

"Nice!" Emma cheered, her applause mingling with Jack's chuckle as they maneuvered to retrieve Steve.

"Round two?" Jack smiled, pulling alongside.

"I'm not stopping now!" Steve beamed, clambering back on.

The sun's warmth became undeniable. Emma stood, peeling off her layers to reveal her swimsuit, catching Jack's soft comment, "Wow."

"Like the view?" she teased, nudging him as he colored in embarrassment.

"Guilty," he confessed, a smile creeping across his face beneath her amused gaze. His flirtation now shone clear and unguarded.

"How about we find somewhere for a swim?" Jack proposed, aiming to distract from his fluster.

"Perfect," Emma said, eyeing the shoreline for a serene spot.

"Party or quiet?" Jack asked.

"Quiet," Emma and Steve said together. "Party," came Sally's lone reply.

"Sorry, Sally. Quite wins. Red Run Cove it is," he said, their destination promising tranquility.

Crossing the lake under the Route 219 bridge and gliding into the cove a few miles away, Steve and Sally were the first to dive into the inviting waters. Their camaraderie was visible in their playful splashing. Steve guided her onto a raft.

Emma's envy resurfaced at their display. Her gaze found Jack, lost in thought in the captain's seat, and wondered what he was thinking. Catching her stare, he shifted his perspective from the water to her.

"Hey," she ventured, a gentle touch on his shoulder. "All good?"

He nodded, a slight grin on his lips. "Yeah, just reflecting."

"On the treasure hunt?" she probed, insightful.

"No," he said, his eyes lingering on hers. "I'm thinking how happy I am you're here."

Emma's heart raced as she considered her following action. Perhaps a kiss would alter everything between her and Jack. Her smile softened; she reached out, cradling his face in her hands, and brushed her lips against his.

"Wow," he whispered, his eyes widening.

"I know you too well. You were holding back something from before, right?" Emma said, soft but insistent.

Jack's eyes flickered toward Sally for a fleeting moment. "Back at the State Park, something popped into my mind, but this isn't the time to discuss it."

"Fair enough," Emma replied, her understanding implicit. She kissed him again, sealing their unspoken agreement to enjoy the day without burdens.

Jack, now encouraged, embraced her. "You're right. Let's make the most of it." He stripped off his t-shirt, revealing his toned physique, and leaped into the lake from the top deck. Emma's gaze lingered on Jack and his scars that served as a reminder of when she almost lost him to a sniper's shot that avoided his vest: one on the edge of his right pectoral muscle under his arm and the more noticeable one running down the length of his sternum. She turned her eyes and caught sight tossing a raft into the water, joined in the laughter and splashing with their friends, setting aside the quest for hidden treasure in favor of the joy of the moment.

"Appears everyone's getting along," Emma whispered, gazing upon Jack from her float. "Still worried about Sally?"

"A bit," he confessed, his eyes narrowing. "It's her situation with Ben. Something's off, but let's not dwell on it today."

"True. Speaking of Ben, we haven't heard from him for a while?" Emma's curiosity piqued.

"We should 'check in' with him," Jack said, using air quotes.

Emma chuckled. "After your failed attempt with Sally last night, could we get more out of Ben this time?"

He tilted his head, his eyes wide, a smile tugging at his lips in pretended surrender. She encircled him with her arms, her lips inches from his, and with a swift motion, plunged him beneath the water.

Jack emerged with a laugh and sent her a playful glare. "Be careful. I'll get you back for that."

Emma, climbing onto his back, shot him a challenging gaze. "Try it if you think you can outsmart me."

Nearby, Steve nudged Sally toward the slide, their chuckles blending in the air. With a mock scowl, she sent a splash his way. "Hoping my suit falls off, are you?"

"Can't blame a man for wishing," Steve retorted with a grin.

Seizing the moment, Emma rallied Sally to go on the slide. She activated the pump and, with a whoop of delight, took the plunge, followed by Sally. When Sally surfaced, missing her straps, she clutched her chest and shouted, "I lost my top!" capturing the carefree hilarity of their lakeside escapade.

Steve cut through the lake, each stroke a masterclass in speed and control. Nearing Sally, her laughter broke free, vibrant, and alive while her hands, nimble and sure, retrieved the submerged strings and fastened them around her neck. "I knew it," she said, eyes alight with a playful sparkle.

"You got me," Steve said, filled with amusement as he edged nearer.

Emma and Sally perched at the stern of the boat, their legs swinging into the cool water below. "Thank you again for inviting me," she said with appreciation. "You and Jack, you've made me feel welcomed."

"You're most welcome," Emma said, her tone shifting with curiosity. "So, I have to ask, what do you think of Steve?"

Sally paused, reflecting. "I find him... quite remarkable... well, he's different."

A sly smile crossed her face, "Be careful. You may be falling for him."

"Perhaps," Sally said with a hesitant grin and confessed, "There's something about him."

She recognized the signs; Sally's glances toward Steve spoke volumes. "Steve's never been happier. I'm glad he met you," she shared, noticing Sally's flushed gratitude as Steve's impromptu cannonball sent a splash their way, inciting laughter and Sally's playful retaliation.

Jack's misjudged flip resulted in an awkward and painful smack. Surfacing, he shouted encouragement and a challenge to the women to follow.

Overcoming a brief hesitation, Emma leaped from the roof deck, her splash punctuating the silence. As she resurfaced to a triumphant cheer, Sally followed suit, executing a graceful one-and-a-half that sliced through the air and water with a splashless entry. The three friends' mouths were agape in surprise, followed by laughter, mingling with the joyous moment.

"Sorry to say this, but it's time to head back," Jack announced, his tone filled with disappointment. A hush fell upon them as they made their way to the boat, each absorbed in thoughts of the evening ahead.

Dropping Sally off, the ride back was contemplative, the day's fun giving way to reflective quiet. At the apartment, Emma probed Jack's distant demeanor earlier in the day near the state park.

He met her gaze, a resolve in his eyes. "I was pondering something," he said, hinting at a revelation. "I think I've pieced together something crucial. Do you have Bill's number, you know, the guy from the museum?"

"Bill O'Connell?" Emma queried, sensing the shift in Jack's priority.

"Yeah, can you call him? See if he wants to join us for breakfast or lunch tomorrow?" Jack asked.

"Why? What's up?" Emma asked, curiosity piqued.

"Your comment about finding a different path earlier got me thinking. The old map we stumbled upon," he said, "It showed trails not on Steve's map. You commented you saw a path that would be now submerged and that it followed the creek past the dam to the river. We've been on part of it."

Emma's eyes narrowed, and asked, "What's this got to do with Bill?"

"Bill's family has deep roots here, dating back to the 1700s; his perspective on the area's transformations might prove invaluable. The lake, by historical standards, is new. He might recall a notable tree, and perhaps one lost to the relentless march of development or the building of Route 219. I wonder if the lake's construction caused a waterfall or cave to go underwater."

Emma said, "Makes sense, but that's a lot to hope for, but you're probably right. Bill's the only one who could point us in the right direction."

"Pitch it as interest in local history," Jack said. "He might share local lore about Braddock's Pittsburgh expedition, why the barrel was where it was, or something else I've not heard before. And, let's not mention anything to Sally tonight."

"Understood," Steve said, grasping the importance of their silence.

After cleaning themselves up, they set off for the Mountain State Brewery, tucked in a lush farm valley. The venue's rustic charm, bathed in the glow of the setting sun, promised an ideal place for their dinner.

Upon arriving, they chose an outdoor table where the restaurant's lively atmosphere welcomed them, complemented by melodies from a local acoustic band. The inviting ambiance suited their mood.

"This place is buzzing," Emma said, taken by the selection of craft beers on the menu.

Jack's grin broadened. "Thought you might enjoy it. It's new since you were here last."

Sally made her way toward them, her smile as warm as the sun's setting rays, with Steve enchanted by her arrival.

Settling into her seat, Sally joined the flow of conversation peppered with laughter and the soft clinks of bottles. Soon, Sally leaned close to Steve, her voice low but audible to Emma.

"Don't drink too much; you're taking me home," she murmured, her fingers brushing his thigh.

Steve hesitated, his wide eyes flicking to Jack and Emma, and he gave a subtle nod. "Yes, ma'am."

Emma caught the exchange, her eyebrows lifting in mild surprise at Sally's forwardness. She turned to Jack, finding him engrossed in the menu, and familiar warmth towards him settled upon her. His glance up and smile reinforced the reasons she fell for him.

Their time together unfolded with laughter and anecdotes, erasing the awkwardness of the previous night. As the evening came to a close, Steve and Sally stood, hands linked.

"Let's catch up tomorrow for breakfast. Text us the plans," Steve said, his gaze fixed on Sally.

"Don't enjoy your night too much," Emma teased.

Walking back to their car, Emma shared her observation with Jack, "Steve and Sally appear to be getting very close."

Jack nodded, his eyes narrowing with consideration. "Seems so, but I worry about Steve's history, remember Stephanie?"

"I almost forgot about her. He does jump in too quickly. Stephanie exploited him because of it."

"Given his frequent travels, his opportunities for romance are few," Jack said, his tone filled with concern. "When he finds somebody, he clings too quickly, almost in desperation. If he lasted a month with someone, I'd believe he'd propose to her then and there."

"True. Yet, Sally's... different," Emma said.

They settled into the car, and she became lost in thought, the night's events leaving her both hopeful and wary for their friends.

The drive back was quiet, the soft hum of the engine and the whir of the road beneath them. Emma found comfort in the silence, resting her hand on Jack's leg, reliving the evening's joy in her mind.

Breaking the quiet, she said, "If Steve and Sally are serious, I'm thinking we should include her more in our plans."

Jack's glance was thoughtful, and he refocused on the road. "I'm not sure, Em. I'm still worried about her connection to Ben."

"I understand," she said, her fingers tapping to the steady rhythm of the music against his leg. "Suppose she's falling for Steve. Her loyalty should shift from Ben to Steve and us. She'd want to keep our secrets. Why would she spill the beans if she thinks she's in on the treasure?"

"Good point," Jack said, his brow furrowed, hands tightening on the wheel. "Let's see how it goes."

"We forgot to check on Ben," Emma said, her head resting back. "We should call him tomorrow."

The possibility of finding the gold both thrilled and unnerved her. "Breakfast with Bill could be a game-changer," she pondered aloud. "Should he know something, we could wrap up this hunt."

"I hope he does. Otherwise, we probably don't have much of a chance except to search the length of every river," Jack said, sounding tired.

"Let's hope he does. Are we doing this together?" she pressed, seeking reassurance.

"Always," he kissed her hand in affirmation and a gentle smile in his gaze, sending her heart racing.

Approaching the apartment building, the light from his unit shined down upon them, welcoming them, but Jack's playful chatter ceased. He stared up at the window.

"What is it, Jack?"

He put his finger to his mouth and opened the door to the stairs in silence. He crept up the steps, placing his feet on the far sides of each tread to eliminate squeaks. Near the top, his attention sharpened, and he gestured for quiet and slow movement, clear from finding the door ajar, unbroken by force.

Chapter 24

Jack indicated with his hands, "Stay put," and edged forward with caution. He peered through the opening. After what felt like an eternity, he pushed the door open and scanned the room. His voice was tense, "Someone ransacked my apartment!"

"Could Ben have done this?" Emma whispered, horrified by the mess.

"Maybe, but let's not assume," he replied. The chaos was overwhelming: drawers emptied, possessions scattered.

"Jack!" Emma exclaimed at the sight of their memories, now fragments on the floor.

"I'm so sorry, Emma," he said, his touch reassuring. "But we need to check the documents."

She nodded, her determination returning. In the bedroom, Jack drew the curtains and lifted the carpet to look at their secret stash beneath the floorboards. A sigh of relief escaped them both as they found the maps and letters safe and returned to the living room.

"We should call the police," Emma insisted, her voice trembling with fear and fury.

He closed the secret compartment and reached for his phone. He briefed Allen on the apartment. "Thank you, Lieutenant," he murmured into the phone before disconnecting.

"They're en route, Em," he said, pacing near the door, his heart racing. He caught Emma's gaze, her complexion washed with fear, her arms wrapped around herself as if to hold herself together. The abrupt arrival of a car outside, punctuated by the closing of doors, broke the tense silence.

"Stay behind me to be safe," he whispered, positioning himself between Emma and the entrance with a protective stance.

"Wow," Jack exhaled, seeing familiar faces. "I didn't expect you so soon."

"We were nearby, assisting with a DUI on Friendsville Road near the interstate when your call came in," Barnes put away his gun, explaining their prompt arrival. "Fortunate timing. What's happened here?"

Jack gestured towards the chaos in his living room. "We returned to find my apartment ransacked."

"Did you spot anyone leaving?" Allen asked, readying his notepad.

"No, but they might have fled upon our approach. There's a back exit," he said.

"Let's take a look," Allen signaled Barnes to follow him inside. They navigated the wreckage with precision, each movement methodical.

"Document everything," Allen directed. Barnes started photographing the scene, capturing every detail. Jack and Emma looked on, silent and anxious, while the officers carefully examined the damage.

"Where's Steve?" Allen said, turning to Jack.

"With his girlfriend, Sally Adkins. They're at her place," he replied, puzzled by the relevance.

"Understood," Allen said and resumed his inspection. "Anything missing?"

"It doesn't seem so. I'm guessing they were after the artifacts." Jack said.

Allen asked, "Where are they?"

"They're… already with the Smithsonian."

The Lieutenant paused, looking at Jack with a tilted head, "Lucky. We can't afford to lose history."

Jack's thoughts darkened with frustration as he watched Barnes sift through the debris. *Who would invade my apartment? Why?*

Allen eyed the door. "Was it locked when you got here?"

"No, wide open," Jack replied.

"Barnes, go grab a kit and dust the door's interior handle for fingerprints," Allen instructed, moving towards the balcony door and sliding it open with his gloved hand. "Do you lock this on a regular basis?"

"No, I thought it was too high. A ladder would be obvious. I never fathomed someone scaling it," he said.

"Could be reached from a pickup truck roof," Allen surmised, gazing at the drop to the street. "I'll have Barnes check the patio door handle for prints too."

"Hold on," he said, a spark of realization in his tone, "Steve mentioned seeing that same truck on the Pawn Run surveillance near a cave at the Yough River this morning."

"Exactly. We're looking for its owner, but it's clear they're either trailing you or aware of your movements. However," Allen's voice carried a heavier note, "there's troubling news."

"What?" Jack felt a wave of unease.

"A park officer found Ben Baton injured today in Lower Swallow Falls. They evacuated him, and he's in the intensive care unit for observation," Allen relayed, flipping through his notebook.

"Ben?" Emma echoed, disbelief and concern etching her face. "What's his condition?"

"He'll be okay, but he had to have surgery to repair his broken leg. He claims someone attacked him yesterday evening, though we've yet to identify any assailant."

"Who would do that?" Jack's mind swirled with the implications, Emma's firm grip squeezing his hand in reassurance.

"We've got no leads," Allen conceded. "It's the wild, so no witnesses or surveillance. It's hard to say. It's possible he fell, and his memory's affected, akin to trauma-induced amnesia."

Jack's face looked sullen from stress over the events: the violence, the breach of his apartment, all interwoven with their pursuit. Emma's eyes met his, her stare of concern piercing his heart.

"Please keep us informed," Jack asked.

Allen shifted gears, "Before meeting at the Bar and cave, where were you?"

Emma's voice rose, "You think we're involved?"

"I must explore all angles, build a timeline, including Ben's last known interactions."

Jack, aiming to soothe Emma, shared their activities, "We parted ways with Ben after searching for a cave near Sang Run and the Yough. We saw the pickup truck but have not seen Ben after he left to visit his dad."

"Afterwards?" Allen probed.

Jack detailed their day, from the cave to the encounter with the bear, the discovery of the cave, and the damaged tires, concluding with their evening at the Honi.

Allen pondered, "Ben might not recall the exact moment of the attack." His gaze fixed on them. "Did you see him today?"

"No, we spent our day boating with Steve and Sally. I've got receipts," Jack said, reaching for his wallet.

"That's fine," Allen waved off the offer. "I'm checking if you might've seen him, trying to pinpoint the timeline of his injury."

Jack, hoping to quell the lingering doubts of their involvement, presented the crumpled receipts with a steady hand.

The Lieutenant scrutinized the evidence, his nod conveying a cautious acknowledgment. "This helps," he conceded, returning them to Jack. "However, our investigation must be thorough. You understand?"

"We do," Jack replied, his pulse racing. The possibility of being implicated in Ben's assault layered additional tension onto an already fraught situation. He caught Emma's eye, her expression awash with concern, and pondered her thoughts.

Allen, rifling through his documents, produced a set of photographs. "They captured these on last night's security footage," he said, handing the images to Jack.

Jack's fingers brushed against the photos, and a chill of realization came over him. The first showed their vehicle; the second, a shadowed person in a hoodie, sabotaging their tires and skulking in the darkness towards the cave. Emma leaned closer, her shock evident as she scrutinized the images.

"Ben?" she murmured, disbelief threading her whisper. "Why would he?"

Jack's mind raced, piecing together inconsistencies. "If somebody assaulted Ben and left him for dead, how could he have done this?"

"Correct," Allen said with a grave nod. "Steve reviewed the surveillance video yesterday. He's certain the figure isn't Ben. He said he determined that based on their size and movements."

"Steve would be able to tell the difference," Jack said. "So, if it's not Ben, who is it?"

"That's what we're trying to determine," Allen replied. "Someone may have donned a hoodie to mislead you, should you review the footage."

Emma's shoulders and head ebbed. Jack met her gaze, offering silent reassurance amidst the storm of unsettling revelations.

Allen's demeanor softened. "You're not suspects in Ben's attack. Given the possible connection to your activities, we ask you to remain in town during our investigation. Your insights might help us identify the assailant."

"We'll cooperate," Jack affirmed, his resolve unshaken. This development would not derail their quest and their safety.

Emma's lip trembled as she absorbed the revelation. Jack met her wide-eyed gaze, his steady stare an attempt to anchor her spiraling thoughts. Beneath his calm exterior, the stark truth loomed between them: someone was stalking them.

"Appreciate your understanding," Allen concluded, noting their agreement. "We'll keep you informed. Remember, please be cautious."

After Allen and Barnes left, Jack shut the door, his hand lingering on the knob. A shiver of fear, old yet vivid as his days under Iraq's scorching sun, crawled up his spine — the terror of a relentless pursuer shadowing him once again. Despite the shadowy presence of their unknown adversary, one thing was transparent to Jack: their path ahead required cautious steps.

"Emma," he whispered, facing her with an intensity matching the gravity of their situation. "We're going to make it through this. Together, we'll unravel this mystery."

She met his gaze, her eyes a tumultuous sea of dread. "I know," she said, her voice quivering. "We have to identify who is orchestrating this mess… who we are up against." In the face of adversity, their unity was their fortress.

With a watchful eye on Emma, Jack grabbed the phone to call Steve. After a long ring, he received Steve's voicemail message and hung up.

"Damnit, he didn't answer."

"Should we drive over there?"

"Maybe." After taking a deep breath, he tried again, successful this time.

"Steve," Jack said, urgency lacing his tone, "someone's broken into our place. The cops are clueless, but they think it might be linked to Ben being attacked at Swallow Falls yesterday."

"Damn," came Steve's concerned response. "I'm on my way."

Emma cut in, worry etching her features. "No. Stay with Sally, keep her safe."

"You sure about this, Emma?"

"It's for the best."

After a brief hesitation, Steve consented. "Alright. Keep me in the loop."

"We will," Jack said before ending the call.

Gazing at their violated home, Jack exhaled. "Time to start cleaning up, I guess."

"Yep," Emma concurred with a heavy sigh, and they set to work, piecing back their disrupted lives.

Returning disorder to order, a sense of violation gnawed at him.

"Who would do this?" Emma's voice was fragile as she attempted to piece together a shattered vase.

"I wish I knew," Jack confessed, his frustration growing. *Who is it? They are relentless in pursuing us, from the cave to the slashing of my tires and now this.*

"It wasn't Ben," Emma reflected, focusing on the fragments. "Not with him injured and in the hospital."

"Who? Why?" Jack pondered aloud, anger simmering within.

Emma's eyes welled up. "I don't know, Jack. It's the violence... it's escalating. Until we find the treasure, I don't think we're safe anywhere. They might track me to DC and try to use me to obtain information from you. We have to find it quickly."

Seeing her determination, Jack's admiration of her surged. "You're right," he concurred. Their path was fraught with hurdles, but together, they would navigate it.

They were pressing on with the cleanup when Emma said, "Jack, promise me something."

"Anything, Em," he replied, their eyes locking in a silent vow.

"Promise me, no matter what, you'll keep me safe," Emma's voice quivered with fear and resolve. "If I say it's over, it's over. We can surrender the journal and letters. That's it. We're done, we escape, whatever it takes."

Jack's gaze hardened with determination. "I promise, Emma. Like you saw with the bear, I'd die for you. However, you're right. Our safety is compromised until the treasure is found. You decide our next move."

Emma discarded a vase into a trash bag and stooped to gingerly collect the torn fragments of their engagement photo from Mount Washington. The damage to the picture during the break-in was not accidental; someone ripped it between them: a clear, menacing message from their intruder.

Jack ceased tidying, watching Emma collapse under the stress, a surge of guilt washing over him.

"Emma," he started, approaching her with caution.

"No!" she protested, the pieces of their shared past in each hand, tears welling in her eyes. "This is my fault. I involved you and Steve, hoping it would end your fixation with the treasure. I missed us and thought this might help you... us move forward. Instead, it's all fallen apart. Your apartment's violated, our friends endangered, and for what?"

Emma's sudden vulnerability and confession left Jack reeling, understanding the depth of her despair. "I'm sorry, too, Emma, but we cannot go back now," he said.

"I'm aware," she sobbed, the gravity of their situation dawning on her. "We're in too deep, paying a price I never envisioned!"

Maintaining his vow, Jack said, "Perhaps we should lay low and find a hotel till things settle. DC, Oakland, Pittsburgh, anywhere..."

"Jack?" She said with scorn, "Do you believe escaping will fix this?"

With a tender touch, he said to her, "My priority is your safety. If that means stopping our search, so be it."

Emma, lifting her gaze to meet his, sighed. "No, I feel safest with you, despite the chaos."

"Are you sure?" Jack wanted to be confident he understood her resolve.

"Yes," she affirmed. "But Jack, something else is troubling me."

"What is it?" Jack implored, prepared to face whatever haunted her further.

Her stare bore into him. Each wrinkle conveyed the level of her anguish. "Remember when we first met? Two college kids dreaming of the future?" Her voice faltered.

"I do. The moment I saw you in class, I knew I had to sit down next to you," he whispered back, the memory bittersweet as thoughts of Braddock's gold and its curse on their lives surfaced.

"We enjoyed our years and planned a life together. The problem is that when your hunt for the treasure intensified, it consumed you. I felt sidelined, your passion for the quest surpassing everything else, including me and your own family," she said, tears marking her cheeks.

Jack's heart sank, Emma's agony now clear. "Emma," he murmured, reaching out, "the search took over, and I lost sight of us. I thought I was doing it for our future."

"By distancing yourself?" Her pain echoed in his soul.

He exhaled, burdened. "I believed the gold would set us up for a better life."

"Jack," she whispered, wiping away a tear, "true treasures aren't buried or hidden. They're with us… in our shared journey. We could have sought it together, but not at the cost of ignoring everything and everyone else."

Her words illuminated his folly, the realization striking deep. He had been blinded but now realized she was the treasure before him.

"Emma, I'm very sorry."

"Jack," her touch was tender, "I don't crave riches, just a life with you."

"I'll leave the hunt behind. Tell me what to do."

"No, we'll seek it out, not for wealth, but to end this. We need to find it to prove it can't be found to stop those chasing us. My biggest fear is if this is left unresolved – it will haunt you and, therefore, us forever," Emma said, a glimmer of hope in her eyes. "We must finish this… together."

"We will, side by side," Jack promised, their hands intertwined.

"Promise?" she whispered.

"Promise," he replied and kissed her. Ahead lay uncertainty, but they would confront it as one.

They tidied their space before nightfall, with Emma succumbing to sleep in Jack's embrace. While she drifted off, Jack was wide awake, contemplating their journey before them, comforted by her rhythmic breathing.

Unbeknownst to him, the dawn would usher in a day to forever alter their course.

Chapter 25

In the quiet of the morning, Jack's phone buzzed insistently, slicing through his dream. He blinked awake, the sunlight's invasion harsh against his eyes.

Emma, undisturbed and serene with her head atop his chest, never shifted as he silenced the alarm. His whispered greeting and a gentle stroke through her hair coaxed her to stir, her smile meeting his as their day started with a shared, soft kiss.

"We should go," she murmured back, still heavy with sleep. "Bill's expecting us."

They disentangled from the cocoon of their bedding, and Jack spotted a message on his phone; his expression changed to amusement. "How about this?" he said, sharing Steve's late-night escapade through a text. "3:20 in the morning. 'Had a late night. Go to breakfast without me. I'll fill you in later.' That's classic Steve."

Emma's amused smile softened her eye roll. "Spare me the gritty details. Steve's adventures aren't my cup of tea."

Chuckling, Jack shrugged off the implications. "Be thankful Steve keeps the worst of it to himself, believe it or not. Anyway, Sally's starting to grow on me. She's got a good head on her shoulders."

Emma, sliding into her attire, said with a laugh. "A good head, but questionable taste in men."

Dressed and ready, they ventured out, the anticipation of Bill's potential

222

historical knowledge fueling their steps. They arrived at Canoe on the Run, greeted by the comforting blend of pancakes, bacon, and coffee wafting through the air.

"Can't beat the smell," Emma said, her hunger evident.

"It's a perfect reason to wake up early," Jack concurred, his hand finding its place on her back as they stepped inside.

The café offered a modern yet warm welcome, the buzz of conversation and the occasional clink of cutlery painting a picture of communal warmth.

Their eyes searched until landing on an elderly man near the window, his white hair and poised demeanor setting him apart. Despite a hint of age in his posture, his eyes sparkled with undimmed curiosity.

"Bill?" Emma ventured, their approach tentative but intrigued.

"Ah, Emma, Jack!" Bill said in greeting, his voice lively as he stood to greet them. "I've been looking forward to meeting you both. And you, Emma, you must be something special to be where you're at the Smithsonian at such a young age."

"Thank you. I've been looking forward to this since our first conversation," Emma said, radiating warmth as she sat across from the elderly man experiencing an immediate connection. "We're interested in learning about your life here."

"Sit down, sit down," Bill motioned to the chairs before him. "Oh, where do I start?"

Enjoying a breakfast of fluffy pancakes and crisp bacon, Bill wove stories from his days as a soldier, farmer, and county official, leaving Jack and Emma captivated by his diverse experiences.

Leaning in, Emma asked, "Bill, what's your secret to staying so vigorous at your age?"

"A mix of genetics and keeping busy, I guess," Bill said with a light-hearted chuckle. "Retired from farming at 83, but this place keeps you on your feet."

"83? That's remarkable," Jack said, his respect evident.

"Other than mild cataracts, which are a nuisance, I've been lucky," Bill said. "I limit my driving to clear days. I'll have surgery soon, but overall, I've been blessed."

Their conversation drifted to more personal stories as they sipped coffee, each anecdote drawing them further into Bill's world.

"Could you share more about your family? You mentioned a long history here," Emma asked, eager for more.

"I'd love to. I live in Swanton but grew up in McHenry near Accident. It all starts with my beloved wife, Sara," Bill said, his tone softening. "She died from cancer 14 years ago. Love and adventure filled our years together."

Emma felt a pang of empathy, reaching out to touch Bill's hand. "I'm sorry for your loss. How did you meet?"

"Thank you, dear. We met back in school," Bill said with a tender smile. "We were inseparable, apart only when I fought in the Korean War. We married before I deployed and raised our sons here upon my return."

"Thank you for your service, and what a beautiful story," Jack said, sharing eye contact with Emma.

"It was a wonderful life," Bill said, his eyes glimmering with unshed tears. "Sara was everything to me. Losing her was tough, but staying active and concentrating on our family, farm, the museum, and the community helped me cope."

Emma said, "Bill, Jack's also a veteran. He served in the Navy and saw tours in Iraq."

"Is that so? My thanks to you as well," Bill said, acknowledging Jack's service.

"You mentioned your farm..." Jack steered the conversation, eager to learn more about Bill's life.

"After I came back, Sara and I took on the farm," Bill said with a trace of pleasure. "It was hard work, but we found joy in it. Even though our sons chose different paths, I've kept it going and now lease it to an agricultural company."

Emma probed about the effects of leasing his land and life in Garrett County. Bill's chest swelled with delight as he spoke of his boys in

Pittsburgh, recounting the visits and skiing with his grandkids into his late eighties.

Jack and Emma shared a glance, unspoken admiration of the resilience embodied in the man before them, as the backdrop of laughter and the soft chime of utensils filled the air around them.

"You've led quite the life, Bill. Your family must hold immense pride," Emma said, her tone of reverence.

Bill's response was humble and with gratitude. "It's been a ride full of highs and lows. But my family, they're my true fortune."

Observing the warmth Bill exuded, Jack yearned for the depth of love and familial connection he described.

Shifting the conversation, Jack touched on Bill's volunteer work. "You mentioned working at the museum. How'd that come about?"

Bill relaxed, a spark in his eyes. "I needed something to fill my days, with the family around periodically. With its history, the museum was the perfect spot for an enthusiast like me."

Emma leaned in, curiosity piqued. "What's your role?"

His smile widened. "I manage exhibits, field visitor inquiries, and sometimes lead tours. It's a way to immerse myself in the past and share it with others. You'll find me helping out, weather permitting."

Jack, intrigued, linked this back to their investigation. "So you were at the museum when the contractor found the barrel?"

"Yes," Bill said, his intrigue about the discovery evident. "I was there when the call came in. Couldn't help being involved with such a find."

"It was," Emma chimed in. "Inside were relics: a British uniform, coins, a journal, and a map. All quite intriguing."

Bill's eyes danced, "You're not fooling an old-timer like me," he said; his laughter caught them off guard. "I don't know exactly what was in the barrel, but I'm sure it's tied to Braddock's treasure. It was found so far south from where his army marched; there's no other reason for it to be here."

Jack and Emma shared a glance, their quiet acknowledgment enough for Bill, who reclined with an air of vindication.

"Aha, I knew it," he smirked. "You're decent folks. Should the gold be found, I'm glad if it's by you. However, remember, the real riches might not be in the gold but in the bonds we forge and the moments we cherish."

"Thanks, Bill," Jack said, his gaze drifting to Emma, their journey together gaining depth. Emma's hand grasped his, their relationship underscoring Bill's wisdom.

Emma, curiosity brightening her features, leaned forward. "What's the story behind Braddock's Gold and its connection here?"

He settled in, his voice dropping to a hush, inviting them closer. "General Edward Braddock, a British officer in the French and Indian War, carried a fortune to cover his campaign costs. Still, fate had other plans."

Bill unfolded Braddock's ill-fated expedition from Alexandria, through an ambush, to his untimely demise, the corners of Jack and Emma's the corner of their mouths raised. Emma's grip on Jack's hand stilled his restless tapping.

"The treasure vanished," Bill concluded. "Some say his men hid it; others believe the General himself did. For years, it's been sought after."

He regarded them with a reflective gaze. "I've known these tales all my life. I looked myself for a bit. Seeing you two reminds me of my younger days, full of hope and seeking adventure."

"Has anyone ever come close to finding it?" Jack asked.

He raised an eyebrow. "Many have tried, but none so far. The legend persists – because it's believed it's still hidden, waiting."

"So, you believe it still exists?"

"You know what? I do," Bill acknowledged, his eyes bright with intrigue. "Folks have been combing through these parts since the French & Indian Ware ended. Had the treasure been found, the word would've spread fast. But I reckon it lay hidden, given the barrel, further south from where any eyes were searching."

Emma's response was a gentle nod, a warmth unfurling within her at the thought of their shared quest with Bill, linking them to his past and the memories of his late wife.

Bill's tone dipped into a solemn whisper, drawing them closer. "Think about Braddock's final resting place? A well-kept secret – over 50 years, he was untouched. Mark my words: should you stumble upon that 'X marks the spot,' be careful around the 'X.' Look at how they buried the barrel. They wanted to make sure it would not be easy to steal their gold."

As the shadows fell, Bill's demeanor lightened. "Enough about Braddock's folly. So, what's got you so curious to bring you here today?"

Jack leaned in, curiosity piqued. "The transformation of this area – how has it shifted with the lake's creation, the developments?"

"Ah, now that's a tale," Bill said, his voice taking on the texture of the stories he wove. "Deep Creek Lake's origins? It wasn't always this vast expanse. Back in the day, it was a long, deep, winding creek. From past Glendale Bridge to a natural dam, somewhere beyond the 219 bridge toward today's hydro dam."

Jack's interest sharpened. "Is that so?"

"Yes," Bill said. "The '20s brought the Pennsylvania Electric Company. Their dam created this lake, along with jobs, tourists, and growth."

Emma glanced around, her eyes reflecting a newfound respect for their surroundings. "It's amazing, the layers of history surrounding us."

"Indeed," Bill said, a nostalgic glimmer passing through his gaze. "The land's face changed, but the essence? It stays hidden beneath the surface."

Their breakfast concluded with a renewed hunger for the adventure ahead, spurred by Bill's insights and tales.

Jack, curiosity never waned, ventured, "Bill, the impact of the lake on the landscape – can you share more?"

Bill's reflection was thoughtful. "The transformation was significant," he said. "They elevated the main road, constructed big bridges, and moved the old Walton house at the top of McHenry Cove so it would have a new lease on life. They needed to relocate it to save it from the rising waters."

"And there are pieces of history which will always stay with me," Bill said. "One was the natural water slide, once a beacon drawing the youth to it in what's now Cherry Creek Cove."

"Sound's incredible?" Emma leaned in, her interest piqued, her eyes alight with the thrill of discovery.

"The old Deep Creek was a bit like Swallow Falls is today," Bill reminisced, a twinkle of fondness in his gaze. "My parents had favorite spots for dates – Cherry Creek was a long natural water slide. My parents also visit a waterfall with perfect swimming holes. One was deep and calm. The other, beside the falls, has a deep pool at a cliff's base. They'd jump in, swim around, and... well," he said with a wink, drawing a laugh from Jack and a shy smile from Emma.

"Sounds like a place out of a fairy tale," she said in wonder.

"It was special," Bill nodded. "Such places were the community's soul, a spot for celebration or basking in nature's splendor. They've faded into history, though the lake and State Park now fill that role."

"Did they ever mention where their swimming hole was?" she asked.

"No, it's lost to me now, a fragment of memory from my parent's tales." He paused and head tilted, "I thought of something. You know, anglers use lake maps to find fishing spots. Such a map might hold clues for you," Bill said.

Their conversation deepened Jack's sense of belonging to the community and its past.

The blaring of "Crazy Train" from Jack's phone interrupted their chat. A stark message read: "911 Sally's place."

"What's wrong?" Emma asked, reading the distress in Jack's quick change.

"Trouble at Sally's," Jack said, urgency sharpening his words. "Steve needs us." He passed her his phone.

"Could this be one of his jokes?" Emma's worry creased her forehead.

"Steve would never joke about 911," Jack said while standing up.

Concern clouded Bill's face. "Sally?"

"Sally Adkins," she clarified.

Bill's worry deepened, his eyes glossing. "Oh, dear. She's a gem, always caring for the museum and everyone."

"We're fond of her too, Bill. Steve would've said if someone was hurt," she tried to reassure him.

"Sorry, we have to leave," Jack cut in.

"Of course, of course," Bill replied, his voice laden with worry. "Do let me know how it goes."

"We will, Bill. We'll visit again," she promised with a smile.

"Thank you, my dear. I'd love it if you would."

They left, and the concern for their friend hastened their steps into the danger awaiting them.

Chapter 26

It was the evening before at Mountain State Brewery, and Steve and Sally said goodbye to Jack and Emma. Steve clapped Jack on the back, and Sally hugged Emma before parting ways.

"Let's catch up tomorrow for breakfast. Text us the plan," Steve said as he turned his attention to Sally, taking her hand and walking to her car. After assisting her into the passenger seat, the engine purred to life, and Steve buckled himself into the driver's seat. The car pulled away from the brewery, gliding smoothly onto the winding mountain road that led to Sally's apartment.

The journey to Sally's apartment was a scenic one, with the bright moon casting a silvery glow over the darkened trees lining the winding mountain road. Sally gave directions and described landmarks as they navigated the twists and turns.

They arrived at Sally's quaint brick home nestled among tall pines. Steve parked the car and walked around to open the door for her. Sally stepped out gracefully, her long legs carrying her up the steps to her front door with a fluid grace that caught Steve's eye.

Once inside, Sally led Steve through a tastefully decorated living room adorned with antique furniture and a large bookshelf. The air was perfumed with the scent of sandalwood and jasmine, creating an ambiance of mystery and allure. Sally stepped out of the room and quickly returned with two glasses of deep amber liquor. They settled on a plush sofa, sinking into its soft cushions as they engaged in light banter, their laughter mingling in the quiet space. The tension between them crackled like electricity, an unspoken desire hanging heavy in the air.

After some time, as the conversation turned intimate, Steve leaned in closer to Sally, his eyes dark with longing. She met his gaze with equal intensity, her lips parting in anticipation as his hand brushed against her cheek, his touch gentle yet charged with a hunger that mirrored her own.

Then, Steve's phone blared the "Raiders March," the Indiana Jones theme, and was a jarring interruption to the charged atmosphere that had enveloped them. *What the hell does Jack want already?* Ignoring it, he continued to lean in towards Sally, his focus solely on her captivating presence. It continued, and he finally relented, pulling away.

"Sorry," he mumbled, his voice tinged with regret as he reached into his pocket to retrieve it. Sally's eyes flickered with a hint of annoyance at the interruption, but softened as she observed Steve's genuine remorse. With a quick press, he silenced it and placed the phone on the coffee table, and his desire for Sally took over.

Just as their lips met again, Indiana's theme played again. Sally let out a playful chuckle at the interruption, her eyes twinkling mischievously. "Looks like someone's more eager to get at you than me," she teased, a sly smile on her lips.

"Yeah... Jack."

"You better answer it, or we won't have any fun tonight."

With an apologetic grimace, Steve reluctantly grabbed his buzzing phone as Sally stood and walked quickly to refill her glass and return.

Steve learned from Jack about the break-in at his apartment and of Ben's attack. After Steve offered to rush to Jack's place, he listened to Emma's recommendation to stay with Sally and keep her safe instead. After a brief hesitation, Steve consented. "Alright. Keep me in the loop."

Turning to Sally, who was quivering, Steve witnessed the fear in her eyes. She asked, "Do you think we're in danger?"

"Not with me here, but I should look around and lock up your house. Better safe than sorry," Steve reasoned, his gaze sweeping the room.

With a slide of his finger, the room darkened as he dimmed the lights and moved to secure the windows and doors, Sally's hand trembling in his.

"Looks okay, but we should be careful," he said to her after a tense moment, his voice a low murmur.

"Thank you," Sally whispered back, thick with emotion. "But why would someone break into Jack's place? What's happening?"

"It's the treasure hunt," Steve said, fixing his eyes on the shadowy street. "Appears like it's put us all in danger."

"Because of the treasure hunt?" Sally's fear mingled with curiosity.

"That's the gist," he kept it vague, unwilling to share too much. "And the break-in might be linked to Ben's attack."

Sally clung tighter to him, shaking, "I'm scared, Steve. I don't want to be left alone while you chase this… treasure."

"Hey," he muttered, drawing her in. "Nothing's going to happen to you." Her trembling body pressed against him, spoke volumes of her unease, a silent cry for reassurance far beyond mere words.

"Can I come with you?" Sally's voice quivered with urgency. "I don't think I'm safe on my own. I'd rather be with you."

He paused, the dilemma heavy upon him. To bring Sally meant exposing her to further danger, yet leaving her isolated was like marking her as a target. With a deep exhale and a decision made, he said, "I'll discuss it with Jack. But regardless, I'll stick by you until this all ends, even at the cost of joining Jack's search."

"I really appreciate that," she said, finding solace in his embrace. "That means everything to me."

"Always, you're important to me."

A brief kiss, a promise in their touch, and she retreated to her room. Steve wrestled with fears for her safety and the uncertain path of their adventure.

Moments later, Sally reappeared, her attire bold and inviting and left little to the imagination, her presence igniting an undeniable tension. She teased with a glass of bourbon, its contents vanishing in a single tilt before reaching behind the doorway again.

She presented two new glasses, along with a bottle of Elijah Craig Barrel Proof bourbon; at first, its label went unnoticed by Steve. Approaching with a playful daring in her eyes, she proposed, "Let's toast to us," breaking the seal and was generous with the pour.

She tilted backward and attempted to pick up the glasses, almost falling off him. Sally slung her arms around his neck as he leaned forward to reach for and grab the glasses. He handed her a glass, her enthusiasm unabated as she drank in one gulp. Steve, feigning participation, pressed the glass to his lips without indulging.

"Relax a bit," she urged.

"Of course," he replied, simulating another drink, mindful of the need for clarity amid looming threats.

Sally's insistence grew, her shoulders slumped in disappointment as she sought to deepen their connection. "What's the matter? Can't we enjoy ourselves?"

"It's just... I'm worried about the danger around us and your safety," he confessed.

"Steve," Sally whispered, her touch gentle against his face. "You promised to keep me safe, and I believe in you. Right now, I want to be close to you."

Sally guided the glass to Steve's lips, and he feigned a deep gulp as he took hold of it before setting it down behind her while leaning forward. As they straightened, she began to unbuckle his belt, retreating to lower his pants before resuming her position atop him.

With a fervent kiss, his hands explored her. As Sally pulled back, locking eyes with him, he slid his fingers under the straps of her lingerie and glided them off her shoulders, baring her to him.

The intensity between them peaked; their lips met with renewed urgency. However, their passionate exchange halted when Sally's head listed and jerked to the side for a split second, her body tensing for a moment. Sensing a change, Steve gazed into the confusion clouding her eyes, a sign she wasn't in control.

With a gentle ease, he lifted her, her faint, slurred pleas for him to carry her to bed and ravish her echoing. Despite his desires, his conscience held firm against taking advantage of her compromised state. He glided her onto the bed, watching as she succumbed to sleep under the blanket's comfort without hesitation.

After ensuring Sally was asleep, Steve's conflicting thoughts consumed him. He dressed in silence, pondering her intentions and his own skepticism, a remnant of his survival instincts from past conflicts.

Was she seeking protection, or was this an intricate seduction? Steve pondered these concerns, trying to discern if she was manipulating him or if his doubts overshadowed reality.

"Stay focused," he muttered, dismissing the suspicion seeded by Jack's warnings. Protecting her was his immediate concern, not unraveling her motives.

Steve flicked off the lights and surveyed the night from each window, his protective vigil unyielding. His heartbeat quickened at the sight of a pickup down the street, its occupant a silhouette in the moonlight, a potential threat lurking outside Sally's home.

"Damn," he said, a chill tracing his spine as the familiar truck came into view. With a quickening pulse, he retrieved his phone, ready to alert someone.

"Lieutenant Allen," he said, urgency lacing his words. "The pickup from before, I think it's outside Sally's place."

"Address, Steve. Which way's it facing?" The Lieutenant's tone was steady, laced with concern.

"125 Accident Bittinger Road, towards 219," his gaze locked on the ominous vehicle, sweat beading at his temple, enveloped by a tangible sense of threat.

"Stay put, keep an eye on it. We're on our way," Allen said as the line went dead.

Steve, glued to the window, peered out as the driver, obscured till now, tilted forward and shifted, the truck's exhaust puffed, and it crawled closer to the house, its lights off. Steve's breath hitched, the driver's head turned, and the shadow focused on Sally's home.

"Shit," he muttered, darting outside as the pickup sped off, its lights flickering to life too late for him to catch the license plate – it disappeared into the darkness.

Refusing to let it end with that outcome, he dialed Allen again. "It left, heading towards 219 after casing the house."

"We're almost to you," came Allen's reply.

Steve's eyes moved up and down the street when they fell upon the flash of the police car as it raced past the house in the direction of the pickup. In a few minutes, Lieutenant Allen and Barnes pulled up, their faces set in grim lines. They huddled with Steve, absorbing his account.

"Sorry, we could not find the truck. The driver might've bolted seeing you," Allen pondered. "We'll stick around for a bit, ensure they don't circle back."

"Thanks," he exhaled, a wave of temporary relief hitting him, yet the unsettling sensation lingered. *Who was driving? And how did they find Sally's place?*

"Keep your phone handy," Barnes said as they prepared to leave. "We're close by."

"Got it," he said, haunted by unanswered questions. He peered into the room where Sally slept, unaware of the night's events.

"Stay sharp," he whispered. The risk was too real, and he had too much to lose with her. Resolute, he stationed himself back at the window, hoping for a quiet remainder of the night.

Needing a momentary escape from his anxiety, he eyed the bourbon. It was not his usual choice, but necessary. He poured a shot, the liquid's warmth spreading through him as he drank, a brief respite from the night's tension.

"Get a grip, Steve," he muttered, pacing the confines of Sally's living room. Each step offered a glimpse into her world: comfortable furnishings, vibrant artwork, and shelves filled with books organized and aligned with precision.

She's quite the reader, eyeing the titles. A stack on the bottom shelf focused on colonial and Revolutionary War histories caught his eye – *She is a teacher*, he concluded and moved on.

He messaged Jack: 'Had a late night. Go to breakfast without me. I'll fill you in later.' *Best not to drag them into this night's chaos.*

A sense of unease crept over Steve, every sound suggesting unseen eyes on them. He realized they weren't safe at Sally's, his paranoia deepening as the night edged closer to dawn.

Despite his resolve, fatigue overcame his vigilance, images of Sally mingling with unresolved mysteries as he surrendered to sleep.

Awakening to Sally's gentle kiss, Steve blinked away the slumber. "Waking up to you... I could get used to it."

Sally, cheeks tinted with color, whispered, "I'd like that too. But why did you sleep here?"

"Didn't want to wake you," he answered, his voice heavy with fatigue.

"Something happened?" her eyes squinted.

Relaying the night's tense moments, he looked at her as she shook and her eyes widened. "Someone was in a pickup outside your house. No one will hurt you while I'm with you. That's a promise."

She took a deep breath. "Thank you. You made me feel better. Will you stay for breakfast?" Her voice carried a hopeful vulnerability.

"I'd like to," he said, as a twinge of guilt struck him for omitting to convey his original plans. "Jack and Emma are meeting Bill O'Connell. I figured we'd join them later."

Relieved, "Oh, that's nice. I love Bill." She offered a comforting embrace before urging him to sleep more. "You're my hero. Rest now. I'll make you breakfast later."

He quickly nodded off.

A piercing scream sent chills down Steve's spine and yanked him awake.

Chapter 27

Adrenaline surged as Steve sprang up, propelled by Sally's shriek from the kitchen. His heart raced hearing Sally's frantic "Go away!" as she brandished a skillet like a shield against an unseen threat outside, with only the glass of the storm door between her and her terror. He rounded the corner and burst out of the kitchen door onto the porch, where he raced to confront a bearded stranger wearing a ball cap approaching the curb of her home.

"Hey!" Steve's roar sent the man, eyes enlarged with fear, sprinting towards a familiar pickup.

"Stop!" Steve's pursuit was futile; the truck roared away, leaving frustration simmering in his wake. Shaking, he fumbled with his phone to alert Lieutenant Allen.

* * *

Gray clouds brooded as Jack and Emma arrived at Sally's, greeted by the unsettling sight of police cars and curious neighbors. Exchanging worried glances, they questioned the safety of their involvement. Jack's lips pierced: *Did I put our lives at risk?*

With a deep breath and stiffened back, he asked with determination and worry, "Are you ready for this?"

"As ready as I'll ever be," Emma said, masking her concern.

Greeted by Sally's shaking figure, they stepped inside and gazed at the two officers inside, the air thick with tension.

"What happened?" Jack asked.

Officers Martinez and Shultz introduced themselves and shared the peculiar situation: they had just arrived after the state police dispatch center received a call. The caller claimed he stopped to check on a wounded deer he struck in front of Sally's house and that he was approaching it on the side of the road when a man fitting Steve's description came charging out of the house at him, screaming, which forced the man to flee in fear of being attacked. Given the rarity of crimes in the county and the frequency of auto incidents involving wild animals, the police suspected a misunderstanding and no real threat.

"Call Lieutenant Barnes!" Steve's demand cut through the room, his hand gestures hinting at his anger. The officers suggested a misinterpretation, but Steve insisted the intruder meant harm.

Emma's soothing touch reminded Steve of the need for clear thinking. The heavy air hinted at challenges ahead, underscoring the urgency of unraveling the truth behind the stranger's visit.

"Sally's safety is paramount, particularly since our friend was recently attacked and hospitalized, possibly by this man. I would think you would want to uncover who this person was, his purpose, and his current whereabouts," Emma said, her voice a bastion of calm. "Can we count on your assistance, officers?"

With a shared glance of newfound gravity, the police nodded. Martinez asked, "What transpired, Miss Adkins?"

Pale, shaking, and troubled, Sally found solace in Emma's comforting squeeze of her hand.

"What happened?" Emma prodded with care, setting aside her own anxieties to bolster her friend.

After a moment's pause, Sally softly recounted the man's appearance, the chilling aura he exuded, and the lack of a deer in her yard.

The atmosphere tensed as Sally's words filled the room, signaling a perilous turn in their journey. This was no mere adventure; they were in a struggle for their very lives.

Fraught with concern, Emma whispered to Jack, "Should we halt our search? The danger appears to be too great."

"It's your decision," he said, a fierce resolve in his gaze. "But remember, you said we are not safe till we find it."

With a heavy heart, she resolved, "Okay… we keep going," and refocused on Sally.

After recording their statements, the officers promised further investigation.

"Were you able to identify the person using their Caller ID?" Steve pressed.

"No. Dispatch failed to identify the number as the call dropped," Martinez said.

Jack asked, "Doesn't that sound like a tactic to divert suspicion – a dropped call from probably a blocked number?"

Emma agreed, adding her support.

"We'll look into it," Shultz assured them before departing.

Once the police were out of earshot, Steve, with a grave tone, led Jack to another room and closed the door. "Look, man, we're facing a serious threat. Someone's looking to stop us at any cost," he whispered with ferocity.

"I understand that," Jack said.

"I'm not sure you do. " Steve pressed. "Violent men are in pursuit of the treasure. They broke into your apartment, attacked Ben, and now they're after Sally, thinking she's involved. They probably wanted to extract information out of her, or worse, maybe take her to use her as leverage. This isn't just about the gold anymore."

Jack, acknowledging the severity, asked, "What do we do?"

"Soldiers, that's what we are," he said, his finger punctuating the air between him and Jack. "We have a duty to safeguard others. Either we band together to protect Sally, or I do it solo, leaving your six o'clock exposed. Your call."

Jack's reply was measured and laced with resolve. "Agreed, we do this together. We've got each other's backs. And Sally's protection is on us." He paused, a nod of agreement. "Emma hit the nail on the head."

"How's that?"

"Last night, at my apartment, she said nobody's safe until the treasure is found or proven a myth."

Steve's grin was infectious. "She's the brains, alright."

Jack extended his hand. "Let's do this."

"By your side, always," Steve affirmed, their handshake morphing into an embrace.

Rejoining Emma and Sally, the duo relayed discoveries from their morning breakfast with Bill.

"His insights were huge, but leave us fishing in the dark, literally – we will have to hunt for a needle in a vast, aquatic haystack. When they made the lake, they submerged several waterfalls under it," Jack briefed. "His tip, using a fisherman's map, was brilliant. He figured the depth charts might guide us to the falls."

Steve quipped, "Life is like a box of chocolates, you never know what you're going to get."

"Thank you, Forrest Gump," Emma interjected, her tone laced with concern. "But remember, diving's a risk. Bill's warning... the code word 'caution' in the letter... both are suggesting there's potential danger, maybe even traps."

Sally's concern was fleeting, yet unmistakable, as the conversation shifted to the lake's lurking dangers.

"We'll be cautious," Jack said. "Prepared for anything the lake hides."

"Agreed," Steve's levity gave way to earnestness. "No treasure justifies a life."

"I agree," Sally said, her voice steady despite her earlier reaction. Then Sally asked, "But... to search the lake, are we snorkeling? Or what's the plan?"

Steve's laughter echoed throughout the room. "Jack's banned from snorkeling!" Regaining composure, he pressed, "Getting serious, Jack. Sally's right, what's our plan?

Chapter 28

Jack's glance at his phone led to a dismissive shake of his head, reacting to Steve's ribbing. "We've got a bit of a trek. Frostburg's dive shop is closest; it's 20 to 25 minutes away. Anything else is a haul – West Virginia, or further out towards Pittsburgh or DC."

"Twenty? Not bad," Steve said.

Emma chimed in with logistical details, "Don't forget we need to swing by Jack's for our swim stuff, plus snacks and drinks."

Steve's playful jab at Jack came with a laugh, "Man, she's thinking of your stomach. You better not mess it up this time."

Warm smiles passed between Jack and Emma.

Their journey to Frostburg, Maryland, unfolded under a now bright mid-day sun, illuminating their path through the scenic hills, alive with summer's palette.

The town greeted them with its historic charm, where the past and present merged in the facades of its buildings, each telling its own story.

Jack, guided by his phone, drove them to the dive shop, its presence on the street corner marked by an elaborate mural of a vibrant underwater scene with colorful fish and coral reefs. The sunbeams created mesmerizing patterns on the sandy lakebed below. It invited people to learn how to scuba and explore the ocean's wonders – a stark contrast to the rural setting.

Upon arrival, Steve's gaze drifted to a Subway across the road, suggesting a quick bite with a "Hey guys, how about we 'Eat Fresh'?"

Emma's agreement was immediate, "Sounds perfect," and her enthusiasm mirrored the group's.

Their meal was lively, filled with conversation and plans, as Sally's smile appeared to shed her concerns over recent events.

With appetites sated, Jack rallied the group, "Let's roll," signaling their transition to obtain gear.

Inside, the shop buzzed with the energy of novice divers boarding a converted school bus preparing for an outing, surrounded by a colorful array of wetsuits. Several of the staff wore dive attire, and all offered welcoming smiles while posters and brochures advertised the local and distant dives.

Approached by a staffer, Jack was straightforward, "We're here to rent some scuba equipment." He turned to Emma, a hint of concern, "Joining us?"

Emma's hesitation was evident, "I'm not sure. Sally, what about you? You dive?"

Sally's response, tinged with uncertainty, "I've never tried. Is it something I can learn as we go?"

"No, they cannot rent to you unless you are certified," Steve said.

Emma said, "I'll stay back with Sally. It's been a while since I've dove. I think it was Belize with the three of us. I'd need a refresher."

The clerk interrupted, "Without diving for two years, a refresher's mandatory. Sorry."

"Understood," he said, addressing the clerk, "We like two sets of equipment and a few tanks," presenting his Navy dive card.

"Never seen one of these. Not quite ocean-side here," the clerk quipped.

"First time for everything," Steve joked, showing his own scuba certification. "We're aiming for Deep Creek."

The employee cautioned, "Deep Creek's murky, with limited visibility. Why not try our local quarry? We have sunken treasure to find."

Jack said, "We're familiar with quarries. But with my friend visiting, we're set on the lake. As Naval folks, we're drawn more to open water. I've free-dived parts of it. The clarity improves beyond 20 feet."

"Yeah, but it gets colder. You may want to join us this weekend when we head to Mount Storm Lake. It's clear, rock bottom, and more comfortable of a dive as a power plant warms it.

"Maybe, but we want to dive Deep Creek today."

"Okay, we can provide the gear. But with a sizeable group headed to the quarry, we're short on tanks."

"We'll work with what you've got. We can come back for refills, correct?"

"Sure, we're here eight to four."

"Sounds promising," Jack noted, then asked about additional equipment. "Got any lights? Maps for diving?"

"We have a few rechargeable flashlights left," the clerk said, placing them on the counter. "No detailed dive maps of Deep Creek, just fishing maps showing depths. The dam's a popular spot. You need to check the hydropower's schedule, though. You'll find a deep channel near the state park with huge catfish, some six feet or more."

"You sure about this lake?" Steve joked. "I don't want to become sushi or dinner for a mutant catfish from hell."

Aware of the employee's rush to catch the bus with the others, the group didn't hesitate to gather tanks, wetsuits, BCDs, regulators, masks, fins, and weights. After completing the paperwork and settling the rental fees and deposit, they packed the SUV.

"Four tanks might limit us today."

"If we keep it shallow, only diving 30 to 40 feet, we might get three to four dives in, extending past dinner with the surface intervals," he estimated, glancing at his wristwatch. "We'll grab extra tanks tomorrow morning when we refill."

"Right, we should arrive early for the opening," they agreed.

Jack suggested Steve drive so he could study the map.

Steve's quick acceptance, "Hell yeah, I'm going supersonic. I'll be there in 30 seconds."

He realized Steve's fast driving would not go over well with Emma and Sally, and he said, "Negative, Ghostrider, the pattern is full," before starting to laugh.

"You two are not *Top Gun* pilots. Stevie, we're already facing enough unknown dangers. We don't need a known danger behind the wheel," Emma chuckled, but it was also the sound of reason.

The SUV's rhythm synced with the breeze as they merged onto the interstate. Jack, silent and thoughtful, pored over the map and made a shaking gesture with his thumb against his pointer and middle fingers. Understanding Jack's signal, Emma snatched a pen from her bag, and he started targeting the most strategic spots around Deep Creek Lake, including Marsh Run Cove by Gravely Run, Cherry Creek Cove, and Carmel Cove by the State Park. Shifting the map, he eyed further to the south, highlighting North Glade Cove near Beckman's Peninsula and the southernmost inlet of Deep Creek near Pawn Run, where they found the cave. Following the original Deep Creek channel, he circled Route 219 Bridge by Shingle Camp Hollow and Red Run Cove. His meticulous planning extended to the lake's broader areas, indicating additional potential dive sites with question marks, with several of them close to the dam.

Leaving the interstate for Route 495, the Suburban followed the winding road, surrounded by frozen waves of hills. Farms and forests stretched out on either side, making for a picturesque drive. After turning onto Rock Lodge and Mosser Roads, a sentinel rose from the earth in the distance – Marsh Hill and the Wisp Resort – towering over the shimmering lake.

"Steve, let's head to Bill's Marina for the boat," Jack directed.

"Maybe we can rent the same pontoon. The ladies might enjoy the lake while we dive," Steve replied.

"Sounds good to me. I liked that boat. It was fun," Sally said.

As they loaded their equipment onto the watercraft, Jack's attention shifted to his ringing phone, placing a temporary pause on the day's preparation.

"Jack, Lieutenant Allen. We have two developments."

Chapter 29

Jack asked, "What's going on, Lieutenant?"

"I've spoken with our team. We have two developments that are somewhat related. First, they've located a suspect vehicle based on the intel Steve provided. A local farmer stumbled upon an abandoned pickup while walking his dog. It's already in our custody, and we've filed for a search warrant."

"Who does the truck belong to?"

"It's registered to Henry Ritter, a known treasure seeker who also owns a nursing home. However, Steve's description of the man by the side of the road does not match that of Henry Ritter, so we are trying to determine if it's a stolen truck or if there is a relationship between the men. Someone may be following you to learn what you know."

"That's concerning. But what's the other development?"

"That's a bit more intricate. We tested a bullet fired by the gun you found in the cave; the markings on the casing matched a bullet from an unresolved murder case dating back to the early 2000s. The prime suspect was Thomas Ritter, Henry's father. Although he owned several guns, all registered, including his handgun, none of his firearms were a match."

"Do you have photos of them?"

"I'll send Henry's. Thomas's might take some time as we weren't digital back then. He also left town after the trial, given the area's suspicion of him. But from what I've been told, Thomas's photo from back then does not match Steve's description of the man on the road."

"So, we do not know who he is yet?"

"No, we don't. We're working on that. Oh, and Jack?"

"Yeah?"

"Just a reminder to be cautious."

"We will. Did you show the pictures to Ben?"

"Not yet, but it's on my list. I'll update you."

Ending the call, Jack lingered at the dock's edge, lost in thought. *Who are these guys? How far will they go? What have I gotten us into?*

Emma wrapped her arms around him. "You can do this, Jack. I know you and Steve can keep us safe and find this treasure. You can bring this to a conclusion."

Taking a breath, he nodded, passing the phone with Henry's photo to each.

With the map in hand, they boarded their boat, drawing Steve into their planning. He outlined their search area, highlighting potential spots in Deep Creek Lake, his finger tracing the lines that held their fate.

"North Glade Cove, near Beckman's Peninsula, could be a spot. It's more east than south of the marker but has significant elevation changes and is on the Native American trails," Jack speculated, a cautious optimism in his tone.

"Indeed," Steve concurred, absorbing the map's details. "Let's not overlook the old Deep Creek. There are many drop-offs on the way to the dam, and it follows a path."

"Pawn Run already has a cave. So, there's favorable rock conditions, and it's on Seneca Trail. We've got two tanks apiece. Multiple shallow dives are possible on one tank. Start there?"

Steve replied, "Makes sense to me."

"Let's head out," he said with resolve, folding the map and securing it in his backpack. "Pawn Run merges with Penn Cove between Penn Point and Pergin Farm. South is our best bet."

While they made ready to depart the dock, Emma glanced at Sally, who had been standing in silence on the pier. "Coming with us? We'll keep an eye out for each other."

"Sorry," she managed, her smile a thin veneer over her apprehension. "It's just... a lot."

"Don't worry, Sally," Steve said, offering his hand. "We've got you. You're safe with us."

"Alright, I'm in."

The boat cut across the lake, and Jack shared his thoughts, fueling the group's anticipation. "The treasure's somewhere around one of these spots. It's going to be a process of elimination."

Approaching their first stop near Pawn Run, Jack asked, "Emma, want to take the helm? Steve and I will gear up. Keep an eye on the depth; it'll guide us where we need to go."

In preparation, Steve presented two hefty knives, securing one to Jack's leg. "We might need these."

"That's not a knife," Jack quipped, only to have Steve beaming retort with a larger blade, "No, this is a knife," igniting laughter.

"Okay, Crocodile Dundee," Emma laughed, indulging their moment of levity.

Nearing the marked location, Emma slowed the boat, allowing Jack to peer over her shoulder while Steve grabbed the anchor.

The depth gauge revealed a gradual ascent from forty to thirty-five feet and jumped to fifteen as they entered the cove.

"Here's good," Jack directed. "Drop the anchor." With a practiced motion, Steve tossed it back and to the right before he secured the dive flag, and they readied for their underwater venture.

"Let's finish gearing up, Stevie. Treasure's calling," Jack exclaimed, unable to hide his excitement. Steve handed Emma a small black bag he pulled out of his backpack and said, "For you and Sally's safety. A clip's already in there. I know you know how to use it as you went with us to the range and target shooting. Let's hope it's unnecessary. Can't go without knowing you're safe. And, as you know, it's unsafe for anyone to dive alone, especially Jack."

Emma hesitated, and Jack insisted he could search without Steve, promising not to do anything risky or stupid. Her vision narrowed on

Jack.

Contemplating the firearm, Emma's hands felt the shape of the gun as her torso rocked, eyes still glued on Jack. "No, I'd feel better if Steve's with you. We'll keep an eye out, and I doubt Ritter would find us here or suspect we're armed."

"Here, take this," Jack said, retrieving an oar from beneath a seat. "If you need us, bang it against the pontoon. Sound travels further and faster underwater. We'll hear you and come right away." He demonstrated to Emma and Sally.

"We'll be fine, Jack. Don't worry about us," Emma reassured him, with Sally nodding in agreement.

Jack and Steve moved to the back, where their scuba gear awaited. The duo equipped themselves, their speed and movements reflecting their deep experience. They checked their gear: straps tightened, air tanks confirmed, a brief hiss from the regulators previewing the air they'd soon rely on. The buoyancy compensation devices, called BCDs, were snug, and the weights they needed to help stay submerged were seamlessly part of the design.

Geared up, they carried the weight of their equipment, including the heavy tanks, with practiced balance. The challenge was navigating to the boat's edge with the awkward fins extending two feet past their toes, yet they managed without faltering. Flashlights, detector, and shovel in hand, they prepared for the dive.

"Stay close," Jack said to Steve as they inserted their regulators, adjusted their masks, and flashed "okay" to each other. They were ready to plunge into the lake's depths, their eyes set on discovering the hidden cave.

Submerging with a giant stride into the lake, the cooler embrace of the water surrounded them, but the clarity diminished. They searched for the old creek bed to guide them to the possible waterfall, their vision limited by the stirred sediment, a mere few feet of visibility challenging their progress.

Amid the muffled sounds of his exhaust bubbles passing his ears while rising to the surface was the distant hum and whine of boat engines as they continued along the lakebed's contours. Silt, agitated with their every movement, created a disorienting haze, a silhouetted view of stumps and tangled underwater plants. The roots of submerged trunks reached out like ghostly fingers, and schools of fish appeared as fleeting shadows in the turbid water, adding to the demanding dive. Amidst the particle-filled chaos, they had to rely on instinct and experience. They moved deeper, following the lake floor's gentle slope, but no drop-off or creek to follow.

Steve signaled a disappointing "nothing," his hand forming a zero.

Jack acknowledged with an "okay," unease creeping in as the murky water led them astray. He consulted his compass and signaled to head in another direction. *We'll find it. We're not giving up until we do.*

In minutes, they found the remnants of a stream hidden beneath the lake's surface for almost a century. Tracing its path, they descended over the ghost of a waterfall and pierced a thermal layer that marked a striking shift in temperature. The summer sun's warmth clashed with the boat-stirred waters, and the dramatic temperature difference crafted a veiled barrier where sediment and organic matter hovered above like the separation of Jello layers.

Beyond this veil, clarity greeted them, unveiling the waterfall's face, now illuminated by the sun's rays filtering through the silt-laden waters above. Ancient stumps soared, yearning for the sky amidst a ballet of fish and swaying plant life. This submerged wonderland, vibrant with color and movement, held them in rapt awe, a silent spectacle beneath the placid surface.

Reaching the base of the waterfall, they peered around to see raised ground encircling them, evidence that a pool once cradled the falls. Jack's dive computer read 39 feet. With hopeful hands, Jack activated the detector, yet the search yielded nothing – no cave. Confirming the absence of another waterfall at this depth, letdown, they turned back to the pontoon.

With detector and flashlight in hand, Jack completed a final quick sweep of the area and joined Steve, who hovered above, ready for the ascent. They made their way up, pausing at 15 feet for a three-minute safety stop before breaking the surface.

Burdened by disappointment as they reboarded the boat, the magnitude of their quest sank into Jack: *This is going to be a long process to check all these possible sites.* Shedding his gear down to his wetsuit, he sought solace in a bottle of water and pretzels, contemplating their subsequent move.

"Where to?" Steve asked.

"North Glade Cove," Jack proposed, mapping their course. "It lies east, following a line due south from the marker, near an old Native American Trail. It's our next spot."

He turned to Emma, "Head towards the Glendale bridge. We're aiming for the second large cove on the right."

As he prepared the pontoon for departure, "Stevie, my watch says we have 27 minutes more of surface time."

"Copy that."

Sally's curiosity broke the silence. "Why the time?" she asked.

Jack seized the moment and directed a playful nod to Steve's expertise. "Well, Steve's our Dive Master," he said, glancing at Steve, "You got this? I'll handle the anchor."

Steve responded with a smile, "Got it, Jack. For Sally, anything."

Sliding closer to Sally, Steve's enthusiasm was evident as he said, "It's not about breathing through a hose." His eyes sparkled with a blend of fervor and wisdom. "Diving introduces us to a hidden realm, demanding respect and an understanding of how it impacts our bodies. Safety isn't just a guideline; it's the foundation of experiencing the underwater marvels."

Emma chimed in with encouragement, "If I can do it, so can you."

"I know you can," Steve agreed. "And I'd be happy to teach you. But to answer your question, precaution is critical – the deeper you go and the greater the time you stay submerged, the more nitrogen builds up in your system and the more risk you are at. Some diving essentials are critical, like managing your nitrogen levels to avoid decompression sickness. You may have heard of the bends," his tone was calm and knowledgeable.

"I have."

"That's where the surface interval comes into play." His explanation was serene and informed, detailing how this pause lets divers' bodies rid themselves of excess nitrogen. "Those three minutes at 15 feet might sound brief, but they're vital for our well-being," he stressed.

Locking eyes with Sally, Steve underscored, "These practices – surface intervals and safety stops – are not just routine; they're essential for safe and enjoyable diving."

Now leaning in, intrigued, Sally questioned the scuba opportunities nearby, to which Steve suggested the Caribbean's enticing waters as an ideal start.

"I've never been further than Pittsburgh." Sally's excitement was unmistakable, and she grinned, "That sounds amazing. I'd like to go with you."

Steve snatched the map, sat beside Sally, and asked, "So, what did you and Emma do while we searched? I hope you were not bored."

Sally leaned in, sharing in a hush about a call that Emma received, a potential promotion, and her request for discretion until a decision about their relationship after the treasure hunt was over. She assured him that she enjoyed time and spent it relaxing and dipping into the cool water, far from boredom.

Steve beckoned Sally closer to inspect the map together. After a few minutes, he called out, "See here, by Penelec Point? It's right by your question marks around the dam," he pointed out, tapping the map. "South of your marker, near the trail by the dam to the river. Look at this depth change."

"Excellent find," Jack affirmed, boosting Steve in Sally's eyes. "We'll dive there tomorrow." He recalled a drop-off in that area, unsure if it led to a pool, but thought the creek feeding it might dry up in the summer, revealing their prize. Still, it was worth investigating as they focused on the most probable to least potential sites.

Approaching Beckman's Peninsula, Jack's anticipation mixed with nerves as they neared their destination. "Ease up, Em. Head to the center of this opening and go straight in," he directed, foot tapping with impatience on the deck.

While Steve had the anchor in hand, Jack watched the numbers indicating the depth swing between 40 and 35 feet. Emma navigated into position; the gauge hit 20 feet. "Now!" Jack announced. Emma reversed for a second and killed the engine as Steve secured the anchor and Jack set their flag.

"Let's go," Jack said, switching tanks with Steve.

On the edge of the boat, Jack briefed, "The map shows two points here: one behind us towards the main lake, one ahead. Deep one first, followed by the shallow site."

They dove, the lake swallowing them into its depths, the surface light dimming and the chill deepening. The first layer of water was warm but cloudy, clearing as they descended, and the pressure compelled them to equalize their ears.

The underwater valley came into view, ancient tree stumps dotting the creek bed, with schools of yellow perch darting away from their lights.

Before them, a drop-off loomed, not a sheer cliff but a steep slope, disappointing in its descent. They ventured down, the incline stretching fifteen feet across as Jack scanned with his detector, Steve shoveling at the rocks, both in search of their quarry.

Encircled by earth, they found themselves in what appeared to be a natural basin. They aimed for the logical exit for the water, a spot about thirty feet away and nearly ten feet higher than the bottom. Their efforts there proved fruitless; no additional elevation drops upon the water's egress as the terrain sloped rather than formed any waterfall.

With a gesture, Jack led them to the second potential site. Following the bed of what once was a stream, they reached their destination, only to discover a steep incline devoid of any cavernous shelter. The slope's face, a smooth stone, served as a natural waterslide in times past, now submerged beneath the lake's expanded boundaries.

Jack's relaxed demeanor vanished when they approached their pontoon for a safety stop. His eyes widened at the shadow of another vessel snuggled up to theirs. His heart racing, Jack motioned for a cautious ascent underneath their boat. He would ascend first, assess the situation, and signal Steve with instructions on their best course of action.

Chapter 30

Monday, June 23rd, 1755

The morning sun shimmered upon the dew-covered ground as Captain Thomas Clarke surveyed the wooded landscape. The air was crisp, and the scent of damp earth filled his nostrils. They rode a long way, and now was the time to secure the payroll they carried for their cause.

"Alright, men. We'll split into two teams to find a suitable hiding spot for the payroll."

Clarke stared at Lieutenant Robert Davis, whose wavy brown hair rustled in the breeze, revealing a determined glint in his eyes. Davis's optimism was contagious, and Clarke believed he was the right man for the task.

"Robert," Clarke said, "I want you to lead your group along the northwestern path. Search for caves or any other locations which may serve our purpose. Any site must be easy to describe in a code but not easy to find. Remember, search till around three this afternoon and return."

"Understood, Sir."

While he gazed upon Davis gathering his men, he sensed pride and concern for the young officer. He trusted Davis would do everything possible to succeed, but many unknown dangers lurked in the area.

Leading his team through the underbrush and down to the trail, every step took them further from the safety of the camp. With each passing moment, he pondered the importance of their task and the payroll his horse carried. Failure wasn't an option.

As his group ventured south along the creek, their eyes scanned the landscape for a secure spot. The sun glinted off the moving current, casting a shimmering light on the moss-covered rocks as Clarke's thoughts turned inward. *We've come so far, but we can't let our guard down yet,* he mused. *The success of this mission is vital, and I must ensure it remains hidden from our enemies.*

The sound of the rushing stream grew louder, beckoning them forward. A cool mist fell upon their faces now, seeing the broad but short waterfall stretching across the hundred-plus-foot width of the creek, except for a mound breaking the falls in half. Below it, another stream joined in from the east, and a massive, long pool of water was before them.

"Look at that beauty," George said, his eyes wide with awe.

"It is, but we have to stay on task, men," Clarke chided, his gaze sweeping the landscape. "We're not here to sightsee."

"Apologies, Sir."

"No need to do so, George. I meant it's unfortunate that we do not have time to enjoy it."

Clarke treaded with extreme caution onto the rocks; his boots had trouble finding solid footing on his way across the waterfall. Scanning the other side, he spotted another trail. His heart raced with anticipation, and he studied the falls and area more thoroughly.

"Anything promising, Captain?" George asked.

"Nothing yet," he sighed. Reaching the middle, he had an unobstructed view to the north and south. "There's another trail on the other side. But let's continue south on the same one. From what I can see, the creek splits into two directions ahead, east and west."

Approaching the split in the creek, the path bent and turned them eastward. However, the roar of water from the west called them to explore its origin. Clarke paused, his brow furrowing while looking at the other side and considering their options. *What's to the west? We can't afford to overlook any possibilities.*

"Sir?" Henry Jones queried, sensing Clarke's inner conflict.

Clarke gestured west. "Maybe we should search in that direction as well?"

"Should we split up, Sir?" James asked, eager to cover as much ground as possible.

"No," he asked, his eyes narrowing with determination. "Stay together. We must protect the payroll. Let's not risk dividing our forces again."

While continuing east, the sun climbed and cast a warm glow on the men. While they trudged further, the gentle murmur of moving water ascended into a discord of splashing and gurgling, announcing the presence of a significant stream. He gazed in wonder at the sight before them: a massive, smooth, inclined stone, slick with water and algae, gliding unimpeded down its surface.

"By God," said Jones, his eyes filled with admiration.

Clarke nodded in agreement, distracted for the moment by the beauty of their surroundings - the falls, trees, and streams. But the relevance of the mission jerked him back to reality, and he squinted at the rock slope and then the far hillside, assessing their potential for a hiding spot.

"Sir?" George asked, sensing Clarke's hesitation.

"Beautiful though it may be, there's no place for us to hide it," he gazed around and shook his head.

Glancing up at the sky, he noted the sun's position. He peered south, and calm water stretched far into the distance, beyond sight, and mountains surrounded them. *Short of burying it under a nondescript tree, there's nothing here.*

"Where do we go from here, Sir?" George said, straining to peer as distant as he could.

Chapter 31

Realizing the need for stealth, Jack removed his regulator and tilted it down to stifle the bubbles that would betray their presence. Steve lingered behind, the boat's bulk shielding him as he awaited Jack's go-ahead. His emergence beneath the pontoon was silent, a whisper against the water's surface.

The authoritative voice broke through, a reminder from the Deep Creek Lake Police about the hazards of diving too close to sunset and its prohibition. Making a swift hand gesture to Steve, he signaled all was well. After they surfaced, Jack's frustration was evident as he haphazardly flung his fins onto the boat. "Nothing," he said, peeling off his mask.

Looking at her watch, Emma weighed their options. "The day's fading. Do we dare another dive, or should we head back?"

Jack, pondering over his dive computer, said, "We need an hour's break before our next one."

"An hour? Haven't the dives been shallow?" Emma asked.

Steve replied, "We're over 2,400 feet of elevation. Our bodies will react like we dove deeper than we did. Therefore, our surface times will be greater than if diving at sea level."

"I guess I forgot about that from my scuba course since we never dove at an elevation."

"That's why you're required to take a refresher course if you haven't dove within two years. Otherwise, you forget critical things. Why not take a refresher course when Sally goes for her certification?"

"I'd like that," Emma said.

Turning to Jack, Steve said, "Okay, as we have some time to kill, want to go to Penelec? I have a positive feeling about it."

Jack hesitated, his gaze on the air gauge. "I realize you do. With only two tanks each, I hoped to complete four dives at shallow sites along the southern trail. The dam required Clarke to cross the creek north of the barrel to follow that path. And they're a lot deeper, so we could only get to two. We can tackle that tomorrow with more tanks."

Steve nodded in agreement, ready to move on. "So, where to now?"

Concern laced Jack's voice as he analyzed their gauges and considered their options. "Cherry Creek might be too deep for what's left in our tanks. Marsh Run Cove at Gravely Run is shallower and due south of the marker, and it would've been the first waterfall they encountered as they headed south. I'd have suggested it first if Pawn Run hadn't had the cave we found."

"Gotcha," he concurred, prepping the boat for departure.

Veering northward, Jack examined his tank gauges. "My first tank's got more air."

"Same here," he said. "Shallow dives were the right call today."

After navigating under two bridges for over five miles, they approached Gravely Run. The depth descended from 40 to 20 feet, their pontoon rocking in the wake of the narrow cove's traffic.

"Emma, don't stay here. Steve and I will dive in. Wait two minutes, so we're clear of the boat, and then anchor in the recessed area over by Route 219. It'll be smoother water for you."

"Can't risk our ladies getting seasick," Steve chimed in.

Sally appeared queasy, her hand over her mouth, urged, "Hurry, or I'll be sick." But then she laughed.

Driven by her mock discomfort, they plunged into the lake. Below, a vibrant aquatic scene unfolded, a stark contrast to their previous dives. Fish weaved through submerged branches, while rocks provided refuge for crustaceans.

Expecting to start near the top of the drop-off, they found themselves at the bottom of a towering wall stretching beyond their vision. Not noticing anything on the western side, Jack gestured eastward toward Route 219 and a dark shadow on the submerged fall's face. Swimming to it, they encountered a massive vertical crevasse resulting from Marsh Run Creek's ancient flow through the rock. At its base lay a deep shelter cave entrance.

They high-fived as they celebrated their discovery – a submerged cavern in a pool beneath the waterfall. The recess, carved out by the waterfall's force, revealed only rocks in the beam of their flashlights.

With air and time dwindling, Jack signaled a split search. Exploring the cave's interior, detector in hand, he scanned as Steve moved rocks and inspected walls, but the treasure eluded them.

Reuniting with Steve, Jack's survey of the surrounding area uncovered signs of previous searches – shifted stones and shovel marks. Exchanging a glance, Steve's gesture spoke volumes: "Zero."

While exhilarating, their find bore no hint of Braddock's treasure. The recess's impenetrable rock offered no sanctuary for hidden wealth.

His gaze fixed on his air gauge as he searched the ground in a frenzy in front of the cave, believing the disintegrating chest scattered its contents over time. Scanning, Jack found nothing but the faint signals of fishing hooks and lead weights.

Steve grabbed Jack's shoulder and tapped his watch. They swam east and searched for the pontoon's anchor line. Jack's rigid jaw set at the safety stop and again on the surface, and the tension in his frame radiated his disappointment.

"Nothing again," Jack said, his head shaking in defeat. "We're out of time and air."

Upon boarding, Emma embraced Jack, her support unwavering. "We've done all we were able to today. We have tomorrow."

"I even checked the front in case the fall's current tore the chest or barrel apart and scattered the gold. Still nothing."

Checking their tanks, Steve pointed out the stark difference between their remaining air pressure; Jack almost depleted his tank, whereas Steve had much more air. "You took a significant risk, Jack. Your rapid movements caused you to burn through your air. That wouldn't have ended well for you with multiple dives. You might've had to surface in that heavy boat traffic."

"Appreciate it, Stevie. I know you've got my back."

After stripping off their dive equipment, Emma thanked Steve with a kiss on the cheek, "I believe he would've been dead several times over without you."

Back at the marina, their gear loaded into Jack's SUV under the glow of the setting sun, the group convened, their faces lit by the fading light. Jack, massaging his temples, tried to rally them.

"Let's focus on what we learned," Jack started, aiming for optimism. "We didn't find *the* cave yet, but Steve, did any of the sites appear promising enough we need to revisit?"

Steve was doubtful. "Nothing at the first two seemed right. The last had potential but was solid rock. If it were here, we'd have found something.

Gazing between the others, Sally said, "You mentioned it was a process of elimination. Do you think we overlooked some possible spots?"

"Wouldn't hurt to double-check," Emma said. "Bill mentioned several waterfalls in the area. One of them has to have the cave we're looking for."

"We still have a lot of spots Jack marked, but we can review the map again tonight," Steve said.

Jack, contemplative yet hopeful, agreed. The pressure on their quest was building, and their time dwindling.

Sensing the group's tension, Sally offered a reprieve. "I know a fantastic Mexican restaurant in Oakland – Don Patron's."

"I'm up for that," Emma smiled.

"I'm game," Jack nodded, the weight of their mission pressing on his mind. "Just remember, we need to have an early night. Tomorrow's going to be a long day."

"Got it," Steve said with a clap on Jack's shoulder.

Emma's gaze lingered on the men, her concern for their safety and Jack's fixation on the prize evident in her eyes.

Settling into the Suburban, Jack spotted a missed call from the Lieutenant.

"Better check that," Steve suggested.

Jack's heart skipped a beat as he returned the call, opting for speakerphone so the group could listen in.

"Lieutenant Allen here," came from the other end.

"It's Jack. Sorry, I missed your call."

"No worries. Just an update on Ben's situation. Ben knows Henry Ritter, a known rival, who he said doesn't play by the rules. He was the one lurking near the cave you found," Allen's voice filled the car. "Ben tried to confront him but couldn't get much from him or convince him to back off."

A cold unease gripped Jack. "You think Ritter's behind Ben's accident?"

"We're investigating. Ben spotted someone suspicious before his fall, a bearded man in a baseball cap watching him from a distance. He doesn't remember anything else, but his description of the man matches Steve's person who approached Sally's home," Allen continued.

Jack's thoughts raced. *Are Ritter, the man in the hat, and Ben's attack connected?*

"Stay alert," Allen warned as the call ended.

"We're up against more than we thought," Steve said, concern etched in his voice. "We'll need to tread more carefully."

The mood was somber as they entered Don Patron's, trying to find some comfort in the evening. Despite the vibrant dishes served, Jack's mind was far from at ease, preoccupied with the dangers that awaited them.

"What's our plan for accommodations for tonight?" Jack broached the subject, aiming to focus on immediate concerns.

Sally voiced her unease. "I don't feel safe staying at my place. I'd feel safer at Jack's. We'd have more people together."

"Of course. We can all stay at my place," he resolved, the protector role settling on him.

"That's fine by me," Steve agreed, lightening the mood. "Though, be warned, Jack's couch isn't the best. However, he has a decent air mattress."

"Hey, don't fret over me," Sally said, her smile brief but genuine. "I'm okay with a flimsy air mattress."

Steve, with exaggerated shock, said, "Okay. I wouldn't let you crash on the sofa. That'd be a crime."

Emma smiled as she followed their banter, a light moment amid the day's relentless quest for treasure, her expression one of entertained relief.

Exiting the restaurant, the night's cool embrace contrasted their earlier pursuits. Jack, burdened by the unresolved mysteries from the day, remained vigilant. In the SUV, his voice carried a mix of concern and suspicion to Steve, "You think we've got a tail?"

"They know where we live," Steve said dismissively, "I doubt they'd dare to approach us together."

No suspicious followers emerged on their route to Jack's. Upon arrival, Steve collapsed on the sofa without ceremony. After bidding everyone a goodnight, Jack withdrew to the sanctuary of his bedroom.

In the meantime, Emma and Sally engaged in light-hearted chatter, and the air mattress setup was underway. As Jack drifted toward sleep, Emma slid close, her voice a soft murmur, "Isn't it strange? How do they know so much about us, yet we know so little about them?" Her words echoed in his now awake mind, stirring a whirlpool of thoughts about their unseen adversaries – their locations, methods of surveillance, and the ominous uncertainty of their next move…

Chapter 32

Dawn's first light came too soon, waking Jack and Emma from their peaceful slumber. Jack's eyes fluttered open to the tranquil scene of her beside him, yet the thrill of the day's quest prodded him out of bed. With a zeal he couldn't suppress, he stomped to rouse Steve and Sally with a soft, eager call.

"Time to wake up," he chimed, his eyes alight with anticipation. "Today's the day."

Steve started groggy but snapped to alertness, mirroring Jack's enthusiasm. "Let's hit it," his arms stretching, ready for action.

Emma, her dark hair framing her face, propped herself up, her voice tinged with humor. "You better strike gold today. I'm done with these early starts," she scolded, nudging Jack in jest.

"We'll find it," Jack said, his smile unwavering. "We should cover all the sites by day's end."

Sally pulled the blankets back over her head before throwing them off her with an audible grunt. "All I want to know is, who's the cruel and sadistic person who decided we should wake up at 6:30?"

"Sorry, sweetie," Steve said as he walked over to help her up. "We need to be at the store's opening to have a chance to hit all the sites."

The four friends readied themselves while Jack calculated how many tanks they would use by running the possible dive sites through his head.

Their journey began with a spirited ride to Frostburg's scuba shop, the early sun guiding them to Route 219 and then Route 40, Braddock's Road, to a McDonald's drive-through for a necessary caffeine and food fuel-up.

"Large coffee, black," Jack asked, a common chorus of orders following as each selected their morning fix. Emma's stomach voiced its disagreement, and she added a breakfast sandwich. The others followed suit.

Pulling forward, the aroma of coffee filled the vehicle. However, Jack's attention was now captured within the map's details, tracing their planned path with a mix of eagerness and intensity.

"Focus, Jack. Food now, map later," Steve reminded, nudging Jack back to the present.

With breakfast in hand, they resumed their trek, the warmth of food and drink dispelling the last of their sleepiness. Conversations ebbed and flowed, turning to dreams of what treasures the day might yield and the promises of undiscovered wealth.

Steve jumped in and voiced his dream of owning a luxury sports car while Emma mused about retiring to travel the world. Jack envisioned buying a retirement home for himself and Emma that all may use. Prompted, Sally hesitated, her gaze dropping. "I'd just like to clear my mom's medical bills – and my mortgage," she confessed, casting silence over the group. Jack's fantasy crashed into reality. Sally, brightening, smiled, "Oh, and I guess, a trip to Europe."

"You're the sensible one," Emma said with a grin.

Seeking a lighter topic, Steve dove into logistics, "Considering the lake depths, we're looking at needing five or six tanks each. Seven gives us a buffer for multiple dives or checking out alternate spots. If we're in the water by nine, nine-thirty, Jack, we might be able to hit all the sites and have the gold by sunset!"

"Right, I estimated the same. And we're ahead of schedule." Jack pulled his Suburban into a parking spot near the dive shop. "Time for tank refills. We've got a packed day."

Emma said, "No objections here."

Stepping out of their vehicle, disarray greeted them – the shop's door ajar, glass littering the pavement.

"Damn," Steve cursed, dread creeping in.

Emma, shocked, clasped her hand over her mouth, "What happened here?"

Jack, heart racing, whispered, "I've got a bad feeling about this." Approaching the store, they glared inside in angst.

"Hello?" he asked into the silence. There was no reply.

"This is unbelievable," Sally muttered.

"It appears there's less gear – regulators, BCDs, tanks." he clenched his fists, trying to stay calm.

"Who would do this?" Emma's voice trembled with fear.

"Someone bent on stopping us," Steve said, his tone foreboding.

While they examined the scene from the door, the store owner arrived. "What the hell?"

"We found it like this, came to refill our tanks," Jack said.

The owner dialed the police, then tried the lights – nothing. "They took all kinds of things, wetsuits, and lots of tanks," he vented, frustration evident. Checking tanks, he started turning valves. "They depressurized all the tanks. Damn it! They even damaged the compressor," pointing out the ripped-out power line.

Jack faced his friends, "Now what?" Their plans were in jeopardy, and they pondered alternatives, with the police's arrival cutting through the tension. Steve paced. Emma wrapped herself in a tight hug, her head moving, while Sally sat silent, reflecting the shock and uncertainty of their disrupted morning.

"Well, here we are again," Officer Martinez said, stepping from his vehicle with a scrutinizing glance. "Appears trouble has a way of finding you, or is it the other way around?"

"Not sure," Jack replied, a hint of nonchalance in his tone. "Though, you might want to chat with the owner first. We arrived a minute before him."

Navigating through the aftermath, Martinez approached the owner amidst the chaos of shattered glass. "I'm sorry you have to go through this," he said, his voice blending professionalism and empathy. "Any idea who did this or what's missing?"

The bewildered owner listed only the damages and losses, clueless about the perpetrator. Martinez, seeking clarity, turned to Jack for his account – from their routine refill trip to the unsettling discovery of the break-in.

"Hold tight," Martinez informed them as he stepped outside and looked around before disappearing into the neighboring store. Moments later, he emerged, signaling them over. "They have some surveillance footage. Come view the video to see if you recognize anyone." He pointed at Jack and the dive shop owner.

Clustered around the tiny screen, the trio witnessed two shadowy figures approach the shop – one in a hoodie, the other donning a cap and a scruffy beard, their identities masked.

"Their vehicle... Is it a red Jeep Wrangler?" the store owner asked, peering closer.

"It is," Jack said, a surge of anger rising. "Those men have been tailing us. The one in the hoodie cased Sally's the other night. Lieutenant Allen mentioned Henry Ritter owned the pickup truck found on that farm. The other, the bearded man, might be linked to a possible assault on Ben Baton and was the one Steve told you was the man approaching Sally's home from the street – he remains unidentified."

Martinez's gaze settled on Jack, mixed with concern and curiosity. "The Lieutenant briefed me of all this, so I take it you're in frequent contact with Lieutenant?"

"We are."

"Good. Seems like he briefed you well, perhaps too well. However, given you may be a target, or at least in their way, it's understandable."

Jack pulled out and showed Martinez his phone, "Lieutenant Allen sent us Henry Ritter's photo in case we run into him again. So we could alert him."

Martinez nodded. "I think that is all we will need from you right now,

Jack. We'll reach out if we need anything else. You can head out while I continue the investigation here."

"Of course," Jack said. He turned to the owner, "I'm sorry for this trouble," and promised to return the gear soon.

As they departed, Emma asked, her voice uneven, "Who was responsible?"

"Ritter, and another. We won't let this stop us," Jack's resolve was unshaken.

"Where's the closest shop?" Steve chimed in, ready to move forward.

Jack grabbed his phone from his pocket. "There are two in West Virginia. There's one by Morgantown and another at Mount Storm. Both are roughly the same from here, but Mount Storm would be closer to the lake after we pick up the tanks. Steve, can you call ahead? If they don't have what we need, we'll redirect to Morgantown."

"Agreed," Steve nodded. "On it."

Route 220 snaked through the Appalachians, a ribbon amidst the wilderness. The dense canopy above painted the road in strokes of light and shadow, a natural kaleidoscope on Jack's windshield.

Driving deeper south into Maryland and crossing into West Virginia, the mountains parted, unveiling the lush tapestry of the valley below. The hills rolled, a green sea under the broad sky, leading them to the quaint dive shop nestled in Mt. Storm.

Parking, a quiet tension settled over them. "I hope they're not cleaned out, too," Emma's soft words mirrored Jack's thoughts.

"They're good," Steve said, "Confirmed before we left."

"I know, I'm just paranoid now."

The door chimed as it opened, and the sight of well-stocked aisles cut through their worry.

"I'll be right there!" came from the back of the store. They soon saw a man walking toward them, smiling, "You must be the divers in need of tanks, right? Frostburg's mishap sent you our way. I've prepped 14 tanks. We have the same tanks as they do. Let's swap yours out, and we'll square it away on the receipt."

Relief flickered in Jack's eyes as he and Steve exchanged their Navy dive certifications for the tanks. The delay cost them precious hours, yet they were back on track.

"Thank you!" Emma said, warmth in her tone.

"Enjoy your dives!" the owner waved them off.

Leaving, Jack had a sense of unease, the premonition of unseen eyes focused upon them. He scanned their surroundings – a serene landscape, undisturbed except for their presence.

"We need to move," urgency lacing Jack's words. "Time's now against us."

Chapter 33

While returning to the lake, Emma's phone shattered the silence. Brows furrowed, her eyes darted to the caller ID. "It's Bill," she murmured and pressed the speaker button.

Jack's gaze flickered to Emma, reading the worry creasing her brow before she pressed the speaker button.

"Hey, Bill," Emma's voice wavered a bit, betraying her attempt at calm. "What's going on?"

"Emma, I have something you should know. I only just arrived at the museum. They informed me that yesterday evening, a peculiar man came looking for me, claiming to be a friend of yours and Jack's."

Jack cut in, "What did he look like?"

Bill's tone was shaky, "In his late fifties or sixties, rough around the edges, bearded, wearing a ball cap. Said he was assisting you both and had additional questions about the area he hoped I would answer."

"Did you give him any information?" Emma asked, urgency in her voice.

"Nothing at all! I wasn't here. I was calling to check with you first before I called him back. So, he's not with you, I take it?"

"No, Bill. He's not. You confirmed our fears," Emma said. "There's a lot more going on here. Our friend Ben was attacked, most likely by this man. He and his partner are treasure hunters who are trying to learn what we know."

"Good Lord," he gasped.

Jack jumped in. "Bill, please listen to what we are about to say. It's critical you remain out of sight for a bit. You should stay with family. Don't head home. This man's accomplice might have targeted one of our friends, and someone broke into my place. It appears that they will not stop for anything to get the treasure."

"Alright, I'll heed your advice. But how's my Sally? Is everything okay?"

Sally said, "I'm here, Bill. I'm okay. This same guy approached me at my house, but Jack's friend Steve chased him away."

"I'm happy you're safe, child. I've been worried. You all, please take care."

"You too, Bill. We'll keep in touch," Emma concluded, her finger lingering on the end call button before disconnecting the call.

No one spoke. Jack's grip on the steering wheel tightened. The adversaries they faced were relentless, and their intentions were clear: stop the quest for Braddock's lost treasure or face the consequences.

Emma's voice trembled, breaking the oppressive silence, "Jack, I'm scared. They're always one step ahead, and we have no idea what lengths they'll go to."

"They've already tipped the scales today by hitting the dive shop," he said. "What's next?"

Chapter 34

Upon their return to the lake, Jack broke the silence. "Before we hit the water, I need to make sure everyone is up for the challenge ahead. If not, we can figure out something, I guess."

Emma's head ebbed as she eyed each team member before speaking up. "There's four of us against two. We know what we're after; they don't... I'm still in."

Steve's response was lighter. "You had me at treasure and certain danger."

Jack shook his head with a smirk.

Attention turned to Sally, who avoided eye contact in her discomfort. "You okay?" Steve asked.

Meeting his gaze, Sally stammered as she whispered, "I'm scared. However, I'm safer with all of you than if I tried to hide alone... I'm coming with you."

"It's settled. To the marina," Steve said, the decision unanimous. "We've got a dive to ready for."

Their drive to Bill's Marina was contemplative; the team was silent, lost in thought amidst the serpentine roads. Arriving, they found their pontoon poised on Deep Creek Lake and loaded it with their gear in unified silence and speed.

Jack, checking their progress, voiced a concern. "This detour cost us hours. Without finding the cave today, hitting every site won't be possible. Let's be efficient, shorten our bottom times, and go as soon as allowed. Agreed?"

Nods of agreement met his plan.

"Keep an eye out when Steve and I are under," Jack said, the gravity of their situation clear. "We're not quite sure what we are up against."

With determination, Emma ignited the engine, the vessel slicing towards Cherry Creek Cove. The journey across the lake was tense, and Jack pondered the potential dangers lurking below and above as he and Steve geared up.

Reaching the inlet, she skillfully managed the boat to a gentle stop, signaling the start of their dive with a shout, "Go, Steve," and the anchor tossed.

Breaking the water's surface, the sensation of being on the correct path was instant for him, a current guiding them toward their goal. At the bottom, a massive rock formation awaited, just as Bill described, a long natural waterslide. Exchanging glances of excitement, they dove deeper, following the flow into the unknown.

"Look, there," Jack gestured with practiced hand signals as they navigated the rocky depths. Despite their thorough search, every crevice and niche yielded nothing close to a cave. Jack's frustration simmered, his breaths growing labored with each fruitless minute.

"Up," Steve signaled, miming ascent with joined pointed vertical fingertips. Hovering during their safety stop, the outlines of Emma and Sally swimming came into view. Nearing the unsuspected pair, they nudged them under, inciting laughter that broke the tension when they emerged, only to have the ladies submerge them in payback.

Regrouping behind the boat, the quartet shared their lack of discoveries, pondering their future moves.

"Maybe you missed something?" Emma pondered aloud.

"Na," Jack replied. "No cave, only solid rock."

"We gotta keep looking," Sally encouraged.

Steve injected optimism, "Let's use our surface time to reassess. What's our next dive site?"

Jack outlined their choices, mentioning the landmarks and potential sites: towards the dam were several possible spots in front of it, and sites with higher potential: Penelec, Red Run Cove, and Deep Creek by Shingle Camp. Carmel Cove, in front of the State Park, was the closest unsearched possibility.

"I vote Red Run Cove," Sally said, eyeing it as a chill spot for her and Emma.

Climbing aboard, he was skeptical about their chances without signs of waterfalls or pools.

Emma, following Jack, theorized, "Carmel Cove is on the Seneca Trail, south of the marker, and the last possible site on the southern path. It fits the description Bill shared about the pool and falls. With two drop-offs, it has decent potential."

"Let's do it!" Steve concurred, shedding his BCD.

Jack asked, "Remember where I turned the boat around to see the turtle?"

Emma replied, "Yes."

"Head to that spot."

"To the first cove on the left, and straight on to Carmel Cove," Steve's attempt at humor with a *Peter Pan* reference fell flat, but he tried to lighten the mood, drawing only groans.

Emma chuckled, easing the tension. "Okay, off to Neverland!"

"Hey, at least Emma's playing along with me," Steve laughed, watching her throttling up the boat.

Approaching the State Park and Glendale Bridge positioning them, Jack and Emma scanned their surroundings: him for landmarks, her for navigation cues. As Jack readied himself to call for a stop, she skillfully slowed the pontoon to a halt, the engine quieting behind them, ready for their next exploration.

"Below us!" Emma's voice cut through the air, her arm extended towards the sudden deepening of the water. "Must be the first drop-off!"

Jack, following her gaze, recognized the nearby homes. "I think you're right. I remember those houses from last time." His tone conveyed both admiration and a hint of playful rivalry. "You've got a sharp eye."

Anchoring at the site, anticipation hung between them.

Jack and Steve suited up in their scuba gear. Standing at the edge, they checked their air pressure, placed regulators, signaled, and plunged into the watery depths.

This dive site presented a stark contrast to their previous explorations. Sparse plant life and a few small fish overshadowed the widespread jagged rocks. Navigating towards the cove's base, they searched for the supposed waterfall but discovered no hidden cave.

"Look, two," Jack gestured to Steve, urgency threading through his movements. They delved deeper, tracing the ancient creek bed to another submerged pool marked by a steep rock face.

Steve's excitement was evident, hands shaking, pointing to a recess at the bottom of the drop-off.

Jack, heart pounding, explored the alcove with his metal detector, shifting rocks where he found nothing.

Steve, still fixated on the recess, caught Jack's curiosity. He pointed to signs of recent disturbance – plants displaced, a shallow hole, and scratched markings on the wall.

A chill of despair hit Jack, fearing they were too late.

Sensing Jack's dismay, Steve attempted to appease him with a gesture, "Safe," mimicking a baseball umpire.

"Safe?" Jack mimicked, followed by palms up in puzzlement.

Steve guided Jack's attention to how he signaled "small" with the thumb and index close and then "distance," taking his hands from together to apart and pointing at the recess.

Jack shook his head and signaled his confusion with his palms up before indicating they should rise.

Back on the surface, Jack's confusion spilled out. "Ritter was clearly here first. What did you mean, 'Safe'?"

Cutting off Jack's speculation, Steve said, "They didn't find it."

"How can you be so sure?"

Steve explained his reasoning, focusing on the absence of significant excavation marks. "You don't start hammering away at the rock if you've already found what you're looking for in the dirt on the ground."

Jack's skepticism lingered. "Or do you think they were trying to move something big?"

"No. The recess is too shallow. The force of the waterfall over a century and a half would've scattered any hidden chests or disturbed any rocks concealing them," he concluded. "And you did not get a signal hit in front of it."

"Makes sense," Jack conceded after a moment, his mind ticking through the implications.

Emma's voice broke into their reflection. "Any luck?"

"No," he said as they approached the boat, their fruitless dive apparent. "It appears we weren't the only ones here, but there was nothing to find. We pieced together what happened in the aftermath from their haphazard search."

"We?" Steve echoed, some amusement in his tone.

"Okay, all Steve. I panicked," Jack said, a sheepish grin crossing his face.

"Thank you," Steve said, chuckling, and briefed Sally and Emma on their conclusions about the other treasure hunters.

"What's the plan?" Steve asked as two officers on a patrol boat approached them, interrupting with a request for their diving certifications.

He responded, masking his concern with calmness. "Do we have an issue, officers?"

"We'll need to see your dive credentials. Some uncertified folks were diving by the dam and were about to dive near Penelec," the officer informed them. "We confiscated their equipment. We have to make sure you're legit."

"No problem, we're certifiable," Steve laughed.

"Sorry, yes, we're certified," Jack assured them, asking Emma to pull their scuba cards from their wallets behind her chair. The police examined and nodded in approval.

275

"Be careful. Boaters may not pay much attention to the diver's flag or even know what it represents. Plus, some people like to buzz anchored boats for fun, rocking them in their wake."

"Thank you, officers," Emma replied.

"No time to lose," Jack said, eager to stay ahead in the hunt for the gold. "Steve will be happy with this, but let's head to Penelec. It puts us in the lead, assuming Henry Ritter will regroup and try to dive the spot again."

"Whoever said we should search by Penelec is a genius," Steve laughed. "However, I think Ritter might do a shore dive next."

Upon reaching Penelec Cove, Emma and Steve repeated their positioning and anchoring routine.

"You're getting good at this," Jack smiled.

Jack glanced at his dive computer, signaling, "We're clear." Together, they descended into the lake's abyss. The darkness began to surround them as they descended to its deepest reaches. The chill of crossing a second thermal layer enveloped them, and the increased clarity of the water was a sharp difference from the rapidly diminishing light. He tapped his watch, now reading 62 degrees – time was of the essence.

It appeared as if the sun had rapidly set as they continued their descent. Powering up, their flashlight beams cut through the eerie dark, unveiling nothing, not even a passing fish, until they reached a desolate lakebed, a seemingly alien landscape. They found themselves in a massive, lifeless bowl, its edges climbing away. Here, at 65 feet, they ventured where few had, far surpassing their prior exploration depths.

Advancing toward the slope exiting Penelec Cove, a solitary, perpendicular stump – a melancholy sentinel of the deep – greeted them. Steve's flashlight pointed up, illuminating the expanse above – a vast cave ceiling stretching beyond them – oblivious to the shelter cave they swam into. Lights cast a shadow upon the wall, but the silhouette on the cave wall appeared disproportional to the stump itself. Moving closer, they realized it concealed an opening, and they responded with a high-five in anticipated discovery.

They moved the stump with concerted effort, unveiling the cave's mouth. Inside, Jack's detector scream pierced his ears, a promise of hidden treasures, sending adrenaline surging through them. Excited, Jack wasted no time digging through the sediment, and visibility dwindled in the cloud of silt he stirred up. Then, the unmistakable clang of metal on metal broke through the murky silence.

Thrilled, he groped in the gloom, his fingers brushing against the corroded steel. Yet, its identity remained shrouded in mystery. Reluctant to risk harm to their find, he paused, hoping the water would clear.

Jack froze his body and hovered to allow the sediment to settle. Yet, his slow, steady breaths caused his body to faintly ebb up and down, coupled with his exhaust bubbles agitating the water, yielding only more clouds of silt. Signaling Steve, he motioned upward, their shared language of gestures calling for a temporary retreat. They ascended to 15 feet, biding time for the sediment to settle, conserving their air, and minimizing nitrogen.

In the stillness of their wait, Jack's curiosity haunted him. He pondered: What echoed so loud against my shovel?

Chapter 35

Monday, June 23rd, 1755

It was still the morning when Captain Clarke strode up next to George and peered south across the body of water. "It stretches for miles, and I sense we will find nothing other than hiding it under a tree along the path, and I don't spot anything that stands out. And any further south, we're off the map."

"I agree, Sir," George said. "Thoughts?"

"It's pushing mid-day. We'll return to the waterfall we passed on the way here and follow the trail I spotted on the other side of it. It may take us to the loud roaring sound we heard back at the bend."

"Understood, Sir."

They headed north, and the familiar roar of the falls greeted them. Clarke wasted no time leading his men over it before turning south and west. The way led them to the end of the vast pool that stretched southward for miles. A natural earthen dam spanned hundreds of yards over the valley.

The far side of the pool drew their eyes to it: a torrent of water cascaded twenty or more feet over a steep slope to another pool below, providing both an imposing backdrop and a soothing melody. In the middle was a mound, and in front of them were deep, calm lagoons separated by the exposed dam and the dramatic change in elevation. However, the stream eroded the rock against the embankment they were standing upon, forming an outcropping that overhung the pool.

They walked down the slope and along the rock shelf over the creek, and George laid down and spied under the overhang, almost dipping his head into the water. "Check out the hollow area underneath us, Sir. The recess goes back five to ten feet; it's a solid hiding spot."

"Indeed," Clarke said. He sensed the men's anticipation, their eagerness to complete their mission pulsing in the air around them. But caution still tugged at his gut, urging him to consider every possibility before deciding.

"Let's explore further," he said, his gaze never leaving the pool and the shadowy space beneath the rock. "There may be more than meets the eye."

Clarke wondered if this was the place they'd been searching for – the perfect spot to secure the payroll and ensure its safety.

Kneeling and peering into the pool below the outcropping, he murmured, "It appears ten to fifteen feet deep, at least." He could make out the bottom in front of him but not in the shaded area underneath himself. Realizing the chests would be hidden from sight if submerged in this darkness, he needed to be confident of its protection.

Clarke began to take off his jacket.

"Sir?" George asked, following his gaze.

"Stay here, men. I'm going in to explore." Clarke stripped down to his breeches; the cool air prickled his exposed skin, and he filled his lungs before diving.

The cold water enveloped him, sending a shock through his system. Swimming deeper, he searched for a suitable place to hide their precious cargo.

Is this the spot? Kicking his legs, he swam further below the overhang. Approaching the back wall of the hollow, he gazed upon an unexpected opening in the rock face – an entrance to a cave was a few feet underwater. Intrigued, he kicked his way closer.

Unbelievable, he mused. Gazing upwards, he could not see any of his men atop the ledge, adding to the appeal of hiding it there. With renewed vigor, Clarke propelled himself upward, breaking through the water's surface with a gasp.

"Men!" he called, catching his breath. "I found a tunnel below, on the back wall! This might be the perfect place."

"Are you sure, Captain?" Jones asked, his eyes widened with surprise.

"Possibly, I must explore it further," he said, determination etched across his features. "We have to ensure it's safe to conceal the payroll within it. Toss me the end of a rope."

"Yes, Sir," Jones replied.

Tying it to his waist, Clarke said, "I may need to pull myself out in an emergency, so no matter what, don't let go!"

"Understood, Sir," George said as he joined Jones holding the rope.

Taking a deep breath, he dove with excitement and apprehension as he swam into the cave's entrance. I hope I can get back out!

Chapter 36

Glancing over at Steve, whose fists were impatiently shaking, Jack saw that his friend's gaze was locked downwards into the blackness concealing the lake's bottom and the cave they discovered. He, too, felt the anticipation building as they hovered at this shallow depth to conserve the precious air in their tanks. They needed time for the solid silt cloud in the cave to settle and unveil to them the mystery that made his detector screech.

Jack checked his watch again: *A few more minutes should do it.* He stared into the abyss and began to visualize he was in the cave, grasping the metal encasing the edges of a wooden treasure chest and extracting out of its centuries-old hole. They were on the cusp of a discovery that promised to transform their lives. As time continued to tick by, he imagined the lavish rewards: a sports car and a wedding with Emma. What seemed like ages was only ten minutes until Steve, unable to contain his excitement, nudged him back to reality and repeated his gesture toward the prize below. Jack nodded, "Okay. Down."

Regrouping at the cave's edge, Jack checked on his friend with a brief "Okay?" before their focus turned to the shadowy interior. Jack's eyes locked on his target: *This is it!* But as he ventured inside, a monstrous six-foot plus catfish burst from the darkness, its whiskers twitching and mouth gaping, sending him reeling back with a startled "aaaahhhh" cry. Steve's laughter, muffled by his regulator, filled the cave, teasing him for his skittish reaction.

Jack signaled, "Okay," trying to regain his composure, knowing he'd never live this down.

They redirected their attention, finding the spot marked with their detector. Using his hands, he extracted the sediment with extreme caution to reveal corroded iron, his pulse quickening. When his fingers snagged on a corroded chain, visions of a chest in a protective wrap of links flashed before him. He tugged, and the chain rose from the soil until it ceased yielding. Squinting through the plume in front of him, he yanked, and it refused to budge. Steve's massive arms reached in to join him, digging in their heels. They were in a tug-of-war contest.

With a final heave, they tumbled backward, and the cloud grew – blinding Jack. Guided by touch, Jack's hands shook when he grasped something sizable and solid, but his hope vanished. He recognized the shape of an old boat anchor.

Discarding the anchor, he grabbed the metal detector for one last sweep – nothing. Signaling the dive's end with a glance at his dive computer, they had only five minutes left. Disheartened, they explored the cave's entrance and the surrounding area to no avail and began their ascent.

Upon breaking the surface, Jack's tone conveyed the letdown as he briefed the women, "We thought we found the perfect spot, deep behind a waterfall, but it turned out to be an anchor." He glanced at his watch. "We'll need to wait a little over an hour before diving again. Our hovering while the water cleared cut our time down."

"What do you think, Sally?" Emma asked, her eyes alight with the thrill of the hunt. "I think it's our turn for some adventure."

"Yeah, we want to do something besides lounge around!"

Jack furrowed his brows, puzzled. "What do you mean?"

Emma's enthusiasm was infectious. "We were talking while you were below. You have to wait for your next dive. Why don't Sally and I take a shot at snorkeling Red Run? It's shallow enough for us to search. Maybe we'll spot something for you to examine later."

Steve, ever the mediator, flashed a grin at Jack. "Are you going to argue with them? I'm not. Sounds like a solid plan to me."

"No, I agree."

Sally, excited, chimed in, "We're on it."

Emma seized the helm, firing up the engine. "Let's roll."

While navigating toward the inlet, doubt gnawed at Jack. *We're running out of probable places. What if we are wrong? Did we miss something in the clues? Are we wasting time looking in the lake? Where else is left for us to search?* He shook off the negativity. *Focus on the positive and take one site at a time*, he coached himself. *We came too far to falter now.*

Upon reaching Red Run Cove, tranquility enveloped them. The secluded area, a stark contrast to the broader lake, shimmered under a golden sun, bordered by a ballet of swaying trees.

Skillfully, Emma guided them through, their vessel gliding past others anchored in the serene waters.

"Isn't this place gorgeous?" Sally said, taking in the scenery.

Peering into the clear lake, she said, "It is." With a swift maneuver, she killed the engine, and Steve dropped anchor.

Emma sprung to action, "Ready? This is where we shine." She scooped up Jack's diving mask and snorkel.

Sally's excitement was contagious but had a hint of nervousness in her voice. "Can you help me? I've never done this."

"Of course," Emma assured her. "It's easy once you get the hang of it."

Grateful, Sally shared a brief kiss with Steve before heading to the water's edge, where he assisted her with the equipment.

Emma, already treading water, said to Sally and Steve, "Leave it to me." She demonstrated the snorkel's use, cautioning, "Keep your face downward to avoid the tube going under, and you end up with a mouthful of water." Sally was a fast learner, and together, they commenced their underwater exploration.

Moments later, Sally's head popped up, her words garbled by the snorkel, "I think...I found something! A steep slope!" Her arms waving in exhilaration.

Emma dove under to verify, surfacing in a minute with confirmation and a splash of water on her face. "It's a long slope. No cave, though." She flashed Sally a thumbs-up, scanning the cove. "Shall we keep looking?"

Sally nodded, eager to continue their adventure.

The two women sliced across the surface towards the expanse of the lake, their movements purposeful, eyes scouring below for hidden depths or caves.

Jack, with an inaudible grumble, peered around the inlet. *Relaxing is overrated*, aware that any delay might let their adversaries gain ground or get ahead. His fingers bounced on the rail, the sense of urgency dominating his focus; they needed to maintain their lead.

"Jack?" Steve's voice pulled him from his thoughts. "I think we need to go on the offense against these guys."

He nodded, considering. "I'm on board, but we can't endanger Emma and Sally. Leaving them alone at my apartment may be risky. They can spot someone coming on the boat."

"True."

"But if we confront our rivals, then what? Beating the crap out of them would land us behind bars. I like the idea, but how do we do it?"

"Let's think about it, keep it between us."

"Agreed."

When the two ladies returned, having explored an area as vast as a football field without finding anything, disappointment was on their faces.

"Nothing here," Emma yelled as they neared the ladder. "This cove's a dead end."

"Then let's make the most of our break before heading out," Steve said.

"Sounds good," Jack said, a smile touching his lips as he gazed upon the women's light-hearted splashing. These fleeting moments of joy amid their quest underscored the value of their bond and the memories woven.

When Jack glanced at the time, his expression turned solemn. "It's past 6:30. We've missed the window for another dive today, as we won't finish before the cut-off. Night diving is risky with the dam and Shingle Camp as options."

"I say we risk it," Steve countered.

Emma interjected, "That's a no from me. It's easier for the police to spot us at night. Plus, we're out of food."

"And I'm hungry," Sally said. "Let's call it a day and pick up where we left off in the morning."

"Sorry, Steve, I believe they decided for us. We'll head to Brenda's and start early tomorrow," Jack concluded, setting the course for the following day.

Steve conceded, his stomach ruling his decision. "Alright, but I'm hitting Brenda's hard. Their Abbondanza pizza won't stand a chance against me – 26 inches of yummy. Want to boat to the restaurant?"

"No. Let's secure our gear first. We can't leave the stuff exposed."

"Okay."

Sally's voice, tinged with disappointment, broke the silence. "What time do we have to wake up?"

"Before sunrise, dear," Steve replied, failing to keep a straight face.

They transferred their gear to the SUV and made their way to Brenda's, the promise of food lifting the spirits dampened by their unfruitful day.

As they entered Brenda's, Steve's chant for his favorite dish, "A Bon Dan Za, A Bon Dan Za, A Bon Dan Za," grew in fervor, his enthusiasm infectious.

"Nothing like a giant pizza to drown our sorrows," Sally quipped, lightening the mood as laughter found its way through their disappointment.

The warmth of Brenda's, filled with the scent of melting cheese and fresh basil, enveloped them, offering a brief respite from their day's failures.

Settled at a lake view table, they bypassed the menus, surprising the hostess with an immediate order of Coors Lights and the Pepperoni Abbondanza Pizza. Drinks in hand, they toasted to a day of closed doors but open windows for tomorrow's endeavors.

Mid-sip, a buzz from Jack's phone interrupted his contemplation. The text from Lieutenant Allen was terse: "Call me when you're alone."

He listened as Emma recounted Steve's past romantic misadventures, eliciting, "Not true," or "I don't think so," and embarrassed laughter from Steve, until Emma's heartfelt "I am so glad you and Steve found each other," brought a warm scene to the table.

Sally blushed and put her head on Steve's large shoulder.

Jack excused himself and used the restroom's solitude to return Allen's call.

"What's up?" Jack asked, laden with worry.

"We've got into Ritter's truck and discovered a lot of fingerprints. We're guessing three or more individuals," Allen disclosed, his voice carrying significant concern.

"Three or more?" Jack's mind raced, piecing together the implications. "Whose?"

"Working on it, but I have more. We found crinkled photo prints of what appears to be the journal pages, along with letters addressed to Elizabeth and Thomas Clarke. Those are the only items that stood out," Allen said, painting a picture of clues left behind from a hasty departure.

Jack's concern deepened. "Can you send those photos?"

"They're evidence now. I'll find out what I can do," Allen promised, procedural caution in his voice.

"Thanks, Lieutenant. Please keep me in the loop."

"Will do. And Jack? Stay safe," Allen said before he disconnected.

Jack lingered, the pieces of a puzzle swirling in his mind: *How did someone obtain those images?*

Realization struck him with the force of a thunderclap. *Who else had access to the journal and letters?* Hands shaking, he dialed Mike Thompson, the contractor, muttering for him to answer. The phone echoed unanswered. "Mike, it's Jack Sullivan. Call me back ASAP," he urged into the voicemail, pacing with mounting tension.

The nagging suspicion of being shadowed crept up on him once more. *How would they know about our dives? Was the break-in also a ruse? Did they bug my place? Did they find my hiding spot and put everything back so as not to tip us off?* The idea of unseen eyes on them was unnerving.

Jack's thoughts raced, circling back to the necessity for action. *Steve was right – We need to go on the offense.* A plan started to form, rooted in the belief their rival compromised his apartment.

To outwit their foes, Jack resolved to keep the details of the Lieutenant's call to himself, fearing that if his friends were in on the diversion, they might overact, tipping his adversaries off.

He returned to the table, appearing calm but still stressing and strategizing. The enigma of the source of the photographs was an incredible concern.

Their dinner concluded in a haze of camaraderie, and they headed back to Jack's apartment to rest up for the next day's dive. His sense of impending danger grew.

"Are you okay, Jack?" Emma asked, "You were too quiet this evening."

He masked his turmoil with a half-hearted smile. "We might have overlooked something today. We dove at the best spots so far. I want to recheck things to determine if some sites need adding to our list."

"I understand, but I don't think you did."

Back at the apartment, the task of storing their diving gear did little to ease Jack's growing sense of peril. The conviction that someone compromised his apartment propelled him toward designing a decoy strategy. He needed to devise a credible play, something to throw their adversaries off their scent.

Then the play came to him.

Hike!

Chapter 37

Jack slipped into his room, pressing the door closed behind him. He moved to grab the journal, letters, and museum map Steve had acquired, taking care to reseal his secret compartment. Back in the kitchen, he spread his findings across the table.

Flipping through the journal, he noticed the curious eyes on him until their silence became too loud to ignore. With a sudden intensity, he said, "There's a piece we're missing in these last entries. I'm certain of it."

He left the journal open, its secrets laid bare, as he unfurled the large printed chart, anchoring its corners with whatever was within reach.

Consulting his phone, he overlaid the fishing and trail maps in his mind's eye, his focus narrowing. His finger traced a path from the marker, skirting the lake's eastern boundary down to Cherry Creek. A memory of Bill's words struck him with a moment of clarity: *His parents adventured 'as far as Cherry Creek.'*

A vital piece clicked; many of the places they searched were wrong.

Scanning the old trails from the county building on his phone, Jack deduced Bill's folks followed a route down the eastern edge. They had to choose their crossing points with care to avoid the deep, treacherous waters further south. *Everything south of Cherry Creek is too distant and tricky. And past Glendale Bridge? It would have taken way too long.*

Gazing at it again, he traced the path down the western boundary. *Shingle Camp is the best option on the trail along the western side of Marsh Run*

Creek.

Puzzled by his mutterings, Emma asked, "What are you piecing together?"

Without breaking his gaze from the maps, he gestured for patience with a lifted finger.

Returning to the fishing map, Jack's finger retreated upon the lake northward, pausing at Gravely Run. A thought emerged: the need to revisit. The map's contours hinted at a raised hump in the middle – *Does a second cave exist on the western half?*

Yet, doubt lingered. *Did I overlook any other sites?*

A detail just north of Gravely caught his eye – a significant depth change buried amongst hundreds of the lines and numbers: 27 feet bracketed between depths of 15 to the north and 20 to the south, creating a secluded pool, an anomaly he missed prior, closer to the marker. He now realized he had misread it as 17 before.

Switching back to his phone, he opened the older trail map from the courthouse and zoomed in on the creek's path, examining it closely. Starting at Cherry Creek, he followed Deep Creek as it flowed northwest until it met Marsh Run Creek. Then, he slid his finger to move northward. His eyes strained as he tried to make out the small marks over the creek just north of where Gravely Run joined it. At first, he thought it was just a wider section of the creek or a pool of water, but he wanted to be certain.

Zooming in even further, the lines blurred and became pixelated, but then he noticed the marks were two faint, wavy lines drawn across Marsh Run. It suddenly dawned on him that these marks indicated the waterfall they had already explored. As he glanced at the fishing map, he realized that due to the width of the channel at Gravely Run, they may have missed a cave on the far west side. *We need to make a quick check there.*

Returning to his phone again, he slid the map a hair further north and spotted a second set of lines. They were in the same potential spot he had just determined he originally misread on the fishing map. *Wow. Much like Upper and Lower Swallow Falls, Marsh Run Creek drops twice over a short distance. So, we have two sites to check that would have been on Clarke's route south along Marsh Run.*

Navigating south along the contours of Marsh Run on the map, Jack's fingers dragged the screen to follow the stream southward till it met with Deep Creek again. He followed it as it snaked its way west. His finger paused over serpentine lines near Shingle Camp Hollow, which was their next target.

Continuing along the creek to Red Run, he saw no lines there. However, as he proceeded to the area around Penelec and the dam, he saw two more sets of lines. There were wavy lines by Penelec where they found the anchor. But there was a second set of lines that were clearly much further west than where the dam was today. *What's there?*

He then recalled their previous searches: *This must be where we found that dry waterfall behind the dam before running into the bear.* Retracing Deep Creek east and then southeast, there were no other signs of waterfalls north of Cherry Creek.

The gears in his mind turned, crafting a strategy to mislead their competitors away from their real potential sites. Now, he scrutinized the fishing chart and noted the terrain by Carmel Cove. They examined it in detail before, suggesting it as a point of interest would be a safe misdirect. Despite its depths, it lacked any additional pooled drops to conceal an unexplored cave, save a small one east of the State Park Bridge.

He rechecked the courthouse map and did not see any wavy lines there. Knowing the creek would dry up at times in the summer, treasure hunters would likely have found and searched it if a cavern existed. *This is the spot!* Luring Ritter and his henchman away from Shingle Camp and Marsh Run was paramount.

Raising his voice to catch the attention of his friends, Jack ventured, "You know, something Bill mentioned to us struck me. Emma, didn't he say he grew up in Swanton, where he resides today?"

With a skeptical tilt of her head, she asked, "Yes, I believe so. Why?"

Sally chimed in, eyes and fingers never ceasing to be engaged in her phone's game, "That sounds right."

"He wasn't clear on the exact location of the waterfall where his parents used to swim. But he said his folks only went no further than Cherry Creek, as it was closer to home?"

Emma, sounding uncertain, replied, "Right. You might be onto something."

Appreciating Emma's and Sally's support, he pressed on, unsure if Steve was on the same page. "So, the central part of the lake would be the nearest, wouldn't it? We know the Native American path followed the east side of the old Deep Creek."

"I'm with you," she said, curiosity piqued.

Jack elaborated, "You mentioned where the trail met the old stream near Carmel Cove, which would have been on the surface but is now underwater. It got me thinking the cave might be beneath the lake. Breakfast with Bill was enlightening; he said many areas became submerged during the lake's creation. His parents' swimming spot, now underwater, was close to their home."

"Yes, that's right."

"He commented about the natural slide in Cherry Creek, still not far from their house," Jack said.

"What are you suggesting?"

"We should revisit Carmel Cove." Jack helped the map flat. "Carmel Creek flows in front of the park, emerging from under the bridge. We searched Carmel Cove's western and deeper half by Glendale Bridge. However, beyond the park's bridge, on the eastern side of it, there is another drop-off, one more accessible to Bill's parents. It would have been easy for Braddock's men to spot that waterfall as they followed the trail south."

Emma, joining him, peered at the chart, "I see your point," understanding the logic in his deduction.

Steve hovered behind, attempting to peer over Emma's shoulders, with Sally squeezing in beside him. The map sprawled out before them became a battleground of fingers and shadows.

Jack, aiming for deception, obscured the map's details with his finger.

"We go back to Carmel Cove," he said, pointing towards the eastern side of the State Park bridge. "It's south, by the main trail. It would have been easier for Bill's parents to reach it from where they lived. And since Cherry Creek was a bust, it's the next waterfall Braddock's men would hit and might have a cave."

Steve, brows knitted in concentration, struggled to follow. "Near where we found those fresh marks on the recessed wall of the shelter cave?"

"Yes, but more eastward," he clarified, finger tracing imaginary lines across the map. "The lake's widest point is by the park. We searched by the center before, around Glendale Bridge. This spot lies beyond the park's bridge on the eastern edge. Consider the era – Bill's folks were pre-auto. They'd walk or ride horses. Proximity mattered."

Steve's skepticism eased into understanding. "So, closer meant better. Makes sense."

Jack, bolstered by the logic of his argument, outlined the next day's strategy. "A quick dive there could do it. We'll check with one of the spare tanks. If we find something, we'll get a fresh tank and go back down."

Emma, stifling a yawn, signaled the end of the discussions. "That's enough planning for tonight. I'm beat. Goodnight, all."

As the group disbanded, Steve's brows furrowed, and puzzled gaze lingered on Jack, who was already gathering the maps and notes, retreating into the night's silence.

Chapter 38

Monday, June 23rd, 1755

It was still mid-day when Captain Clarke swam into the cave; the reflecting light cast eerie shadows on the walls as he entered the watery depths. Swimming as fast as he could, arms forward, feeling along the wall, he realized it climbed upward and to the right.

Just as his lungs began to burn, and thoughts of pulling himself out using the rope crossed his mind, he broke through the surface and emerged into an air pocket. The air was damp and heavy in stark contrast to the sunlit world he had just left behind. Echoes of his splashing reverberated throughout the cavern, masking the sounds of his labored breathing.

Clarke turned and peered down the tunnel shaft and the dim light of the opening. Although they may have found the perfect spot, he asked himself: *How could they get the gold into this cave?*

After descending through the cavern's entrance and ascending to the surface, he relayed his findings to his waiting comrades: "There's a passage that goes into what sounded like a vast chamber. I believe we can use it to keep the payroll secure. George, I want you to see it for yourself."

"Understood, Sir."

George stripped down and dove to the cave entrance, where he stared at it with concern before surfacing. "How far up to the air pocket, Sir?"

"It's not. 20 or so feet. I'll tug on the line when it's safe to follow."

Clarke dragged the rope with him into the cave. After arriving there, he moved out of the way and pulled on it several times. A few moments later, George's silhouette began to climb toward him.

"Excellent choice, Sir," George said as he started to shiver in the cool air. "I don't think anyone could ever stumble upon it by chance."

"My thoughts exactly, but it'll be hard to get the payroll in here," Clarke's voice heavy with relief. "Let's head back to the tree. That will give us some time to figure out how to get everything in here. I'll decide where we're going to hide it once I hear what Davis found. Maybe he'll find something as secure but dryer and warmer."

The men dove and sped their way out of the tunnel, their excitement radiating off of them as they emerged into the open air. While they helped each other out of the creek, streams of water poured from their now wet breeches. Clarke grinned, feeling a sense of pride and achievement. They found the ideal site to hide the cache – one that would protect it and keep it safe.

"Remember," he cautioned his soldiers during their return to camp, "not a word about this location to anyone outside this group, including Davis."

"Yes, Sir," the group replied in unison, their loyalty unquestionable.

The sun dipped lower in the sky as Clarke and George hung back, allowing the others to forge ahead.

"George," he whispered, a little louder than the rustling leaves. "We must figure out the best way to carry it into the upper chamber."

"Agreed, Sir," George's eyes scanning their surroundings for potential threats. "I've been thinking about it. We could use ropes to hoist the crates up one at a time. It'll be slow, but it can be done."

He nodded, envisioning the plan in his mind's eye. "Once it's in place, do we need to fortify the entrance?"

George scratched his head, "We could place some branches and stones to camouflage it."

"Go on."

"How about we booby trap it, Sir?"

"I like the sound of that."

"We can rig the entrance. Using ropes, we could set a massive slab rock and a lot of rocks on top of several branches, and after we have those propped up, we can add more tree limbs so no one knows which one to pull out without studying it in detail. If someone triggers the wrong support, they won't be around to realize they've made a grave mistake."

A smile crept across Clarke's face as he pondered the idea. It was daring, even devious, but there was a certain elegance to its simplicity. The cave would become a silent sentinel, guarding the payroll from those who dared to trespass.

"Excellent idea," Clarke clapped George on the shoulder. "Let's implement this plan if Davis has found nothing better. We have no time to waste."

As they caught up with the others, he felt renewed confidence.

The sun was approaching the peak of the western mountain as he and his men returned to camp. The gnarled branches intertwined above them like a giant's twisted fingers, casting eerie silhouettes on the ground.

"Lieutenant," Clarke called out, firm but soft. He beckoned to Robert Davis and George, gesturing for them to leave the group for a private discussion. As they huddled together, his eyes focused on Davis. "Your report."

"Sir, we searched to the Youghiogheny River and a little north," Davis said with a hint of pride. "Along the way, we spotted a cave up the hill, just off the path."

"Interesting," he said, his brows furrowing. "Tell me more."

"Of course, Sir," Davis replied, eager to share his findings. "The cave is sizable and empty. There's no dirt in it, so if we hid the payroll there, we could gather and pile rocks over it."

Clarke's thoughts raced as he imagined it. *It would be easier to hide the payroll in Davis's cave, but would it be a better, more secure location?* "How can we conceal it?" He glanced at George, who appeared to be pondering the same issue.

"Rocks, you say?" George asked, putting his hand to his chin.

"Yes, there are plenty nearby," Davis said. "We could place the chests in one of the small nooks and then make it look like a collapsed ceiling to conceal them. Or, we could collapse the entrance after placing them deep inside."

"How confident are you that the French or Natives could not discern something hidden under or behind the rocks?" Clarke asked.

"Based on George's experience, he would be the best to secure it, Sir."

All eyes locked on George, who said, "It's easier than the alternative. Collapsing the opening could be the most natural looking, and it would make stealing it very hard. However, recovery will be a problem, and we would need an army to reopen it."

"Or we both bury it inside and collapse the entrance," Davis said.

"How visible is the cave from the trail?"

"It's not easy to spot as it's over several hundred feet above it. I hand men walking above the path as part of the search. They found it."

"Thank you, Robert, George. Let me ponder our options. In the meantime, Robert, I want you and Edward to prepare to set out at first light. The two of you will ride back to the head of the trail to place the first marker and hide a code under the stone by the tree. We need speed and stealth, and I trust you to complete this vital task. On horseback, you should make it there and back within a day. Take a day's provisions. The rest of us will work together to secure the payroll."

"Understood, Sir," Davis said. "Edward and I will be ready."

"Good," Clarke said, nodding. "Now, let's join the others."

He sat and surveyed the landscape, allowing the details to etch themselves into his memory. The setting sun cast long shadows across the ground as it approached the far mountain peak. He knew he had to choose wisely; the fate of the payroll depended on it.

Turning, his eyes fell on the men gathered around the fire and those of Davis and Edward exchanging uneasy glances over their upcoming journey.

Robert and Edward stood and walked up to him. "Sir," Robert said, his voice laced with uncertainty, "May we discuss your orders?"

"Proceed."

"I'm concerned it is a greater distance to ride and return. Edward reminded me that we took two days before."

Edward nodded in agreement, his stoic expression betraying his concern. "That leaves fewer of us to guard the payroll… It could be risky."

Clarke studied their faces and understood their apprehension, so he met their gazes with unwavering determination. "I appreciate your comments, but you will be riding unencumbered. You will be able to travel light and fast. Therefore, I trust both of you to fulfill this task."

They hesitated, searching Clarke's eyes for any inkling of doubt. They found none. With a shared nod, they swallowed their fears, driven by loyalty to their commander.

"Very well, Sir," Robert said, firm and resolute.

"Thank you," Clarke said, clapping each man on the shoulder. "Now, let's get some rest. We all have a long day tomorrow."

"We will be ready, Sir."

Staring at his soldiers around the dying fire, he still had some nagging concerns. *After my decision that cost Samuel his life, will I make the right choice? Which is the best option? Davis's cave or the one we found?*

Clarke knew the payroll's safety depended on their success, and the thought gnawed at him like a persistent itch.

Since he was struggling to decide, he knew he couldn't sleep for a while. "I'll take the first watch, men. Robert, I'll wake you when it's your turn. Followed by Edward and Henry."

"Yes, Sir," Robert tried to mask the exhaustion tugging at the corners of his eyes. "Just alert me when you're ready."

He took up his post, eyes scanning the darkness beyond their makeshift camp. He took out his journal and made a few entries.

Realizing he needed to create a code for Braddock to find the payroll, he had no idea what to write nor where to direct them to it. His thoughts drifted to his family, and he pulled out and read the letters from his wife and sister again.

Fearing he might not return to England to see them one day, he contemplated writing a letter to his wife for someone to convey to her after his death. As he considered what codes and ciphers to use, it dawned on him he could accomplish both in the same document: saying farewell to his life's love and including the code.

But where? He then remembered the general's words: *Trust no one.*

Clarke crafted an eleven-word message highlighting direction, turns, and landmarks. After recording the codes on a page, he started to write to his wife, crossing off each code word as he used them.

Folding the completed letter and placing it in his coat pocket, he again wondered if his decision would cost more lives. He was looking at the glowing embers when he tore out the page of words for the code, stood, and ignited it in them. Returning to his post, a noise from the edge of camp broke his concentration. He strained his ears for several minutes but heard nothing again…

Chapter 39

Emma joked as her gaze swept over Jack, Steve, and Sally, each cradling their coffee, "Six in the morning is cruel, Jack. These early starts and endless searches are taking their toll. I'm surviving on caffeine at this point." The dawn light bled through the window, casting their steaming cups in a warm glow. They prepared for the chilly embrace of the mountain morning, wearing sweatpants and shirts thrown over swimsuits.

Jack, leaning in to peck Emma on the cheek, countered with a mix of apology and excitement, "I get it. But think, we're close. Today should be it. We're narrowing down the last few spots for the treasure."

Steve smiled, "I'm here for my best friend and a slice of that treasure. Count me in."

Sally, more reflective, nodded, "True. I'm in."

Emma, affection laced with a hint of exasperation at Jack's fixation, added, "For Jack, it's the thrill of history and the hunt. But I'm going to win either way. Finding the gold or getting Jack's obsession to end."

After breakfast concluded, Jack checked his phone for missed calls – none. He cleared the remnants of their meal, and they planned to head to Carmel Cove, the next item on the agenda.

"Let's get a move on," he urged, their day packed ahead.

An agreement was silent but unanimous as they headed out, Emma maneuvering the SUV for an easier load-up of their diving gear.

"Everything accounted for?" Steve eyed the gear.

Jack scanned the equipment, confident, "Yep. If not, we improvise."

Emma's worry, "Improvise? That's your plan?" clashed with Steve's confidence, "Jack's plans have gotten us this far."

With that, they drove off, only to hit a snag. An accident on Route 42, the most direct, rerouted them, the delay chipping away at Jack's patience.

Steve tried to ease the tension, "It's just a detour, Jack. Only 15 or 20 minutes more. We'll make it."

Jack's teeth pierced his lips in frustration, "It just feels like we're running out of time."

Emma's reassurance broke the tension, "We'll find that gold. It'll all be worth it in the end."

Jack, surrounded by the steadfast Emma and Steve, felt unwavering support despite the setbacks. They were more than just a team; Emma and Steve were family.

As they approached the marina, urgency propelled everyone to load and board the boat quickly. Jack steered the pontoon with a seasoned hand. The cool air tousled his hair, a shiver of anticipation running through him.

Emma, concern etched in her voice, broke the silence. "What's our plan, Jack?" The boat's engine thrummed beneath her words. "We need to ensure we're not watched."

Jack glanced toward the shore, strategizing. "We'll skirt by the state park boat ramp and head to the cove. It would mislead anyone watching from the land. And it'll allow us to check if they're already there."

"Clever," Emma nodded, her gaze sweeping the landscape for any hint of danger.

Approaching the park's bridge, the absence of anchored boats struck Jack, a gut feeling that trouble loomed. His eyes scanned the surroundings and caught a red Jeep at the Deep Creek State Park Welcome Center. Its familiarity set off alarms in his mind.

"Is that the Jeep you saw in the video the other day?" Steve's voice was tense with worry.

Jack's grip tightened on the wheel. "It looks like it. They've figured out our plans and beat us here."

Emma leaned in, her voice a whisper. "They could've bugged your place, Jack. Should we sweep our gear?"

The realization hit Jack hard, and the stakes of their quest suddenly became more perilous: *Did they do more than just bug my apartment?* He motioned for Steve and shared his fears. "Steve, search our stuff. I suspect Ritter's listening in or tracking us."

Steve's concern mirrored Jack's. "Seriously?"

"Yep," Jack said, his mind reeling from the implications. "You wanted to go on the offensive, right? I only thought about creating this diversion last night. Didn't want to risk an open discussion. I don't want them to know where we are going."

"Understood."

They veered away from the State Park.

"I had a hunch you'd catch on to the bluff about the map, especially since it confused you, and I was somewhat casual about hiding it with my finger. Emma considered this morning the chance Ritter planted bugs or trackers on us. Given they broke into our apartment, they likely know about our boat and gear," Jack said, his voice low but steady.

Steve's confusion from the previous evening dissolved into admiration. "I was trying to read you, looking for your tell. But you were solid. I trust you, yet this clears up a lot. And man, you'd clean up in poker with that stone face," he chuckled. He then began meticulously examining their boat and equipment.

As Jack moved toward Marsh Hill Cove and the Route 219 Bridge, Sally's curiosity peaked. "What's happening, Steve?" she asked, glancing up from her mobile device.

"Give me a second, Sally. Jack's onto something. Mind standing? Need to check under your seat," Steve said without pausing his search.

Sally complied, and Steve inspected the now exposed compartment and found nothing. He thanked her and moved on to thoroughly search their belongings.

Moments later, Steve held up a sinister-looking GPS tracker, no bigger than half a deck of cards, extracted from the depths of a pocket on Jack's backpack. "Found this hidden away," he said, the gravity of the discovery was evident in his tone.

Visibly shaken, Jack directed Emma to take control of the boat. His search then intensified.

"What are we searching for now?" Steve queried, scanning the boat.

"Anything that can float and hold the tracker," Jack replied, his gaze sharp.

Steve humorously chose this moment to pull out a sandwich, prompting a light-hearted comment from Emma about him being a Hobbit wanting Second Breakfast. But his actions were deliberate; he replaced the sandwich with the tracker in the Ziplock bag, leaving a small opening to inflate it and then sealing it with precision.

They navigated deep into Cherry Creek Cove and towards the shore, guided by Jack's subtle hand directions. As the boat approached shallow waters, Jack signaled for a halt.

With careful movements, Jack set the tracker adrift on the lake's surface before they retreated, steering back towards the main body of water.

Sally, her patience worn thin, demanded, "Can someone please tell me what's going on?"

With a reassuring nod from Jack, Steve took a moment before gently taking Sally's hand. "Last night was a diversion. Jack suspects Ritter, or one of his people, bugged his place. And now, finding this tracker in his bag confirms they're on to us, trying to figure out where we're heading. They must have tracked us to realize the treasure may be beneath the lake."

Sally absorbed the plan with a nod, asking if they could do more. Jack outlined their strategy of misdirection, using a tracker in an incorrect location to buy them time for a thorough search of the remaining better sites.

"So, where to first?" Steve chimed in, arms folded across his chest, embodying impatience.

Jack unfolded the fishing map, fingers tracing their imminent journey. Enthusiasm thinly veiled, he shared that their initial target was just north of Gravely Run, explaining his discovery on the map the night before. "Not deep, 27 feet at most. We'll check there, and if we don't find it, it's onto the next site."

"Let's go," Emma said, decisively pushing the throttle forward, propelling them into action.

Speeding to Gravely Run, Jack and Steve suited up, calculating their air for the shallow dive ahead. Jack's voice carried a mix of excitement and caution over the sound of their preparations, reminding Steve of the darkness awaiting them and the limited visibility they'd face.

"Be careful. It will be dark as the sun's not very high yet. We won't have great visibility due to it being shallow. I'm hoping the sediment in the water settled overnight, especially with very few boats out this early," he said.

Steve, now ready, replied with a solid "Got it," securing his gear.

Emma's pierced lips of concern were evident as she wished Jack luck and stressed to be safe, to which he said, "We'll be fine," before signaling Emma for the final approach.

While approaching their destination, the anticipation surged in Jack. Failure meant losing to Ritter. He called for Emma to ease off as they drew near, cutting the engine and drifting only.

"There!" Emma identified the spot as the depth gauge dipped, and Steve slid the anchor into the water.

Jack and Steve grasped their equipment and prepared to step off on opposite sides as the boat slowed.

"Ready?" Jack asked with a supportive thumbs-up.

"Yep," came Steve's concise response.

With a splash, Jack and Steve plunged, the creek bed greeting them with a tapestry of rocks and sand, while Jack directed them towards a promising ledge, both enveloped by the silent underwater world, their quest just beginning.

Steve nodded, trailing Jack through the murky waters towards the deep. Their fins stirred the bottom, veiling their path in clouds of silt.

Edging around the underwater precipice, a silent world unfolded below – a fossilized waterfall, boulders, and sediment locked in an eternal cascade. Sunlight barely reached this depth, casting an otherworldly glow over the scene.

"Look. Around." Jack pointed at his eyes and waved his finger in a large horizontal circle. With his metal detector in hand, Jack probed the waters while Steve eyed the surroundings for clues. Their search yielded only an ancient tree stump, its roots entangled with the discarded lines of long-gone fishermen.

"Zero," Jack's gesture conveyed his disappointment.

Steve pointed, "Up."

Reaching the anchor, Jack eyed his dive watch – fourteen feet deep, their dive so brief that their ascent and approach doubled as their safety stop. He shared a signal with Steve, confirming their status.

Emma's worried face greeted them. "Everything alright? You weren't down long."

"No luck," Jack said as he climbed aboard. "Let's head to the west side of the wall across from Gravely Run, near where we dove before. That wall was the first major fall they would have encountered heading south."

Emma nodded, setting their new course.

Checking his tank and watch, Jack said to Steve, "No need to wait; we can dive again immediately."

With scuba gear still on, they moved swiftly. Steve hoisted the anchor, and they sped towards their next target.

As they approached the next dive site, Jack's anticipation grew. He glanced at the surroundings and then over Emma's shoulder at the gauges. "Stop here."

After a quick look at his air levels, he said, "About thirty minutes of air left. I'll scout for a waterfall and cave – back in five, tops." With fins in hand, Jack moved quickly to the edge of the boat and took a giant stride into the water.

Steve watched Jack stride off the deck. "Sometimes I question why I'm friends with this guy," he muttered and smiled, following suit.

After donning his fins, Jack neared the wall and plunged past the edge and the noticeable hump separating the wall in half. While preparing to search west, Steve arrived in front of him, stirring up the bottom.

Realizing they had not searched the entire face before, their excitement was building.

"Look around," Jack signaled. Yet, as minutes ticked by, optimism waned. The wall and lakebed revealed no secrets; the metal detector remained ominously quiet, yielding nothing.

Frustration gnawed at him. Dead ends were a luxury they couldn't afford. Time and luck were slipping through their fingers.

Five unyielding minutes later, Jack signaled their return to the surface. Growing disappointment seeded doubts about the treasure's existence and his pursuit of it.

Don't give up now, he silently rallied himself.

At their safety stop, Jack sought reassurance in Steve's steady gaze, finding a silent pledge of unwavering support.

Surface-bound sunlight, and Steve's sharp rebuke met Jack, "Jack, what the hell were you thinking of jumping off the boat without me? Never dive alone!"

Surprised, Jack wiped water from his face, struggling for words. "I... I wasn't going to be reckless. Just a quick look. Once you joined, I figured we could explore."

"You bet I joined you," Steve's rebuke was sharp. "You know the risks."

"I was trying to beat Ritter to it."

"I get it. But never dive alone in unexplored areas. That's when you get in trouble. Get caught on a stump, tangled in fishing line, or run out of air."

"I promise. Never again."

Steve's frown eased into a reluctant nod. "Just... be safer, okay?"

"Understood," Jack whispered, sharing his next lead. "Bill's childhood home was Accident, and a northern waterfall would have also been easier for Clarke."

Steve leaned in, their conversation barely audible. "And what now?"

Jack checked his dive watch. "Next is the falls between Route 219 Bridge and Shingle Camp Cove, following the trail to Yough River, or in this case, the dam."

"Got it."

Jack glanced at his watch, "We need a short break on the surface and to swap tanks. Twenty minutes up top."

"Okay," Steve replied, hits of agitation remaining in his tone. "Remember, safety first, buddy. Check your gear twice, stay aware of your surroundings, and maintain line-of-sight communication. Got it?"

"Got it,"

Climbing back into the boat, Jack and Steve began peeling off their dive gear, stripping down to their wetsuits. Jack's gaze lingered on Emma and Steve, his closest companions, feeling a rush of anticipation for what lay ahead and a deep appreciation for their love and friendship.

As their surface interval ticked by, Jack checked his phone for updates from contractor Mike Thompson, finding none. He stowed his device, catching snippets of conversation between Sally and Steve.

"Jack?" Emma's concerned voice broke through. "You alright?"

"Yeah," he replied, mustering a smile. "Just waiting for a callback."

Emma nodded, squinting her eyes, showing she wasn't fully satisfied with the answer, but was willing to let it go.

While their surface time wound down, Jack felt a prickle of unease. He surveyed the waters to the south and the western shoreline, but nothing out of place caught his eye. Yet, as he turned north and east, his gaze fixed upon two figures standing at the open hatch of a red Jeep along Deep Creek Drive, both clad in wetsuits, one with a distinctive beard that caught his attention.

"Guys," Jack's voice carried a sharp edge of concern as he gestured towards the men. "Over there."

Emma, Sally, and Steve looked where he pointed, their focus narrowing on the unfamiliar divers.

"Who are they?" suspicion laced Sally's voice.

"It's Ritter," Jack said, a sense of urgency propelling his thoughts. *How did they manage to track us here?*

Chapter 40

Tuesday, June 24th, 1755

The sky was beginning to glow when Henry Jones stirred, his eyes flickering as he tried to peer into the dim twilight. He blinked; confusion gave way to worry as he realized Edward Smith had failed to rouse him for his duty.

"Damn it, Edward," he muttered under his breath, pushing himself off the ground. His muscles ached from the hard surface and the previous day's search, but he pushed the discomfort aside, focusing on answering the question of where Edward was. He scanned the camp, irritated and realizing everyone else was still asleep, and walked to where the lookout should be.

"Edward!" he called out, trying to keep his voice soft enough not to wake the others. No response came, only the distant chirping of birds and the rustle of leaves in the breeze.

Henry's gaze swept over the camp again, and he started noticing unsettling details. Edward's horse was missing. *Did he abandon his post and leave the group?*

He continued to search. His eyes landed on one of the payroll crates, and panic set in – its lid was ajar, much of its contents gone.

"Son of a..." Henry whispered in disbelief. When the realization settled in, he gritted his teeth, anger bubbling beneath the surface. The thought of betrayal crossed his mind; stealing payroll while everyone slept was unthinkable. *Why would he do such a thing?*

Determined to confront the turncoat, he sprinted to grab his rifle and roused his horse, ignoring the groans of disgruntled men disturbed by his actions. He swung onto the animal's back and followed the trail they had arrived on.

"I'll bring the traitor, Edward, back," he yelled to his fellow soldiers.

Disappearing into the distance, Henry's thoughts mulled over the events leading to this moment. Edward had always been quiet and unassuming. Never would he have suspected Edward being capable of such deceit.

The steady rhythm of hooves pounding against the earth matched the beat of his heart, both racing towards an uncertain confrontation. The encampment disappeared behind him, and he steeled himself for what was to come: *Why Edward? Why did you betray us?*

His ears strained to pick up any sound over his own thunderous heartbeat. A whinny reached him from a distance ahead, and he knew he was right – the betrayer wasn't far ahead.

"Traitor!" he bellowed, gripping his gun tighter in one hand as he raced on.

The camp erupted into chaos, and disoriented soldiers scrambled to their feet, trying to understand what had happened. Although still half-asleep, Clarke was quick to grasp the gravity of the situation. His eyes darted from the open crate to Henry's shouting figure, putting the pieces together.

"What the hell did you do?" Clarke muttered, the bitter taste of betrayal stinging his tongue. He sprinted to his horse.

"Captain!" a fellow soldier exclaimed, concern etched on his face. "What should we do?"

"Guard the remaining payroll!" Clarke shouted in urgency. "I'll go help Henry bring that traitor to justice!"

After mounting, a gunshot split the air the moment he urged the animal forward. His heart leaped, and he pushed his steed to go faster. *Did Henry fire at Edward, or did Edward fire on Henry?*

While Clarke disappeared down the path, he asked himself: *How could a man shatter his loyalty to his comrades?*

Clarke's stallion thundered through the underbrush, his chest pounding in time with the beast's hooves. Sweat trickled down his brow as he concentrated on following Henry's trail, the crisp autumn wind biting at his cheeks. A second gunshot reverberated through the valley.

"Damn it," he muttered, pushing his steed harder.

"Captain, coming up behind you!" Davis's voice rang out, cutting through the chaos like a knife. However, Clarke's gaze was on the scene before him, and his stomach clenched in horror. He brought his stallion to a halt.

Henry stood beside a fallen Edward, blood streaming from the man's battered head. Edward's horse lay lifeless nearby, its once-majestic form now twisted and broken. Clarke dismounted, his face filled with shock, as Davis joined him.

"Why?" Clarke demanded, his hands raised, shaking with anger and disbelief.

"Braddock's mad... going to get everyone... killed." Edward wheezed through labored breaths; his eyes clouded with pain. "And the colonies... deserve freedom."

A pained silence fell over them, and Edward's words settled with grave concern.

"Freedom?" He whispered, his mind racing. "Is this why you took the payroll? To aid the colonists? For what?"

Edward nodded weakly, coughing up blood. "Independence... from a tyrant... worth fighting for."

"Even if it means betraying your comrades?" Henry spat, his eyes blazing with fury.

"Betrayal or not, the cause is just," he rasped, his body trembling as death approached. "You'll see... one day..."

With a final shudder, Edward's eyes rolled back, and he breathed his last. Clarke closed his eyes, grappling with the torrent of emotions threatening to consume him – betrayal, anger, and a nagging sense of doubt.

"Captain," Davis said, placing a hand on his shoulder. "What do we do now?"

"We carry on," he said, his jaw set in determination. "We'll hide the payroll as ordered and face what challenges come next."

"Whatever it may be," Henry said with a grim stare of furrowed brows, staring at Edward's lifeless form.

Clarke and Davis stood over the body, uncertain what to do. He gazed in thought, scanning the horizon, spotting the first rays of the sun striking the tip of the massive oak tree back at camp, and he took a deep breath. Clarke's conscience spoke to him. *Despite this man's actions, I have to do the right thing.*

"Edward betrayed us, but we owe him a burial," he said, firm and resolute.

"Agreed," Davis nodded.

They draped Edward over Clarke's horse and walked back to camp.

When they arrived, Davis approached Clarke. "Captain," breaking the heavy silence. "I'll ride back to hide the code – alone. If I don't return, you must assume I've failed, and you will have to place the marker yourselves. However, if I fail, I'd recommend you go to Fort Cumberland and inform General Braddock of the hiding spot upon his arrival."

"Are you certain?" he asked with concern on his face. "It's risky."

"Braddock's orders were clear," Davis replied, determination evident in his eyes. "We have to protect the payroll at all costs. Besides, it might be safer if I go alone. My horse is the swiftest, after all."

"Very well," he conceded. "Grab provisions and go. Hide it under the rock, in this small pouch to keep it dry," Clark said as he presented Davis with the leather bag and placed the coded message inside.

"Before I go, Sir, can I be so bold as to make a recommendation?"

"Proceed."

"I say this as I'm unaware of the payroll's location once you complete the task of hiding it. I am, therefore, suggesting a ruse when we head north."

"A ruse?"

"Yes, there's a greater chance we'll run into the French the further north we travel. As you are now a Captain in a Lieutenant's coat, I suggest you take Edward's to wear and leave yours behind. Should we be captured, they would most likely torture the senior officer to find out what we were doing this far south. Their focus would fall upon me. I have no wife or children, so they would get nothing from me. Plus, a lieutenant on a patrol mission is more believable than a captain. The higher rank would lead them to believe it was more important; therefore, we would be more suspicious and dangerous. Same if we have two lieutenants."

Clarke went silent and gazed at the mountain gap to the northwest. After a moment, he turned and offered his hand to Davis and said, "Thank you, Robert. Your reasoning makes sense, and your bravery is unmatched. I'll do as you suggest. Godspeed on your journey, trust no one, and good luck."

"Same to you, Captain," Davis saluted and mounted his horse.

Clarke's eyes followed him gallop away until he disappeared, praying Davis and the payroll would remain safe.

An unexpected cold wind whipped around Clarke, and a chill went down his spine. He hoped it wasn't an omen. He turned and explained to the troop what transpired and ordered them to bury Edward at the hill's peak, away from the hole for the payroll. He took his uniform coat from him.

They finished covering Edward's body, and he wondered if Edward's final words would haunt him for the rest of his days.

"I know we are all tired from digging, men. Let's take a short break, and then we'll head out," he said before turning to write in his journal. Once completed, he grabbed the promotion letter Braddock handed him, stood, walked to the fire, and threw it in. He turned to address the group.

"Men, we must focus on the task at hand," he said. "We've come too far to falter now. William and Thomas, dig the hole here." He pointed to a clearing between the massive tree and several other trees. "I'm hopeful you will find fewer roots. The rest of us will hide the payroll and return it by nightfall. Gentlemen, let's grab the chests, ropes, and shovels. We've still a lot of work to do."

Chapter 41

Sally glared at the two men and their red jeep on the hillside and asked, "Why didn't they go after that tracker?"

Jack conceded with a sigh. "I chose the wrong place to ditch it. If they had followed the tracker's signal from where they were in Carmel Cove, they would've driven through the state park and wouldn't have seen our boat anywhere in Cherry Creek. They probably continued on to their next spot. Damn it! I should've chosen a better, busier spot. Something further away."

"Or... did they anticipate us stopping to look after finding one and planted a second?" Steve asked, a hint of frustration in his voice.

"Shit. You may be right," he said.

Steve's energy surged. "Either way, I say we go and confront them!" He punctuated his resolve with a loud smack of his fist into his other palm.

He pondered and shook his head. "Not yet. Let's try to stay ahead of them. Confronting them might tip them off that we're on to them, and they may get aggressive. And if we go after them, we'd land in jail for beating them into a pulp."

Steve, clenching his fists and itching for action, took a deep breath before consenting. "Maybe we should," he said as he shook his head and his shoulders slumped. "Okay, let's get away from them."

"Agreed," Emma supported the cautious approach. "You two focus on diving and finding the treasure. Sally and I will keep an eye out for them."

"We're on it," Sally said, her gaze fixed on the distant foes.

Jack directed Emma, "Take us towards the dam."

Steve couldn't resist a cinematic quote, "I feel the need, the need for speed!"

Emma chuckled, "Okay, Maverick." And she pushed the throttle down.

Distancing themselves from Ritter, the lakefront homes soon obstructed their pursuers' view of their direction.

Concerned, Jack suggested a thorough check for additional trackers.

The trio combed through their gear, finding nothing until Steve insisted on checking under the pontoon's deck.

"Stop the boat," Steve demanded, eager to investigate further. Diving in, he emerged underneath, echoes of hands slapping on the metal frame as he moved around. From time to time, he called out, "Nothing yet!"

Moments later, "Shit!" resonated in all directions.

"You okay, Stevie," Emma cried out with concern.

"Yeah," Steve surfaced behind the pontoon, small device in hand. "Found one mounted on a bracket."

Jack's frustration building. "We need to dispose of this one better."

Soaked but determined, Steve climbed the ladder, grinning ear to ear.

"What?" Sally asked.

"Let's head to Bill's Marina. I'll put it on another boat," he laughed.

Arriving at the rental dock, they pulled up to a gas pump. Steve eyed a nearby, almost identical pontoon beginning to buzz with the activity of a half dozen boaters climbing aboard as an attendant arrived and the pump thundered to life, fueling their vessel. With a swift motion, he donned his mask and slipped into the lake unseen.

Jack caught a glimpse of his friend underwater before resurfacing, pointed at the pontoon's number, then vanished again. Moments later, he emerged and hauled himself onto the dock's far side without issue and away from prying eyes.

Rejoining their boat, Steve helped the attendant untie the boat from the dock, and he jumped onboard.

Emma edged the boat away before pushing on the throttle and heading westward for their next dive near Shingle Camp Hollow. While she navigated them under Deep Creek Bridge, Jack strode over to her and pointed between the map and the surrounding landscape. "Keep heading west. After we pass Marsh Run Cove on the right, we will almost be at the site. See where the mountains slope down to the lake's shores on both sides? Notice how the lake narrows and then widens again?

"I do."

"The underwater natural dam is near its narrowest point. Can you head to the right side? That'll put us out of the way of most of the boat traffic."

Peering from the chart to the mountainside, Emma acknowledged with a tense, "Got it."

Edging closer to shore, Emma studied the depth gauge until it jumped and stabilized. She reversed the engine to bring the boat to a stop and signaled Steve to drop anchor.

Impressed by her precision, Jack half-joked, "The navy might be calling your name."

She rolled her eyes, "Very funny."

Then, turning earnest, he posed, "Given Ritter's threat, would you prefer to stay here or return in 30 minutes and circle back every 10?"

Emma's gaze locked onto him, and she made her decision as she reached for Steve's bag, securing his gun. "We'll hold the fort here. The water's not too choppy. Plus, we're in the wide open and visible to passing boats."

"Okay with you, Sally?" Steve asked.

"Yeah, we're fine," she said, her voice blending courage and caution.

Steve chimed in, with a pragmatic edge, "If things go south, remember to give the pontoon a good whack with the oar."

"Understood," came Emma's firm response. Positioning the paddle within arm's reach, she and Sally sat strategically. Emma was scanning the area ahead, and Sally was at the rear.

In a calm tone, Emma whispered a heartfelt, "Be careful" to Jack. Their gazes locked, a silent acknowledgment of the risks before them.

"Always," Jack murmured as he and Steve donned their dive gear.

Laying out the map on the table, Jack outlined their strategy. "This dive's tricky, Steve. We're at 10 feet and near the shore, so the water will be rather murky from being churned up by the boats. We'll head south and descend towards the natural dam. I expect clarity should improve before we arrive where the original creek flowed over the waterfall."

Steve stood, nodding.

"The top of the dam's around 20 feet. A hill or hump that splits the dam into two parts," he detailed, his finger tracing their underwater route. "The target area is on the western side of this dam. The southern side is slightly lower and appears to have a gradual slope like Cherry Creek that flows into a deep pool, around 45 at the bottom. We'll aim for the northern side closest to us; it looks like a sheer drop, offering us a quicker way to the bottom and has a greater chance of a recess or shelter cave at the bottom of it."

Steve absorbed every word, and the strategy crystallized in his mind.

"We'll circle the area counterclockwise," he proposed, eyes locked on the table. "Passing along the northern edge of the first, as it also has steep walls. Both the falls and the wall may hold a cave. We have 49 minutes, max. I'll set an alert for 45 to give us a cushion. Ready?"

"Yes. I understand why we needed to plan this dive," Steve said. "Looks like you're finally growing up!" He slapped Jack on the back. Jack could only smile and shake his head as he inserted the regulator into his mouth and took a deep breath from his tank.

With a giant stride from the boat, they submerged into the lake, hearts racing from a mixture of thrill and apprehension. Below, visibility turned opaque; the sediment-filled water appeared like a thick fog. Every move became an unknown – they bumped into or pushed away in panic from stumps that popped up in front of them without warning.

Minutes later, they ventured deeper and past the thermal layer where the water's embrace became colder; however, their vision cleared. Before them, a ghostly forest of stumps and entwined roots sprawled, a haunting reminder of life once flourishing here, now submerged and silent.

As they moved further south, the lakebed flattened and became devoid of trees – a clear indication they reached the channel's bottom, scoured clean by relentless currents. Unease over Emma and Sally intruded, but he shook it off, refocusing on the mission.

"Okay?" Steve signaled.

"Okay."

Jack and Steve looked around and realized that although they found the submerged creek, they arrived on the wrong side. They were at the earthen dam's eastern edge, staring down into a 20-foot deeper, massive expanse of calm water below. They were at the end of the original Deep Creek's lengthiest pool that stretched miles to the south.

Having their bearings, they veered west and traced the water-smoothed path to the precipice. The massive force necessary to sculpt these cliffs from rock-filled Jack with awe and a sharp sense of the hurdles ahead.

Dropping over the western edge, the water turned colder, signaling another thermal shift. A shudder passed through Jack, excitement eclipsed by the penetrating chilly temperature for the moment.

"Cold!" Steve's signal was clear.

"Okay. Onward," Jack gestured, despite his own struggle against the chill.

They entered a natural amphitheater at the waterfall's base, its floor littered with stumps and logs like the aftermath of a colossal battle. No visible cave at the bottom prompted a westward move along the towering rock faces to their north.

A second, deeper basin unveiled itself, its depths shrouded in mystery.

On their right, a vertical face sculpted by the might of water rose beyond the thermocline and out of their sight. Awestruck, they hovered before a shelter cave. They probed the cavern, but it yielded no secrets.

"Anything?" Jack signaled.

"Zero."

Gripping the metal detector, its hum a constant in the silent underwater world, Jack persisted, scanning the rocky bed with unwavering focus. Encountering only fishing remnants deepened his frustration.

Steve gestured southward, urging on.

"Okay," he acquiesced.

Their exploration of the pool's far edge revealed the steep incline, yet no cave or passage. Their circuitous search brought them to the dam's natural slide – a geological wonder that lifted Jack's spirits despite their fruitless endeavor. They continued their search till they reached their original entry point below the waterfall.

Damn it! The repeated failures gnawed at Jack, a silent battle raging within as despair began to take hold. The further they swam, the heavier the specter of defeat loomed, a constant companion in their ascent to the channel over the earthen dam. With each thrust of his fins, his mind teemed with doubts.

They depleted their list of high-potential sites except one and now moved closer to poor chances and mere guesses. *Diving every part of this lake will take weeks! Weeks we don't have. Is the treasure beneath these waters? Or did I lead my friends astray and into a dangerous quest for a treasure that someone else has already found?*

Beaten, they rose against the vertical wall and swam across the earthen shelf, following the underwater streambed toward their pontoon. Searching for the boat's anchor line or the shadow of the boat itself, they saw neither as they reached the dam's eastern edge and gazed upon the vastness of Deep Creek's original body of water.

Jack checked their progress on his dive computer, starting their safety stop at 15 feet. Suspended in the lake, the extent of the original Deep Creek and its massive depth behind the dam drew his attention. He crept out over the edge and peered down as Steve joined and hovered beside him.

The sharp beep of his alarm signaled the maximum bottom time and jolted him out of what was almost a trance. Silencing it, he noted they needed another minute as he drifted further over the expanse.

With an exhale, pivoting to return to find the pontoon and ascend, something unusual in the depths caught his eye – a distinct shadow against the dam's wall, drawing him with the promise of discovery.

He silenced the safety stop alarm, his heart daring to hope. Staring at the rock wall, he asked himself: *Is that a shadow from above or something else?* The glimmer of optimism sparked within him as he pondered: *Is that a shelter cave? Might this be what the cryptic message meant, a cave in a pool of water behind the waterfall?* Perhaps this was the breakthrough they needed.

Fueled by this newfound possibility, Jack edged lower and closer to the cliff, his eyes straining through the murky waters, desperate for a clearer view. The need to confirm his suspicion drove him forward.

But as he started to dive deeper towards the shadow, Steve's hand clamped around his arm, yanking him back with decisive force.

He turned to meet Steve's urgent gaze, his expression stern, his message clear: "STOP! UP!" The silent command, unyielding and fierce, halted him in his tracks.

Chapter 42

Jack's heart thrummed against his ribs as they rose northward and in the direction of where the pontoon should be when they caught sight of the boat's silhouette looming above them through the lake's murky water. A rush of excitement surged within, the thrill of the hunt electrifying his senses. He was sure they were on the brink of discovery.

Surfacing and pulling off his mask and ejecting the mouthpiece, Jack called out with urgency and anticipation, "Emma! Sally! We didn't find the cave, but we found something promising on the bridge side of the dam. We didn't get close enough to figure out what it is – we ran out of time."

Bobbing in the water beside him, Steve said, "I saw it, too." They glanced up to see Emma and Sally smiling and wide-eyed, peering over the boat's edge.

Emma said, her voice edged with skepticism and intrigue, "How long till you can dive again?"

Jack consulted the computer and said, "Needs an hour and twenty to be safe."

Sally's surprise was evident. "That's quite the wait for such a brief dive."

"Don't want to risk the bends," Steve chuckled.

Once aboard, Jack beamed as each dive narrowed their search, edging them nearer to the treasure that eluded so many. This one was different; it held more promise than the others now.

Catching Emma's eye, he saw the strain of his obsession tempered by a mutual excitement for what lay beneath. Her weariness had been a constant shadow over their relationship, yet now, there was a flicker of shared hope.

"We have to prep for our next dive," Jack said. "This may be the moment."

The enforced wait was agony for Jack. He paced the deck, trapped by his own racing thoughts and the tantalizing possibility of success. Each step echoed his inner turmoil – was this it or just another false lead?

Emma's command snapped him out of his reverie. "Jack, sit! You're driving me nuts."

Plopping down beside her, he apologized. Sally's silent observation from a distance puzzled him. She was an enigma, yet her presence was soothing, the opposite of the typical, more overt, and superficial personalities Steve attracted. However, he sensed an impending connection between their quest's outcome and her.

After a deep breath, Jack's eyes met Steve's, reflecting a shared anticipation.

"Before we go down, we should move the boat past the drop on the dam's eastern side," Steve proposed, the thrill evident in his voice. "It's deeper and clearer at that spot, and it will be easier to reach the cave."

"Agreed, but let's head into Shingle Camp Hollow now," Jack countered, scanning the lake as he leaned on the railing, the sun warming his back. "It's smoother, less watercraft traffic."

"Got it," Steve said, retrieving the anchor.

Emma took control, guiding them toward the inlet with a focus that spoke volumes of her strength, a stark contrast from the woman Jack once knew.

After anchoring, they gathered for a quick lunch, helping them to prepare for the dive ahead.

Finishing her meal, she stood, gestured to the back of the pontoon, and asked, "You in, Sally? I'm tired of sitting. Time for a swim."

"I am," Sally said, grabbing a life vest to use as a float and heading to the ladder.

Jack's head tilted in confusion, and his eyes followed Emma's moments as she climbed to the top deck. He received an answer in the form of a deluge as Emma's cannonball doused him, drawing laughter from all. Emma, consistently successful at calming and grounding Jack, grinned as she resurfaced.

"Don't just stare," she teased, calling for a life jacket to use as a float. He complied, tossing one to her.

Soon after, Jack and Steve joined in, diving into the refreshing, cool water. Conversations and playful splashes made them forget their quest for a time, immersing them in the joy of friendship.

Jack's alarm buzzed, a jolt to remind him of their mission. "Time to gear up," he said, the resolve clear in his voice.

"Let's do this," Emma said.

Back on the pontoon, his brief hope faded at the sight of his silent phone. Droplets fell from his hair as he messaged Mike, "Who took pictures of the journal the day you found it? That may have something to do with who dug up your site." Hitting send, he proceeded to text Allen for an update on Ben.

"Everything alright?" Steve asked, pulling himself up the ladder. His gaze, filled with concern, met his as water cascaded from his face.

"Just texted the Lieutenant about Ben," Jack said, a strained smile playing on his lips as he tucked his phone away. "Thought we should check on him."

"That's good. We could drop by if Ben's still in the hospital," Emma said.

"He's such a nice kid," Sally said, her down-turned mouth betraying her sympathy. "Do they know who did that to him yet?"

"Not yet," Jack replied, catching the worry etched in Sally's expression. Once Steve helped Sally aboard, he moved to retrieve the anchor.

"Now that we're all onboard," he said, reaching for his wetsuit. "Emma, can you hit the spot Steve mentioned?"

"Of course, are you doubting me?" she quipped with a smirk, steering the boat with practiced ease, her gaze flitting to the navigation tools.

The depth gauge nosedived when they passed over a submerged ledge, indicating deeper waters. "That's it! Go, Steve!" Emma directed.

Steve obliged, sending the anchor plunging into the depths. They anchored about 100 feet offshore in 41 feet of water, an ideal location for their expedition.

"Time to suit up," Steve said, clapping Jack's back. They quickly geared up, checking and rechecking each other's equipment before signaling readiness.

"Be careful; remember Bill's concern," Emma reminded them. "We're here if you need us."

"We've got this, Em," Jack said, kissing her cheek as he passed.

Jumping into the lake, the cool undercurrents enveloped him. The sound of distant boats blurred into the background as they descended, the bubbles flowing across his cheeks and clarity greeting them past the thermocline. The vast shadow of a rock shelf emerged, stirring Jack's excitement.

"There!" He signaled to Steve, pointing towards a thick rock overhang stretching out to greet them. Under it, a deep, shadowed recess awaited.

Glancing at his watch, it read 20 feet. He reasoned that the ledge was once just above the waterline, shaped by centuries of relentless flow, and surmised this would have been an ideal location for Clarke and his team.

Powering up, their flashlights illuminated the entrance to a cave. However, entangled branches and debris veiled the entrance.

"Yeeesss!" Steve's exhilaration bubbled through his regulator.

Jack led the way, adrenaline urging him forward.

"Slow," Steve cautioned, "Look. First."

"Okay," he acknowledged. Together, they approached the cave, hearts racing in anticipation of the secrets they were about to uncover.

Now facing the cave's ominous, shadowed mouth, a beam from his flashlight sliced through the dimness as he searched the depths beyond the entangling branches. The cavern's throat stretched upwards, a silent challenge, yet any treasure remained elusive.

"Look!" His voice, muffled by the regulator, pierced the underwater silence, his arm outstretched towards the enigmatic entrance.

Steve, ever the voice of caution, gripped Jack, spinning him in the watery gloom. Peering into Jack's eyes, he signaled, "Stop. Danger. Up. Together. Talk."

"Okay."

As soon as they surfaced, a wide-eyed Jack started, "Holy shit..."

Chapter 43

It was late in the morning when Captain Thomas Clarke set off from camp with his most trusted men: brothers James and John Miller, George Williams, and Henry Jones. They had been with him throughout the journey, and it was still not over.

Edward Smith's betrayal still bore down on them, but the group's mission drove them on. They walked their laden horses to the trail and turned toward the falls.

The group crossed the creek atop the nearby waterfalls and soon arrived at the more significant waterfall to the south and west. They understood each other so well they went to work without any orders.

George and Henry gathered the ropes and placed them on the shelf above the cave's entrance.

The Miller brothers carried the chests to the edge as well.

The soldiers started their tasks, and Clarke admired their resilience.

Clarke then opened his pack and grabbed several items: his flint, knife, and a vial of lantern oil. Retrieving a short cask, he knocked off the hoop ring to open it up and insert the vial and pieces of wood he had brought from camp. Ripping pages from his journal, he positioned them inside the cask before resealing the lid. He then tucked the knife and flint into his tight breeches.

"What's that about, Captain?" George asked.

"Just giving us some light when in the air pocket."

"No, Sir. The pages?"

"Oh, just some entries about what transpired the last few days," Clarke replied. "If we don't return to meet the General on the battlefield of Fort Duquesne, they'll learn what happened to us when they retrieve the payroll."

"Makes sense, Sir."

"Let's go to work!"

Clarke started by securing the cask to one of the chests and tied one rope to one side and another to the other.

"You ready to get wet, George?"

"No, Sir. But I'm happy to do it," he replied with a smile.

He chuckled and turned to look at his men. "I cannot describe what your loyalty and friendship have meant. What we are about to do is dangerous. If something should happen to me, it's been my honor and privilege to serve alongside all of you."

"You as well, Sir," James said.

"James and John," he continued, "you lower the chests in one at a time, the one with the cask first. I'll tug when we are in position. Henry, try to monitor and pull us out if you think we are in trouble."

"You can count on us, Sir," Henry said.

Clarke started to tie the rope's end to the cask and the chest to his waist, indicating George to do the same.

"Ready, George?"

"Yes, Sir."

"I'll go first. You follow, but not too close to me. I don't want to kick you."

"Yes, Sir."

They dove in, and the cold shock almost took Clarke's breath away. As he swam deeper, he could feel his heart racing as they entered the tunnel.

Reaching the cave, they crawled away from the water and took a moment to breathe. Clarke then pulled on his rope, "Be prepared for a lot of weight."

"Yes, Sir."

Working together, they began to pull. In a minute, as they peered down the shaft, the silhouette of the chest appeared. Judging by the glow around the chest, they tried to keep it in the middle. However, between the brothers lowering and their pulling, the chest and cask repeatedly banged against the floor and ceiling of the tunnel, and the cask broke loose. Lucky for them, it was buoyant, and it rolled up the top of the passage with the sound of a splash, greeting it to the surface.

Continuing to pull, the chest broke the surface. Dragging it out of the water and setting it aside, they could hear the water streaming out of the chest. George pulled on his line. Soon, the second chest followed, and they struggled to slide it onto dry ground. Walking back to the water, Clarke grabbed the cask and brought it to a flat spot.

He pulled the knife from his breeches and used it to pop off the hoop. Shaking the excess water from his hand, he pried the lid off. Reaching in, he found the vial and some wood by touch. Stacking the wood on the ground, he opened and poured some of the oil onto the wood and resealed the vial. Reaching for the flint, he struck it with his knife, and the wood erupted in flame.

"Well, that helps," he said. The light was enough for them to discover they were in a larger area, which continued upwards to the right. A trickle of water was running down the side of it, escaping into the creek below.

"Suggest we go further to find a more level spot, Sir. I'm afraid flowing water made this cave. We need a drier location so water does not damage the chests."

"Excellent point."

They freed themselves from their ropes and carried the chest up the slope until their feet were dry on the flat rock. At this distance, the light from the fire below was dim. However, the echoes of each footstep took some time to return, indicating they were in an enormous cavern.

"I think this should do, he said.

"Agreed."

After setting down the first chest, they returned and retrieved the second one.

Clarke retrieved, sealed the cask, and placed it with the chests.

"Ready to go up?"

"Yes, Sir!" a relieved George replied.

"Don't become too excited. We need to help set the trap now."

Picking up the rope, he tied the ends from the chests together and then attached one end to himself. "You go first." They tugged on their ropes to alert the men above that they were on their way up.

James and his brother pulled the excess rope until Clarke broke the surface. James teased, "Those are some odd-looking fish we caught!"

John said, "I hope they're good eating."

Clarke turned to the group, smiled, and said, "That's funny. Now, the hard part is setting a trap."

"What do you have in mind?" Henry asked.

"George and I discussed using a massive slab of a rock. We'll tie three ropes to it. Two are for lowering to the entrance, and the other will be utilized from the inside to pull it to the top of the cave's opening. George will use several branches to brace it in place. We'll need a bunch of heavy branches, four to five feet long."

"How big of a slab?" John asked.

George interrupted, "Sir, I can take a branch down to measure the opening. We would then have measurements of the width and height. We can remove the stone's thickness to determine the braces' length."

"Excellent idea," Clarke said.

"We should make them about a half inch or so longer than needed to wedge them under the stone."

The men went to work, gathering rocks and branches to prepare the trap. Henry grabbed a branch from the ground, used his hatchet to remove the twigs, and handed it to George.

George dove in with a branch and used the knife to mark the width of the top. Given the variation of the bottom of the entrance, he scored a range for the height.

After he surfaced, George said, "We have to find a rock slab no wider than about five feet." He handed the branch to Clarke.

The men studied the markings and set out to find a slab. Clarke watched as they worked, his mind already working on the next steps. John and James found a perfect stone, around three hundred or more pounds, and it took three men to carry it to the edge.

George used a saw to cut the branch at the end of the longest range mark and then held it to the slab. "We'll need several branches four to three and a half feet long."

The men started to go into the trees and forage for thick limbs, and George cut them into different sizes. He then said, "I think we have enough."

"Alright, let's set this trap," Clarke said. "Henry and I'll go into the cave and pull with the middle rope to hold the stone to the roof while George props it open with the branches."

George paused, "I have some thoughts."

"Yes, George. Go ahead," he said.

"I can start instructing the brothers on when to stop lowering the slab. I'll then tug on your rope when you can take up the slack. You should be able to tell it's in the right place when its silhouette when it's lodged at the top. I'll signal you to pull more by knocking the cave wall once, but just a little each time. Twice means a little slack. Three will mean it's ready done and for you to come out, but be careful to go through the hole I'll leave for you."

"Perfect. George is the point. Everyone got that?"

"Yes, Sir."

The men worked with speed and precision, each understanding their role in the operation. The slab was in position within minutes, and George began to prop the stone up. George wrapped three times, surfaced for air, and returned to guide Clarke and Henry out the exit so they didn't knock a brace out.

George and Clarke took a few more dives to add more branches as props and some loose ones as disguises.

"The slab sticks out over a foot, Sir," George said at the surface. "We can place more rocks on the top as well."

"Agreed."

On their next trip, they cut and removed the ropes. They then made repeated visits to add more stones to the top of the ledge.

Clarke pulled himself out of the water and said, "Great work, men. Now, let's head to camp and have some rest…" His eyes spotted George standing motionless, lot listening and peering down into the water in silence.

"What is it, George?" Clarke asked.

"I just realized I left our hatchet in the tunnel. Sorry, Sir."

"No problem. It's no longer safe to retrieve it. So let's ride. Tomorrow, we begin the long ride to catch up with General Braddock."

The group nodded in agreement and mounted their horses. Clarke stared at them with a sense of relief and accomplishment. They secured the payroll and set a trap for anyone attempting to follow them.

The sky was glowing from behind the mountain when they arrived at camp. They peered down into the massive hole dug by Willian and Thomas, almost nine feet across and about five or six feet deep.

"Excellent work. I'm impressed."

"Thank you, Sir," William said.

"Have you spotted Davis?"

"No, Sir,"

"Well, we all deserve some rest tonight. In the morning, we'll have to bury the barrel with the coded clue as I used the small cask to leave a note should we not make it back."

As Clarke gazed upon stars above, he wondered: *Where's Davis? Will he return to camp, or did he take his chance to flee like Edward?* Then, he realized he had failed to check the level of the gold after they had replaced what Edward had taken: *Did he steal some and run?*

Clarke then put those thoughts aside and focused on the task at hand: preparing for their journey north to rejoin the army.

After a hearty meal, the men settled in for the night. Deep in thought, Clarke sat by the dying fire and couldn't shake off the suspicion something was off. Although he couldn't pinpoint what it was, he understood the need for caution. He made a mental note to keep his gun close at hand.

Just as he was about to retire for the night, he heard the sound of slow hooves on the ground from the trail below.

George was on watch duty and said, "Sir, someone's approaching."

Chapter 44

Breaking the surface, the rush of fresh air filled their lungs. Jack's eyes widened as he could not contain his excitement. "What the hell's all that about?

Steve's brows formed a crease between them, "The entry's rigged like a Jenga Tower. Pick the wrong stick, and it all comes crashing down."

"How do we tackle it?"

"Extreme caution! We'll remove whatever's loose, then reassess."

"I guess it's better to be outside than trapped beneath a collapse."

Steve nodded, "Absolutely. But if it collapses, we'd need equipment to move the rocks, and that would draw unwanted attention."

"Not good... Not good," head shaking. Jack asked, "Did you notice the hatchet by the entrance?"

"No, what about it?"

He pondered, "Must be Clarke's. He likely discovered this cave while hiding the payroll and used the hatchet to pound the branches into place. Why else would it be in the opening?"

"That's got to be it."

Jack said, "I'm taking the hatchet as proof this is a man-made barrier and a trap. Remember, Clarke's coded letter alluded to the cryptic word 'caution.' Our challenge now is that Clarke had six or more guys to set this trap up, and we are just two. So this is going to be difficult. We have to be careful."

"Agreed."

They returned and, with a delicate touch, tested and removed branches one by one. With the remaining supports wedged too tight to risk further removal, they paused and gleamed upon an opening just big enough to squeeze through.

"Small. Hole. Tank. Off," Steve assessed, his eyes measuring the gap. Jack nodded.

Removing his BCD, he signaled his intention to explore alone and for Steve to remain outside. Steve protested but, after several exchanges, acquiesced, realizing it was safer for just one to chance it. He had to stay to be a lifeline to summon aid. Venturing in together risked a deadly delay; Emma might take over an hour to sense trouble, so any chance of help would vanish.

He unzipped the back of his wetsuit, released his grip on the BCD, and began to ascend as he struggled with buoyancy. He handed his friend one weight pouch from his vest, and Steve helped by inserting the weights into his wetsuit. Steadied, he zipped up and activated his flashlight, the beam slicing through the darkness ahead.

"There," Jack pointed at the hatchet, excitement surging.

Steve's thumbs-up quivered with expectation.

"Watch. Back. Okay?"

"Okay."

After a series of quick, deep breaths, Jack removed his regulator. Releasing tiny bubbles from his mouth, he leveled himself to the entrance. Steve's hand on his back guided him through the treacherous entry, ensuring no accidental collapses would seal his fate.

Once inside, Steve passed the BCD and tank with extreme caution. Jack placed the regulator again into his mouth and donned the BCD. He turned, and the flashlight pierced the cavern's shadowy silence. Despite the eerie quiet and previous setbacks, an unyielding sense led him to believe this cave harbored the pivotal point of their quest.

Jack gestured towards Steve's hand. Steve understood the silent communication and handed him the metal detector. This device might be their last chance to ascertain the truth of the legends.

Emotion welled up in Jack as he glanced back at Steve, placing a hand over his heart before pointing at him – an unspoken assertion over their bond.

Steve mirrored the gesture, an unspoken acknowledgment of their shared hope that moment this was not their final farewell.

Let's do this! Jack faced the depths of the cave. Adrenaline fused with the sterile tang of the tank's air, marking the onset of the discovery of the veiled mysteries that lay ahead. He began to kick, his fins flapping and stirring up sediment.

After bidding farewell to Steve, Jack ventured further into the cave's embrace, noticing its northern bend and the widening of its walls. The once constricted passage yielded to a spacious chamber, stirring Jack's curiosity about its destination. The change in pressure urged him to equalize his ears as he ascended from the entrance's depth. Glancing at his dive gauges, it tracked his rise through the water column – 20 feet, 15, 10 – until a dark expanse loomed overhead. The odd reflection of light against his bubbles breaking the water's rippled surface quickened his pulse with anticipation.

Could this be the place? Jack surfaced, scanning the cavern that stretched upward, inviting further exploration.

With his mask and regulator aside, he drew in the damp air, tinged with the scent of stale water and decay, yet the mystery invigorated him.

Steve would love this! He considered, still he pressed on, driven by an unyielding resolve. After shedding his diving gear except his neoprene suit, his feet embraced the chill of the stream winding its way beneath him towards the lake. Though frigid, each step on the slick rocks propelled him closer to the revelation he sought.

Jack clawed his way up through the oppressive blackness, his flashlight his only savior. His heart hammered in his chest like a desperate plea for escape. His ragged breath and the relentless drip of water blended, creating an ominous symphony that echoed through the enormous chamber. A long pool lay to his left, and the reflections from his light danced upon the walls.

He panned right, and the beam revealed an otherworldly sight — towering stalagmites and stalactites casting silhouettes like guardians over the vast cavern. Then, an odd shadow further to the side caught his attention and sent a chill down his spine. With widened eyes, he looked for the source. They fell onto two ancient wooden chests and a small cask nestled together beside the wall of the chamber. His breath stuck in his throat as he realized the magnitude of his finding.

"YES!" His triumph resonated against the walls. However, Emma's cautionary advice echoed in his mind: he should be wary of hidden perils guarding the treasure. *How else did they protect them? What trigger awaits me?*

Despite the warnings, the allure of discovery drew him forward with hastened steps.

This is it! He reassured himself, bracing for the chests' secrets.

His hands, trembling with anticipation and fear, hesitated before the first chest. Taking a deep breath, he pressed upon the lid with his palm – no traps sprung. A forceful tap elicited no response either.

Closer now, he fumbled with the rusted latch, its fused resistance mocking his efforts until, with a determined thrust and jerk of his knife behind it, the lock snapped free, falling away in a loud crash.

Excitement surged within Jack as he pried open the lid. The hinges gave way with a sharp snap, the top tumbling aside with a resonant crash onto the rock.

Before him lay a treasure beyond imagination. The light of his flashlight made gold, silver, and copper coins gleam like stars in the night sky. His hands trembled with anticipation as he lifted a gold coin, its surface bearing the regal imprint of the long-deceased British monarch, King George II. Without hesitation, he forced open the second chest, revealing more coins amidst an array of golden and silver artifacts – jewelry, cups, and trinkets, likely intended as gifts for Native Americans.

"General Braddock's gold," he whispered to the shadows, his voice a mix of reverence and disbelief. The legend he spent years chasing was true.

Steve... Emma... they have to see this! They'd been with him through the good and the bad, and this moment of triumph belonged to them, too. Clutching the gold coin, he turned back, eager to share the discovery. *Steve will lose his mind,* picturing the astonishment on his friend's face.

This discovery promised a new beginning. Yet, as the thrill coursed through Jack, it was like a Heavyweight Champ punch stuck a blow: *How do we transport all this fortune from this hidden depth?*

He kneeled and sized up the chests, their ancient wood and metal bindings creaking and groaning under his lift. The weight of their contents – and their historical significance – sank in.

With one last glance at the chests, he turned and quickly retraced his steps, anticipation building with each stride toward the entrance. *Almost there,* Jack thought as he navigated the cave's passageways. The promise of Steve's disbelief spurred him on. This treasure wasn't just about wealth but the unbreakable bond of their mutual adventure.

Arriving at the water's edge, Jack reached for his metal tank and BCD.

Chapter 45

Steve tracked Jack as he turned and moved deeper into the cave behind the barrier he just slid through, his flashlight radiating the long tunnel. Steve was harboring concerns about the risks his friend embraced. Unfortunately, he knew this particular journey was something Jack needed to pursue, regardless of the potential outcome.

Please be safe, Steve's eyes lingering on the shadowy void where his friend vanished.

Rising and hovering around 15 feet deep, he sought the thermal layer's relative warmth and the efficiency in air consumption while keeping the cave's entrance within his sight.

As minutes dragged on, each tick of time lingered on into infinity. Then, without warning, the metallic *clang, clang, clang* striking upon a scuba tank pierced the silence. It was a distinct signal he recognized all too well, one that spelled urgency in the language of divers, a sound he experienced dozens of times during training and adventures together.

Jack? What's happened? Where are you?

He plummeted toward the cave's mouth, his flashlight sweeping through the murk and darkness of the tube in search of his friend. His heart raced as the cave remained devoid of his friend's presence.

Come on, show yourself, he pleaded, anxiety heightening with each rapid breath.

The clanging sounded again, more insistent. Steve spun in the water, deciphering its direction – it wasn't originating from the boat but appeared to emanate from over the earthen dam. *It has to be Jack,* he concluded, the thought sparking a rush of determination. *He must have found another opening to the tunnel!*

With resolve, Steve navigated westward, eyes peeled for any sign of a secondary cave entrance. But as he neared the dam's western half, the banging ceased.

He searched the murky waters where he expected the tunnel to lead, finding nothing – not a diver, not even the telltale bubbles of an exhale. Only the whine of distant boat engines broke the silence. Steve's training popped into his mind after a tense minute or two with no other signs: *Never leave your dive partner behind. I better return so Jack can find me.*

When he raced back toward the cave, Steve's heart leaped as he spotted a faint, hazy silhouette against the shore's glow – Jack beckoning from the cave's entrance, urging Steve to join him.

Thank God, he exhaled in relief.

A wave of adrenaline hit him as he gazed upon Jack, disappearing back into the tunnel, the beam of his dive light slicing through the water. *Jack's in a hurry. Did he find it?* The possibility ignited a thrill of anticipation within him. But as he followed, a shadow of unease crept in alongside his excitement. *He must have! He needs my help!* Then, a suspicion that something wasn't right made his heart skip a beat.

Steve's flashlight pierced the darkness following Jack's progress through the barrier. As his friend slid through the narrow opening, chaos ensued – a misplaced kick from Jack dislodged a branch, triggering a cascading rumble and shattering the silence. Dust and debris clouding the water, beginning to mask a valiant effort to escape, erased Jack from sight. His chest thumped. "Nooooo!" he screamed, muffled by his regulator as he clawed through the settling haze.

However, it was too late. His best friend was trapped… or worse, buried!

Steve swam upwards, using his powerful flippers to force the floating particles downward, clearing the water as much as possible. The sediment began to disperse, revealing the grim reality: Jack's fins protruded from between the rocks; his kicking was at a dead stop, the fallen slab trapping him.

"Jack!" Steve yelled through his regulator in panic. A small opening above the pile, the telltale bubbles of Jack's breathing, a haunting sign of life in the stillness. Searching, he found no other signs of movement, no glow of Jack's flashlight.

Desperate, he banged the shovel upon the stone entrance, expecting to elicit a response. Silence answered him. Steve's mind raced, his body springing into action. He needed to free Jack, and time was against them.

Steve assessed the rock, searching for any advantage. Finding a crevice, he wedged the shovel in, hoping to leverage the slab off of Jack. "Come on!" he urged, as much to himself as to Jack. With every ounce of strength, he heaved with the handle, willing the stone to move.

But fate turned cruel. The shaft snapped, and he tumbled backward, the broken tool sinking away from reach. The failure was a tangible blow, leaving him adrift for a moment in the fight against the immovable stone.

"Shit!" The curse slipped from him, his words distorted under water. Steve seized the spade, striking the slab once more in desperation, a silent plea for any indication Jack was still with him. Yet, the response was the same – silence, punctuated only by the slow dance of bubbles.

Think, Steve, think, his mind raced, eyes locked on the sight of Jack's fins, caught in a grim tableau. *What can you do?*

A surge of resolve gripped him. The only choice left was to break the surface, to summon any help within reach. They needed more hands, tools, perhaps even machines – anything that might tip the scales in their frantic bid to pull Jack from the brink.

I'll be back! He vowed a solemn oath to the friend he refused to abandon.

With that, Steve turned, pushing through the water with all the strength he could muster, driven by the stark realization of what was at stake. Ignoring the protocols for a safety stop, he knew each passing moment thinned the thread by which Jack's life dangled.

***

Emma and Sally relaxed in solitude as the boys were submerged, exploring the lake's depths. Emma was floating in the water next to the pontoon, releasing a sigh to the rhythm of the gentle waves, seeking calm. Bathed in sunlight and digital distraction aboard, Sally remained oblivious to the world beyond her screen. The sun glinted off the water's surface, casting a shimmering reflection upon the boat.

Climbing the ladder, Emma broke the silence, asking, "Hey, do you have a favorite movie?"

Sally's gaze lifted a spark of engagement. "Tough call, but *The Shawshank Redemption* wins. Morgan Freeman's voice is just something else," she shared with a light laugh. "Yours?"

"*Eternal Sunshine of the Spotless Mind*," she said, toweling off her bikini-laden body. "It's beautiful and heartbreaking."

A ding from Jack's phone clipped their conversation. Curiosity piqued, she took a few steps and reached for it, only to be stonewalled by a passcode. Moving to sit in the captain's chair, Emma's frustration mounted as she cycled through the last passcode she remembered and then familiar family dates, each attempt as futile as the last.

Sally, watching the struggle, said, "Something personal to him, maybe?"

"I've tried his and every family member's birthdate, everything..." Emma's voice trailed, laden with irritation.

"Did something more recent happen or something he was trying to remember?"

Then, an idea sparked. *Could it be that simple?* Her hands shook as she keyed in her own birthdate. The phone unlocked, and a surge of emotion washed over her. "That sentimental bastard," she murmured, blinking back tears, both touched and heartbroken by the realization Jack had never forgotten her.

"You okay?" Sally asked, filled with concern.

Forcing brightness into her tone, Emma nodded, "Ya-yeah, fine." She refocused on the text from Lieutenant Allen about Ben's discharge. She crafted a prompt response, "Carl, It's Emma. Thanks for the update on Ben. The guys are underwater, diving. Sally and I are hanging out on the boat. We spotted Ritter and the bearded man at the state park and then again near Gravely Run on Marsh Hill Cove. Steve found a GPS tracker in Jack's backpack and one on the bottom of the pontoon. We got rid of them. Should we be worried?"

Finishing, she told Sally, "I'm happy to say Ben's coming home tomorrow."

"That's fantastic news!" Sally's focus shifted from the virtual to the real, a shared relief bridging the gap between them.

Emma's sigh broke the silence, her fingers brushing a loose strand of hair back as they tried to distract themselves with casual talk of films. Sally's voice rose mid-conversation, recounting the plot of her favorite action film, *Enemy of the State*. The soft ding of Jack's phone sliced through the air, pulling their attention.

Lieutenant Allen replied, "Where are you? I'll send the Lake Police to keep an eye on you."

"We've got some backup coming," she relayed to Sally, a note of relief mingling with her words. She rushed to text their location via Google Maps. Her comfort turned into unease as she glanced at Steve's bag, the juxtaposition of safety and danger unsettling her.

"Backup is good," Sally said, her voice floating over the familiar sound of Candy Crush emanating from her phone.

Emma clenched her fists in the moment of fraught silence. Her thoughts had just wandered to Jack and Steve beneath when Steve erupted from the water, his emergence cutting through the calm. Flopping his fins onto the deck, he raced up the ladder and to the boat's console. Panic etched into his features, he seized his phone and dialed.

"Listen to me," he barked, hoarse with urgency. "We need help! My friend Jack's trapped in a cave, and the entrance collapsed! He's underwater and buried by rocks. We need help to rescue him! Now!"

A sudden shock enveloped Emma and Sally, the gravity of Jack's peril descending upon them. He paced, his words painting a desperate picture of Jack trapped and soon out of air beneath them.

"We're on the lake between Deep Creek Bridge and Shingle Camp

Hollow. Our pontoon has an upper deck and waterslide," he replied. "No, we are on a boat; Jack was in the water scuba diving! He's trapped underwater! He has only so much left in his tank. Please hurry – time's running out!"

As Steve ended the call, looking at Emma, she became weak in her knees. Her grip on the boat's wheel was a lifeline against the chaos. Reality hit hard; Jack was in grave danger. "Is he okay?"

"I don't know," Steve's admission deepened the dread, "Something's wrong. I waited while Jack went into the cave – but soon after, I heard clanging on a scuba tank from somewhere over the dam below. I went to investigate, thinking he located another way out, but I found no one. I returned to find him hovering outside the entrance, waving me over. I'm now worried someone lured me away from the entrance so that they might get at us or you. You and Sally need to stay safe."

"What?" Emma asked more as a plea.

Steve grabbed the bag behind the chair, reached inside, and thrust his Sig Sauer P226 MK25 into her hands, a gesture underscoring the severity of their situation. The weight of the gun in her grip, cold and somber, transformed the threat from a distant danger into a pressing reality.

With resolve hardening her gaze, Emma met Steve's eyes.

"Emma, listen," Steve was steady and calm amidst the storm. "Start the engine. Hold tight, but don't move – yet. I'll be back," he said, his words a promise as he disappeared once more into the depths.

The engine's growl filled the silence as Emma's fingers tightened around the pistol, her heart thundering against her ribs. She caught Sally's eye and saw Sally's fear mirrored her own.

"Stay close!" Her command was soft but firm, betraying a tremor of uncertainty. "We need to look out for each other."

"I'm here," Sally said, setting her phone aside to sit opposite Emma. Her gaze never strayed from the weapon, which appeared to hold their fate.

With a sense of urgency, Steve grabbed another tank and slid on his fins in haste. He glanced back to ensure his message was clear. "Be ready!" he called before thrusting the regulator in his mouth. His figure sliced into the air as he flung his body into the water, landing on his back while clutching the spare scuba tank to his chest.

Chapter 46

Steve slammed into the water, its chill mirroring his escalating dread. He raced downward with a desperation born of life-or-death stakes, his gaze darting, hunting for Jack. Frantically equalizing the pressure in his ears as he arrived, his eyes fell upon the sporadic trail of exhaust bubbles offering a sliver of hope.

Come on, hear me! His teeth clenched, a muted plea underwater. Clutching an extra air tank, he struck its bottom upon the cave's blocked entrance, a frantic bid for Jack's attention. The hollow sound echoed, met only by silence and the indifferent dance of bubbles. His heart raced as he shoved the spare tank into the crevice, a lifeline extended into the abyss. *I hope he can reach it!*

How do I get this massive slab off of Jack?

Steve's eyes darted around for anything that could help. When they fixed upon the anchor line, something clicked inside his mind, and he marshaled all his resolve. Quickly grabbing the line, he hauled the anchor with a force that belied his fear, each kick, each pull, a battle against their predicament – the weight of it trying to pull him into the depths of doom.

Let's do this! Determination steeled his jaw as he took command of the anchor. Once the cold metal was in his grip, he thrust it into the opening, past the barricade, and twisted it until the prongs wedged themselves behind the slab. Casting a final hopeful glance at the bubbles, he propelled himself upwards.

A silent prayer accompanied his ascent, fate pushing him downward as he broke through the surface, gasping for air and salvation.

* * *

Emma was shaking, her heart hammered in her chest as she raced to the back and readied herself to help haul Jack to safety. Her eyes darted for any sign of Steve and Jack rising. Time stood still.

Moments later, Emma heard Steve screaming her name in front of the boat. She sprinted to the other end, where his gaze locked onto hers with a piercing intensity that sent a chill down her spine.

"Emma!" His voice cut through the air, droplets cascading off his face. "No time for questions! Head for the bridge!" His rapid gestures pointed past himself. "Go at full speed! Floor it! Now! You'll know when to stop!"

A flicker of panic sparked in her eyes, but she sprang into action without a moment's delay. Clutching the wheel in the captain's chair, she braced herself against the fear threatening to engulf her. The engine's growl deepened as she veered the boat toward the bridge.

She reassured herself amidst the creeping dread: *Steve has to have a plan. He'll find a way to save Jack. He always does.*

As she slammed the throttle down, the boat sped into motion. A breeze began to whip through Emma's hair, signaling their hastened departure past Steve's position. *But how does this help Jack?* The vessel surged ahead, only to shudder to a violent halt, slamming her into the console and Sally against the front railing as the bow suddenly dropped and plowed into the water and aft went airborne and swung around unimpeded.

"Agghh!" Emma's scream wrenched from her lips as a towering wave loomed, crashing over the bow and engulfing Sally in its frothy grasp. She braced for the impact as the swell surged over them, the boat buckling under the onslaught.

As rapid as the pontoon's bow succumbed to the lake's embrace, it exploded upwards with a defiant lurch, shedding the water that once claimed it. Emma's heart raced, each beat a deafening echo of her fear and resolve.

"Sally!" Emma's cry went unheard over the tumult of engine roar and the churning lake. "Enough!" The command was a ragged tear from her throat as she cut the motor and turned off the ignition key, the pontoon rocking in the calming aftermath.

"Steve better know what the hell he's doing," Emma muttered, he body trembling from adrenaline and terror, knotting in her stomach. Collapsing into the chair, the thought of Jack trapped or killed was now too much for her to bear.

"Emma," Sally's voice was a soft lifeline in the chaos.

Emma's eyes fell upon Sally as she pulled herself up off the wet deck, dripping water and blood from several lacerations to her head, arms, and legs. She then shifted her gaze, now fixated on the troubled waters beyond.

Battered yet resilient, Sally moved closer, embracing Emma, who had been a shelter against the storm. "Steve always pulls through for Jack," she said with a blend of pain and comfort. "You have to have hope."

"I know," Emma's reply was fragile, a thin veil over her anguish. "It's just... I can't lose Jack. Not now. Not like this."

"There's always hope," Sally said, her arms tightening in support. "Trust Steve."

Emma nodded, a silent vow to cling to hope, even as her voice faltered. "Yeah," she muttered, the acknowledgment a glimmer of faith in the unyielding darkness. "I just wish I knew what's happening..."

"Here," Sally cut through the tension, her eyes flicking down to the firearm still gripped in Emma's trembling hands. "Do you feel okay holding that? We don't want it going off by accident."

Emma paused, and in an instant, the gun's weight became magnified in her grasp. With a shaky exhale, she passed it to Sally. "You're right," she said, the relief in her tone masked the underlying strain of her ordeal.

Sally tucked the pistol within the confines of her swimsuit's waistband. "We should keep our eyes peeled for them now. The moment we see them, we'll need to act fast to help Jack aboard."

"Okay," Emma's response was faint, almost lost to the sound of the lapping waves. She moved towards the boat's bow, brushing away her escaped tears. Her gaze locked on the location where Steve submerged, each second stretching into infinity as she searched for any sign of their return.

***

The second after the pontoon passed him, Steve plunged into the depths, propelled by a rush of adrenaline. His heart pounded in his chest, and with every breath, he struggled against the increasing fear of failure. The lakebed changed beneath him, and the massive slab, now dislodged, had slid into the gloom below. A veil of sediment clouded his vision, obscuring the cave's entrance.

He kicked with ferocity, his fins stirring the murky waters into clarity. As the dust settled, Jack's prone figure emerged, a grim statue half-buried in stone, his leg entombed up to his waist. A dark stain of blood marred the back of his friend's head, sending a spike of panic through Steve's resolve.

Stay calm! Steve commanded himself, drawing in a deep, steadying breath. *Assess. Focus on what you can do, not what you can't.*

Jack lay motionless, yet the periodic rise of bubbles offered him some hope. He approached, wary of causing further harm. He freed Jack's air gauge and found some relief upon reading that two-thirds of a tank remained – a small miracle in their dire straits.

Upon checking his own supply, Steve's heart sank. With only a fifth of his tank left, time was a luxury they couldn't afford. Fueled by desperation, he set to work, hands trembling as he excavated Jack from his rocky prison; each stone removed a victory against time.

Amid Steve's frantic efforts, something unexpected pushed upon his head. Reflexively, his hand shot to the knife strapped to his leg.

Chapter 47

Emma's heart thudded against her chest, and there was a silent prayer on her lips for Jack's safe return. Clinging to the boat's railing, her gaze locked onto the water's depths where Steve vanished. Each passing second stretched into eternity; her whispered chants of hope were barely audible over the sound of her own pulse beating in her ears.

"Come on, come on," she urged under her breath, her grip on the rail so tight her knuckles blanched.

Then the aft dipped, and the clanking of someone climbing the ladder grabbed her attention. Hope surged, but Sally's terror-laden scream shuddered Emma to her core.

"Emma!" Sally's voice, filled with panic, spun Emma around to confront their nightmare.

A man, clearly not Steve or Jack, was shedding his BCD and tank. He turned, removed his dive mask, and tossed it aside. Henry Ritter now stood before them; his expression twisted in malice as he drew a long, ominous knife. His slow, deliberate steps, the blade glinting with malevolence, set Emma's heart into a frantic gallop.

"Get off our boat!" Fueled by raw fear, Emma's demand broke against Ritter's cold, mocking laughter.

"What? You think you can stop us?" his words, laced with contempt, pierced the heavy air. "We've searched for this treasure for generations. You receive one lucky phone call and think you can just take it away from us? I don't think so!"

"Please," Emma pleaded, her voice quaking. "We just want to leave. We're not going to fight you. We'll give you the gold."

The wicked snort spewed from Ritter was like jagged ice slicing through Emma's skin. "No chance," he growled, his clasp on the blade tightening. "We need… *leverage*… to ensure your boyfriends surrender what is ours."

He edged toward them; each wet slap of his foot made her tremble. The sudden appearance of Sally's rising arm, steadfast gun aimed at him, sliced through the despair. Her unwavering stance and steely voice halted his advance for a moment only.

Ritter's smirk twisted further, and he inched closer – slap – the knife now twirling in a menacing dance. Emma's heart pounded, a desperate look exchanged with Sally, who stood resolute, finger now tensing around the trigger.

Slap.

The deck echoed again with another taunting step, his sneer growing as he goaded Sally. "Be a good girl, Sally. Give me the gun," he coaxed with a familiarity that sent a shiver down Emma's spine.

Slap.

"STOP!" Sally shouted, her voice unyielding. "I'm not afraid to use this!"

"Sure you will."

Slap.

"No one was supposed to get hurt," Sally shot back, her words sliced the tension like the very blade he wielded. Emma's mind raced as she digested this revelation: *Are Sally and Ritter allies? Or is one the chess master and the other a pawn?*

Slap.

"Stop, Henry. It ends now!" Sally's plea, though fierce, carried an undercurrent of desperation. The pressure of the standoff appeared to suspend time itself.

Slap.

Ritter's predatory advance brought him closer, now just over two body lengths away. His dark eyes locked on Emma with a hunter's focus. "Sally, do something! Shoot him!" Her imploring scream cut through the stifling air, her voice almost unrecognizable.

Sally's hands, once steady, now quaked, her frame buckling under the strain of the moment. Her gaze wavered, the firearm in her grip erratic, its aim untrue.

"We've got a problem now, Sally," he taunted, his eyes flashing with a menacing glint. "You just spilled our little secret. Can't have any loose ends now, can we?" His voice sliced through the tension, fraying the last threads of Sally's resolve.

With a roar born of urgency, Ritter surged forward, his knife poised for Emma. In a burst of protective fury, Sally screamed, "No!" and refocused the gun on him as she took a half step forward. Ritter stopped and scowled at her for a moment; but his eyes slid back to Emma.

Slap.

Sally pulled the trigger. Click – then nothing. Her eyes and mouth gaped in horror as she glanced helplessly at Emma.

Ritter's smirk widened into a cruel grin. "This does end now!"

Slap.

His head lowered, blade hand recoiled, poised to strike.

Sally's face twisted as she unleashed a cry of rage and lunged at Ritter, their bodies crashing together in a chaotic struggle.

Emma stared in horror as the pistol slipped from Sally's grip. Her eyes widened as she lunged in desperation, and they locked onto the gun as it tumbled and fell just beyond her fingertips. Her heart hammered in terror as it clattered to a stop.

A guttural cry tore from Sally as they hit the ground, their desperate scuffles and gasps echoing in the charged air.

Driven by survival instinct, Emma scurried for the weapon, the fingers of her right hand wrapping around its cold steel. She stood, facing Ritter, who flung Sally aside with a grimace of pain and fury. Extracting the blade from her chest as the gushing blood painted his hand.

Tears blurred Emma's vision, and a tumult of dread and determination steeled her as she raised the gun. "STOP!" Her voice cut through the chaos as her left hand grasped the top of the gun and drew the slide back with a sharp, deliberate motion, the metallic slide lock clicking into place with a resounding snap – the chamber now loaded.

Yet Ritter, undeterred, lurched up.

Emma's eyes narrowed ablaze, acting without a second's pause; she brought her hands together and guided her aim, her finger squeezing the trigger. The first shot struck Ritter's knife-wielding shoulder, his body recoiling, the blade clattering from his loosening grip. His glare fixated upon her again as he began to reach out with his other arm.

Slap.

Her second squeeze targeted his thigh, anchoring him to the spot as if chained, his form crumpling to the deck.

Groans escaped Ritter between labored breaths while Emma, adrenaline surging, stood firm. The realization of what she had done – what had to be done – crashed into her with the force of a tidal wave.

The world shrank to the echo of gunfire and the sharp tang of gunpowder in the air. Ritter, now a pained figure clutching at his wounds, became a peripheral blur as Emma's attention turned to Sally, struggling for each breath. With hands still quaking, she kept the gun pointed at him as she made her way to Sally's side.

"Stay with me, Sally," her voice wavered as she helped Sally roll over, her eyes instantly drawn to the grim blossom of blood against Sally's ghostly skin. She dropped to her knees, an instinctive effort to stem the life seeping out from the knife wound, her hands pressing upon the warmth, spreading the stain.

"Emma..." Sally struggled even to whisper, her eyes searching amidst the pain.

"I'm here!"

"I'm sorry... tell Steve I'm sorry."

Emma's vision blurred with tears as she held Sally closer, witnessing the vibrant spirit drain from her friend's face, replaced by a haunting resignation. A lone tear escaped Sally, blending with the blood on her lips.

"Hold on, Sally! Help is on its way," Emma implored, her voice cracking in despair as she pressed on the jagged hole in her chest.

"I... had to..." Sally's confession trailed off, her body surrendering, her gaze fixing on the void above as the last breath slipped from her.

"Thank you, Sally," Emma whispered, closing Sally's eyes with her blood-covered hand. Trembling, she turned her gaze to Ritter, her grip on reality as shaky as her hold on the gun.

"Drop the gun! Hands where I can see them!" The authoritative and clear directive and the roar of a boat motor reversing thrust snapped her out of her malaise. Emma's eyes found a patrol boat, a female officer at the bow, her firearm steady, aiming at her.

With a numbness, she let the gun slide from her hand, pushing it across the deck, distancing it from both her and Ritter. She raised her hands, watching as the officers made their approach, their boat scraping against the pontoon in a harsh greeting.

"Miss Wilson?" The officer's tone was firm, underscored by urgency as she surveyed the grim scene.

"Yes," Emma's response was faint, a thin thread of voice in the thickening plot of death and deception around her.

"You can lower your hands. I'm Sergeant Jackie Meyers, and this is Officer Jones. Lieutenant Allen sent us. He warned us about two men with ill intentions. And we received a 911 call about a trapped diver. Is that you as..." Her words dissolved into silence, the magnitude of the situation overwhelming her.

"Miss Wilson?" Sergeant Meyers prompted, her voice cutting through the haze of Emma's shock.

Emma's gaze flickered to Meyers, finding a semblance of solace in the officer's steady presence. "Carl feared for our safety."

"What happened here?"

"Ritter attacked us," Emma stammered as she pointed at him. "He had a knife... went for me, but Sally... she tried to stop him, gun didn't fire, and she dove in front of me."

Meyers's expression hardened at the mention of Ritter, and she stared at him as he contorted on the deck in pain.

"Sally... she's gone. She protected me..." Emma's voice broke, and the reality of Sally's sacrifice rendered her speechless. She stared at the still form of her friend.

"And Ritter?" Meyers pressed.

"In the struggle... Sally fell on him, and he... stabbed her. She dropped the gun. I... I grabbed it... He came... shot him," Emma recounted, the surrealness of her own actions resounding in the void that Sally's bravery left behind.

Meyers nodded, absorbing the gravity of Emma's words before turning her attention to the immediate crisis. "The others, are they still in danger?"

"Steve, he's trying to rescue Jack. He's trapped in an underwater cave. The entrance collapsed."

"Jack Sullivan?" Jones's recognition was instantaneous, his brow furrowing with concern.

"Yes, please. You have to help them! He'll run out of air soon." Emma's plea was desperate. Her hands reached toward the dark water, which held more than its share of secrets.

"We have to deal with Ritter," Meyers assured her, her tone leaving no room for doubt.

"You better! I need a hospital!" Ritter demanded, his voice hoarse from pain.

Jones's boots thudded onto the deck as he boarded, a bulky medical kit in his grip. His eyes darted between Ritter and Sally, assessing with a trained rapidity that spoke of experience in chaos.

Meyers, ever vigilant, secured the scene, her tone commanding assistance over the radio. "We need two ambulances to the southwestern end of the Route 219 Bridge. ASAP."

Jones kneeled beside Sally, his fingers probing her neck for a pulse. After a moment, he shook his head before turning to Ritter, who was grimacing, his wetsuit darkened to a deep shade of red. With a clinical detachment, Jones snapped the handcuffs around his wrists with a decisive click, causing Ritter to scream.

Emma gazed at them, her breaths shallow, fighting to keep her emotions in check. Her eyes flickered between Sally's lifeless body and Ritter's, now flinching under Jones's firm hands as he applied pressure bandages.

"Officer," Emma found her voice, despite it trembling, "Are you going to help them underwater?"

Jones, who had been focusing on treating Ritter's wounds, looked up at Emma. "Do you know where they are?" he asked.

"Yes, about fifty feet in front of the boat," she pointed with desperate precision to a spot on the lake, her finger shaking.

"Got it," Jones responded. "With Ritter contained and you safe here, we can now focus on your friends below."

She nodded, her gratitude mixed with a burgeoning impatience. Every second seemed like an eternity, each tick of the clock a reminder of Jack's peril beneath the water.

"We need to act quickly," Meyers interjected. "You should sit down, Emma. Let us take it from here."

Emma did not move as Meyers and Jones exchanged a quick strategy, and Jones made his way to the police boat, readying his scuba gear with swift, practiced movements.

Then, the unmistakable "hiss" sliced through the tense silence when a diver drew breath through a regulator upon surfacing. Heart caught in her throat, Emma hesitated before turning, half afraid of what she might see. Moving to her knees, she braced herself for what was to come.

Chapter 48

Jarred by the unexpected contact, Steve's instincts kicked into high gear, his hand flying to the knife secured at his leg. His heartbeat pounded in his ears, adrenaline surging as he drew the blade, muscles tensed, eyes scanning for the assailant.

In an instant, his movement ceased, his eyes widening in disbelief. *Wait!* He stared not at an enemy, but at a familiar face. Floating before him was Jack, alive and conscious, his hands raised in a universal gesture of surrender. *What?* He shook his head, Steve's mind racing to piece together the scene.

His confusion spiraled. *How is Jack in front of me if he's beneath the rocks at my feet?* His gaze dropped, the sight below offering a chilling answer. He turned the man's head; the bearded man, their adversary, was lying under the debris.

"Help!" Jack's signaled plea cut through the uncertainty, gesturing towards the trapped man.

Reluctantly, Steve nodded, understanding the importance of their situation. Rescuing the man was imperative, not just for justice's sake but also for their conscience. They had to act, and they had to act now.

They worked together to free the bearded man, and Steve's thoughts were a whirlwind of disbelief and determination. Their combined efforts, powered by necessity, made quick work of the rubble.

But at that moment, a stark realization struck Steve when he had to suck the air out of his regulator. He knew that sensation. He signaled to Jack, pounded a warning fist against his chest, thumb pointing up before slashing his raised arm across his throat in an unmistakable signal – "No Air!"

Jack responded without hesitation, handing him his spare, yellow emergency regulator as Steve sucked the remaining breath from his tank. Steve grabbed and inserted the lifeline into his mouth, and they went to work. With practiced coordination shining through, they grabbed the spare tank and switched Steve's out.

With fresh air coursing through his lungs, Steve's resolve hardened. They continued their efforts, removing the last of the obstacles. But then, a new fear gripped him – the absence of the bearded man's exhaust bubbles. A quick glance confirmed the worst.

"Not. Breathing," Steve signaled to Jack.

They tossed the final rock, urgency propelling their actions. Despite the past conflict, a wave of sympathy washed over Steve as they secured the bearded man, his body eerily limp in their grasp. *No one deserves this fate.*

With no time to spare, they propelled themselves towards the surface, the weight of the situation pressing down on them. As they ascended, Jack's grip on the man tightened, a mix of guilt and determination fueling his strokes. Steve's thoughts drifted to Sally and Emma, hoping it was the police he called next to their pontoon.

Ascending into the light, Steve surfaced first, dragging the lifeless man beside him. Jack emerged seconds later, blinded by the boat's motor.

Emma's voice, laced with terror, pierced the air. "Jack? NO!" Her words echoed in despair.

Jack's chest burned with anguish at hearing her wretched cries. "I'm alright, Emma!"

Relief melted on her features, but switched to confusion as her eyes fixed on the motionless figure.

On deck, Jack and Steve, with Jones's aid, laid the man down, noting the grim mixture of water and blood streaming from his suit. They attempted CPR, their actions a testament to years of practiced emergency training. The harsh reality set in as Jones checked for a heartbeat, only to find none. "Stop," he said, voice low. "No pulse."

The finality of Jones' words struck Jack, the sight of the man's lifeless face a stark reminder of the day's harsh truths.

"From the looks of his swollen legs, he also had internal bleeding," Jones surmised, noting the swelling.

Jack's frantic gaze shifted, finding Emma in distress, Ritter detained, and then – the horror – Sally. Her stillness, enveloped in blood, stopped him cold. "Sally!" he yelled in despair as he grabbed Steve's arm.

Steve's shock mirrored Jack's as his eyes landed on Sally, bloodied and unmoving. The once vibrant eyes were now closed with blood-covered fingerprints on them.

"Don't touch her," Officer Meyers intervened as Steve raced to her side and reached out, desperation in his voice.

"Can I at least hold her hand?" Ignoring the order, he moved to her and took Sally's hand.

Emma wrapped him in a consoling embrace. "Sally saved me from Ritter's knife. The first thing she said was her thoughts of you," she said, a gentle conveyance of Sally's final act of bravery.

"Thanks, Emma." he looked up at her, his tear-soaked eyes red and puffy.

Jack, placing a comforting hand on Steve's shoulder, "We all know how much Sally meant to you."

Steve's grip on Jack's hand tightened in a silent fellowship of shared grief and the poignant realization of Sally's sacrifice. The weight of the moment left them grasping for solace amidst the sorrow.

The friends stood in peace, mourning their loss.

A sudden impact and loud thud of another vessel breaking the silence snapped Jack back to the present. The other police boat impacted with theirs. Two figures boarded, one recognizable. Lieutenant Allen stepped onto the deck with another officer from the Lake Police.

Allen's eyes darted, scanning the scene before calling out to his companion, "Riley!"

"Yes, Sir," Riley said, moving closer to Allen.

In a hushed tone, Allen directed Riley's attention to Sally and the bearded man, his words inaudible to the rest.

Without delay, Allen's focus shifted to the task at hand, his voice firm with the urgency of gathering facts about the day's events.

Jack intervened, "Before we dive into this, I have something rather urgent. Steve, look at me," his gaze locking with Steve's, "You might've been underwater too long or ascended too rapidly."

Steve's brows lowered in confusion, evidence he was processing Jack's worry, "What?"

"Are you experiencing any fatigue, itchiness, joint or muscle pain, dizziness, or shortness of breath?" Jack's tone was laced with concern.

Steve said, "No, I'm good. Thanks."

Allen, intrigued by the interruption, asked, "What's all this about?" just as a distant siren started to wail.

"Checking for decompression sickness," Steve said, his voice heavy.

"So, what happened?" Allen persisted, his inquiry undeterred.

Jack's gaze wandered, catching sight of Sally and the bearded man. Allen's call refocused him, "Jack?"

Regaining composure, Jack said, "Sorry, Lieutenant, are you familiar with this man?"

Meyers chimed in, "Thomas Ritter. When I confiscated their scuba gear the other day, he didn't have identification, but Henry referred to him as 'dad.' Background checks at the station confirmed it."

"Wasn't he implicated in a murder case?" Jack asked, seeking confirmation.

Allen nodded, "Suspected, yet wasn't convicted. The gun was missing until Emma discovered it."

Steve, unable to contain his shock, blurted out, "Fuuu... So, he might've tried to kill Jack in the cave!"

"I can't speculate on that," Allen maintained, his tone neutral.

The siren from a distant ambulance breached the air. Meyers interrupted, "Sorry, Lieutenant. We got to go. We'll take Ritter in our boat to the bridge. The ambulance is meeting us there."

"Proceed," Allen directed, but assigned Jones and Riley to handle Ritter and the Sergeant to stay for questioning. Using his finger to summon Jones over, Jack overheard the whispered conversation. "On your way, call for the coroner to report to the state park boat ramp. Or they can transport Sally with the other ambulance."

Jones and Riley's attempt to escort him was clumsy, resulting in them dropping Ritter without ceremony onto the boat's deck. Riley's apology missed its mark as Allen shook his head in disappointment and turned back to the group, tinged with frustration, "For a third time, what unfolded here?"

Jack struggled for a moment, his concern over the events heavy on his voice, "It began with a cave... we thought it might hold Braddock's treasure." He paused, careful not to unveil too much, "Inside the cave..."

Steve's interruption cut through the tense air. He recounted someone luring him away, and the mistaken identity beneath the water's surface, the collapse, and the dramatic rescue, concluding, "...and we had to perform CPR on him."

Emma broke into the conversation, her tone laced with fear and determination. "Worried about what they might do to Sally and me, Steve unpacked and handed me his gun. I took it because of your message about sending help. Wondering why you thought we needed protection terrified me." She paused, the weight of the memory evident. "It was just Sally and me on the boat. After learning about Jack, panic set in. Sally asked to hold the gun so I didn't have an accident with it."

Her eyes flickered to the other police boat as she recounted Henry's threatening approach. Tears began to flow as she described how Henry climbed aboard and was coming at them with his knife, the verbal confrontation with him, the gun not firing, Sally's courageous act, the gunshots, and Sally's last haunting words.

Steve moved to Emma, his embrace a silent vow of protection and understanding. "Emma, this wasn't your fault. It's possible the Ritters manipulated Sally, but she chose to protect you. That choice... it says everything about her final stance. You meant something to her."

Emma said a heartfelt, "Thanks, Stevie," her voice was a mix of grief and gratitude.

Allen's analytical gaze swept over them. "I think Steve's right, and there's more to Sally's actions than we know," he said, the pieces of the puzzle aligning yet incomplete. "But the pressing question remains – how did the Ritters find you here?"

Emma recounted their earlier sightings of the Ritters, adding, "We thought we lost them after disposing of the tracker."

Allen, picking up the thread, pointed out, "But they must have known more than just your location."

Jack gestured towards a damp map by the captain's chair. "Our apartment may have been bugged. Knowing our search areas, maybe they predicted our search here."

Allen absorbed this, his focus narrowing. "And how did they pinpoint this moment to strike?"

Emma suggested, "Maybe when we put the tracker on the other boat, they followed it and saw us sitting here when they crossed the bridge. This pontoon is quite distinctive."

"It's possible," Allen said the possibility, his mind racing ahead. "We have more to unravel here. We will take your individual statements when we return to the marina to drop you off."

His gaze settled on the group, a silent acknowledgment of their ordeal. Turning to Steve, "Oh, Steve, I'm assuming you have a permit for your gun?"

"Yes, it's in my wallet in my backpack. Want me to get it out now?"

"If you would. We'll need it and will be holding your gun as evidence."

"Understood. But you said there was more to Sally's story. What is it? I need to know. Please!"

Allen exchanged a weighted look with Meyers, then turned, his demeanor shifting to one of reluctant revelation. "I wanted to wait till tomorrow to delve into this, but given your concern and urgency, here's what our investigations have unearthed. It turns out Henry was somewhat entangled in Sally's life, owning the nursing home where her mother died. According to staff, their relationship, marked by months of dating, ended ugly."

"Sally mentioned her struggles with her mother's medical expenses," Emma said, her voice a whisper of memories.

"That's part of the investigation," Allen continued, "but it aligns with our findings. Our conversation with contractor Mike Thomas, who's on vacation, revealed that Sally came to the site looking for the items out of fear the Smithsonian wouldn't return them – her agitation was quite visible."

"We intended to return those items," Emma cut in, her protest clear.

Allen raised a hand for patience. "Understood, but the situation is more complex. He said Sally documented everything in detail, fearing the loss of these artifacts. I'm not sure, but we're investigating if Sally's photos *may* have ended up in the Ritters' hands, which could be how we found the few pages in his truck. And that is why I believe they may have had some leverage on her."

Steve, absorbing every word, could only utter, "Wow."

Allen nodded, summing up the twisted weave of motives and desperation. "I'm speculating they backed her into a corner, and she could have thought aligning with you might offer her a way out, a safety net she couldn't find elsewhere. This is all compounded by the aggressive tactics we've seen from the Ritters, confirming her fears. I suspect now Sally believed Henry would stop at nothing to obtain the treasure. She told Emma she had no choice. Maybe she felt compelled to do what she did to save you."

Emma's tears flowed anew, the reality of their bond with Sally hitting home. "She did care about us, then," she sobbed, Steve wrapping an arm around her in silent support.

"We must get going, folks," Allen said, signaling the shift in focus. Meyers headed to her vessel as Allen took the helm of Jack's boat.

Jack, however, lingered, concerned. "Just a moment. I have to check on Steve once more."

With a nod from the Lieutenant, Jack turned to his friend. "I'm sure I'm okay," Steve assured him. "We can go."

"Alright, we're ready to leave," Jack conceded, his gaze drifting towards the Deep Creek Bridge. The day's revelations and implications unfolded in his mind as he looked over to Emma and Steve, their sodden faces etched with the day's burdens. He looked at Emma and Steve, who stared in silence into the distance.

Jack stared at the lake and began to contemplate their next steps: *How the hell are we going to recover the gold in the middle of a police investigation?*

Chapter 49

As the day tipped into its afternoon descent, Lieutenant Allen steered into an open slip at the marina, and Jones and Riley glided their vessels into an adjacent spot. Jack leaped from the pontoon, ropes in hand, just as an attendant approached. The boy's offer of assistance dying on his lips at the vision of blood-stained tarps concealing a grim situation.

Lieutenant Allen took the lead, his voice measured as he briefed the marina staff on the unfolding drama: their watercraft turned crime scene, now under the scrutiny of law enforcement. The revelation hit Jack hard – the potential loss, the financial burdens of damages, and how Renter's Insurance doesn't cover boat rentals, which only added to the situation.

"Steve!" Allen called, cutting through the tension, summoning him for a task to retrieve the tracker.

"Of course," Steve said, his demeanor unflinching as he scanned the lineup of boats, seeking number 11. With a swift dive, he retrieved the submerged tracker, a small victory amidst chaos.

"Much appreciated," Allen said, as he patted Steve on the back. He then turned to address the group. "Alright, everyone, take your gear off the boat."

Jack and his friends removed their belongings in haste, and as soon as the last item hit the dock, Allen shouted, "Jones! We need to process this pontoon as quickly as possible. You and Riley take this and your boat to the state park. Call to arrange for a trailer to haul it to the impound. Meyers and I will follow after questioning these folks and meet you at the park's ramp."

"Yes, Sir," Jones replied.

In the shadow of Jack's SUV, the interrogation unfolded with Steve first in line. Meyers looked at Allen, raising an eyebrow. Allen gave a subtle nod, indicating he would handle this part of the interrogation, and placed his hand on Steve's shoulder as they started walking away. Jack overheard the first question Allen asked, "What's your relationship with Jack?"

He listened to Steve's response, "We're friends. We've been through a lot together," but he was unable to discern any other portion of the conversation. It was clear Allen took charge while Meyers looked on and took notes, but asked a few questions. Jack gazed upon Steve's nervous body shifting.

Emma's turn revealed a different tact, her composure unwavering under Allen's occasional smile, a stark contrast to Steve's visible tension.

When Jack stepped forward, the gravity of the moment bore down on him.

"Jack, can you summarize the events from the barrel find to this morning for Sergeant Meyers?" Allen asked, crossing his arms over his chest.

Jack inhaled, embarking on his tale with a deliberate omission of the treasure, wary of legal hands that might claim it.

"The need for a diversion today," Allen probed, "why was that?"

Jack wove a story of deception designed to mislead potential surveillance, hinting at their discovery of a bugged apartment and subsequent false leads. He detailed their maneuvers around Carmel Cove and Gravely Run, conveying he was not present during the cave's collapse and Sally's defensive actions.

"Anything else, Officer Meyers?" Jack ventured, his narrative complete.

"No, Jack. It's clearer now," Allen said, his tone suggesting a puzzle falling into place.

Jack, despite sharing their tale, harbored lingering doubts under the officers' scrutinizing gaze. *Are they going to arrest us?*

Meyers and Allen spoke with hushed voices, with the latter offering a tempered relief. Allen informed them they wanted a detective to question them further about Sally's passing and the shooting of Henry, even though they were not being considered as suspects. However, he was unavailable till the next day. "Please present yourselves at the Oakland station tomorrow morning. But that's all for today," Allen said.

Turning to look at Allen, Meyers's brows furrowed, "I take it you don't think they will leave the area, Lieutenant?"

Allen's reply was laced with a wry chuckle, "No, their quest for the treasure keeps them here," underscored a trust in their honesty. "However, we'd appreciate it if you wouldn't go too far in case we need you. Yet something tells me you can finish what you started."

Their departure, with a parting reminder to stay local, left Jack mulling over their predicament. The law saw them as victims, not culprits, a temporary solace. Yet, the looming challenge struck him: *How do we retrieve the gold now?*

Back at his vehicle, Jack's mind drifted to his Navy days, the adrenaline of past missions a grim contrast to this unforeseen quest. Glancing at Emma, her expression vacant and weary, he recognized the toll of the day's ordeals.

"Emma," he muttered, reaching out, "are you alright?"

"No," tears traced lines down her cheeks as Jack enveloped her in his arms.

"Stevie, you okay?"

"I'm... it's just hard. Did Sally care about me, or was it all a game to her? I thought we had something real between us." Steve's voice cracked, laden with doubt and hurt.

"I believe she did, Steve."

He paused for a moment, "After everything you two endured..." Jack's comments trailed off, his gaze firm yet sympathetic. "I hate to ask both of you to do more today. We need to go to the cave again now before the authorities arrive to investigate."

Steve's head drooped. "I can't, Jack. I just can't."

Emma's distress erupted in a flurry of motion and sound. "Jack, have you lost your mind? I'm past my limit here. I want to either sleep for a week or drown my memories in alcohol. We've witnessed death, believed I lost you again, and now you're proposing another dive into madness? Plus, the looming police interrogation... And the boat! The cost of repairs alone…" Her voice broke under her anger. "This is the shit that drove me away the first time!"

Jack, his tone a calm anchor amidst the storm, faced them. "Listen, Emma, Steve," he said, capturing Emma's gaze with his hands on her face. "We'll make it through this. But we have to go now."

"How the hell can you even say that?" Emma's protest softened, but her disbelief remained.

With a cautious glance around, he drew a gold coin from his pocket. The ancient coin gleamed.

"Jack, is that...?" Steve leaned in, and his jaw dropped.

"Yes," he whispered, never taking his eyes off Emma.

Steve's stance shifted from resignation to resolve. "Damn. I also assumed you lost it altogether. I'm in."

His eyes were still locked on hers. Her initial shock gave way to a dawning realization, and she nodded. The fire of newfound purpose in her eyes. Emma said, "We're going to need a bigger boat."

"You nailed the quote!" Steve chuckled.

"Alright, you heard my lady. Back to the rental desk," Jack said, the coin now a talisman of their shared conviction. They approached the desk, their spirits buoyed for the moment.

The attendant's scowl stopped them short. "No more rentals. Not until you return the boat and pay for the damages to it first."

Steve stepped forward, "What if I rent it?"

"None of you can rent another boat here," the attendant was firm.

Jack sighed, signaling a discreet retreat. "We'll find another place."

"Where to, now?" Emma's worry creased her forehead.

"Deep Creek Marina in McHenry. They'll have what we need," Jack said.

In the charged atmosphere of Jack's Suburban, the group sped towards the marina, the car's hum the only sound amidst their collective anticipation. Arriving, they found a single pontoon swaying on the lake, the last of its kind for the day.

"Looks like we're missing the waterslide today," Steve quipped, unable to suppress a laugh.

"Steve, take care of the rental. Emma and I have to grab some gear from across the street," he said, and their determined strides carried them to the boat dealership.

"Try to relax," she said, though her pace betrayed an equal urgency. The image of the gold coin ignited her imagination.

Inside, they made a beeline for the supplies, necessity never waning. He scrutinized the equipment with his gaze drifting to the ceiling in contemplation, prompting Emma's curiosity.

"What's on your mind?" she asked.

"Calculating lift."

"Lift?"

"It's about buoyancy. Think of how a beach ball behaves underwater. It wants to go to the surface," he said, sparking a glimmer of understanding in her.

Then, with precision, Jack assembled their peculiar arsenal: eleven 5-gallon gas cans, four hefty boat bumpers, and eight lengths of 100-foot anchor rope.

Emma, puzzled, asked, "What's all this for?"

"We'll talk outside," he murmured, catching the cashier's skeptical look as they completed their purchase.

Once on their way to Jack's vehicle, he shared his strategy. "The integrity of the chests might be compromised by age. The ropes are for reinforcement. The cans have a dual purpose: they could either aid in floating the treasure out or serve to transport the coins."

Emma marveled, "When did you come up with this?"

"To be honest, ever since I saw how much treasure there was, I was clueless. That was until I looked over what items were available."

They returned to the SUV, where he retrieved shopping bags and a bicycle pump. Laden by their haul, they made their way back to Steve and the pontoon.

Steve's laughter greeted them. "Think you've got enough crap?"

Jack, focused, replied, "I hope it's enough."

"You kidding?" Steve's expression was one of disbelief.

"No. I cleared out their stock. If it's not, we'll have to improvise," he said as they loaded the boat.

Emma, taking the helm, paused prior to starting the engine, lost in reflection.

"Everything alright, Emma?" Jack's concern in his soft tone.

A moment passed before she shared, "I was thinking about Sally."

Steve interjected, "I'm struggling too, but as a soldier, we focus and power through to complete the mission. It's the only way."

Emma said, "I have an idea. One which should make us, or at least me, feel better. Let's honor Sally. Assuming the treasure is large enough, we dedicate this find to her, supporting the museum in her memory, maybe even naming a part of it after her. That way, people will well think of her and remember she sacrificed herself for others."

"I'd like that, Emma," Steve said, embracing her.

Jack chimed in with a supportive nod, "You're right, Em. That'd be a fitting tribute."

With a determined breath, Emma keyed the ignition and steered their course toward the cave.

Steve's gaze fixed on Jack, tension threading his words. "What's our plan?"

Jack paused and unveiled a smile. "Simple," he said. "You'll help me figure it the F' out when you see it."

A light chuckle escaped Steve. "Classic FITFO strategy. But really?"

Jack's grin waned to a serious line. "One word – Buoyancy. We'll fill cans with water and tie them together when we arrive. We have to deflate the bumpers to sink them. Can you handle that as we head out?"

"On it," Steve said.

While Steve worked to expel air from the bumpers, Jack packed ropes and the pump, securing them.

Curiosity piqued, Steve asked, "Never asked – how heavy are those chests?"

"Each one? Over 250 pounds or so, including the chest."

Steve whistled low. "With water, we're talking 300 or more."

Jack tied two long ropes to the pontoon, and Steve tethered the now-deflated bumpers. Slipping into their wetsuits, they prepped for the dive, the anticipation tangible.

Anchored at their destination, they flooded the cans, linking and tying them alongside the boat.

"I'm all set here. You?" he asked, eyeing the water's edge.

"Born ready," Steve shot back, his excitement tinged with a sliver of apprehension.

Their mutual confidence wavered for a moment. "Just remember," he said, "slow and steady."

Jack tossed the ropes into the water. With a shared glance, they strode in.

Below, the gas cans trailed them like tin cans following the auto of newlyweds, but with an eerie sound of banging and thudding. The containers humorously fought against their bindings, eager to seek the sun or plunge into the depths. Jack and Steve exchanged a disbelieving look, pressing on toward the shadowy entrance ahead.

They navigated to the cave's mount, securing their long ropes with care before venturing into the darkness. The thrill of discovery propelled them forward, each breath a mix of adrenaline and awe.

Inside, the cave unfolded in mystery. "Incredible," Steve breathed, his voice bubbling with enthusiasm. "We'll need to explore this place sometime."

Jack smirked, leading on. "Knew you'd like it. Just wait for what's next."

Approaching the chests, a chill of realization still swept over Jack.

Steve's reaction was immediate; his eyes went wide, and his mouth opened. "Holy shit, we've it the motherlode!"

He clapped Steve's shoulder, his excitement mirrored in his friend's wide eyes. "We did it!" But then, a sobering awareness dawned. "Now, how do we haul all this out?"

Steve grunted under the weight of the chest, his tone betraying a hint of strain. "Thought it'd be heavier," he half-joked, eyeing Jack with concern and determination.

Jack felt a twinge of apprehension. "I hope we have enough to get it all out of here today," he murmured; the extent of their challenge became more tangible.

Peering into the chests, Steve nodded. "We should make it."

Jack glanced at him, the plan forming in his mind. "Carry or float them out?"

Steve, ever the pragmatist, asked, "Check my calculations on how much a 5-gallon can, can carry."

Jack couldn't resist, "A European or African can?"

Smirking, "We're not in a Monty Python sketch, and we're not in a mental joust with the Holy Grail's Bridge Troll today. Yet, it appears I'm jousting with a witless child."

"Ouch," Jack said with a smile.

After a moment, Steve said, "A 5-gallon should give us about… 41 and 2/3rds pounds of lift."

"I came up with the same amount."

"Keep it under 21 pounds, and they float. More, and they'll sink. With ropes, we can manage heavier loads."

Jack pondered aloud, "Do we max out the cans with coins and use bags for the bulky items or try floating everything in the chests as they are?"

"If we secure the chests well, we can use the cans and bumpers as buoyancy aids. Direct lifting into the boat is out of the question. We'd have to drag them ashore first to lift them aboard," Steve analyzed. "But if a chest breaks open during the lift, we'll be diving to recover each piece of gold instead."

Understanding dawned on them at the same time. "Cans!" they both affirmed.

"Worst case, we leave the chests behind," Steve said.

"Right. They'd be interesting for a museum but not worth risking the gold for," Jack agreed.

"And an empty chest can be lifted straight onto the boat."

"We have to secure the lids first," Jack pointed out.

"What about the cask?" Steve asked, focusing on the smaller container.

"It appears to be intact. I'll test it for leaks. If it holds, we take it as is; if not, we'll repack its contents."

While Steve prepared the treasures for transport, Jack tested the cask in the water. No bubbles escaped, indicating it was leak-proof. Satisfied, he placed it on the shore.

Together, they took care to sort the treasure into gas cans and cloth bags, emptying the chests to prevent any breakage. Steve secured the bags with rope to avoid any loss.

Their hands worked with practiced efficiency, securing the chests for the journey. They knew one wrong move might send their precious cargo tumbling into the lake's depths, and he refused to let it happen. Jack thought: *I don't want to dive again to retrieve anything.*

Together, they transported the treasure to the lake's edge and submerged each chest. Tying the bumpers to them and using a pump to add air, they balanced the chests on the bottom before discussing their strategy. Jack suggested moving the items to the entrance and assigning tasks for pulling them up from the boat or retrieving them from shore.

"Sounds like a plan. You take the lines; I'll handle the haul up, weakling," Steve chuckled.

Jack's laughter echoed back, relief in sharing this moment of levity. "Try taking a can with you. I'd guess each is 30 to 35 pounds dry, but underwater, that'll drop to 10 to 30 pounds. Just watch yourself climbing the ladder – hauling it out of the water will be awkward."

"35 pounds? That's child's play for me," Steve boasted.

"We'll see. I'm securing another anchor line to each rope at the cave's mouth. I'll signal when you can pull it up. Once you secure a can, attach a lead dive weight so I can track its descent. I'm sending the bags in two clusters after the cans, then the chests. So remember, water resistance will be a factor, so be gentle when bringing them up to avoid damage. I'll follow the last chest."

"Understood!" as Steve went to insert his regulator.

"Wait!" Jack paused, a new idea dawning. "Drop a fresh tank down on the first return. I can swim up the tunnel to swap it out if needed."

"Smart thinking. Better safe than sorry. I wouldn't have considered it."

"That's right; you couldn't, muscles," Jack said, and both laughed.

* * *

"Almost there," Steve panted, each breath a battle as he approached the boat. Despite inflating his vest for extra buoyancy, the weight he carried made ascent arduous; his buoyancy control device (BCD) stretched to its limits, leaving no room for a safety stop.

He managed to rest the can on the ladder and set his fins onto the pontoon with a practiced motion. Grasping the bottom rung, he heaved the weighty can from the water: *Jack was right. This small ladder is making it cumbersome.*

"Steve, where's Jack?" Emma's voice carried a note of worry over the sound of the waves.

"He's fine. He's down there, sending up the treasure. Needs me up here for the heavy lifting," Steve assured her.

"Okay, stud!" The laughter in Emma's response lightened the air, her steps quickening to assist.

Turning back to his task, Steve positioned himself upon the next rung and, with a concerted effort, lifted the treasure-filled can onto the deck.

"On second thought, should I dive down to monitor him or stay here with you?" Emma pondered aloud.

Steve, removing his gear, contemplated. "My BCD won't fit you, and it's a 20-foot free dive to be able to see him. Jack knows what he's doing, and he's only 25 feet deep. He's not off searching and getting lost. Just stay, help me here."

"Okay."

Emma and Steve worked together to haul cans aboard. With each pull, Steve's rhythm found ease. Once all the cans were safe, they secured a chest against the boat and waited for the last one and Jack's return to assist in lifting them onto the boat.

Surprise flickered across his face as he discovered Jack's used tank on the next pull. No concern shadowed his features; Jack could stay at a depth longer than his tank would last due to the exertion of moving everything around.

"Your boyfriend sent us a present," he announced to Emma, a chuckle in his voice.

"What's he done now?" she asked, half-joking.

"Sent his tank. Guess he's holding his breath now," Steve said, laughter coloring his words.

Emma's smile was both amusement. "Let's hope he doesn't hit his head this time."

* * *

Following the final load, Jack lingered at fifteen feet below the surface, his gaze drawn downward to the cave one last time. The entrance, a gateway to years of relentless pursuit, seemed to mock him with its darkness. Mixed emotions swirled within him – triumph, nostalgia, and melancholy. The quest that devoured so much of his life was at its end, leaving behind fulfillment and a void. His eyes focused on the crate as it was now secured to the pontoon; his heart caught between hope and fear for its survival.

At last, it was his treasure: General Braddock's Lost Gold.

He ascended to the boat with measured strokes, enveloped by a profound sense of completion. Emerging from the water, the sight of his friends, weary yet alight with victory, greeted him.

Together, they lifted the chests aboard, draining them to preserve their integrity. The deck became a scene of jubilant reunion as Emma wrapped Jack in an embrace. Steve clapped him on the back, their faces aglow with the bond forged through adversity.

Emma's voice cut through the air, "Great job, guys!" Her eyes sparkled with joy.

Jack said, with warm gratitude infused in his tone, "I couldn't have done it without you. Both of you." His glance encompassed Steve and Emma, understanding the grievances lingering within them. "I know I caused each of you pain in the past, so I hope I've made up for it. And there's plenty to do right by Sally."

Steve's bear hug was hearty. "Dude, we're square now," he said with a deep sense of closure.

Emma's embrace followed her kiss a seal on their reconciliation. "I'm just glad to have you back. This is all behind us now," she whispered, optimism tinting her voice.

In that moment, surrounded by his friends and their hard-won treasure, Jack allowed himself to savor the triumph. Unaware that Emma's words of finality would soon prove premature.

Chapter 50

It was just after midnight when Captain Clarke stood and reached for his pistol in response to George's alert. His eyes narrowed, scanning the darkness, ready to defend himself and his men. When he took his first step toward George, a piercing snap of metal made him cringe. He sighed as he knew his bayonet was broken.

Turning his attention back to the situation, the thuds of slow steps of hooves grew louder.

"Captain?" Davis said as he was halfway to camp.

"Davis?"

"Yes, Sir, sorry I'm late. I pushed on in the moonlight rather than waiting till morning. I think a moving target is harder to catch."

Clarke gazed at him, "We worried something happened to you."

"I figured so," Davis said, looking contrite. "But it was further than both of us thought. I would have to guess we are closer to 20 miles from the start of the path than 15, Sir. If it weren't for the bright half-moon and a clear night, I would have had to stop and wait until dawn, a few miles short, near where we met the Native. I assumed I wasn't in a safe place."

Clarke smiled and nodded. "I'm glad you made it," he said. "But had you not called out, someone would have fired upon you."

"Thank God they didn't."

He turned, "Henry, get Robert some food."

"Yes, Sir," Henry said.

After a brief tale of his journey, the men earned a good night's sleep.

As dawn broke, they focused on burying the barrel and rejoining the General. William and Thomas started digging a hole large enough for the barrel at the bottom. The others walked over the top of the hill, found a grove of sizeable oak trees, and began cutting off several massive branches. They made five logs about eight or so feet long.

Clarke folded and placed his Lieutenant's coat inside and put on Edward's. He emptied his pockets of a few coins and shot before grabbing his journal. Thumbing through it, Clarke sighed and ripped several blank pages from it to use later.

Reaching into the barrel, he hesitated and set the journal and the final marker inside. He smiled at the thought of hiding the clue in plain sight within his letter to his wife, should someone pay extra attention to his writing.

Clarke replaced the lid, secured the hoop ring, and banged it tight with the stump of his bayonet. The men carried the oak logs next to the pit so they would be ready to be rolled in. He tossed his broken blade into the hole.

William and Henry covered the barrel, slamming their feet to compact the soil while the others inserted the massive tree branches. They all went to work, tossing shovel after shovel and stomping upon the earth as the bottom grew to meet the surface.

Once it reached the top, the group walked around to spread the extra dirt on and around Edward's grave. They removed all signs and barriers of the camp and reconstructed them at the bottom of the hill to draw away any attention from the top of the hill. George began to sweep the area using a downed branch and scattered the leaves and ground cover to camouflage the cache's spot.

"Well done, men," Clarke said in appreciation. "I doubt anyone would detect the barrel is below."

"I agree, Sir," George said.

"Now, let's catch up with General Braddock."

The group mounted their horses and embarked on their journey north. The moment they stepped on the trail, Clarke started to laugh.

"What is it, Sir?" George asked.

"I just realized something."

"What?"

"I left Washington's map in my journal. We'll have to rely on your navigation skills, George."

Davis said, "The Youghiogheny isn't far away. We can follow the path from there."

"I can find our way from there," George said. "Just one question, Sirs. Should we head south or north when we see the river?" he laughed.

Clarke could do nothing but shake his head and chuckle.

They enjoyed the cool, crisp afternoon air, and the sun shone down upon them. Clarke felt a sense of accomplishment as they rode. They were successful in hiding the payroll and created a trap for anyone who may try to steal the payroll. He was proud of his men and their dedication.

Soon, they came across the clear but fast-moving Youghiogheny River and discovered why the Native man warned them not to float down it. The rushing water turned to loud, raging rapids a little downstream. The horses were thirsty, so they stopped to let them drink. Clarke took a deep breath and enjoyed the scenery and peace of the moment, even though he knew it wouldn't last.

His eyes came to focus on his broken hilt. He stared at it and sighed. Taking hold of it, he made a few rapid steps forward and hurled it across the river in one smooth motion.

"Why'd you throw it away, Captain?" Davis asked.

"It's the only item I have identifying me as an officer. And, if they find it on that shore, I hope it will cause them to search along the river for what we were doing instead of back at the hill."

Without expectation, he heard the echo of a steed galloping towards them in the valley ahead. Clarke ordered his troops to ready their guns and aim. The reverberation of hooves pounding on the ground grew louder, and a rider dressed in red came around the bend. Clarke grasped that they stared upon a British soldier who stopped and his horse reared.

"Stand down!" Clark commanded.

"Captain Clarke," the messenger said as he neared.

"Yes."

The confused messenger's gaze went from Clarke and then to Davis.

Davis intervened, pointed at Clarke, and said, "He is Captain Clarke."

"What's the message?"

"I'm Joseph Moore. The General sent me to find you as he expected your return already. We received word that the French and their Native allies learned about a British patrol to the south and were searching for you and your men as we speak. He expects that you should have completed your mission and orders you to ride in haste to join him."

Clarke nodded and said, "We were successful." He turned to his troop, "Gentleman, the General needs us! Let's ride!"

They began to gallop northward as fast as they could.

Little did Clarke know their fate lying ahead.

Chapter 51

Standing beside Steve as Emma turned to the captain's chair, Jack paused to soak in the evening's tranquil beauty. The evening sun painted the water in hues of gold, its rays illuminating their newfound treasure, and reflections from the water danced upon them. Gazing around, this moment etched itself into his memory as a testament to their journey together.

"Another challenge is just beginning," Steve said, breaking the silence.

Jack nodded, believing his thoughts mirrored Steve's. "It's one thing to retrieve the gold. Another to secure it – and then what? Where does it all go?"

"Perhaps a bank's safety deposit box? Or a vault service might offer more privacy."

"A vault is a long-term play, likely in New York or DC. Tomorrow, we'll scout local banks for boxes."

But Steve's concern lay elsewhere. "It's not the treasure's logistics troubling me. It's if the police will think we shot Henry and killed Thomas to get the treasure?"

"No way. They attacked Ben. Henry stabbed Sally. They suspected Thomas of murder before, and the officers said they also had confrontations with them. I think we'll be okay. We answer with the truth, but not volunteer, like we found it."

They reached a consensus, shifting their focus to departure. "Emma, ready to take us home?" Jack asked.

"Absolutely!" she said as they prepared to return the boat.

Steve's chuckle broke through the tension. "Dude, you're a madman. Those gas cans? Genius."

Jack smiled at the memory. "Inspiration struck me at the store. Necessity indeed is the mother of invention."

"FITFO," Steve quipped, their shared laughter easing the stress of the day.

Approaching Deep Creek Marina, Jack handed the Suburban keys to Steve. He directed him to a secluded dock in McHenry Cove, a quieter place to offload their haul.

After Steve disembarked, Emma steered toward the tip of the northeastern most cove, where Jack tied off their vessel to a lonely dock. "Sorry, but we'll need to move quickly," he urged, adrenaline fueling their efficiency.

They passed the treasure between them, a silent symphony of movement under the fading light. At this moment, Jack's admiration for her deepened, witnessing her determination and her focus. This journey bound them, heart and soul, ready to face whatever lay ahead.

"Last one," Steve said, his voice strained from lifting the final piece into the Suburban. They stood for a moment, looking at each other with fatigue and satisfaction painting their faces. United, they unearthed more than treasure; they discovered the depth of their resilience, the strength of their bonds.

Jack eyed the dive equipment strewn on the shore, a puzzle unresolved in his mind. "The snag is, there's not enough room for all the tanks and the chests now."

Steve glanced at the Suburban. "You've got a roof rack."

Emma, the pragmatist, suggested, "Lay the wetsuits on the top of the roof, zippers up. Even if we can afford a new paint job, let's not waste money. If that doesn't work, I guess were paying for the tanks that don't fit."

"Yes, ma'am," Jack said, tipping an imaginary hat. "Told you, Steve, she's the brains."

"No doubt!"

"Hey, Steve, could you return the boat? Emma and I will tackle securing the tanks on top."

With a nod of consensus, Steve returned the pontoon. The treasure was snug within the SUV.

Once reunited at the marina, he said, "Next stop, Lowes. We need better containers for the gold, ones that are easier to haul."

"I never imagined we'd be on such a shopping trip," she said with a smile.

Inside Lowes, he zeroed in on two heavy-duty collapsable dollies capable of navigating any terrain, imagining them filled with their precious cargo. He also picked up straps and blankets for a more secure transport.

"Jack, look." Emma's call drew him to her find – stackable, heavy-duty plastic containers with locking lids. "This should do the job."

"Excellent choice, Em. Let's grab two dozen. It'll be tight in the Suburban," he said, admiring her quick thinking. Their efficiency as a team filled him with pride.

While they made their way back to the SUV, laden with supplies, Emma's voice was soft. "This has still not sunk in."

Jack squeezed her hand in response, sharing in the moment's surreal quality.

Approaching the truck, they found Steve asleep. "They'd court martial you for sleeping on watch," Jack joked, tapping upon the window.

Steve groggily joined them, and together, they reorganized the roof's load, securing the dollies and their new containers.

The drive back was quiet, the day's excitement giving way to exhaustion. He looked around the vehicle, and his friends were sleeping.

He hated to disturb them when they arrived, but they had the grueling task of hauling everything into his place for the night. However, when Jack pulled up to his apartment, the sight of two police cars and a van, with Lieutenant Allen standing at his door, greeted them.

Chapter 52

Jack announced as they pulled up to the curb, "Houston, we have a problem," prompting the groggy friends to wake up.

"What's going on?" Steve mumbled in confusion.

Stepping out into the cool night air, Emma, concern etching her features, Lieutenant Allen approached them.

Emma asked, "What's wrong, Carl?"

Allen glanced at the officers near their vehicles and said, "The team wanted to make a joke about arresting you guys. However, I guessed it wasn't an appropriate time."

"I would've laughed," Steve said with amusement.

"Well, we have several issues. One, I am still struggling with how the Ritters knew where you were at. And two, I told Jack we found at least three sets of fingerprints in Ritter's truck."

"Understood, but why are you here?" Jack asked.

"We're concerned someone else may still be out there and might try to do you some harm."

Emma gasped, "Oh, my."

Allen said, "Barnes and I are about to go off duty, and I must be at the station in the morning for your interviews. We're going to leave two officers for protection. The other two are investigators here to sweep your apartment for the listening devices you believe might be here."

Jack replied, "Thank you, Lieutenant. After they do that and we unload, we're ordering some food. Since you are already here, would all of you care to join us? It's our treat."

"I'm sure the two young officers will accept your offer. My partner and I are going off duty. Yet I suspect you may be able to afford to pay for dinner for everyone now." He put his two hands up, "This isn't a shakedown. I know you two are reputable Navy officers who offered out of courtesy."

"We were."

"Now, Jack. During my questioning, you paused when describing your underwater search for the treasure. I've been doing this for over 20 years, and I can tell when someone is holding back information. You didn't lie, but I suspected you found what you were looking for. That's why I said I believed in your ability to finish the task. And if I'm right, congratulations are in order."

"Well, thank you." Jack took a deep breath. "We did, so having your fellow officers protect us tonight, I thought offering dinner was the least we should do."

"I figured as much. Plus, I'm concerned that if word leaked out, more folk might try to come here wanting to see it, beg, or do harm. Now, Jack," Allen said, his tone sterner, "we'll check for the third person. It's also for your protection in case it's bugged and to prevent future issues. We don't want any prosecutor trying to make a name for themselves by putting you on trial. This way, we can state we thoroughly investigated all three of you."

"Thanks, Carl," Emma cut in just as a tall, lean figure with silver hair approached.

"Mr. Sullivan, I'm Lead Investigator Barton. This is Carter," he introduced, pointing towards his colleague.

Their footsteps echoed inside the dim stairwell. Jack unlocked his door, offering a tense smile. "Sorry, I don't have much in terms of refreshments for our guests, but please come in," he said with unease.

Carter unveiled a device resembling a thick book, energizing the room with an anticipatory buzz. Jack's eyes followed them, pondering whether he was a visitor in his own home as they searched.

"Something's here, Lieutenant," came from the bedroom, pulling Jack to the discovery.

"This was behind your headboard," Allen said, revealing a listening bug in his gloved hand.

Emma blushed with a beaming gaze that met Jack's in silent conversation.

In the kitchen, Carter's scanner hovered near the light fixture above the table, where Barton extracted another device, "Found another, with a camera," he said.

Emma and Steve exclaimed, "Wow," overlapping in shock.

Carter made another pass. "That appears to be all," he said.

"We need your fingerprints for elimination purposes," Barton said, shifting to the procedure.

Emma frowned, confusion and concern knitting her brow. "Why?"

Barton explained the need to eliminate their prints from the ones recovered from the pontoon and the apartment break-in. "It's needed to separate yours from our suspects."

"Okay," Jack consented, masking his unease for Emma and Steve's sake.

With a gesture to the table, Barton began collecting their prints.

In the meantime, Carter announced plans to inspect their vehicles for locators given the ones found on the boat, which Barton agreed was prudent.

Wiping the ink from their fingers, they joined Cater outside. He greeted them, stating. "I detected signals. Trying to find one now," he muttered, though the tracker remained elusive.

"They're not easy to spot. I discovered the one by touch," Steve said, describing the size of the units from their earlier discovery.

"Thank you." Then, triumph from Carter: "Got it!"

Jack's concern etched deep lines on his face, and he sought clarification, "You mentioned *signals*, meaning multiple?"

Carter's announcement of trackers on all three vehicles sparked an exchange of alarmed glances between them, the unease over the situation settling in with a newfound gravity.

"Located another one," Carter said, extracting a small black device from Emma's bumper, revealing the stealth with which someone had been shadowing their every move. The revelation darkened the air around them, a tangible cloud of unease.

"On each vehicle?" Emma's tone was of disbelief and fear.

"Yes, all of them," Barton said.

Carter soon presented the last one, his action punctuating the grim reality of their predicament.

Allen's assurance came as a sliver of relief. "These findings should prove others were the aggressors in this matter. We've secured your home, and officers will keep guard. Rest easy tonight," he said, preparing to leave.

"Thank you, Carl," Emma said with a grateful smile and a hug.

"It's all part of the job," Allen nodded.

Allen accepted Jack's request for a delayed start the next day. However, he advised them they needed to arrive prior to noon, and the police would also escort them to the bank.

With the Lieutenant departing, Jack pivoted to the immediate concern of dinner. "Friendsville Public House?" one of the younger officers said, which became the unanimous choice.

"Perfect! Let's put in our order now before we drag everything upstairs," Jack said, taking in everyone's preferences and calling them in.

Moving their treasure to the apartment took some effort. Emma collapsed into the worn cushions of the living room couches and chairs, exhausted but exhilarated.

"We'll be back," Jack said as he and Steve ventured out for their pickup, one officer accompanying them.

The pub greeted them with the comforting aroma of burgers and beer. After grabbing their food and returning to the apartment building, Jack offered an invitation to the officers to join them in his kitchen. They declined – they were for protection and not authorized to socialize.

Their return was a quiet procession, the night's events a vivid backdrop to the simplicity of their meal, shared in the solace of their temporary sanctuary.

Jack eased the door open to find Emma wrapped in the peaceful embrace of sleep. He tiptoed towards the counter and set each order in distinct groupings. However, Steve, brimming with excitement, couldn't contain himself.

"Alright!" Steve's voice boomed as he unveiled his cheeseburgers and fries. "Let's dive in!"

Emma, now awake and bleary-eyed, joined them. When they settled with their meals, Steve cut to the chase, "How do we split the treasure?"

Jack ducked into his bedroom for a second. Returning, he asked, "What do you think, Steve?"

After washing down a mouthful, Steve said, "Let's save a part for Sally and divide the rest into thirds."

"Sounds fair. But don't forget Bill O'Connell, Mike Thompson, and their crew. He kick-started our quest," as he shoveled in a mouthful of mashed potatoes.

Sipping her iced tea, she agreed, "Their help was crucial. And let's not overlook Ben's contribution. He confronted the Ritters. He may have held them off us for a while, but now he has the medical bills for his efforts."

"Definitely," Jack nodded.

Steve proposed, "First, let's take the boat damage off the top."

"Why not buy the boat?" Jack asked, envisioning future fun for the group.

She hesitated, the memory of recent events shadowing her thoughts, "I'm unsure about *that* boat..."

"We'll find another," Jack said, sensitivity tinting his voice.

Her expression brightened, "Let's donate a chest and a few items to each the Garrett County Museum and the Smithsonian. And let DC replicate the journal and letters."

Steve then remembered and asked, "What about the cask?"

Intrigued, Jack fetched the small cask and pried it open with a knife.

Inside, they found pages that extended Captain Clarke's narrative – a harrowing account of Samuel Rogers' sacrifice and their encounter with White Hawk, a solitary Native.

"How tragic," she reflected. "I never thought of the hardships they endured burying the treasure."

"It adds perspective." Then Steve asked. "But just one man? Not a tribe?"

"I would have to guess the man was traveling alone or was a scout sent out to determine if Clarke and his men were friend or foe."

Steve said, "Clarke's journal sheds light on their formidable journey."

"Anything else?" she asked, drawn into the unfolding saga.

"Yes, *Tuesday, June 24th, 1755…*" Jack told the story of how Edward Smith attempted to commit treason by stealing the payroll. "Incredible, but here's something even more shocking. *The fear of the payroll being stolen by the colonial militia to fund a revolt against the crown was the reason Braddock asked me to hide it for protection.*"

"Wow, crazy," Steve said. "As Emma said, I never thought they had to go through all this."

"There's more. '*Although I trusted Lieutenant Davis, a regular British Officer, I took General Braddock's order to heart and was cautious about whom I shared information with. Towards the end, I was not comfortable with some of Lieutenant Davis's men. I am glad he and his men did not know the payroll's final resting place.*

"'*I did not share the location with Lieutenant Robert Davis. Because of this, he suggested I take Smith's uniform and wear it, as I had a lieutenant's coat and not a captain's. In doing so, if the French captured us during our return to rejoin the army, the French would try to gain the location from him, not me. The Lieutenant is a truly honorable and courageous man.*'"

Emma's voice, laced with shock, cut through the tension. "Ben's comments about their being captured were correct. It appears their plan kept the gold from the French."

Jack nodded, the weight of history on his shoulders. "Yes, the question is: did Clarke and his men fall in battle or not survive their capture? Either way, they never made it back here, leaving the treasure lost."

Steve chimed in, "Their fate remains a mystery."

Jack's tone softened, "I can't blame Ben, though."

"Neither would I," Emma said, a shadow of solemnity falling over them as they shifted into more comfortable attire. Jack returned last to the room.

They pushed the furniture aside for more space. Emma took up the tablet and pen, offering to document as they sorted the treasure into sturdy containers interspersed with thoughts of future dreams.

"Well," he said, running a hand through his hair. "As I said before, I was considering buying a home on the lake for us. Big enough for everyone and their families to stay. We can all hang out and relax together."

"Sounds amazing," she said, warmth spreading through her chest at the thought of a sprawling house filled with laughter and love.

"Then, once I finish my master's, I'm thinking about finding another place to teach," Jack said with vulnerability. "DC's good, or even here at Garrett County College, if you're tired of working in a big, congested city."

Emma stared into his eyes, her voice quivering with strong feelings, "I like the idea of a new home and possibly getting married one day. But I'm scared. I'm still a little worried we'll never return to how we were before. Would you mind if I took some time to decide – about staying in DC, moving, or maybe something different?"

Jack's assurance was unwavering. "Whatever path you choose, Emma. It's our journey together that matters. You helped me accomplish my dream; now, it's my turn to help you follow yours."

Emma's emotions overflowed. "I *do* have my Jack back," she whispered, tears of joy and relief streaming down.

In response, Jack, with a gentle smile, grabbed a peculiar shiny ring from the treasure. "Since you mention marriage, maybe I should ask you to marry me with this ring?"

Emma's eyes widened and said, "Not with that ring. I loved the one you first gave me."

Jack rose and reached into his pocket. He then knelt and asked, "Oh... Since it is a matter of the ring... What if I asked you again with the ring you cherished?"

Overwhelmed with joy, Emma cried, "Yes!" her tears were a testament to their enduring bond. She admired the ring, her gaze of adoration mirroring the depth of their connection.

"I didn't think you would keep it. You had so many bills piling up..."

Jack's affirmation cut through the uncertainty, his stance resolute as he kissed Emma's forehead – a gesture brimming with the promises of their future. "I found a way because I never lost hope," he said, encapsulating resolve and reassurance in his tone.

Emma glanced at Steve. His smile was peculiar. "Sorry, Steve, perhaps Jack's timing wasn't ideal, all things considered."

Steve's response was gracious and tinged with a hint of longing. "No, I'm genuinely happy for you two. Sally was special, but I only knew her for a few days. I'm still on the lookout for my own Emma, I suppose."

Emma's embrace was warm. "Don't worry, if you don't meet her soon, I'll hunt her down for you," she offered, half-joking.

"As long as you choose better for me than you did with this guy," Steve chuckled. They shared laughter, and soft light cast a serene backdrop as they delved back into their treasure.

Jack's meticulous nature shone through as they organized the treasure for transport. The coins, under the dim light, seemed to await their fate.

He broke the silence, and his voice rose in excitement. "It looks like we're staring at a fortune – might be over six or seven million dollars." He detailed the value of the Gold Five Guinea coins and the bulk worth of gold and silver, the potential figures dancing in the dim room.

Emma and Steve both had their mouths open, stunned. The magnitude of their discovery dawned on them, lightening the room's atmosphere as the shock of their newfound wealth settled.

Jack, buoyed by joy, teased, "Now that we tasted treasure hunting, why stop here?"

Steve's eyes widened as he asked, "What do you have in mind?"

Jack's eyes sparkled with the thrill of the hunt. "What about searching for the Lost Continental Army Gold in Granby, Connecticut? Another quest, which may be worth millions, awaits us."

Their laughter and shared glances spoke of deep bonds, adventure, and the endless possibilities lying ahead.

Leaning in, his eyes alight with enthusiasm, he revealed his discovery. "I've checked into it. That treasure was to support the Continental Army during the Revolutionary War, but it vanished. Finding it would be monumental."

Jack's effort of a stoic facade quickly crumbled into laughter.

Emma, half-annoyed yet intrigued, gave him a playful smack. "What, Jack? Are we doing this again?" Her eyes, however, lingered on the coins and artifacts scattered before them.

"It was just a joke, Em," Jack said, catching her expression.

Emma paused, her gaze flitting between her friends. "Well, Jack," she started, a tentative smile forming, "searching together, the three of us might be fun. Think about it – adventures, travel."

Jack and Steve, stunned, stared at her. "Are you joking?" Jack managed.

"No," she affirmed, "but let's plan for summer when you're off from teaching."

Steve's silence met Jack's grin and his failed attempt at a high-five as Steve left him hanging in the air.

"Let's not get ahead of ourselves," Steve cautioned, his tone grounding. "We still need to get through the investigation and the questions tomorrow. We need to stay sharp."

Chapter 53

After an early breakfast, Jack and his friends started loading their newfound treasure into the back of his Suburban. The morning air was crisp, and the presence of the police escort to the bank in Oakland added a surreal quality to their journey. Jack's right hand tapped in anticipation on the steering wheel; securing the gold was pivotal, and he hoped nothing would go wrong.

"Alright, let's do this," Jack announced with resolve as they arrived at the bank. The scent of fresh coffee and the sight of polished floors welcomed them. The bank staff stared oddly at their cargo and officers and offered cautious smiles.

Jack approached the counter, requesting several large safety deposit boxes with a calm he didn't quite experience within. Emma and Steve's anxious glances didn't escape him, but he kept focused.

"We'll start with six," the teller suggested after a moment of disbelief at the size of their haul.

"Yes, that'll do for now," Jack said, signing the paperwork with a steady hand.

Filling those boxes, it became clear they would need more. In the end, they secured the last of their treasure, which required renting all the remaining large boxes and several medium ones.

Back in the Suburban, the air was thick with tension as they headed a short distance to the police station. "It's time to face the music," Jack said, a determined grip on the steering wheel.

The station was imposing, a symbol of the official scrutiny awaiting them. As they stepped inside, the robust scent of freshly brewed coffee mingled with the sharp, antiseptic tang of cleaning agents. After introducing themselves at the front desk, an officer approached and led them into a conference room. They gazed upon Lieutenant Allen, Sergeant Meyers, and a man they assumed was a detective. They shook hands with each of them, and Detective Mark Smith introduced himself. He was a handsome, tall, athletic individual with white hair and a goatee.

They took their seats around a wooden table and tried to appear calm and confident. Three stern law enforcement officers looked upon them from across the room, but Smith's penetrating stare from his blue eyes made it clear he would not allow any lies to slip by unnoticed.

Taking his gaze off Smith, Jack swallowed hard, looked at the Lieutenant, and posed his own question, which he believed was necessary to bring up before proceeding. "May I ask something that's on my mind?"

"Go ahead, Jack," Allen encouraged, his tone sincere yet reassuring.

"Do we need a lawyer?" Jack's voice held an edge of caution.

Allen shook his head. "No, Jack. Our goal is to finalize this investigation and clarify your involvement as targets. This is only a formality to ensure we have no future disputes."

After a nod of agreement from his friends, Jack consented, "Okay, then. We can start."

The three officers questioned them individually again and in the same order. Jack believed his interrogation was thorough yet familiar, with Sergeant Meyers and Detective Smith introducing new questions. Meyers asked, "Would you detail how you searched for the treasure without harming the environment or the lake?"

Jack outlined their meticulous approach, noting that they only displaced a single stump by a few feet near Penelec. He mentioned Thomas Ritter's unintended collapse and disturbance of the lakebed and clarified that their search did not disturb any other natural areas.

Smith's pointed question: "Regarding the collapsed entrance, what did you have to do last night to retrieve the gold?"

After a pause, knowing Smith asked for a reason, Jack said, "Thomas Ritter caused the collapse, and clearing of it happened during our attempted rescue of him. Yesterday, our entry and exit were through the already created opening. Nothing else had to be touched. Does that address your concern?"

Smith exchanged eye contact with Allen, who gave a noncommittal shrug, then nodded. "Yes, that clarifies it. Thank you."

Allen softened. "Your cooperation has been invaluable. Please wait outside while we confer."

Once seated in the hall again, the tension between Jack and his friends was evident from them shifting in their seats or their legs bouncing. It was a subtle but persistent sense of unease, a mixture of worry and hope that hung around them like a silent chorus.

The sounds of a chair sliding back on a tile floor and footsteps approaching reverberated through the door. The Lieutenant opened the door and waved his hand, signaling them to return. The officers' bodies appeared relaxed and the room calmer when they retook their positions.

Returning to their seats, Allen affirmed, "We all agree you were the Ritters' target. We came to this conclusion because of finding the bugs and trackers and what happened last week at The Lodges at Sunset Village. Your stories align with the victim, Ben Baton, who may have been attacked by the Ritters. You also came forth right away when you found the gun. Forensics proved the gun matched a murder predating you being in the area."

He gazed up and down the table at his fellow officers, "Based on our ongoing investigation, you are free to go. Please enjoy your findings, and we hope you spend much of it here in the community."

They exchanged handshakes, and the group departed, a weight lifted from their shoulders. With a sense of relief and newfound freedom guiding their steps, Jack led the way to the 3rd Street Diner. They left behind the looming shadows of suspicion and emerged into the bright atmosphere of the day.

"Why aren't we heading to Englanders?" Emma asked, a playful tilt to her question.

Jack offered a smile. "Thought you'd appreciate a change, Em."

Steve's laughter broke through. "More like he's scared you'll end up buying the place."

Emma chuckled and joined in, teasing. "Guess that's one way to have me move to Garrett County."

Jack conceded with a nod, turning towards Englanders, but Emma stopped him. "No, let's try 3rd Street. I don't fancy watching you two brood for hours while I shop." She laughed.

A gentle breeze brushed against them as they entered the diner. The enticing scent of sizzling bacon and freshly brewed coffee wafted around them. Warm wood paneling and exposed brick walls adorned with vintage photos and kitchen tools welcomed them in. The cheerful chatter of other diners and the clink of utensils upon plates created a soothing ambiance. It offered them a much-needed respite from the tense atmosphere they had just left behind.

"Being in DC has its perks, Jack. You'd be closer to Norfolk now for when I'd visit," Steve said, a sly grin spreading.

Emma set her menu down. "Don't you worry, Steve. I also have an uncomfortable couch with your name on it."

Their laughter filled the brief silence before Jack went serious. "After lunch, we should go to the bank. I've got some ideas for Mike Thompson, but Bill and Ben need their shares, too."

"Agreed," Steve nodded.

Jack leaned in, sharing his plan. "Bill should receive one of the Gold Five Guineas and a few smaller coins. One Gold Five Guineas sold a year ago for $50,000. And for Ben, I'm thinking we give him around $150,000 in coins and items."

Emma and Steve shared approving nods.

"Let's eat up, and then let's go share the wealth," Jack concluded, the decision made.

Their generosity continued with a $50 tip left on the table, the waitress's surprised gratitude marking the start of their journey to deliver their gifts. Jack called Bill, setting up a visit, a fitting conclusion to their adventure.

"Hey, Bill," Jack said with anticipation as they reached the porch. "We've got something for you, a token of thanks."

"Really?" Interest sparked in Bill's eyes.

"Yes," Jack replied, unveiling a Gold Five Guinea coin, a silver farthing, and a halfpenny. "For you, my friend."

Bill's eyes widened. "You found it?"

"We did," Jack affirmed.

"I'm speechless," Bill managed, emotion swelling. "Thank you, both of you."

"Thank you, Bill," Emma said, her gratitude confirmed with a kiss on his cheek. "Your stories, the ones of your parents and the waterfalls, were our final clue. Keep these small tokens as a memory, or sell them and take your entire family on an enjoyable, expensive vacation. One, they'll remember you for forever."

Tears glistened in his eyes as he pointed to the chairs beside him on the porch. "Tell me everything," he urged, yearning for their adventure's recount.

Over iced tea, they regaled him with their tale, laughter and suspense filling the air.

"You should write a book," Bill said.

"Perhaps we will," Emma replied.

Their next visit was to Ben, who sighed in relief at their news about Sally. "The Ritters..." he trailed off, his disdain for their actions evident. Ben's history with them had been fraught with tension, their pursuit of the treasure relentless.

Ben's initial refusal of the gifts they offered turned into heartfelt thanks, promises of wise use, and care for his family. His father, by his side, extended apologies, "You and Grandpa were right. The gold was real. Sorry for discouraging you."

"It's okay, Dad. This is more than I expected to find. I enjoyed going out with Grandpa all those years, listening to his stories."

He turned to Emma and ended with, "Don't feel guilty. What Thomas Ritter did to me is not your fault. From my perspective, I'm sorry to say this, but I would have shot to kill him. I believe that if you had not stopped him like you did, he would have killed you like they tried to kill me. I think they trapped Sally, and she did what she did to protect you."

"Thanks, Ben." Emma leaned over and hugged him.

"We should head out," Jack declared, and they said their farewells and gave parting embraces.

As they left, Jack's thoughts turned to Mike. He sent a message, hinting at a surprise. But silence met his anticipation.

"Maybe he's still on vacation," Emma said, a hopeful note in her voice.

"Maybe," Jack conceded, skepticism threading his voice despite the uncertainty. "However, I can't shake the suspicion something's off. What if he ran into the Ritters? Or he's the third party we've been wary of?"

When evening approached, casting elongated shadows across the landscape, they found themselves back at Jack's, the day's tension unwinding in the familiarity of his living room. With a playful critique of his outdated furniture, Emma made herself comfortable on the couch, gesturing for Jack to join. Steve, claiming the recliner, soon succumbed to the room's serenity.

Settling beside Emma, Jack saw the fleeting glance she gave her ring before she nestled against him, finding solace in his presence. As sleep claimed her and Steve alike, Jack remained awake, the glow of the television painting his thoughtful face. Amidst the silence, a question lingered, unspoken yet heavy with implication – *Was there more to this story?*

Chapter 54

Jack tensed as the unmistakable echo of footsteps on the stairs crescendoed, followed by the ominous creak of his door swinging open. "Who's there?" he muttered.

Steve jolted from his slumber, and his hand darted to his sidearm, his body coiled and ready as his gaze pierced the darkness. "Show yourself!" Steve commanded, his voice betraying no hint of the adrenaline surge within. "We know you're here!"

Henry Ritter loomed in the doorway, his figure marked by shoulder and thigh bandages and a malicious smirk. "Sally played you fools to the end. What you claimed is now mine, as it should have been all along."

Steve's hand clenched around his gun, a storm brewing in his eyes. "Explain yourself."

"Relax. It's over," with a disarming laugh. Henry gestured with his hands raised in peace. "Sally was my ally the whole time. Here, as a token of gratitude," he said, tossing them each a coin, "consider these parting gifts from your misadventure. And now, I don't even have to share it with anyone! It's the least I can reward you as a thank you."

Jack's eyes widened as he recognized the King George II coin, the reality of the betrayal sinking in. "How did you...?"

Henry's smirk broadened. "A simple seduction of the bank manager by Sally. She gave him a *really* good time. Several damning photographs later, and voilà, your treasure was mine for the taking."

"Like hell!" Steve countered, disbelief and anger lacing his remarks. "Sally was loyal to us."

"Was she?" Henry's grin became twisted. "She played us all, securing herself three chances at the gold: you, Ben, and me."

Steve cut in, weary yet defiant. "Jack, this man's word is worthless."

Henry's retort was icy, his confidence unshaken. "Deny it all you want, but the gold in your hands is proof enough of Sally's deceit."

Steve erupted, his patience shattered. "Lies!"

Henry's face turned to stone, his words dripping with a dangerous warning. "You failed to realize how *desperate* Sally was, Stevie."

Steve's resolve crystallized in the next breath; his lip twitched, and he fired. Henry crumpled, his demise as swift as it was violent.

Jack startled awake, drenched in a cold sweat, his heart racing.

"Jack, are you alright?" Emma's voice, laced with concern, cut through the remnants of his bad dream.

"Sorry, a disturbing and vivid nightmare," Jack said, laden with unease, stirred from the depths of a restless dream. "I can't shake this feeling. Could Sally have planned all this? Played us? Ritters, Ben, and us?"

Emma rose, a beacon of calm. "I don't think so," she said, guiding him to bed. When her head found its place on his chest, her presence became his solace, lulling him into a peaceful sleep.

Dawn's light spilled into their modest apartment, heralding a day of departure. With meticulous care, they packed their findings into a nondescript suitcase, a silent pact of caution between them. "Leave the chests. It will help keep the treasure under wraps for now," Jack said, contemplating the impact if the Smithsonian knew about the gold.

"Understood. But you and I will have to clean and preserve the chests when we return here. I'll order what we will need," Emma concurred, already planning the next steps in their preservation.

"Did you pack for two weeks?" she asked, pausing at the doorway.

"Three. I'll take the bags down and pull the Suburban up."

"Three?" Emma asked with a smile that quickly morphed into concern. "Wait, when are you due back at Penn State?"

"I've got three and a half weeks. I figured I'd stay with you as long as I could. Then, I'll come to DC on weekends except when we decide to come to Deep Creek together. After I finish my master's this year, I'm figuring I can move to DC."

Emma smiled again, "But we need to find a new place here. This is not where I want to stay when we come to the lake."

Jack looked around and chuckled, "What? You don't like my luxury apartment with high-end furniture?"

Laughing, Emma said, "It's too small, but maybe we can buy the furniture from the landlord if you're that attached to it."

"He might give it to us if we hauled it out of here," Jack laughed.

The sight of Steve interrupted their moment of fun, his focus on packing with a purpose that suggested imminent departure. "Off to another adventure?" Jack asked, concern masked by jest.

"Just a trip to Norfolk. The rear admiral has some ideas he wants me to work with him on and test out," Steve said. Curiosity piqued, yet Jack knew this mystery belonged to Steve alone, another narrative unfolding parallel to theirs.

"Seems like you're skipping the DC excitement," Emma quipped, joining Jack with a serene presence. Her eyes flicked to Steve's duffel. "Sure you don't want in? DC's more than just suits. Plus, my disaster of a couch is all yours." Her laughter softened the offer. "But seriously, I have a spare bedroom for you."

Steve zipped his bag with conviction. "Sorry, I've got commitments, Emma. I should be in Norfolk when they roll out the training program I developed for recruits to the new class, and the admiral's *project* is something else."

Emma walked over to her purse and started to rummage through it.

"Remember us when you're hobnobbing with the brass," Jack half-joked, masking the sting of Steve's absence. Despite understanding, he missed their untroubled days as a trio.

Steve locked eyes with Jack, smiling. "I'll be back to help escort the gold to the auction and for the exhibit. I wouldn't miss seeing Sally's face hanging at the new museum gallery."

"Counting on it," Jack managed, a smile breaking through.

"I'm on it," Steve said, slinging his bag over his shoulder. "Have some fun for me."

Emma returned to Steve's side and turned practical. "Steve, you're always welcome. If you're up for it, we'd like you to join our house hunt." Her hand brushed Jack's arm. "Here. Take this. It's a key to my place. As I said, you are family and can show up anytime."

"Thank you. You two mean the world to me." Steve reached in and hugged her.

"Sorry, we need to wrap this up. We've all got to get on the road."

"Will do," Jack said, though his gaze followed Steve. Spotting his backpack near the kitchen, he fetched it. "Em, let me sort through this so I can throw some things in it for the trip."

"Alright."

While Jack emptied the bag on the table, each item: a knife, a hand shovel, a brush, and worn leather gloves – told of past discoveries. Dirt from countless digs dusted the surface as he pulled out a cloth bag, heart racing. "Steve, please grab the broken bayonet blade from the suitcase?"

Emma's voice, tinged with intrigue, filled the room. "What's up?"

"In all the chaos of the finding of the barrel and chasing our treasure, I almost forgot about this object. I discovered it by the Yough River the same morning Mike Thompson found the barrel."

Steve approached, laying a blade on the table, his expression one of fascination. "What's this about, Jack?"

Jack, hands quivering with anticipation, and didn't answer. Instead, he produced the hilt from his bag and aligned it with the blade. The connection was instant and undeniable.

"Holy shit," Steve gasped, the pieces fitting seamlessly. "It's a match!"

Jack, with a tone of reverence, said, "This has to be Captain Clarke's bayonet. Its ornate handle indicates it was an officer's. He abandoned it to conceal his rank."

"Wow. This will be a huge addition to the museum display," Emma said, excited by the potential.

Steve's gaze lingered on the reunited bayonet. "If only Sally were here to see this."

"We all wish that," Jack echoed.

"I'm going to rush the restorations and begin working with Bill O'Connell on setting the exhibit up."

"Anything else you can do to make a bigger splash? Draw more people into the museum?" Steve asked.

Emma stared at the table, "Let me find out what we have at the Smithsonian." Running a finger through the dirt on the table's surface, Emma said, "Jack, I think you should leave the backpack here for our next adventure. It's not coming into *our* place in DC."

"Yeah, Indy," Steve chuckled, "You have enough dirt to bury another ark at Tanis."

They all laughed.

The trio of friends, Jack, Emma, and Steve, descended the stairs and emerged into the crispness of the morning air. As they loaded the last few items into their respective vehicles, Jack threw his arms around Steve in a tight embrace and patted him on the back. "Take care of yourself, brother. I'll see you when we transport the treasure." His voice was thick with emotion.

"I always do, and I'll be waiting," Steve said, returning the pat on Jack's back before letting go of the hug.

Emma and Steve hugged, tears streaming down their faces. "Remember, you can come and stay with us anytime. Just show up. No need to ask," Emma said.

"Thanks, Emma," Steve tried to smile.

They sped away with Fleetwood Mac's *Tusk,* filling the space amidst him and Emma. The sunlight bathed them, illuminating the journey ahead and the silent, shared understanding of their bond.

"Everything okay?" Emma asked, catching Jack's admiring glance.

"Better than okay," he assured, his smile reflecting a deep contentment. "Just savoring the moment."

Emma's warm and comforting smile met Jack's as their hands found each other, resting between them. The world outside melded into a serene blur of greens and blues, their silence a shared happiness.

The tranquility shattered as Jack's phone buzzed, an intrusive vibration against the dashboard. Emma, battling the sun's glare, relayed the message from Mike Thomson, their contractor.

"Typical Mike, always on his own time," Jack quipped with a chuckle, "I already got my answer from the Lieutenant."

Emma shared Mike's brief apology, "Sorry for the delay. Still away with the family. I'll call you when I get back."

"I guess his present will have to wait."

They drove across I-68 and enjoyed the views of the rolling hills. It was not long before Jack glanced over and saw Emma sleeping against the window, her jacket balled up like a pillow. About an hour out of DC, when traffic started to pick up, Jack's phone vibrated with life - it was Lieutenant Allen on the line.

"Hey, Lieutenant, what's up?" Jack asked.

"Jack, Emma – how are you?"

"Good. We're on our way to DC to take the items from the dig site to the Smithsonian," Emma replied.

"When are you planning to be back in town?"

"In two or three weeks – my car is still at Jack's place."

Allen's voice turned stern as he said, "I have more to discuss with you." The tension shot up as the Lieutenant revealed more information regarding the fingerprints analyzed. "As you know, we have fingerprints of the two Ritters on everything. In their truck, we also found Ben's print. However, we also found his prints on those photos we discovered in the truck..."

Jack shifted in his seat, showing he was anxious.

"I questioned Ben," Allen went on, "and he said he sat in Ritter's truck when he confronted him after seeing his truck at the cave. Given they attacked him, I am inclined to believe him."

"Makes sense. Ben did say he faced him," Jack said. "I believe Henry may have shown him the photos to lure him to the falls to eliminate him, and they hoped to make it appear to be an accident."

"I agree, and that is our theory at this point. But we have bigger issues," Allen said with concern. "We found another set of prints in the truck."

Emma asked, "Who's prints are they?"

Allen paused before answering, "Sally's. Her prints were also in the mix."

The words landed like a sucker punch, Jack's mind reeling. "Sally? That doesn't make any sense." He glanced at Emma, whose eyes widened, a silent testament to their shared shock.

"Clear as day, we matched them from the state's school teacher database," Allen insisted, his tone firm.

"Her role in this... it may be deeper than we thought," Jack muttered, the revelation casting a shadow across Sally's beguiling image. "Was she the chess master playing a match we haven't even begun to comprehend? Or was she a pawn in the Ritter's strategy?"

Allen's tone was cautious as he spoke, "We also don't know the age of the fingerprints. Remember, they used to be in a relationship." He paused, the importance of the investigation evident even over the phone. "We're working on it, Jack, but it feels like trying to solve a puzzle with important pieces missing. Just so you know, State Attorney Cunningham is meeting with Ritter today, and things could become more complicated. Stay ready; we may need your assistance."

"Will do, Lieutenant," Jack said, the line going dead. He exchanged a glance with Emma, both their faces etched with concern.

"Can you believe this mess?" Emma's voice was a whisper of disbelief.

"I still think she was a pawn, Em. Why else would she save you?" Jack's gaze remained fixed on the road, thoughts racing.

"If caught in the middle, her stepping in front of me... it could've been her play to pin everything on Ritter if things went south."

"It's possible..." Jack's grip on the steering wheel tightened, his mind teetering on the brink of what dark revelation lay ahead. *Is another shoe about to drop?*

Chapter 55

Jack and Emma exited their SUV into the stifling embrace of the Washington, DC, summer. They navigated through the Smithsonian's employee parking to bring their findings into the heart of the Museum of American History. With a blend of urgency and excitement, Emma handed over the artifacts for swift preservation and hinted at cloning the historical documents for an upcoming exhibit.

Wandering the galleries, they immersed themselves in the quiet grandeur of the past, their conversation weaving between the artifacts' stories and their own discoveries. "Can you imagine being part of something that ends up here one day?" Jack was half-serious as he pondered beside a display of Revolutionary War artifacts.

Emma, catching his gaze, teased, "With the Braddock treasures, I might know someone who might be able to help make sure it makes the cut."

Their laughter, a brief respite, mingled with the museum's ambient sounds, allowing Jack a momentary peace amid the relics of yesteryear.

Emma guided them to the National Mall, where the monumental landscape lent a surreal backdrop to their intimate exchange. "It's like we've stepped right into history," Emma said, her eyes alight as they settled on the Capitol.

Jack squeezed her hand. "And we're writing our own chapter in it," his voice carried their shared journey's excitement.

Yet, the past's echoes were never far behind.

The abrupt ring from Jack's phone pierced their moment of serenity. It was Lieutenant Allen, his tone heavy, signaling the urgency of his news. "Jack, Emma, brace yourselves," he warned.

"Ritter sang like a canary just now," Allen said, and the shuffle of papers carried over the line. "Claims Sally was pulling all the strings."

"Go on," Jack urged, his gaze never leaving Emma's.

"He explained that Sally told him to share the photos with Ben as he was helping them. Sally was the one who slashed your tires and attacked Ben at the falls.

"Really?" Jack asked.

"He also insists they were searching at the final site for the treasure because Sally provided them with the location. When things went south, and Henry found his dad trapped under rocks, he went to the closest place he thought he could call for help. Which was your Pontoon. However, here's the kicker…"

"Keep going," Jack pressed, his focus sharp, while Emma listened, her expression a mix of shock and anticipation.

"Ritter claims Sally pulled a gun when he sought assistance on your boat. He says it was self-defense when she lunged at him," Allen relayed.

Emma scoffed. "Self-defense? Not even close."

"That's his story," Allen said.

"Does it make any sense to you?" Jack pressed, skepticism etched across his face.

"It's doubtful. Ritter also contends he posed no danger to Emma, yet she shot him."

Emma raised an eyebrow. "He alleges he wasn't advancing on me when I fired?"

"State Attorney Cunningham doesn't believe Ritter's self-defense claim. Your actions, targeting his knife arm and his leg, indicated you aimed to neutralize a threat, not to kill," Allen said. "Facing these facts, Ritter is not pressing charges against you, suggesting you acted under distress and confusion after discovering Sally's betrayal."

Emma shook her head in disbelief.

"Cunningham thinks Ritter believes that if he paints himself as reasonable, it might sway a jury for him and versus Sally."

"That's appalling," Emma countered.

"They're wrapping up the investigation, planning for trial. I'm sorry, but we're asking you to return by Tuesday."

"We'll be there," Jack said, resolve in his tone.

"Concerned about Ben?" Allen asked, offering security.

Emma glanced at Jack. "Ben's not a worry for us."

"Agreed," Jack affirmed. "We spent parts of two days with him. Ben's caught up in this; he's not a threat."

"And Steve?" Jack asked.

"Already spoke to him. At this point, as he was not on the boat at the time, we don't need him back till the trial. Cunningham will handle his questioning via a web meeting. We'll need you, Emma, for a day or two for depositions and the entire trial. We'll depose Jack next week as well."

"Understood. We'll see you Tuesday unless you update us to do otherwise," Jack concluded, and he ended the call.

"Our adventure just got more complex," Jack murmured, tension lacing his voice.

Emma's hand found his, a gesture of solidarity. "We've never backed down from a challenge."

Jack said with unwavering conviction, "We should make the most of the time we have."

"Yes, please," Emma echoed, their strides matching as they left the mall's thrum behind.

After their stroll around the mall, they returned to Jack's SUV, and Emma guided Jack to her new apartment.

Entering, Jack surveyed it with quiet admiration. Its spacious layout and modern aesthetics, punctuated by selective artwork and sleek furniture, were the opposite of his homier setting. The apartment's grandeur, crowned by the expansive windows revealing the city's heartbeat below, both awed and unsettled him. Yet, a touch of familiarity lingered in a few choice pieces; he presumed they came from Englanders.

Emma's touch, gentle and reassuring, brought him back. "It's different, I know," she whispered. "But we can make it our own."

Jack managed a smile, acknowledging her effort to ease his unease. "Impressive, though," he said, the corners of his mouth lifting in amusement.

"Well... after we broke up, I believed I needed a change," Emma said with pride and melancholy. "I've done well at The Smithsonian, so I thought I should upgrade."

Jack's heart twinged with guilt as her words sank in as she entered the bedroom to pack. "I understand the need for a change," as he remembered why he joined the Navy. Staring out at the sprawling city, he wrestled with his past decisions and their future together.

Their conversation paused as Emma attended a call, her tone tense. Jack's concern deepened, overhearing snippets of her anxious dialogue.

"Problem?" he asked, his brows furrowed with worry.

"It's complicated," Emma sighed. "I told her I was a witness to a murder. I explained they needed me there for a day or two this week to interview me and later for the trial. I'll explain more to her when I am in front of her. It's too intricate for a phone call. "

"How was she?"

"She sounded somewhat okay, as I could be at the museum for three days this week to oversee things while she's out. We try not to be out at the same time."

Jack nodded, understanding the delicate balance of professional commitments and personal crises. Their shared glance spoke volumes, acknowledging the intricate weave of their lives, intertwining once more against a backdrop of challenge and change.

"Understood," Jack carried a note of resolve as he moved towards Emma's bedroom, the air filled with the subtle bustle of her unpacking.

Her voice, loud in the house's quiet, broke through: "Do you want to go out for dinner?"

"Sounds good," he said, his footsteps slowing as a shelf caught his attention just outside the bedroom.

Photographs of Emma's life were laid bare in frames – laughter with her sister at Hershey Park and proud moments with her parents at her Penn State graduation.

It was the third photo that halted Jack, drawing him in. A picture from their scuba diving adventure in Belize – Emma, Jack, and Steve, encapsulated in joy. A surge of warmth rushed through him, a smile breaking across his face as his tears threatened: *She never forgot about me.*

Lingering at the doorway, Jack beamed at Emma, lost in her world. She thumbed through her closet, pausing periodically, trying to see what struck her fancy. After glancing at and passing on several outfits, she lingered, her head oddly tilted in thought. With a smile, she pulled it from the rack but then proceeded to reach to the top shelf to extract a framed memory. Gazing upon it, she walked over and placed the photo on her nightstand with reverence before returning to her wardrobe's depths – now trying to find the perfect shoes.

Curious, Jack stared at the photo, a tear coming to his eye. Jack looked upon their moment on Mt. Washington, the day he proposed, framed by the backdrop of Pittsburgh and sealed with the promise of forever. He cringed when he remembered that the Ritters' callous hands tore that same photo in his apartment.

The very dress she pondered wearing, the one that triggered the memory of the photo, was the same one she wore for their engagement.

In that instant, Jack felt at home.

Chapter 56

Back in Garrett County, Jack, Emma, and Steve found themselves amidst the bustle of the grand opening weekend. They were the quiet force behind the scenes. Having lent their strength to unload trucks and set up the Braddock exhibit. Their efforts diminished by Saturday, the day it all came together.

"Amazing," Steve said, gazing at the meticulous display in the rotating room. His focus fell on those applying the final touches.

Caught in the whirl of preparation, Emma said, grateful, "Thank you."

Jack's gaze swept the room. Artifacts on loan from the Smithsonian's *The Price of Freedom* collection filled the room. British and French uniforms from the French and Indian War, rifles, and a canon surrounded them.

Alongside them were depictions of historical generals, bringing the past alive. In the middle of the displays, a print showing the generals: Sir William Pepperell, Sir Jeffery Amherst, James Abercrombie, James Wolfe, and, in the center, Major General Edward Braddock.

Yet, the photographs lining the walls held Jack's attention. He smiled at their own faces around the treasure chest. His grin continued over the photos of Mike Thompson and his men displaying the red coat. Bill O'Connell was holding his coins. Ben was smiling, embracing his coins while sitting in his chair with casts on his legs. Each immortalized in shared victory. Jack then stared at the photo of Sally, whose legacy would soon expand the museum.

Reflecting upon Henry Ritter's trial, his actions cast a shadow over these achievements. Found guilty of first-degree murder and extortion, Ritter's manipulations unraveled in court. Forensics traced his schemes through encrypted communications, which police had not discovered on Sally's phone. However, evidence showed a controlling and untrusting Heny installed a tracking app on Sally's. It had been active since they were dating.

Evidence also surfaced that Henry took advantage of family members when they were most vulnerable. Henry coerced them into signing documents to pay for their parent's care. They signed even though they should have been able to use Medicaid or wait for the funds from their parent's estate.

A staff member who was afraid to speak up before Herny's arrest testified. They provided valuable information to the police and aided in the search for physical proof. Without them, Ritter might have gotten away with it.

Despite a thorough investigation, there was no indication Sally signed any agreements regarding her mother's care. Based on the number of people who have already come forward, police believe there are additional hidden records. Many showed they had either signed or pressured by Ritter to sign.

From all the evidence, the jury concluded that the Ritters trapped Sally in a web they had created. She was a pawn in their game. Jurors believed she lunged in front of Emma to protect her, also believing she would face dire repercussions from the Ritters if she didn't comply with their demands.

Jack took a deep breath. *Thank you, Sally, for saving Emma.*

His gaze examined the exhibit, a chronicle of their journey. He lingered over each: the barrel, the worn journal, a restored red coat faded by time, and a bayonet dulled yet dignified. A smile came to his face, glancing at the coins that glittered with tales of old, the chest, and its once-hidden trinkets.

The coins triggered his recollection of the auction in New York. It had been a campaign-filled spectacle, with the final bids ringing in a hair over $9.7 million. They retained a few pieces, relics too personal to part with, and others destined for museum halls.

After donating to the museum for expansion and the subtraction of fees and taxes, they divided what remained: $5.9 million. The sum was staggering, but Jack's eyes lingered on each artifact. He knew the true value of their find transcended any figure.

On the evening of the unveiling, a collective silence embraced the attendees. Anticipation and excitement were in the air when Bill O'Connell, the master of ceremony, announced the entrance of Jack, Emma, and Steve. They opened the doors into a hall that whispered of history, the artifacts a testament to their remarkable quest.

"Can you believe this?" Emma's voice was a blend of awe and disbelief. Her gaze swept over the exhibits that narrated their adventure.

Steve could not contain his own astonishment and offered a quiet affirmation. His hand found Emma's in silent solidarity in their shared amazement. She lent support to him, knowing this event would open the wounds over Sally again.

The familiar faces then drew Jack's attention. Mike Thompson and his team gathered by the barrel. The O'Connells joined Bill, standing on the platform. Ben and his father mingled with the officers from their journey, and Lieutenant Allen among his peers. "It appears everyone's here," he said, the sense of community cracking in his throat.

The evening unfolded into a symphony of laughter and chatter. The air was light with jubilation, a stark departure from the shadows of their past endeavors.

Champagne flutes found their way into eager hands in anticipation of a toast. Steve, alongside Bill, Jack, and Emma, stepped forward. His voice cut through the murmur, capturing the room's attention.

"Thank you, everyone, for being here," Steve said, his words echoing a sentiment of gratitude and reflection. "Tonight is more than a celebration; it's a tribute to friendship, determination, and the collective effort that led us to uncover a piece of history. Jack's knowledge, relentless pursuit, and Emma's invaluable collaboration with the Smithsonian."

"A thank you to Mike Thompson and his crew for finding the long-buried barrel. Tonight, all started with them. Thanks to the Baton family for their insights. Their family passed their insights down for almost ten generations."

"Let's not forget Lieutenant Allen and his fellow Garrett County officers. Thank you for going above and beyond to protect us."

"And we cannot forget our ageless wonder and our host, Bill O'Connell. His unmatched knowledge of Garrett County's history was the key to our discovery. Each of you played a pivotal role in this exploration and solving the 262-year-old mystery of Braddock's treasure."

"Yet, our greatest gratitude," he paused, gaze anchoring on Sally's photograph, "belongs to one irreplaceable soul. Sally Adkins, your former museum director, and our cherished friend. Her dedication was the cornerstone of our success."

"Sally's passion for this museum was unparalleled; she was the shield that protected these artifacts. She and Bill sparked the interest that drew the Smithsonian to us. They lead us to this remarkable find and the museum's expansion."

"But it was her selfless act, stepping in to save Emma at the cost of her own life. This action embodied her true spirit. She cared more about others than herself. Let us toast to Sally, her memory, and the legacy she leaves behind."

With champagne glasses raised and sipped in solemn homage. Emma sought Steve's embrace, acknowledging the tears welling in his eyes. The evening proceeded with conversations that wove through laughter and remembrance, commemorating the bonds Sally forged.

Epilogue

The following morning, the sun pierced through the blinds. Emma awakened, the remnants of last night's museum over-celebration clouding her senses. She battled the grogginess enveloping her.

"Daylight already?" she whispered to herself, rubbing the sleep from her eyes, almost not audible.

Her limbs were sluggish as she forced her body upright. The room's brief spin settled as she planted her feet on the cool carpet, sending a shiver up her spine.

The sound of Steve's routine, the hum of ESPN, barely registered as she glared at Jack's intense focus on his computer. His fingers danced over the keys with purpose.

"Hey, guys," she greeted them, her voice still soft from grogginess. She leaned in to kiss Jack, the stubble on his cheek brushing her lips.

"Hey, Em." Jack's response was quick, with a flash of a smile in his glance.

"Morning," Steve's greeting floated from the background.

Emma moved toward the kitchen at a snail's pace, allowing her body to wake. Her hand cooled against the counter as she poured coffee, and the rich aroma promised clarity.

Turning back to them, coffee in hand, she ventured, "Breakfast plans, anyone?"

Jack half-joked from his digital trance, "Want me to whip up some pancakes?"

She chuckled, "Only if you plan on serving them as burnt hockey pucks."

Steve's laughter joined hers, teasing, "You're right, Em. We better steer clear of Chef Jack's specials."

Jack, undeterred, flashed a grin, "Well, I did offer."

"True," she smiled back prior to adding, "Let's hit Canoe on the Run before we meet with the realtor. When are we meeting him?"

"Ten-thirty," Jack said without looking up from his monitor.

A pause filled the space, the day's potential hanging in the balance, their imminent house-hunting adventure stirring excitement and apprehension.

Jack corrected himself, eyes leaving the screen, "Sorry, Em. It's eleven."

Emma cradled her coffee, letting its warmth seep into her bones. She gazed upon Jack, the morning light casting a gentle glow on his features, accentuating his focused demeanor.

"Have you scoped out some properties for us to visit today?" she ventured, her interest sparked by the idea of a house search together.

Jack paused, his gaze meeting hers. "Yeah, I've sifted through a lot online," he confessed, a slight hesitance in his tone. "I wanted to ensure we only see places that meet your criteria."

"May I review them?" Emma asked, her excitement uncontained. While she appreciated his effort, she wished he had included her more from the beginning.

"Sure," Jack said. He passed her a collection of printouts, his enthusiasm breaking through. "I marked an X on the ones that don't have everything you said you wanted."

Emma was grateful and accepted the papers, her eyes dancing over every page. The properties unfolded before her, each promising a shared future she longed to build with Jack.

"You've done your research," Emma said, her eyes widened, impressed by his dedication, a stark contrast to her prior feelings about his treasure-seeking adventures. It was clear to her that Jack did pay attention to her various comments about her ideal house.

"I wanted us to have options," Jack said with a modest shrug, his commitment to their search evident.

Emma reviewed the listings, and a specific property caught her eye – a serene, lakeside cottage surrounded by nature.

Her excitement was visible as she spoke. "It appears perfect," she said, pointing to the listing. "Not only is it located on Red Run, but it also has a second primary suite for Steve."

"No need to worry about me," Steve insisted.

"Nonsense, you're family and part of this, too," Emma said as she smiled at him.

Jack leaned in, nodding in agreement. "That one stood out to me as well. It appears to be the ideal retreat."

"It does," Emma concurred, her affection for Jack deepening with their shared vision.

Yet, as Emma lingered over the listings, she caught Jack returning to his computer, his focus intense as he navigated through pages of analysis.

Curious, she studied the concentration etched on his face, his keystrokes rapid and deliberate.

"Jack?" Emma asked, breaking the silence. "What are you looking into now?"

"More research," he said, his voice laced with a thrill, making his blue eyes sparkle with promise as he gazed at her. Emma leaned in, attempting to make sense of the jumble on the screen, but the text blurred into an enigma, deepening her intrigue.

"What's it this time?" she nudged, a mix of support and concern in her tone. The lure of a fresh start by the lake hung between them, fragile against the gravity of Jack's latest obsession.

"It's too early for a reveal," he said with a smirk. His tapping foot a tell over his excitement behind his playful demeanor. "Just know, it's monumental."

An internal sigh escaped Emma, echoes of past pursuits shadowing her thoughts. The rush of discovery, the weight of setbacks, and the all-too-familiar sensation of being sidelined haunted her. She found herself at a crossroads, her faith in Jack's visions warring with her fears of neglect.

"Jack," her voice softened, revealing her vulnerability. "Is this a journey we're on together? I can't be an afterthought this time."

"You won't, Em," he said, his grip on her hand firm. "This won't be like before. Remember, you said we could have an adventure in the summer? We're in this as a team."

"That's right, Emma. You did say that!" Steve said, eyes glued to the television.

Her pulse quickened with hope, the prospect of a shared quest igniting a spark within.

"Okay," she said, a cautious optimism in her smile. "Is this the legend from New England you hinted at? And I reiterate, and promise me, we're in this together, through and through."

"Not New England, but yes, we're a team," he said, his gaze tender yet resolute. Emma sensed a surge of belief that things would be different this time.

"Show me what you've found, Jack," she said, moving closer to his workspace. Curiosity drew her to the documents sprawled beside his computer.

"Okay, Em," he said, allowing her to explore the findings.

Emma's slender fingers picked up the first stack, and they brushed over the details of the legendary *Lost Gold of the Lewis and Clark Expedition.*

ABOUT THE AUTHOR

David R. Leng is the international best-selling author of four business books and has written numerous short stories over the years that friends and family enjoyed.

As a lifelong resident of Southwestern Pennsylvania who spends considerable time in Western Maryland, David has long been intrigued by the local legend regarding hidden treasures buried deep in the region. His passion for history and this subject inspired him to construct this historical fiction thriller based on the centuries-old legends of Braddock's Lost Gold.

You can learn more about David and his upcoming book releases at www.DavidLeng.com.

Made in the USA
Monee, IL
19 November 2024

70652133R00233